CHILDREN

*Also by Bryan MacMahon*
*and available from Butler Sims Publishing Ltd*

HERE'S IRELAND

# CHILDREN OF THE RAINBOW

BY

BRYAN MACMAHON

BUTLER SIMS PUBLISHING LTD

DUBLIN

First published 1952 by Macmillan & Company Ltd
This edition published 1983 by
Butler Sims Publishing Ltd, 24 Anglesea St, Dublin 2, Ireland



ISBN 0-946049-03-3

Printed in Great Britain
by Richard Clay (The Chaucer Press) Ltd, Bungay, Suffolk

To
Séamus Wilmot

In little towns, lives roll along so close to one another, loves and hates beat about their wings almost touching. On the pavements along which everybody comes and goes, you must, if you walk abroad at all, at some time pass within a few inches of the man who cheated and betrayed you, or the woman you desire more than anything in the world. Her skirt brushes against you. You say good morning, and you go on. . . . Out in the world the escapes are not so narrow.

*Willa Sibert Cather* in
" LUCY GAYHEART"

The Highlander whistled very softly a bar or two of a wild melody with longing and a poignant sorrow in it . . . he said, " I fight for the old ways and the old days that are passing."

*John Buchan* in
" THE PATH OF A KING"

# CHAPTER I

I

THE young women of Cloone had not come to see the hares die: rather had they come to see the young men live.

Swaggering, Finn Dillon and I left the frosty sunlight and entered the marquee. A smell of liniment and spirits hung in the brown-yellow air. Beneath the handlers' boots the deep fresh straw slow-crackled. Men were lying full length on the straw, their arms arched over their sheathed hounds. Here was mystery and conspiracy.

From all sides the soft queries came to me: " Chestnut! Ches Macnamara! Your hound . . . ? "

Smiling, I walked on. Beside me, smiling too, was Finn Dillon, in-a-jest called Prince of Cloone, wearing the studded Belt of Cloone, having the clean-cut profile of Wolfe Tone, alert and well-limbed. Both of us were swaggering because of the virtues of my hound and because we were dodging our fathers' trades—Finn farriery and I saddlery. Swaggering, too, because by thus walking we denied by implication the statements of our oldsters who were continually making lovely dialogue by the turf fires of thatched Cloone, pausing only to whisper with malice: Ah, the lovely world of youth and soon enough the buckos would be brought to heel! Swaggering, too, because in the year 1925, after the bitter centuries, Southern Ireland had decided to take stock of the measure of freedom she had gained.

" Ches! Ches! "

Kneeling close by the side of the marquee, Galileo, an old cobbler from Cloone, his throat double-corded with memories of Fenian rebellion against Church and State, watched the coursing through a slash in the canvas. The gilt of a sunlight shaft had completely taken his features. As I began to peer here and there I heard the judge cry a decision from the bright field. Galileo lay down and the sunshaft struck rich and long into the high tent spotlighting my greyhound bitch, Tidy Woman, where she stood, meek, black, blaze-breasted and compact. Her eyes softened in my direction. Watching with ready affection I saw the jaws of my hound pulled apart by a pair of sun-bright hands and then transformed to a narrow cave complete with stalagmites and stalactites, a floor of pink sand and walls of dark purple. To this, the cleated, lighted cavern of my hound's mouth, Badger Breen brought the conspiratorial planes of his face, his deep-visored cap and soiled yellow scarf. Of a sudden from his pursed lips a mouthful of brandy spurted down the hound's throat. On the act, hound and man spluttered away from the light and the beauty of the scene was lost in the anonymous dimness. Badger growled. Finn laughed ; I laughed. The hound was in good hands. We walked away.

" Ches ! Ches Macnamara ! "

This was when I had reached my twentieth year and Finn his twenty-third. This was when I was suffering because of the nameless black-haired girl who had begun to knife St. Andrew crosses on my breast. This was when every square inch of my skin was growing clamant because I was coming into the full inheritance of the Cloonies which was the ability to become transfigured on small pretexts. This was when I, called Chestnut Macnamara because of my chestnut-coloured hair, was desiring more than anything else in the world to make the errand of my life less lonely.

The coursing field lay on the inchland across the river from the hundred thatched cottages of Cloone. The crowd stretched along the line of lattice. The young judge, wearing a huntsman's scarlet coat, white breeches and black cap, was mounted on a bay hunter. From the peak of the cap ribbons dangled over the nape of his neck. His silk cravat was dazzlingly white. A pair of handkerchiefs, one white, the other cerise, protruded from the breast of his jacket. He galloped hither and thither on small pretexts. Once, when a course was about to begin, the judge faced his horse to the slipper's box. When the midday Angelus rang out from our red sandstone church of Mary-without-Stain which stood in dumpiness above the clay cliff, overlooking the mouth of Cloone, the young judge raised his cap and cut a careful sign of the cross on himself. Behind him as the prayer ended a shower of 'finches fell, irregularly touching the grass in light-brilliant units.

Near the wicket that led to slips, Three Cheers and his wife were boiling soup over a turf fire ; from time to time our erect bearded bellman, whom Old Font the carpenter had nicknamed Metal Belly, glanced in the direction of the pot that was slung on a tripod over the flames. Metal Belly's throat was dry from clarioning the names of the hounds wanted by the slipper. The new timbers of the roughly-erected course-bar glowed cleanly. For an ultimate delight the southern peaks were white with the first of the winter's snow.

Long since the sun had forsaken the limestone houses of the town and had picked out the brown roofs and whitewashed walls of Cloone ; it had also found the twin painted pubs guarding the mouth of Cloone—Palatine Abernethy Bovenizer's with the larger-than-life Chinaman we irreverently called Flung Dung over the doorway, and Murray Folan's with the Maid of Erin in a similar position—the Maid deep-breasted, mastiff-faced, wryly suggesting Ireland's traditional defiance.

The huge countrymen kept their hounds on the move. Each man, too, was alert for his hound to relieve itself before its name was called for coursing. For the most part the men wore greatcoats of frieze : their collops were walled with red gaiters —glancing down at their inch-thick shoe-soles I thought of the coursers' trick of pouring unracked whisky into shoes to keep out the cold.

The bookmakers kept chanting monotonously: " Even money Green Rushes and the hare to die ! " Scraps of conversation reached me: Old Font the carpenter said softly as he tugged at his white pointed beard: " My stick is after fallin' out of my frosty fingers. I'll shortly be fallin' myself." Beside him, his son, Young Font, looked upon his father with affection and pride.

With arms linked, the girls walked up and down on the frosty ground. I saw Shoon Lawlee and Madcap O'Neill in the company of my sister Mary: Finn Dillon had eyes for Shoon only—her eyes were on the hills. Mary was chestnut-haired like me: she was inclined to fall into flesh and the possibility that a similar fate would befall me disturbed me at times. Trick-acting the girls were, with little attention for the coursing field. " Forever Cloone ! " they said, which was a password with us of the cottages.

The excellence of my hound was meant to be a secret, but judging by the type of greeting I received as I went through the field the world and his mother knew all about her. Although it was my first time coursing Tidy Woman I had tried her several times on the mountainside. Behind a hare she had top pace: her sense of anticipation was a delight and her close-in workmanship a treasure.

The money to back her had been collected in the Rookery the evening before. The Rookery was a long thatched lodging-house standing beside the bridge and boreen in mid-Cloone. Finn Dillon had entered each subscriber's name and the amount contributed in an old rent-book. Almost everybody had chimed in: Tom and Martha Goggin, the childless old couple who owned the lodging-house; fiery Galileo the cobbler, Streaming Blood the Pick-and-Win merchant and his side-kick Dicky Hickey the mannikin, Shemus Goff, the red-haired ballad-singer, Metal Belly, the bellman, Jody Shea the little wheelwright, John Brophy, a mallet of a man who owned a hearse and a jaunting car, and many others. For once in his life My Lord Caherdown's cupidity had conquered his distaste for the lodging-house—he was there with his clean hard hat, his fat-jowled face and his general air of tyranny and patronage. Old Font the carpenter who had modelled himself on Saint Joseph and had nicknamed most of the inhabitants of Cloone stood by while his son Young Font handed in his contribution. The money collected was four pounds seventeen shillings and sixpence; Finn Dillon had brought the total to an even five-pound note.

Outside of this amount I myself had put three pounds on the hound. For me that was an enormous sum: it had been realised by raiding my cache under the mattress and selling among other things, a mule finch, a seasoned hurley and the faulty reel of a fishing-rod.

On the morning of the coursing Finn Dillon and I had waited at a small distance from the red-gold board of a bookmaker. When the prices were written up we saw that Tidy Woman was quoted at twenty to one long odds to win the stake. It was my privilege as owner of the hound to have the first of the market, so I quickly moved in and placed my bet. Finn was straight at my heels with the investments of the people of Cloone. The bookmaker looked hard after the pair of us, then spat on his little finger and erased the number twenty which stood in front of the bitch's name. Turning we saw that the odds against the hound had shortened to 10 to 1.

Coursing was now brisk and earnest. Whenever a hare was released the idle hounds began barking in a savage mechanical anticipatory manner that travelled immense distances in the frosty air.

Erratic cheering blazed and died. For the most part the applause was for a sterling hare that punished a pair of poor hounds. The gay little animal kept dodging death while she dusted the frosted field with her hind legs. The spurts of frost-powder set me thinking of a woman dusting her floury hands after breadmaking. As often as not the hare dived into the straw rampart and was safe. Baulked and weakened the hounds floundered and leaped wildly. On the escape a white flag was raised to indicate that the hare had gone home.

At the wooden bar I had a drink with Finn Dillon. The old men of Cloone were beside us : they missed the normal atmosphere of tobacco-smoke in Folan's and Bovenizer's ; they missed, too, the silver-painted mock-barrels, the insistence on drinking out of pewter vessels and the saying " Ah, Delightful God, the taste is different and may the devil send us novelties ! " Dicky Hickey missed the atmosphere of the pub too : there he could climb up the rungs of a bar-stool and having drawn level with Streaming Blood's face, speak cryptically of money they had made together at races, fairs, markets and patterans.

Men from the town beyond gibed us :

" Murderin' rogues, the Cloonies ! "

" Don't fall into the river goin' home, Sonny Macnamara ! "

" Kissin' an' bleedin' like the Cloonies ! "

I looked at a bookmaker's board : Tidy Woman's price had again shortened. She was now 8 to 1 to win the 16-dog All-Aged Stake. Four clear courses to win. The favourite, a dog called Mister Honey, was quoted at threes. The braces of dogs were still flowing past me. Finn Dillon and I were but moderately interested.

II

I then heard Metal Belly ring his bell and call out my hound's name ; Finn Dillon and I hurriedly finished our drinks and went to the wire. Badger took his time about replying ; at last I saw the pair of hounds go into slips.

The hare was unslotted and the hounds slipped. Tidy pulled away from her brindled rival with facility. Nearing the hare she gathered herself low. I found myself crouching in sympathy with her. She seemed to be sending all the muscled venom of her body into her head and urgent mouth. My dark little lady went into the hare in a long harsh thrust.

Her throat tightened on her game. She held her grip, then rolled over and over in a flurry of black legs. I saw the star on her breast flash.

Too late the brindled dog joined. Old coursers nodded: with certain reservations they gave my hound a grudged approval.

In the marquee, Badger was unenthusiastic. " Too bloody handy with her teeth," he said. " If she overruns she'd never smell puss again." He was truculent because of the bitch's initial victory. From Tidy's mouth came jets of condensing breath. Her tongue was curled. When I spoke to her she made no effort to greet me but closed her mouth abruptly and set aside her weariness.

Her rival in the second course was a strong blue hound. Hip to hip they buckled into the hare with Tidy putting a nose in front at the vital first turn and having the better of the exchanges thereafter. By now the Cloonies were quietly jubilant: some of them were already cracking their knuckles with glee.

The semi-final was a disaster! Not that Tidy was beaten! After she had knocked up enough points to win two courses the pair of hounds were still behind a hare that continued to ladle out punishment until I thought the dogs would drop from sheer exhaustion. I cursed the hare that refused to live or die. Time and again when I had despaired of Tidy's running another yard, she resumed coursing with a fresh brilliance. Every turn, wrench, flick and go-by knocked hell itself out of my little bitch and lessened her chances in the final. When the dogs were gruelled to a standstill the hare moved with a mocking fluency to the escape. I had to concede its gallantry, even though it had almost murdered my own hound. Badger picked up a listless Tidy.

In the marquee Badger again made the bystanders pander to his craving for conspiracy. Jody Shea was at his side: terriers were Jody's main delight but on occasion he could make-do with hounds.

Tidy Woman was in poor trim. However, when she gathered herself together she could look as fresh as a daisy. That was the mysterious thing about her : one minute she looked good enough to win the final course and the next minute all the weariness of the world seemed to rest upon her. I asked Badger directly : " Will we draw the bitch ? " I received no reply.

Sharply, I said : " I asked you a question ! "

" She'll run ! " Badger snapped.

" I don't know," I said, turning away.

" I know ! She'll beat that animal there if she had only three legs."

I looked to the far end of the marquee where the other finalist—the favourite, Mister Honey—was being handled. He was an upstanding brindled-and-white dog that had had an easy passage to the final. He was owned by the Mallorys who lived in a great house in an upriver demesne. A small immaculate man wearing riding breeches, check coat and canary-coloured socks, whom I knew to be an ex-point-to-point jockey, was doing up the hound.

The Cloonies had forgotten their dissensions. They were looking sharply at my face.

This was my quandary : whether to run the hound and so trade unfairly on her kindness and keenness, or withdraw and leave the Cloonies poorer than poor. A third course of action lay open to me : to ask the owner of Mister Honey to agree to a division of the stake money and thus ensure that the Cloonies would at least secure half of their winnings. There seemed to be a poor chance of securing the agreement of my rivals to a division since they held the advantage of a comparatively fresh hound. Among the faces that ringed me around only one appeared to favour the division of the spoils : that was the face of Jack the Hibe.

" A pity to withdraw," said Shemus Goff. " If she wins, there's a ballad in it."

Shifting from one leg to the other, John Brophy growled :

" A night of gaiety gone west, with a half-barrel queenin' it on the table of the Rookery."

Displaying his white prominent upper teeth, Jody Shea the wheelwright said: " Didn't God fashion a greyhound for runnin'? Aren't her legs her all?"

" I don't know," said Jack the Hibe diffidently, glancing away.

Galileo the old cobbler broke in: " The Mallorys have always been out of tune with national aspirations!" He then spat out as if ridding his mouth of the taste of the Anglo-Irish. " Five years of my life I'd give to beat starlight out of their dolled-up dog!" A fierce old man this—he couldn't countenance the freeing of our island by measure. Always an utter rebel and intransigent, from the moment our Church had condemned the Fenians he had never again crossed the threshold of Mary-without-Stain.

Finn Dillon, although he was Prince of Cloone, stood without venturing an opinion. He knew that the decision was mine only.

Shemus Goff began to rally our hopes by humming an old coursing song:

" *The Rose got the first turn according to law,*
*But the second was given to Master Magrath. . . .* "

I looked through the ope of the marquee. Madcap O'Neill passed by. When she saw me looking at her, she walked away over-quickly. I turned again to where the gloom was—after my glance at the sunlight the place seemed the colour of ale.

" I wouldn't like to wrong the bitch," I said to the men.

Badger's edged voice stilled the contentious tent: " Blast you, Ches Macnamara, d'you think I'd wrong her? I took her into my bed last night. As sure as God is over me I'd rather have her in my arms than a gamey woman!"

" Ssssh!" said Jack the Hibe.

" I'll not ssssh! For you nor for no man!"

I looked down the tent to where the rival dog was; the Mallory girl was standing to one side. Her figure was good. Her blonde hair ran free over the collar of a white riding-coat. She was young.

Uppermost in me then was an inverted snobbery that has always been my predominant sin. I gloried in the fact that I was a saddler's son. This Mallory girl's breed was niminy-piminy: that was my consolation: what it sorely needed was vitality and violence. We of Cloone belonged to a folk who grew angry in the old style.

The Mallory girl was looking at me coolly, quietly resenting my staring. Her skin was flawless. Her hands were deep in the pockets of her coat. We stood there for a while with our eyes locked in the beginnings of antagonism. Most of the group around us must have noticed it. The small man handling her dog glanced quickly from one to the other of us.

Leaving the linimented air of the marquee, I walked a step or two into the sharp sunny day. The sun had swung into the higher sky and everywhere a cascade of light was spilling prodigal silver. Two old coursers came up to me. One was a mountainy fellow with a peg leg.

"A right smart hound you have," Pegleg said. "What breedin' is she?"

"Smart Daniel out of Woman of Three Cows. Smart Daniel is by. . . ." Then I stopped. As far as the litany of breeding went, here I was, a pup teaching its father to suck eggs.

"What trim is she in?" the other man asked.

"Average!" I answered. Then: "Will ye look at her?"

Badger grew deferential in the presence of the two men. The Cloonies silently awaited the verdict. The pair handled Tidy, rubbed her tentatively to see if she would wince, looked at her toes, pulled her black rat tail and finally walked her up and down the tent.

"About do it! Run her!" Pegleg said, with a sigh.

" She's a distressed dog : I wouldn't destroy her," said the other.

The pair fell to arguing with one another. I was as wise as ever.

" A man's life is his will ! " said Pegleg.

" No denying it ! The goose said it ! "

" So did the gander ! "

" He'd be a brisk fellah if he could get the Mallory girl to divide."

" If she was mine, she'd gallop," said Pegleg.

" I'd cut my throat before I'd draw," said Streaming Blood thrusting his head into the rattle of words.

" Or divide," said tiny Dicky Hickey.

" Things have indeed come to a sorry turn," said John Brophy morosely.

" No song at all ! " Shemus Goff was bewailing.

" Bred to be baulked we were," said Dicky Hickey suddenly removing his cap to prove to all that he was bald and consequently an adult.

" What's half ? We want all or nothing ! " growled Streaming Blood.

" I hold we should divide," Jack the Hibe ventured.

Galileo hawked in his throat, then spat. " Divide with the Mallorys, is it ? " he said. " Her great-grandfather shot a man the time of the Famine for stealing a turnip ! "

John Brophy said : " Supposin' the bitch was mine an' she was balanced on only two claws—would I hell divide ? "

" I'll break one of yeer faces ! " The knot of wranglers fell silent at Badger's threat.

Dolly the Rose was looking into the tent : she was a foolish road-woman, forever addicted to nosegays and litanies, who lodged at intervals in the Rookery. I saw the bent stupid-crafty pose of her as she cunningly examined the faces of the men. Her grey hair was painted a queer brown with stale tea.

I thought : an old Gaelic triad has it that the three sharpest things in creation are the thorn in the marsh, the sneer of an Englishman and the word of a fool.

Drawing near her, I said : " Dolly, will I draw my hound, run her, or try to get the Mallorys to divide ? "

Dolly began to cry. " Why do you ask me ? " she complained. " What am I doin', Ches Macnamara, beyond collectin' a few pennies to buy a bottle for my chest that's torn in two with cold ? "

" The Bottle ! " said Badger, as if inspired. " The Mad Bottle ! "

The crowd of partisans took up the word. Bottle, bottle, bottle, bottle, receding.

(There is a legend among coursing followers that there exists a magic elixir that can make the poorest dog gallop like the winds of the highest air.)

" Utter God Above ! " said Badger. " Why didn't I think of it before ? Back, men, an' let the bitch see green grass ! "

Badger brought the hound to the tent-opening, where she remotely put her nose to the ground. She was trembling. From all sides rose the barking of restless hounds. A course was in progress. Tidy was but moderately interested in it.

" Try to force a divide," I said to Badger. " If you fail I'll run the hound."

" Rest the hound," Badger said, listlessly thrusting the leather at Streaming Blood. He then sidled over to where a knot of watchers had gathered around the Mallory hound.

Galileo was complaining : " To shed the blood of the heart of man for an ordinary purple turnip ! "

" Such talk is not fair ! " I said wearily to Galileo.

" Fair ? " Galileo shouted. " Was it fair when our population was halved by foreign hucksters ? Was it fair when Father Murphy's belly-fat was used to grease yeoman's boots ? Was it fair when our country was partitioned by upstarts and foreigners ? "

" Surely to God," I said, " you can't interpret every trifle in terms of this stagnant island of ours ? "

" Enough ! " Galileo ranted. " Until this country is free and united from the centre to the sea I'll interpret every bloody thing I please in terms of what you call this stagnant island. You base-bred bostoon ! How dare you refer to our noble country in such terms ? Did we who were Fenians countenance defeat ? To one another we cried out as the conqueror's boots passed over us : ' We shall rise again ! ' "

Young Font nodded a dignified approval. Straightaway Jack the Hibe, the lobe of whose right ear the quiet Young Font had once bitten off in a maul between the two families, curled his mouth in a sneer of opposition ; yet he did not venture to speak. Old Font stood to one side, silent and bright-eyed.

" For the love of God's Blessed Mother," I said wearily, " will ye give Ireland a rest ! Talking about greyhounds we are, not about politics."

Galileo remained maniacal : " Nothing is greyhounds, I tell ye ! Everything is Ireland ! Night is Ireland ! Day is Ireland ! Grass is Ireland ! Sky is Ireland ! Blood is Ireland ! That bitch there is Ireland ! Until we have possession of our four green fields, the very air we breathe is Ireland ! "

Jail had crazed the unrepentant old Fenian for sure.

" You daft bastard ! " Jack the Hibe said under his breath.

The twin cords on Galileo's throat stood out then. Anger, too, had scooped a sudden cavity on the back of his neck. The cobbler threw himself at the speaker. Remembering the feud between their two families, Young Font readied his fingers to tear at Hibe's throat.

I came between them. They were half glad to hush : nervousness about the hound was telling on them.

Meanwhile Badger was strutting around the Mallory dog. The fancy jockey was running his accurate hands over his hound's haunches. The way he did it, it was a rite.

The jock's hands stopped rubbing as Badger's boots came to a halt.

" What is it you're tryin' to do, moderate jock ? " Badger inquired.

The jockey's features were excellent but diminutive. " Easily answered, that inquiry is, tangler and half-handler," he said. " Giving the winner the last rub-down I am."

" The winner ! Still colour-blind as ever ! Still size-blind ! God's knockers, that reminds me ! A fellow the spit of you rode the wrong course in a lightweight at Ballyroe. Are you a half-twin, jock ? "

Indulgently : " That was me at Ballyroe. I got my eyes attended to since then."

" Your teeth it'll be next, my white child. An' after that, maybe, 'twill be the bridge of your nose."

" A matter of opinion ! No more : no less ! " The jockey had resumed the grooming of the hound. Edith Mallory stood quietly to one side.

" I'm still waitin' for the message," said Badger.

" And the nature of the message is . . . ? "

" That ye're dividin' the stake."

" The world is full of awful animals," the jock said loudly ; " and the skies are thronged with laughable birds."

The knot of bystanders guffawed heartily.

" Wheesh ! " said Galileo, at our end of the tent. " Badger is givin' it to him."

" Still waitin', jock," Badger said primly.

" We're running our fresh hound," the jock said sternly.

" So are we, you bothered knob of an ex-jockey," said Badger with peculiar logic.

The jock looked sharply up : " What are you doing here ? " he asked suddenly and with truculence. " Go back and run your bitch."

Badger blustered : " You think our little woman is ribboned after her last course ! I'm telling you, quarter-jock, that you're makin' a mistake ! For, by hell, smart as you are, you're forgettin' one thing ! "

" Yes ? "

" The mad bottle ! " Badger's eyes had narrowed in triumph.

The jockey screwed his face into a small encarmined snout.

He was still astride the hound. He made several preparatory passes with his hands and then chanted: "Mumbo jumbo: hocus pocus: gilly gilly gooly: gilly gilly gooly."

A laugh went up at Badger's expense, mostly from the Mallory retainers and the sons of their servants. Edith Mallory—I watched her—had smiled distantly for the first time.

Badger was frantic: "For the last time, are you goin' to divide?"

"Divide hell," said the jockey, "into two hot halves!"

"Before I give her the mad bottle?" Badger was now the centre of a loud gibing ring.

"Badger!" I called.

Badger was involved in random argument. "Once let me strip the brown cork of that bottle and then . . . yes or no? Are ye goin' to divide?"

"Badger!"

With a bad grace, Badger returned. "The curse of the seven orphans on the top of you," he growled. "Just when I had the lard frightened out of them! You!"

"Get on the hound," I said. "We're neither dividin' nor drawin'."

Word went out that the Cloone bitch was running.

I searched the crowd until I saw Abernethy Bovenizer, the Palatine, standing at the wire. He was at his usual tuneless whistling. Anyone in Cloone had only to look at Abernethy in a certain way and he understood. This understanding had never made him the poorer in the long run.

"Have sense, son," he said quietly. "Your dog is be't to the ropes."

"The man with the scarlet jacket will tell it," I replied.

"I'll lend you the money," said Abernethy, with a sigh.

He gave me five pounds out of his wallet. I'd have to work myself to the bone for a long space freeing myself if Tidy lost. As an afterthought, Abernethy gave me an extra three pounds. "Put that on for me," he said. "I'll stand or fall with the thatch o' Cloone."

The bookmakers were calling two to one against Tidy Woman to win the final course. That was a bad sign. The Mallory dog was hard to back at seven to two on. I backed Tidy with what was a small fortune for a saddler's son.

III

At the pocked muddy wicket Metal Belly, the bellman, was clanging his bell and solemnly calling for Tidy Woman and Mister Honey. Badger came out of the tent with a crowd of Cloonies at his heels. I whistled to him to wait up for me.

"I'll take her in," I said.

"You'll change the luck." He said it regretfully, not arrogantly as if denying my rights.

The Mallory girl was already near the slips leading in her great hound.

At the wicket I heard: "Good luck, Ches!" It came from the lips in Metal Belly's short black beard. Then: "Good luck, Ches!"—that was Madcap O'Neill, daughter by the second of three wives to Dark Jack O'Neill who had his farm at the back of Cloone. Madcap was leaning against a post; her body was good, her lips well-shaped and her black hair was gathered to the waist of an hour-glass at the nape of her neck. Eighteen she was then and ripe for life. Her voice sounded off-key—that was because between her and me there had always been a strangeness that defied resolution.

By the fire Three Cheers raised his timber spoon.

Nothing mattered now but my hound. As I walked slowly to slips I was willing her to win as if my doing so could travel down along the leash and enter her body. Behind my back the bookmakers had redoubled their roaring. My eyes enfiladed the dark press of people against the wires. Over their heads were the immediate low-backed hills, while to my left hand, staunch above the glitter of the river, the white cottages of Cloone had redoubled their brightness.

In the small three-sided canvased enclosure, the tall slipper took my hound from me. The bitch was cool as I slipped the red knitted collar over her head. Tolerably eager she was, too; no longer frail nor shivering with tension. I ran my hand over her back a few times in order to reassure her ; this caress she accepted with her usual workaday apathy. Edith Mallory drew the white collar over the neck of her hound : for a moment as we crouched our heads were close to one another. The slipper ran the loop on to his wrist and doubled the leather under the hounds' bellies.

Edith Mallory was beside me as we walked away. We did not speak to one another. As was our privilege as owners, we walked outfield on to the coursing ground. The gap between us widened. Now and again we glanced back over our shoulders. Instinctively we were making for a point opposite the place where the hounds would first break the hare off his line. The judge was galloping into position.

An old white-marked hare festooned with ribbons was then released. The laughing slipper blinked the daft hounds and did not slip them. This hare of legend was called Joanie and the club kept her as a pet : in her day she had beaten the best hounds the barony could offer. The crowd welcomed Joanie with huzzas : when she had reached the escape, the Cloonies began to cry out in fierceness : " Forever Cloone ! "

The Mallory girl looked across in their direction. She had been bred to be cool.

A stag of a red hare came racing out the field. His legs were so long that he seemed stilted away from the earth. He moved fast with a high disdainful ease. Confidently he faced for the straw of the distant escape.

The slipper was dragged out on to the run-up ; the long lead from his wrist held the struggling hounds. "Hulla-hulla ! " came from between his teeth. The slipper's head was high while his heels were digging deep into the sod. The dogs kept staggering on, rolling awkwardly in the grip of primitive desire. When their passion could no longer be bridled, the slipper began to crown their frenzy. " Yeh ! Yeh ! Yeh-yeh-yeh-yeh ! " came from between his teeth.

Abruptly, sharply, the slipper's wrist was lifted aloft. We heard the clack of the releasing metal. We then saw the dead leather on the slipper's wrist and the apparatus idle on the field. The hounds came pelting away. I choked with pride to hear the Cloonies roaring :

" Ti—dy ! Ti—dy ! Ti—dy ! "

Neck and neck they came, the brindled-and-white hound and the black bitch. Tidy was buckling tight and true against the Mallory dog as if resting against him. The hare was now in full flight.

" Tidy ! " Despairingly the sound came, for my dark lady had begun to lose ground. Then, my sorrow ! I saw daylight plain between herself and the Mallory dog.

I was twenty. As yet I wasn't accustomed to having the knife of disappointment turned in my breast. After a quick glance, I turned my eyes to the hills. I did not wish to stand witness to the defeat of my hound.

From the people came " Ti—i—idy ! " with faint hope in it ; then, when I had reckoned all lost, I heard " Ti—i—idy " with glory in it !

I turned : Tidy was close in. I was taken by a fever of excitement. I shot a quick glance at the Mallory woman. Her experienced eyes quietly chided mine. Tidy was now lying mouth to mouth with Mister Honey. Both hounds were on top of the hare. The hare broke off his line. Only the judge could say which of the two had broken him first. I was confused. I could only watch Tidy's red collar as the neck shot low. Mister Honey took command. Turn upon turn mounting, pounce upon pounce, flick, wrench, turn, go-by. After Mister Honey's span of winning there came a spell during which at one moment the hare favoured the dog and threw the bitch away and at another favoured Tidy and left Mister Honey eating empty air.

Tidy suddenly came into full possession. She piled merciless point on point. It was all Tidy then. She continued to punish the thistledown hare that seemed to be enjoying his narrow escapes on the sunlit powdered ground. Generously and with a kindness of spirit Tidy gave everything she had to the coursing. All the while the Cloonies kept up a continuous hoarse tide of noise. Point upon point still scoring! The Mallory hound as idle as a piper's little finger. Flick, wrench, turn, go-by. Go-by again. And yet again! All Tidy!

As if tiring of the sport the great hare turned easily and faced for the straw, home and salvation. He moved in a long cool run that reminded me of fast-flowing water. The hounds straightened after him: Tidy was slightly in the lead, with the Mallory dog straining behind. Inexplicably the hare came to a different decision; turning in a right angle he thrust towards the lattice and there, in the cornering and miniature coursing that followed, tricked the Mallory dog into driving fully at him. When Mister Honey had ventured his all in a gambler's throw, the hare at the last moment leaped into the air, free high and buoyant and sent the great hound sprawling heavily into the loose tangle at the foot of the lattice.

Tidy was left to course the hare home. Between that point and the straw, singlehanded she broke the hare twice and piled up an additional few valuable points. At last the hare dodged under the straw and was safe. From inside the escape the flag of salvation went up. The crowd spared a moment to cheer the gallantry of the little animal, then turned to look in the direction of the judge.

A close decision, I thought. As close as could be, depending on which hound got the first turn. The judge galloped his horse towards the wire; I knew and the crowd knew that as he galloped he was mentally totalling the number of points each dog had made. In complete silence we waited for him to draw the handkerchief from his breast—cerise for Tidy Woman or white for Mister Honey.

For me everything seemed to stand still. The hills seemed dark sages under their skull-caps of snow. The thin winter river was heard. A woman stood soundless on the cliff of Cloone. There was no noise whatever except the drumming of the hooves.

Then I saw the white handkerchief held high above the judge's head. "Brindled-and-white dog!" he roared. I caught Tidy. She stood still on the field. I put on her collar and led her away.

I walked towards the wire. I dodged the Mallory girl lest she should say "Hard luck!" I knew she would pronounce the word "luck" in the English fashion. As I went I heard a medley of Cloone voices raised questioning the decision. I heard Galileo's cracked voice calling me: "Ches, boy! Ches!" Out of the corner of my eye I could see his stick raised aloft to attract my attention. To hell with the old dotard! I didn't want to notice him. Why was he always chewing the same rag?

"Ches! Ches boy! Ches!"

I did not want to raise my head. I did not wish to look in the direction of the voice. I knew well that he would offer me the traditional password of an undefeated people: "We shall rise again!" This slogan of Galileo's was the whipped dog's tongue on the raw wound and the shine of the pike thrust into the thatch. But I was then twenty and defeat seemed an enormous tragedy. "I shall look back at it and laugh!"—that was how I comforted myself. The Cloone money had been lost. I went out by the lower wicket so as to avoid the people. To hell with sympathy! What I wanted was victory! I was twenty. Good girl, Tidy! We shall rise again, eh? Look, with every day the tragedy will grow less.

The first of deadly sins is pride. I had put my pride on the bitch. The story was told. Tidy looked up at me in the accepting fashion in which a beaten woman looks at the man who has beaten her. I kept thinking: to hell with it all, it is of no consequence. The world seemed old. Into the black pit of hell with everything. I was twenty. Good girl, Tidy!

Badger was hobbling down inside the wire. His cap was clenched small in his hand. His dirty trenchcoat was flapping in such a manner as gave him grotesque wings. He was calling on me to wait for him. To hell with him, too! Victory I wanted. I was fit to burn him alive if he sympathised with me.

As I closed the wicket I saw Edith Mallory leading her hound across the field. And, oh, the way she walked! I froze in my crouch over the gate. Behind her the jockey was perfunctory in victory. Not so if we had won: we would have roared and raised aloft the trophy our black hound had gained so that all the world might stand and wonder at it.

So long was I watching the Mallory girl that purposely I had to fumble with the catch of the wicket to afford myself an alibi. I saw then that her eyes were fast upon me. Despite my utmost endeavour to prevent it our souls moved towards one another across the winter grass. For a moment they fused in a strange warmth. Implicit in the fusion was a promise of further richness. My spirits rose. Perhaps, in the long run, I had won. I thought: a woman is less happy in victory than in surrender. There was a truth!

Knowledge had come riding high upon a tide of disappointment. I pondered the truth again. I articulated it so that there could be no chance of my forgetting it—the most precious thing a woman possesses is her surrender . . . it is a jewel given her to bestow. I laughed aloud. The sound of the laugh sounded strange even to myself.

Badger was close beside me as we walked towards the river to cross by the stepping-stones and mount by the boreen that led up into Cloone. Badger was pricked of his valour. Half-angry he was when he saw me smiling. A second time he looked up into my face as if to analyse the smile, to see if I was a better actor than he thought I was. It was comical to see Badger's open mouth when his mind was quizzed. When he realised that I was smiling from gratification, he began to sulk.

To hell with Badger ! I put my legs firmly under me, so that he had to break into a half-trot to keep pace with my pace.

# CHAPTER II

I

"STREAMING Blood! The little fellow's wife is streaming blood!"

The country people halted. Involuntarily they made a ring and prepared their faces for laughter. It was the great feast of Mary in the Harvest and we were spending Patteran Day in the seaside village of Fanore.

"Streaming Blood!"

Streaming Blood's declamatory voice stilled the cries of the morning Patteran. Even the noise of the restless sea was temporarily unheard. The people strolling on the strand halted and looked up to the seawall where the bulky figure of Streaming Blood, pound notes pinned in profusion to his jacket, was spreadeagled against the sky. Behind him were the heavily-slated houses that abutted the promenade.

"And, ladies and gentlemen, permit me to mention in passing that the lady is seven inches high, seven pounds in weight and twenty seven years of age. In a few moments you will see her for yourself when my tiny colleague here releases his miniature wife from the attaché case. Coming as she does from a torrid climate the atmospheric conditions in Ireland are scarcely to her liking. But, hey! hey! hey! Hallo! Hallo! Hallo! Look! Look! The lady is streaming blood!"

Streaming Blood frenziedly directed his pointer at an attaché case on the ground. Immediately Dicky Hickey crouched and set up a mad racket by turning a vibrator on the cover of the case. Suddenly the noise ceased and Streaming Blood, wearing an air reminiscent of the schoolmaster, rapped on a large board on which was painted a series of numbers set in squares:

beneath certain of these numbers were written sums of money varying from 6d. to 7/6d.

The country folk gathered round but remained impregnably neutral. Streaming Blood then spied Finn Dillon, Lord Caherdown and myself seated at the edge of the promenade. Covertly he winked at us, imploring us to give him a start.

"Hey! Hey!" The din of the vibrator increased. "Hold her, my friend! Look! Every pore in her unfortunate body! Every follicle in her head! Streaming, streaming blood!"

The crowd of onlookers pressed out as far as the old rust-eaten rails below which lay the stretch of fawn sand with the sunlight full upon it. The waves were heard turning gently. Streaming Blood looked up at the cloudless sky, then glanced around at the circle of shining sea. In a quiet voice, he said: "My good friends, while we're waiting for the weather to improve. . . ."

Everybody laughed. The laughter signified that Streaming Blood and Dicky Hickey were well on the way to success—if only some countryman braver than his fellows would step forward and give them a start.

Streaming Blood coughed, then spoke swiftly: "Now perhaps I can interest you good country folk in a business proposition. I have here in this tin vessel a series of spills each containing a number corresponding with a number on the board. These numbers, you will readily appreciate, carry with them valuable cash prizes. For example, Number 53 on the board . . ."

The country people shook their heads and shuffled their boots preparatory to departure.

For God's sake, Streaming Blood's eyes implored Lord Caherdown, come and take a spill. Don't deny a Cloone neighbour before a throng of bumpkins!

How the green water tumbled! How we revelled in its glassy falling!

Caherdown ignored the silent entreaty. Looking out to sea,

he turned supercilious. " Infernal roustabouts ! " he muttered, flicking a speck from his black sleeve. Nevertheless he was tempted. He knew he would be allowed to win. The question agitating him was how much he would receive for his initial investment of sixpence. He was determined to hold out for the highest possible stake on the board. He pointed at the sea with his black polished walking stick and began a quotation from " The Corsair." Finn Dillon and I realised that we could be of little service to Streaming Blood : our appearance would carry small weight with the country folk.

Streaming Blood was now finishing his briefing ; if Caherdown didn't come to his rescue he was beaten for a further dole of language. The countrymen were prodigal with their laughter but niggardly with their money. With a gambler's throw, Streaming Blood turned directly towards Lord Caherdown :

" If the aristocratic gentleman on the seat will give us a lead. . . . "

Finn and I prodded Caherdown. He stood up. He shot his cuffs, then stalked forward. Watching him go I asked myself how it was that beshawled Cloone had thrown up this sham aristocrat. For a moment I feared that Caherdown would denounce Streaming Blood as a charlatan. He made a pathway through the people by brandishing his walking-stick. One tall country fellow he struck fully on the forearm. " Out of my way, rustic ! " he said. In the heart of the throng Caherdown spied Dicky Hickey. Then he smiled, for he and the mannikin were fast friends. He groped in his pocket, then tendered Dicky sixpence. With a nose-tightened innocence His Lordship took the marked spill from the honeycomb of spills confronting him. He unwrapped it ill-humouredly, then compared his number with that on the board. With an excellent show of histrionics he beamed as he handed up his ticket. Straightaway he set about deluding himself that he had won the prize fairly.

Streaming Blood set off with a gallop of words : " Hallo !

Hallo! This gentleman wins seven shillings and sixpence! Hallo! Hallo! . . .

"Do you know me, sir?" he said to the smiling Caherdown.

With a sudden arrogance, Caherdown said: "Give me my money, you confounded impostor!" Over-hurriedly, Caherdown was paid. He was in excellent spirits as he walked away. "Quite a presentable fellow, that Streaming Blood!" he conceded.

The waves curled over in the rich bloom of breakage. The air, the sun, the sea, the people, all were partners in a rich conspiracy to lift us up. Finn Dillon and I were exhilarated beyond measure.

One on each side of him, swinging from Caherdown's arm, we walked around the small town. We had begun to laugh at nothing at all. It was too early to start drinking. We saw an old woman with a festoon of seagrass falling from the corner of her busy but useless mouth. We smiled at the sudden bounce and aplomb of a country girl whose bare calves were of a fiery red. Shemus Goff the ballad-singer we discovered in an alcove between the houses with his quota of listeners surrounding him. As we drew near we heard him singing "The Low Lowlands of Holland." I pleaded with the others to dally so that I could hear the naïve verse that pleased me more than all the others:

"*Says the mother to her daughter, 'What makes you so lament?*
*Is there ne'er a man on Ireland's ground for to aise your discontent?'*
*'There are plenty men in Ireland's ground but there's ne'er a wan for me,*
*Since the Low Lowlands of Holland have parted my love and me.'*"

I had trouble prevailing on Caherdown to stand and listen to this verse. His Lordship lived alone: women were grapes rich and blue away above his head. As I had anticipated, the second line amused him inordinately. When the verse was ended he uttered the Raheela Roar which was an outmoded faction cry. The cry startled the morning street. " Yeeow ! " it came, and again " Yeeow ! " As a result of this roar Shemus Goff was in danger of losing his audience. We drew Caherdown away. Walking with us thus was what he called his peripatetic school of philosophy.

My sister Mary, Shoon Lawlee and Madcap O'Neill approached us. They were swinging arm in arm. We halted to swap a sentence or two with them. " For God's sake, go away and don't spoil our chances," the girls said laughingly. The country fellows seated on the low walls outside the houses were meditatively chewing ginger bread or plum duff. The crumbs fell idly on the lapels of their navy blue suits as they watched the laughing women swaying away from Caherdown's stick.

Passing the only hotel in the village I saw young women drinking tea : they were seated on slender chairs beneath a large red and black sunshade on the small lawn where the white croquet hoops were. Edith Mallory was there : she had a delicately made teacup poised in her white fingers. She looked cool in the sun. Our eyes met but we did not salute one another.

We walked past the pubs that before nightfall would sway with tipsy song, and at last emerged at the end of the breakwater which had been rigged to resemble a promenade. Before us the sea was coloured rich greeny blue to the right of the cove and silver to the southeast where the sun was beginning to assume dominion. The hue of the sand seemed now to have altered to a true tawny except where it had faded to fawn beneath the rounded stones at the head of the cove. Behind the patch of southern dunes a river met the sea. Landward from these dunes and on a bushy promontory over the river stood a church. Over the bushes in which the little church was embowered projected the stone roof of a ruined oratory, beside which lay the well where pilgrims were already beginning to pay " rounds " in honour of their patron saint. Northwards across the sand of the cove the cliffs were ochreous-stained and had forbidding-looking caves scooped at their bases: the entrance to the Great Cave was deep in green water.

Parallel to the placid skyline lay a low dash of cloud, beneath which the black curraghs were moving in from the islands. The satin breeze from the sea pleasantly fretted the sweat patches on our faces.

Metal Belly, the bellman from Cloone, came towards us, walking majestically along the promenade: he was dressed in his father's black suit which boasted shiny black out-of-fashion buttons. The jacket was opened to display the chain of his father's watch. The bellman's black beard jutted over his stiff shirt front. He had modelled himself on Charles Stewart Parnell. The women turned to look after him. Although middle-aged he possessed a striking carriage. Metal Belly had high standards of morality: since it was Patteran Day he would allow himself a few glasses of wine as a concession to Mary-in-the-Harvest. While drinking he would remain aloof and reserved. I always reckoned it good to see his wine-touched tongue move out upon his lips that were miraculously free of beard.

It irked Caherdown that Metal Belly was such a brave figure of a man. He began to tug at his lapels as if irritated by the set of his stiff collar. He had suddenly become an old gamecock momentarily revitalised because of jealousy. The salute we gave to Metal Belly had reservations.

As Finn Dillon and I were swimming in the sea, our exhilaration mounted with the tide's flowing. The young men with us gave themselves over to horseplay. After the bathe we lay where the sand was bone-dry just below the stones. Caherdown sat on his ample handkerchief and kept saying: " And the valley lay smiling before me . . . smiling . . . the word is felicitous ! " He had removed his hat and treasured it on his knee the while he took deep breaths of the splendid air.

A tinker's cart had come down the small boreen that led to the foot of the cliffs. A man was leading the donkey. The cart was filled with golden-haired children. A tall old tinker-woman and two men followed. The children leaped out of the cart when it reached the stony portion of the passage directly before the strand. They began to cry out in gladness. The holiday-makers stopped to look. The earth-stained children tore off their rags and raced naked to the sea. They were awkward bathers. When they took the water in their cupped hands they treated it as if it were precious and incredible. Then they flung themselves at the waves. Their parents paddled. The thin donkey put his nose to the inhospitable sand while the tinker children splashed themselves with the water, screaming and laughing all the while. The seawater coiled the children's hair into golden springs. The tinkers had no need to look outside their own intimate circle and the strand might have been empty for all the notice they took of anyone. Then all the children raced out of the water together. As their young burnished bodies came forward their heads of hair trembled. Except for the tinkers everybody seemed suddenly to have grown poor and strangely lacking in the precious things of life.

In the pie-shop Caherdown rapped fiercely on the trestle table with his cane. With spoonfuls of soup halfway to their mouths the people stopped to wonder at him. The maid who came to serve us was a trim little body: she had sound teeth in a healthy face, laughing eyes and a pleasing personality. Caherdown was so charged with anger at the dilatory nature of the service that he failed to see the maid approaching: it was grand to see his face that was darkened and thunderous fill with light at the sight of the smiling young woman standing in front of him. "Aha, Beatrice," he said, extending his arms to clasp her. This exaggerated courtesy and the subsequent comic words of reparation pleased the young woman mightily. Yet she remained well out of his reach and kept saying through her shy laughter: "You have your health, sir! You have your health!" She turned one eye on Finn Dillon to see how he was taking the banter ; the other eye kept straying to the door behind her lest her mistress should emerge and catch her enjoying herself. The whole room was filled with laughter. As on a signal Caherdown grew unaccountably quiet. In his face, suddenly drooped, I saw the beginnings of a tear of regret for approaching old age. He covered his weakness on the pretext of placing his hat in a safe place.

When the maid had gone to get us the mutton pies, Caherdown said under his breath : " There is a historical insinuation that Samuel Pepys. . . . "

He pronounced the surname Peppis. Finn Dillon came at him lazily. His legs were stretched out beneath the table and his chair back was poised dangerously against the distempered wall. Balanced thus, he was a deliberate temptation. " If I were you, I wouldn't make that observation in a loud voice," he counselled : " some educated person might hear you."

" What do you mean ? " Caherdown asked sharply.

" The name is Peeps ! I was there when a pair of schoolmasters laid a wager on it."

Caherdown placed his hands over his eyes, then rocked his head from side to side. He had begun to moan. I saw that he was peeping through the open fingers. The people in the pie-shop were looking at him. He recovered, miraculously so it seemed, then spoke in a loud voice for the benefit of all present.

" It is suggested that the diarist Peppis on one never-to-be-forgotten occasion—this is apropos of my little encounter with Beatrice—had a difference of opinion with his good wife, whereupon, ha-ha-ha, it is alleged that the diarist surreptitiously spied upon the neatly-turned ankles of the chambermaid. And believe me, gentlemen, our friend Samuel Peppis. . . . "

" Peeps ! " said Finn Dillon.

Outside the door and over the railing beyond the sand lay the sea. The air continued to be thronged with glad cries. Holiday boots were noising on the sun-drenched promenade.

With menace in his voice, Caherdown continued : ". . . came to the conclusion that they contrasted over-favourably with the beefy hockey-sticks upon which his lawful mistress did her perambulations. Yeeow ! The result was unadulterated murder ! " Everybody laughed. Caherdown took advantage of this laughter. He lowered his voice at Finn Dillon : " By the way, you god-damned booby, on what grounds save that of the obscure wager of a duet of semi-illiterate hedge-schoolmasters, do you propound your astonishing mispronunciation of the famous diarist's surname ? "

Finn spoke loudly to the people : " I was there when the bet was made," he said. " I was wearing corduroy pants at the time. Don't be misled, my friends. The name is pronounced Peeps."

Irrelevance could set Caherdown afire : I settled the four legs of my chair fully on the floor. He pretended to be cool, as he said : " Pssh-wssh-wssh ! Corduroy pants ! "

" Corduroy pants with buttons below the knees ! " Finn was addressing the occupants of the pie-shop. " Ye all saw the like ? " Some fool nodded confirmation. Caherdown eyed him fiercely while his hand tightened on his cane.

However, he refused to be drawn. Laughing, as at a secret joke, he continued : " Boswell, a little runt of a fellow ! A boot in the buttocks wherever he went ! But the rascal brought the story just the same. An immortal story ! " A feint this. To me, he said swiftly : " There are some bostoons born of woman and neither God nor man, bamboo, Holy Father nor black draught is a match for them when it comes to a public display of ignorance ! " He gave the Raheela roar : it detonated like a shot in the pink-washed compartment. Of a sudden he grew sad, poured out water from a carafe and took a sip or two with sorrowful lips. He spoke with feeling. " Gentlemen, I suggest I was well reared. A gracious father ! A tender mother ! " After the inevitable tear in his eye, he clamoured : " Almighty Father of Heaven and Earth, the maid's ankles ! Ha ! Ha ! Ha ! Her ankles ! "

Perhaps it was the holiday. Perhaps not. Caherdown's laughter was proving infectious.

Man, woman and child were taken with uncontrollable glee. People were sprawling over the tables. A freckled boy began to laugh without knowing the cause of his laughter: his opened face immediately set his neighbours laughing too. An old farmer with a wart on his nose spluttered suddenly into the soup of his pie. A farmer's heavy wife, dressed in black with a cameo brooch bright in her black blouse, leaned backwards in her chair under an oleograph of the Virgin Mary and got stuck in a corner with the dint of her own weight. The water of laughter filled her eyes. Caherdown was now King of the eating-house. The holiday spirit and his volatile face had won him through to transient royalty.

The people passing the door stopped to look in. " What's up ? " they queried. Soon they too were laughing. Inside and out the laughter mounted to the crescendo. Finn Dillon and I were not deceived. We were both watching Caherdown narrowly. Of a sudden, his face still wholly painted with laughter, he rushed at Finn Dillon and, securing a tight grip on his windpipe, began good-humouredly but forcefully to guzzle him. His Lordship's expression insinuated that the guzzling was an operation replete with merriment. " Peeps ! " he shrilled. And dutifully, off went the people into hegs of capital humour.

" Let me go . . . you fat rascal ! "

Laughter was everywhere like a daft disease. The pie-shop that, on our entrance, was quiet and normal had suddenly turned to a loud rowdy-house.

The woman of the eating-house hurried out from an inner room. She was flushed from drooping over the fire. Her man, a large fellow with the breed of a fisherman lurking in him, stood directly behind her. " Stop that, you ould divil ! " the woman roared at Caherdown, giving him a lusty thump in the shoulder blade.

On the blow, Caherdown released Finn. He looked fiercely at the woman, then glanced over her shoulder and discovered her husband. His fierceness vanished. " Madam," he said, with dignity, " allow me to give you the King of Spain's embrace." He kissed her slowly beneath each ear, after which he cleaned his nose on his generous red handkerchief. He then dismissed the woman with a snap of his fingers. " Back to your regions and bring out the mutton pies, you menial ! " he commanded.

" Well ! " she said. For a moment she was balanced between anger and laughter. Someone was helping the heavy woman to gain a forward position on her seat. Although wart-nose's soup was cold he had resumed his spluttering with over-compensatory assiduity.

Still nursing his throat, Finn rose. Caherdown poured water into the three glasses on the table, handed one to Finn Dillon and another to me. Raising his own glass he adjusted his mouth to the doleful attitude it always assumed before giving a toast.

" Gentlemen," he said, " I pledge you Boswell ! "

" To Boswell ! " we echoed.

The man of the house glanced around at the occupants of the room. He looked at the points beneath his wife's ears where Caherdown had kissed her. His mouth hung open: after a delay he reckoned it desirable to clamp his lips tightly together lest he should stand convicted of idiocy in his own pie-shop. As he stalked to the door, the crowd of onlookers melted. The maid hurried up with the mutton pies but Caherdown ignored her. Her face wore an air of having been cheated. She banged the pies on the scrubbed deal table and flounced away.

After the meal we felt drunk with the goodness of life.

## II

Caherdown had yet to pay his rounds at the holy well. We accompanied him along the road through the dunes until we reached the little church on the bushy promontory of the river. Beside this church stood the oratory and well of Saint

Lachtain, where, on this day every year, the patron rounds were paid. The great doorway of the church almost filled the front wall of the building : over this doorway the ornamental chevrons had been eaten by the years. Within, the church was seated with rope chairs. The press of people hearing the last Mass of the holy-day could not be accommodated within the building, so that many of them knelt on the gravel before the doorway.

As we came down the small curve of sandy road we heard the prayers after Mass pouring up to us. Mostly in Gaelic they were : then we saw the white tweed jackets of the islanders speckling the congregation. When the prayers had ended the islanders took up positions majestically aloof and looked in the direction of the sea. The majority of them were spare-boned lanky fellows—their trousers were hitched up and held in place by brightly-coloured belts of fast-dyed wool which they themselves had woven. Soundlessly they moved on their skin pampooties. Being conscious of the inadequacies of their knowledge of English they rarely spoke to outsiders. They looked at every man with independence, frankness and dignity. In the islands they had great devotion to Saint Lachtain and took their oaths by his right hand. The older men among them wore the bawneen or white woollen jacket, also a black hat crimped to three hollows in the crown.

After a while they moved across the open ground to a stile in the church wall. Outside the wall lay the oratory and the well. The oratory—it was in a good state of preservation—stood on the rising ground beyond the churchyard wall. Beneath it, noising softly at the foot of the little hillock, was the blessed well.

Above the well stood a large stone : its sides were fretted with the prehistoric writing called Ogham. On the stone rested a conical polished piece : this was known as Saint Lachtain's Cap. The credulous believed that if this cap were placed on a childless wife's head and certain ritual observed she would become fertile. Down the years the priests had banned this practice with bell, book and candle. One priest, I recalled, had gone to the extremity of removing Saint Lachtain's Cap to his own presbytery in an effort to stamp out superstition. Local belief had it that the cap had flown through the air during the night and had again settled on the top of the Ogham stone. At length the people had compromised : now the observance was reduced to a token touching of the stone with the finger tips, after first having paid the traditional rounds and drinking from the well.

On a stone at the well side, Dolly the Rose was seated ; without ever moving her head she kept gaping into the clear waters. If she saw the trout in the blessed well she would be certain of the Kingdom of Heaven ! The bush over her head was gay with votive rags.

Caherdown had begun to pay his rounds. We watched him as he circled the well and prayed at traditional stations or stopping places. The priest emerged from the little church : he was an old man—erect, too—with apostolic gracious hair. He delayed for a while conversing with the old women who were loitering in the church doorway. Finn and I were curious to learn from his glance what his personal attitude to this well was. In our minds the absence of a clear directive from the church buttressed the rumour that in the case of some of these wells a pagan custom had been adapted by Saint Patrick to fit Christianity.

Finn and I kept watching the priest. Drawing clear of the people, he stood for a few moments on the gravel path. I saw him look over the wall and then wet his lips meditatively. Just as Saint Patrick must have wetted *his* lips. The priest must have seen, as I saw clearly, the young islandwife's fingers grope eagerly upwards to caress Lachtain's Cap. Three passing things I knew I would recall with clarity—the priest's lips pursing, the woman's fingers trembling, the grey stone unchanged by the years. Fleet as the picture was it had completeness. Faith, false or otherwise, was in it, together with hope in abundance : the priest's attitude supplied the charity. He walked away suddenly, covering his apostolic hair with his biretta. The gesture postulated that the church had an accretion of precedent to give it wisdom. There was no phenomenon of human nature beyond its understanding. It saw human frailty in a woman's fingers. And had charity.

Dolly the Rose kept looking into the clear waters of the well. At any moment the brown back of the trout would appear and then, with a heigh ho and a leap to glory, she would be nearest the throne chanting an unknown canticle.

The short underfoot grass was decorated with trefoil and heartsease. The grey-clad islanders moved like ghosts. Beside each man moved his islandwoman. As each woman rose after having completed a station there was revealed the isosceles triangle of the brilliant red flannel of her petticoat. This flame quenched as the woman again knelt at the next station.

Dolly the Rose was distracted by the wind-stirred rags, yet she dared not take her eyes from the well. People asked her questions : she replied angrily ; always her eyes were firm on the water. There she would remain until darkness walked in out of the sea, moving silently, imperceptibly, like the islanders themselves.

Laughingly the young men and women moved into the old oratory. The front elevation of the oratory was roughly triangular and the side walls had merged into the roof of stone. From the brown gloom within came laughter that was low pitched. The boys and girls had begun to pass through the small ope in the eastern gable. If one passed through Lachtain's Light one would get one's wish. A dishonest man could not pass through, though he were as small or as thin as could be. The light was the shape of a lamp chimney, wide near the base and narrowest at the top.

Finn and I joined the boys and girls. We passed through the window. Doing so I lost a button from my jacket. Out in the sunlight once more we saw Caherdown looking here and there as if searching for us. He had completed his stations. Hiding from him we stood close against the spotted limestone of the oratory gable. Suddenly Finn laughed ; he told me to remain where I was while he walked forward to trap Caherdown. Young people were still passing through the light, stumbling out into the green-gold light of the day from the murk of the cell. As they stumbled out they wished with all their hearts that their difficulties would be resolved, that God through the intercession of Lachtain would grant them fertile ground and a fertile mate.

Finn had begun to argue laughingly with Caherdown. The word wish was repeated several times. Caherdown shook Finn off. Though he continued to laugh uproariously, his laughter had not the genuine ring. He uttered a small Raheela roar which was interrogatory in tone. At last the pair of them went around to the small door of the oratory. Crouching, I set my ear close beside the window in the gable. I heard sounds of prudent merriment coming from within : that Caherdown's laughter was not so sure-toned as it should be pleased me greatly.

The boys and girls in the oratory were not reluctant to have as much time as possible in the adventurous gloom so they let Caherdown try the light long before his turn had come. I heard his obese breathing come closer. I heard his well-polished boots seek purchase in the holes in the wall. Then his plump fingers, strained to whiteness, appeared clutching the stone on the side of the window. I heard Finn's small ejaculations of exertion as he pushed Caherdown up. Sideways His Lordship came, his bald poll emerging to receive the sunlight. Fortunately his eyes were turned away from me. So close to me was his neck that I could see the few acne holes of which he was mortally ashamed. Jet dark under my opening and closing hand was the single lock of grey-dark hair pomaded to his upper brow.

When he heard my laughter spurting from behind his head he knew he was trapped. Frantically he tried to retreat. But I caught him by the shoulders and dragged him forward. With the aid of the country lads, Finn pushed doughtily from within. Before long we had Caherdown firmly wedged in Saint Lachtain's Light.

His ears turned crimson : then he began to roar. Finn ran out among the pilgrims. "A rogue is jammed in Lachtain's Light !" he shouted. "Lord Caherdown, the English ruffian, is trapped for ever and ever !" The islanders set up a low whirr of astonishment.

Caherdown was a spectacle ! On the pretence of freeing him we wedged him tighter. The cry went out that an English lord had become wedged in the blessed window because he was a robber and an unbeliever who had arrived in the country for the sole purpose of pirating the downtrodden Irish. Caherdown had now begun to curse like a trooper. His face turned puce. A charitable tinker-woman hearing mention of the English lord had a sudden daylight dream of guineas so she rushed up with a panny of water and offered the trapped man a drink. Caherdown's eyes knifed her. Again and again he roared loudly. Dolly the Rose, out of pure curiosity, was forced to take her eyes off the water : when she had pressed forward through the people and seen Caherdown of Cloone imprisoned in the light she began to storm and run her fingers through the dyed coils of her hair, lamenting that her chance of winning the Kingdom of Heaven had now vanished for ever.

Finn and I went away. We sat on a mound on the roadside within sound of the sea and waited for Caherdown to arrive. The sparse grass was sweet as we spaced it with our teeth. Rabbit droppings were dry at the toecaps of our scuffing boots. Caherdown walked past us in a high anger. We followed him, whistling a tune in time with his strut. He proceeded up the road towards Fanore, an outraged fat man wearing an arrogant bowler hat. He was scowling at the countryfolk who saluted him graciously and in the spirit of the patteran. We kept at a safe distance behind him. All the while we were saying : "Lord Caherdown, we're sorry !" but he refused to turn. Undismayed we reiterated our expressions of contrition :

" Don't spoil the patteran by falling out with us," " Honest to God, Caherdown, we're dead sorry," " We couldn't resist it, that's all," " Make friends with us again," " As sure as the sun is shinin', we're sorry," and most powerful plea this, " We'll stand you a ball o' malt each if you'll rub it out ! " We were hard set to hold our faces straight as we spoke. At times we came too close to him : then he tightened his grasp on his cane and moved it menacingly so that it bore a distinct resemblance to a cat's tail when it is stirred by a rigid anger. There were *buachallans* or ragworts flowering on the sandy roadside : you should have seen him decapitate these with vicious blows of his black walking-stick !

After a while he ceased swinging at the *buachallans :* we knew then that his anger was ebbing. One at each side, we walked directly after him, still repeating how sorry we were. Suddenly he stood. We stood too—at a safe distance—with our eyes firmly fixed on the cane. Caherdown turned fully. First he threw a dog's eye at each of us, then unpredictably the old light broke on his face. He extended his arms to their full length and uttered the Raheela roar. We rushed at him and clasped him close.

Now truly we were drunk even before we had begun drinking.

But no sooner had we reached Fanore, for such is the whimsy of man, than I had to confess myself fallen into the pit of desolation. I kept remembering a quotation I had once seen framed in passe-partout in the fancy-goods window of what we called an " Italian warehouse." The heading "*LOST*" on the legend had given me pause. Drawing nearer to the window I had read : " *Lost, yesterday, somewhere between sunrise and sunset, two golden hours each set with sixty diamond minutes. No reward is offered for they are gone forever.*" The quotation was from Horace Mann.

The full recollection now made me queasy with a sense of futility. On first reading the quotation I had tamped its significance in my mind, smooring it over as a fire is raked.

Now despite the potent distractions of sun and sea, despite the erratic windblown exhortations of Streaming Blood, despite the glee inherent in the whoop of the Raheela roar, despite the sense of comradeship that lay between us three on that brilliant patteran day, an uncanny loneliness began to have its way with me. By inversion it became almost a type of happy treachery. Thief and robber it was, turn and turn about, filching and tearing from my bright excitement. Sycophant and stormer it then became, taking from me what I held dearest. Nothing could banish it, not even the high electric pub-talk nor the coins smiling in the half-dark nor yet the yellow drink luring me to stay and stay for ever and for ever.

" *Each hour studded with sixty diamond minutes. . . .* "

Dared one stand passive, praying that life in all its plenitude would come and greet one ? Or should one go out with fists closed and soul that was game to gamble and thus meet what should be met where it should be met—halfway ? How far was choice offered to man ? Could man determine what the choice would be ? I looked upon the holiday folk striding between me and the darling sea. Their boots were thumping out the word loneliness. Never, never was it possible by any alchemy to achieve anything approaching congruence with even the most unpretentious of the passers-by. That was a lonely thought. God had created man in His own image. The mind is the most valuable part of that image. In it the soul is bared, almost. Approach the mind of another, closer and closer, stealing, squirming, feinting, dissembling, stumbling, confiding and we approach the mind and the God that is shadowed in that mind. What was the knack or plot or plan of it ?

The schoolteacher had dinned into our brains the end for which man was created : " To know and serve God here on earth and afterwards to see and enjoy Him for ever in Heaven."

Shemus Goff was chanting : " *Is there ne'er a man on Ireland's ground for to aise your discontent ?* "

Heaven ! Discontent ! What a pair of evocative words they were ? Between them they called up the factors most powerful in the struggle of man.

I walked away from the others : they made no bones about my going nor did they question me. Abrupt departures were always understood in Cloone : the closely-knit type of life we led encouraged a respect for one another's moods. I walked away because I wished to grapple with the old loneliness ; I was determined to inch forward to a clear statement of the cause of my inward turmoil. For me the patteran's splendour had become temporarily flawed. Not even the people's huzzas as five canoes were for a moment enthroned on the wave-crests could cheer my desolate heart. Dully I looked at the canoes as they made their way to the outsea stations for the race. On another day I would have been caught up by the glory of the coloured guernseys of the rowers. Turned partisan because of a trifle, I would have grown hoarse shouting at this annual outcome of coast rivalry. Not now ! Etched on the air between me and the sea she was—the ripe nameless black-haired girl. In her hand she held a long-bladed knife and continued accurately to cut Saint Andrew crosses on my breast. Her face dominated the space between me and the boats as they lifted to their recurrent and irregular enthronements. I could not see her face closely but because of the torture she was inflicting on me the day greyed and the sun became a poor plaything.

III

Night came. The air was warm. The boathouse, a roomy building standing on a green *plawsawn* above the strand, was filled with boys and girls dancing the Kerry sets. The old boards were sounding lustily. The light from the oil lamps barely touched the king-trusses of the rafters overhead. The dancing was free, except for a voluntary donation thrown into the musicians' caps.

I stood in one of the doorways. Between the bodies of the

dancers I saw intermittently the honey-coloured fiddle dripping music : it held the country girls and boys in a trance of delighting movement. No other light but the lamplight would have suited. How good it was to hear the sound of the ebbed sea sieving through the cluster of watchers with which each doorway was loosely crowded. Now and again one of the dancers gave a yell born of animal spirits and followed his yell with a leap into the air.

In the third figure of the set, as the dancers swung in and out, Madcap O'Neill was thrown face to face with me. The laughter on her face instantly died, and the smile with which it was replaced was such as she might have readied for a pleasant stranger. She pressed more closely to her partner as they began the wheel. As her laughing face spun away from me there was complete remoteness between us.

Through the intricacies of the dance my eyes followed her body's grace : I was still hoping against hope that something would break into beauty between her mind and mine—between her body and mine. But, despite my most ardent willing, there was nothing.

Far out, at the strand's limit, behind my shoulders, the waves were bringing their bulks heavily down on the sand. Before my face the joyous fiddle-music kept falling drip on honey drip.

For a span I watched Finn Dillon dance. He was the best dancer in Cloone : the idle women standing by the walls rarely took their eyes from his shoes. From my ambush at the doorway I covertly watched Finn's face, noting first his obvious eyes, then his less obvious eyes. His less obvious eyes were constantly roaming to find Shoon Lawlee who was dancing in the same set with another man. Once I saw her look up into her partner's face, laugh with a full heart, then bring her long eyelashes wholly down over her almond-shaped eyes so that they were closed to slits with good humour. After her laughter was ended she kept her bright red lips parted so that the shine of spittle took her teeth ; also she held her small head with its wealth of rich hair so that it was well-poised over her lithe body. Her every movement was acutely personal. Abruptly I swung my gaze and saw Finn's less obvious eyes wince as with pain.

It was midnight. I was standing on the grassy level outside. I was smoking a cigarette and looking down at the moonlit tide which was full out and soon would be at the turn. The waves were breaking to a white rage on the cliff promontory across the cove.

Finn came out of the boathouse. " Where the hell did *you* vanish to ? " he said sharply.

" What is it ? " I asked.

" While you were standing at the door," he said, " the girl I was dancin' with told me to tell you she was askin' for you. She's the loveliest little woman you ever laid an eye on. Come as far as the doorway and you can see for yourself. She's only waiting for you to crook your small finger."

I was lonely, brazen and contrairy. I didn't know what it was I wanted. " I'll pick my own women," I said shortly.

" But you don't understand," he said, as his fingers essayed an explanation. " Her nut-brown eyes are merriness itself and nothing could be whiter than her good teeth."

I walked away.

" Blast you for a cross-grained chestnut bostoon ! " said Finn. " When I go out of my road again to do you a turn the stars will drop out of the sky."

Step by step, my boots digging into the grass, I descended to the strand. Overhead a faint powder was dusted over the million stars. Between me and the moon the sea showed a golden road. Finn called after me with puzzlement and contrition implicit in his tone : I did not turn.

Leaving the dry sand, I went on to where the sand was damp from the ebbing tide. I walked to the tide's edge. There I verified what I had already deduced while standing at the boathouse : that the waves were breaking in short powerful jabs which lost their force in the downward blow and consequently did not thrust far along the strand. Turning my face to the cliffs I strode along the tide-lip. My boots anticipated with accuracy the limit of the short scurry of the breaking waves. The music and the thumping from the boathouse was now full in my right ear : in my left was the pounding of the sea. Whenever an inshore wave crashed over there was a small rush of air. The sea began its task of dwarfing my mental immensities.

I then grew conscious of a knot of people moving along at the cliff-foot : they were laughing and clear-calling as they made their way out towards the sea. At the edge of the tide they dallied ; I saw a single torchlight leap alive to red-yellow and show clearly the warped inverted vee of a cave's opening. And then I recalled that on Patteran Night if the tide suited young men and women were accustomed to making an incursion into the recesses of the Great Cave.

As the torchman moved forward the light scooped a blazing apartment from the base of the jet cliff, and as the man turned, the blaze showed too the stubby churned wonder of a breaking wave. I heard a voice urging the dallying boys and girls to hurry before the tide turned. Silhouetted against the torchlight I saw the young people pass in. The reassuring bass laughter of the men was mingled with the skittish contralto or alto of the women.

Hoping to catch up with the laughing band before they had disappeared into the cave's recesses, I sprinted forward. Something within me cried out for just such a small adventure.

The boots and shoes of the men and women were serried on a rock above water level. I dragged off my own boots and stockings and threw them on the ledge beside the others. Drawing my trousers-legs high, I imprisoned them on the muscles of my thighs. At the threshold of the cave was a knee-deep pool. As I splashed through it, a breaking wave brought the water over my knees. Within, the floor was of soft heavy sand and the air cold on my face. Everywhere there was an intermittent roaring.

It was eerie in the cave. I had never before been beyond the opening. By this time the young men and women were out of sight but in the diminuendo of wave-clamour their jittery laughter was thrown about haphazardly, jingling and neighing in the high vault over my head. Through a flaw in the northern cliff-wall I saw chaotic waves of the full sea strive and toss in the secondhand moonlight. About this opening hung the smoke of spray. Then I saw a wave that had mastered its jostling comrades run in towards me: it was gleaming with a queer white in the darkness. It continued to slide with a soft hiss over the floor of the cave, and before it reached my bare feet, fell away into the unseen recesses to my left hand. Another wave began the same antic. My inability to see the exact point at which each such wave ended touched me with apprehension. Through an unexpected silence voices came clashing in a hilarity that was sharp-edged.

Casting aside my queasiness I padded in the direction of the moonlighted gate in the cliff. Before I reached it I saw the tunnel giving to the right. The torchlight was in this tunnel, its flame hung wicked and high on the dark red and ochreous vault. The torch, a lighting sod of turf impaled on the tines of a hay fork, had obviously just been replenished with oil for as I came upon it, it was chuckling and spitting sprays of blue fire. A breeze from an unseen opening then broke the torch flame. I saw the crouching light touch a nest of brown marine nipples on the ebon sides of the cave. The light showed, too, where some adventurer had torn initials of rugged Gothic with a stone on the accretion of miniature shells which flawed the walls. All the while I was conscious of the tongue of foam running into the left hand of the darkness behind me and the sullen thunder of the waves contending in the open sea.

The boys and girls had formed a swaying, laughing crocodile behind the torchman. The light was so erratic that it was not without difficulty I succeeded in catching on to the last man in the file. As I caught him by the hips, he turned his bright face to me. I did not know him. In similar fashion he was holding on to the girl before him, and she, in her turn, to the man in front of her. Man, woman, man woman : thus to the torchman.

We moved forward through the narrowing tunnel. Now and again we splashed through shallow water. The wavelets, entering at some point we could not determine, were ebbing and flowing in runnels at the base of the walls. The girls were regaining their confidence : now and again one of them gave a shriek of bogus terror as a man hullahooed into a side-cavern where belief had it that seals slept on ledges above the rounded stones.

As we moved inland away from the sea the menace of the waves became reduced to a low boom. When the girls laughed the noise resembled a quick flurry of notes snatched from the treble of a xylophone.

With the widening of the tunnel a movement of air indicated that far to the left amid the twistings of the passages there was another opening about which the open sea was also warring. When the voices had taken a more rotund echo a man near the head of the file sang a snatch of an old ballad. This ballad I had been hunting for a long time : it was called " Mary of Loughrea." I thought it strange that I should hear it under such circumstances.

" *The sun shall miss the glory of your glossy shining hair.*"

The singing continued : the way it moved over our heads, banishing our gnawings of fear as it swelled or narrowed ; the way it surely rode the never-quite-absent insidious sssss of the water ; the way it tricked and pealed and pranked high in the red-yellow roof of the cave, seemed to me to be wholly memorable. The sincerity of the singing bound us together as nothing else could, for it rendered us full kin in the uncanny light.

We had reached a great cave-hall, the roof of which was dimly discernible. Tunnels branched off in different directions. The torchlight was now wan so that once again it had to be replenished. The bodies of the other members of the party bulked black between me and the blinding flare.

We crossed the hall. Some of the tunnels were cul-de-sacs : into one of these the torchman walked, bidding us remain in a huddle in mid-floor. The retreating light showed us the wrack imprisoned on what seemed enormous rounded pebbles. I grew uneasy lest a seal should come out and drive the women frantic with its flip-flapping and slithering. The torchman returned, saying that he could find no seals. We went on into one of the tunnels—as far as I could judge we were moving slightly inland. I was still at the end of the file.

As I entered this tunnel I glanced into the darkness behind me, and tried to memorise by which opening we had entered the great hall. The hall was unquiet with water moving by its walls. The air grew still colder. The dark had draped itself on my shoulders in what appeared to be a curtain of jet velvet. All-powerful it was, though all-soft. The passage before us narrowed : when a person yelled or chirruped the echoes behaved astonishingly. Then the passage widened and began to veer slightly towards the sea. The sand underfoot was rippled and my bare soles tickled me. I relieved them by rubbing each sole in turn on the instep of the opposite foot.

We had proceeded about a hundred paces from the spacious cave-hall when the torchman halted. He turned to us and said : " 'Tis above the knees here ! " He then waded slowly into a pool. A girl followed him, squealing as the cool water bit the flat of her thighs. Suddenly I saw the torchman stumble : the moving torchlight colour-crazied everything, red, black and yellow spinning as the man staggered in the water. When I thought that he was again firm on his feet, he pitched heavily sideways. The torch quenched with a single sudden hiss.

Everywhere then was the jet velvet curtain. The voices of the women, coming from unexpected directions, proved that they had broken file. I tightened my grip on the hips of the man in front of me and sensed that in his turn he too had clutched more firmly at the hips of the girl before him. The torchman had begun to blubber and swear in the darkness. For a moment we stood silent. In that silence an unusually heavy wave broke in the long gallery behind us. Its forward hiss seemed aimed at us in our quandary. The water at the foot of the tunnel walls took insidious life. The hissing came steadily onwards as it consumed the level unseen sand. Louder it came and louder, water clashing on water, until at last the strange world that held us had taken full terrifying tongue.

When the menace had reached its climax a young woman began to scream in such a fashion as I had never heard a woman scream before. The mouth must have been held loosely open for the unquavering sound emerged steadily almost of its own volition. I heard the rip and tear of a light garment in the utter darkness. The torchman shouted: "Hold the bloody woman!" Then our black existence became possessed of a primal flux. A second woman melodied her terror. "Jesus!" she screamed, and again, "Jesus!" I lost my grip on the man in front of me. Cloth brushed by me, burning my side-face in its urgency.

I stretched my two hands out in the darkness: I was resolved to clutch firmly whatever the darkness should send me. Amid the hurly-burly I felt a hand touch my left hand. I had no need to grasp it: it stayed there in strangeness and in confidence. It was a woman's hand. I ran my palm along her bare forearm and took her by the elbow. The fingertips of my right hand then encountered the woman's breast. The touch was fugitive: yet how sweet it was when the fingertips were young and the touched breast, too, was young. My right hand found her left hand and our forearms were lying flat against one another. A sudden scream came unexpectedly from the right. A second wave stepped towards us, low, low in the darkness. Its coming drove the woman closer to me. I measured her height from the passing warmth of her breath. My arms were now imprisoned in her armpits. On a flick of intuition I felt that I knew her. And that she knew me! In that instant of recognition the motive for her coming subtly altered. No longer was she seeking an instinctive protection. Her left hand was now on my right shoulder caressing it slowly. I drew her out of the crazy press of bodies, dancing oh-so-slowly backwards to the wall of the cave. Step by step she came, sure-footedly answering to the rhythm we had mutely agreed upon. There was no misunderstanding. Around us was the bedlam of voices, dying and being re-born. We were calm, eager, joyous and sure. My back met the rough casting of small shells on the projecting cave wall. An outbreak of cries and swears greeted the mounting menace of a new wave's on-coming. The noise offered her the excuse of drawing still closer to me. She was neither underbold nor overbold. Slenderly built though she was, my arms seemed filled in her deep armpits. Closer she came until she had fitted my body perfectly. I signalled to her there in the tumult. She came to tiptoe. The kiss was warm: it was known and unknown. A further wave broke in the northern passages. To us two it seemed to make a friendly noise as it drew nearer.

I had a sudden memory of an unarticulated promise therein fulfilled. My mouth was full against her neck: I felt her hand come up to my hair and comb its shock with sure fingers. It was the way she reacted to my hair that made my former flick of knowledge a certainty. Roughly, quickly, I ran my fingers over her face, delaying longest at the volutes of her nose. The matter was then beyond a doubt.

On my fingers staying to indicate clear recognition, her body seemed to nestle into sureness. I knew that she was smiling. I did not know whether to be angry or glad. The darkness was her very sure ally. While it was there, she was serene, for she lived in a medium that was all-cancelling. She came to me again, nuzzling naturally.

Someone lighted a match: the puny light failed to reach us. For a moment or two the match-flame held its tiny life within a limited compartment of green air; then it died to what appeared to be the smallest possible point of gallant scarlet. Then the matchlights sprang up everywhere. I tilted the woman's face so that the nearest light would fall across it. I was eager to verify what I already felt certain of—that I was holding Edith Mallory.

Concealed beneath her resting eyelids were the twin points of catlight in the pupils of her eyes. As the light died she made an effort to draw closer. Her sleepy but confident assurance that I would welcome her caused me to experience a transient anger. Savagery throbbed under my fingernails. I had to fight against a temptation to hurt her. The lights quenched. I found my body trembling as with a peculiar laughter. Her body answered mine in full joy and our lips cried together again.

The torchman had tied an oil-soaked handkerchief to the tines of the hayfork. As the transient flare sprang out the passages were robbed of extreme menace. With swears that had a touch of good-humour in them the torchman rallied us. Behind me in the darkness a man was comforting a young woman: he was holding her tightly and saying: "Are you all right now, Eileen?" In a listless voice, the woman kept repeating: "For God's sake, Mylie, take me out of here!"

As we retraced our steps Edith Mallory and I dallied as much as we dared. We were arm in arm, well away from the flare, the light of which failed to reach us. Sometimes our bodies broke away from one another: the reverberation of a wave in the hollow place gave us the excuse to come hip to hip together again.

We padded across the great cave-hall and passed the dim openings of the seal recesses to our left. We saw the break in the cliffs where the waves contended under a green spotlight of distorted moonlight. Beneath the arch of the entrance the pool was appreciably deeper, and the wave by the unseen wall had gained a backrace of foam to add novel danger to its slither and hiss. In the open strand, the moonlight, by comparison with the darkness in the cave, seemed almost as bright as daylight.

It was good to hear the fiddle music floating strong across the sand and to hear the dance-thumps coming from the boathouse.

After a quiet word to one of her companions, she remained behind with me. The throng of young men and women were so delighted to be out in the open once more that they paid us little heed. When they had drifted away we went to the head of the cove, and there, sitting back to back on the dry sand, donned our boots and shoes. Up to this we had not spoken.

A pathway ran zig-zaggedly up the cliffside. The climb demanded sureness of eye and of foot : this Edith Mallory had in good measure. On the cliff-top the world seemed fair and free. Underfoot the grass was bone-dry—it would rain on the morrow. In the high south hung the gibbous moon, its edge cut clean against the sky.

We walked along a sheeptrack until we reached the limit of the headland. Beneath our feet was the recurrent thud of a wave breaking in a cavern far below. The woman began to hum ; now and again I had to falter in my stride to make sure that the humming was a reality. The tune she hummed has remained hidden in my mind down the years, revealing itself on small excuses—at the sight of a sheep starting away from me, at the smell of seaweed thrusting up from a hidden cove or at the boom of a wave on a rugged shore.

We had begun to talk desultorily. I found that her world was poles apart from my world of Cloone. A topic chanced between us : it was Darby's Bed. The bed was on a low headland jutting from the cliff : I pointed out where it lay low above the water a little distance to the north. She had never heard of it before. For her the world of Gaelic legend had no existence. I was eager to tell her of Leaba Dhiarmuda but feared that in the telling I should sound precious. At last, her live interest conquering me, I told her of Diarmuid and Grainne, the loveliest lovers Ireland had ever known ; of their flight, of the pursuit, of the bracken beds in which they had passed a single night, to be up and away as day whitened in the east.

We walked on until we were close to the Bed : after twenty centuries it was a place still sought out by lovers. We stood on the narrow isthmus that led to the headland on which the Bed was : here it was that when the pursuers had almost stolen upon their game, a fairy boar had come racing out before them and had roused out the sleeping lovers with the sound of its grunting. Diarmuid had grasped Grainne, had leaped on the boar's back and gone swaying into the morning sky. At the foot of the cliff breakers were falling on a tiny strand. There, at evening, Grainne had bathed while Diarmuid had kept guard on the cliff above. At times he must have turned from the point of danger to glance downwards to where she stood at the mouth of a little cave—a wisp of new moon a spring night had left behind.

Below us the tide was filling Grainne's cave. I glanced in the direction of the snug hollow in the peninsula—in the sector of countryside that lay within a swing of five miles of where we were standing, Darby's Bed had broken the traditional dowry system of marriage. Rich married poor in that area—for the love of the lovers of legend. Land and cattle and house and gear were secondary considerations. Diarmuid and Grainne were only fifty story-tellers away ! Grey man telling apt boy : apt boy becoming grey man. Of the hapless pair, the old story-tellers said : " They lived : they loved. They are remembered because they died for love." The young women of the locality loved Diarmuid ; the young men Grainne. In their secret hearts, the young men said : " O, the mouth of honey ! " and the young women : " O, the mouth of gold ! " The legend they saw as a green eternal tree. In the countryside around Fanore bizarre deeds were done on the head of love.

Fanore is Gaelic for Ring of Gold.

Silently we stepped down, walking on the soft grass of the isthmus. Then we climbed the not-steep acclivity that lay beyond it. I held the woman's arm. Reaching the highest point of the small peninsula we saw the Bed directly below us. In it (for a moment I thought Diarmuid and Grainne had leaped living across the centuries) were a young man and a young woman. I recognised them at once—Finn Dillon and Shoon Lawlee. At first my heart gladdened at seeing them there: then it sorrowed. I signalled to Edith Mallory not to speak. Finn and Shoon were not courting. Shoon was sitting up, erect and stiff, looking out to sea. Always it was said of her that she had distances in her eyes. Finn was turned on his side and was plucking angrily at the grasses. The moonlight made the details of the scene as clear as could be. For an instant then I was taken with a dark premonition: Diarmuid had died bitterly and Grainne had grieved to the full. The parallel was intolerable, so I refused to accept it. We four were young and the world was filled with happiness.

I drew Edith away. We kept to the grass lest we should rattle a pebble on the narrow pathway. We came out on the cliff-top and strolled northwards where we could see the lighthouses winking along the shores of the great estuary.

A late seabird flew in the direction of a flat rock that lay some distance from the shore. Edith looked out to sea; I stood beside her, my shoulder behind her shoulder. Her head came backwards to meet mine. The night sea was prone before us. I was tempted to cup my hands about my mouth and trumpet the world's wonder. Standing thus, my heart kept crying halloo and halloo and halloo.

It was three o'clock in the morning when the last train left Fanore. Edith smilingly remarked that she would have a host of explanations to make, but that her mother, at least, would understand and forgive. The railroad that joined Fanore to our town had to be seen to be believed. The train had been invented by a Frenchman and was unique: alone among the peoples of the world we had had the wit to put the invention to practical use. The train resembled a series of elongated jaunting-cars running on a fifteen-mile-long trestle or raised monorail. The seats in the carriages faced outwards: at ear-level the wheels made the black racket of hell behind a thin partition. The twin-funnelled engine was blood-brother to the carriages—it also was slung in two parts over the rail and seemed endowed with eyes. If God had granted us the boon of seeing this train of ours with an alien eye we would of a surety have died of immoderate laughter.

Pat Gillick, one of the two train guards, a stick of misery if there was ever one, stood at the rear of the train and ran his eye along the carriages ("sighting the dado," Old Carpenter Font called this operation) to see if they were in equipoise. Outside an open carriage-door stood My Lord Caherdown: he had a gay head of drink on him and was conspiratorially telling Galileo how Caius Julius Caesar had insulted his niece under an apple tree. Metal Belly, tall and detached, was standing beneath the blue-green light of a station lantern: he was secretly ashamed at being out of bed at such a roystering hour and was thus wearing his morality like a cloak.

Pat Gillick was wearied from trying to get the last train away. One moon swung high in the sky: another swung in the lantern in his hand. The open-air rolling stepladder by which we crossed from one side of the train to the other was festooned with the tangled bodies of men who had refused to enter the carriages. Unavailingly Pat blew his whistle. The pair of engine-drivers added their ultimatums on the whistles attached to the twin funnels. The cobalt night continued to be replete with good-humoured yowling.

When the long-awaited moment had arrived that the whole train was in balance and Pat was on the point of signalling to his fellow-guard on the other side to slam the doors and wave his flag, a drunken latecomer tumbled into our carriage and upset everything. Pat Gillick was exasperated beyond measure. It was little use arguing with the latecomer, so he shone his lantern on Edith Mallory and myself where we huddled in a corner. His plea to me to hurry to the other side set up a laugh at my expense. " Ches Macnamara," he said plaintively, " deny yourself a small bit o' coortin' so that the train can get movin'. I can't set ye goin' while the off-carriage is cocked up for height." I compromised : I took one half hundredweight from under the seat, while Pat took another. These weights we carried to the other side of the train and dumped them unceremoniously on the floor of the carriage corresponding to the one in which I had been seated. I then rushed back and took my place beside Edith Mallory. At last all was ready. The train for its entire length was in balance. The unearthly whistle of departure was greeted with a cheer.

Bearing a yelling, chanting, swaying burden, the train in full throttle tore through a countryside the colour of the bloom on the first frost-touched sloe. Hoarsely we went and with a delighting racket. I held the woman fast. The carriages were without light but we faced the moon.

# CHAPTER III

I

I CAME close to Madcap O'Neill on the night of the American wake in Littero. The closeness was that of a swinging pendulum.

An aunt of Finn Dillon's was married in Littero, a townland by the shore of the great estuary. The invitation she sent us was generous : " Let the boys and girls of Cloone come out on Saturday night to give my daughter Bridie a good send-off before she goes to America." This invitation caused excitement and rejoicing among the young people of Cloone.

Littero is a district of small holdings on rich estuarine loam : at that point the estuary is five miles wide. It was once a noted place for herring until the local people had dug up a tyrannical landlord's body and cast it into the sea : after that the net-men were desolate because of the empty tides.

But the people of Littero had not given way to despair : the ground under their boots was too good to admit of that. From being fishermen gambling with water and weather, they became industrious smallholders. They had the reputation of being as cute as pet foxes and as thrifty as squirrels. " Cosy farmer-eens," this is how they were described in the adjoining town-lands. Their long low cottages were roofed with Gurranagore half-slate. Sometimes the Litteros, as they were called, rose to the luxury of stepping-ponies which they raced on the strand when the harvest was home.

Because their loam was sandy and warm, they had the earliest potatoes in the barony. The day the first Littero potatoes of the year arrived in Cloone, on all sides there were smiles and snatches of song. " God grant we be alive to see the new spuds again ! "—this fervent prayer arose from every dinner-table. The fervour of the prayers was not to be wondered at since the security of the potato crop was reckoned a matter of transcendent importance in a land where history has had to record that its failure had halved the population. Exiles from Cloone often spoke feelingly in this fashion: "Ah, how I should like to be at home today and see my mother's face smiling at me through the steam of Littero potatoes!"

It was about four o'clock on the evening of an autumn day. On every lip in Cloone was Littero, Littero, Littero. We who were going to the American wake had arranged to meet at the crossroads of Cloone at half-past four. We had decided to walk cross-country the five Irish miles between Cloone and the estuary. The young men poured out great basins of hot water and, setting these vessels on backless chairs in the haggards, stripped to the waist and began to scrub themselves frenziedly. In the back rooms of the cottages the girls were making their secret preparations.

At last we were assembled. We linked arms and made a chain. Facing for the hill road out of Cloone, we went off, singing and skipping as we went. Caherdown came to his door: he was dressed in snow-white shirt and black pants. Shaving-soap was islanded on his good complexion. "Hey!" he roared, "where are ye off to?" "To an American wake in Littero," we sang out in reply. He looked at the full dozen of laughing faces. "My right arm I'd give to be twenty again," he said; "By God but I would!" "What a man I was at twenty!" said Finn Dillon, mocking him. "Have it your own way, my laughing prince," Caherdown said; "but I'll tell you the truth of it. Youth has the meat of enjoyment but lacks the sauce of experience; with age, it's the reverse: plenty sauce but precious little meat. Meat and sauce we'll have only in the Eternal Place." He then showed signs of tears. Concernedly, Finn put his face close to Caherdown's as if examining his Lordship's features for a secret blemish, and said: "Can it be, my lord, that your kidneys are behind your eyes?"

Laughingly we stepped out from him when he showed signs of anger. All together then we gave the Raheela roar. This he accepted as a tribute. " Good luck, chickens," he said; " God keep the blood high ! " " The blood high ! " we echoed as we danced away.

On the road to Littero on that fine autumn evening we got fits of sham fighting among ourselves. " Kissing and bleeding like the Cloonies "—that was a saying in the town beyond us.

We took the short-cut to the estuary, crossing fields by mass-paths and well-paths and traversing small overgrown boreens. Travelling thus made our journey three miles shorter than by road. For the most of the way Madcap and my sister Mary linked arms with Finn Dillon. I walked with Jody Shea, the wheelwright. Shoon Lawlee was behind me, linking one of the others : a nigger-brown beret was clinging precariously to the waterfall of her hair. Her almond-shaped eyes were alight with mischief. Coming down a long field with the path broad before us and the furze brilliant above us, the girls got a fit of mocking. I pricked up my ears to see who it was being impaled.

To my sister Mary, Shoon said : " Seven mattresses and a pea, is it, Mary Macnamara ? "

Mary laughed. It was a tentative but warm laugh. All the women came alive. It was clear that they had been at this mockery in secret and were now producing the rehearsed playlet so as to grill one of the men. I looked at Finn and Young Font. They were alert. Who was on the rack ?

Mary said : " Yes, dear; seven mattresses and a pea ! "

Shoon said : " There'll be considerable difficulty in getting the mattresses, Mary Macnamara. Feather ticks we have in Cloone."

Mary said : " True, a-girl, but look how easy it will be to provide the pea ! "

" May God protect us from small praties ! " said one of the young Hibe girls. The women all laughed at her full intonation of prayer.

My sister Mary stuffed her emerald beret into her pocket and shook out her chestnut hair as if preparing herself for battle. Jody Shea was afraid to laugh lest it be himself the women were pecking. He held his upper lip close over his small buck teeth. His eyes were rovers both. Finn knew exactly what the women were at—I knew by the confident set of his head. Madcap was taking no part in the game.

Shoon sighed, and said : " That I may never die till I die in a fourposter ! "

Mary said : " Far from fourposters we were reared."

And again : " May God protect us from small praties ! "

In order to bring the battle outfield, Finn said : " This is a subject I'm blind and dull on. I'd rather be hit square."

" Me, too ! " said Madcap, in a small voice.

This should make the women come out of their shells. The next sentence should tell it.

With lovely wickedness, Shoon said : " Will you salute poor people, then, Mary Macnamara ? "

" I might, and I might not ! " Mary tossed her head. " Blue blood is blue blood ! " she said primly.

Shoon came up to her and curtsied : " We're thankful to you for your consideration, Miss Macnamara."

" Indirect the relationship may be," Mary said, " but undoubtedly the connection will be there."

" The relationship will be so strained," said a third, " that a greyhound would be hard set to catch it."

" May God protect us from small praties ! " Mock-deep the voice.

The climax was now near. Drawing abreast of Jody Shea and myself, Shoon flashed a glance of triumph at me and then turned to Mary : " Can Mr. Breen have a day's fishing in your Blue Pool ? " she asked with the refinement of provocation. All laughed at this sally.

My face flamed. The Blue Pool was in Major Mallory's estate. I had been meeting Edith Mallory infrequently on the cliff above it. I didn't think the stones of the road knew of my secret. On seeing how my face had reddened, the women were exhilarated. Finn licked his lips. Madcap still continued to play a wan part in the baiting.

The band of mocking women halted. The autumn hillside grew quiet as Mary signalled for the laughter to end. In the nearness and in the distance the year was swinging home. Mary then put her hand close to the grass, about the height of a mattress above it, and called : " One ! " She then raised her hand four or five inches. " Two ? " she said. So on, she counted till she came to seven. She was generous in allowing height for the last three mattresses. Then she gathered her coat about her as if preparatory to climbing into a grotesque invisible high bed. You should have seen her try to lever her ample rump into position. " A leg into bed, Miss Lawlee ! " Mary said, with counterfeit dignity.

Then all of a sudden the play fell asunder. With tears of mockery in their eyes, Shoon and Mary embraced and fell towards the furze. I was utterly isolated : the others were in a shouting, gesticulating, mocking ring around me. But, with two swift tongue thrusts, I more than held my own.

" Maybe 'tis Darby's Bed you're thinking of ? " I said to Shoon Lawlee. " Yourself and the royalty of Cloone ! " That silenced Shoon and Finn both. Mary, my sister, still remained, guffawing incontinently. She seemed reluctant to allow the comedy to end. As she was about to resume her mockery, I extended my arms to the sky, spread my fingers wide and said in a high falsetto : " Oh, Dolly dear, I'm wild to be married ! Keep talkin' ! Keep talkin' ! " This was a tag of conversation between my sister and Dolly the Rose which I had overheard. I was reckoned a useful mimic.

The blow was only semi-fair, but it went fully home. Mary's face turned blood-red. The other girls laughed. It was a novel shy laugh such as women use when only women are present. A hint of malice or serve-you-right was clearly implicit in it. Shoon and Mary were punished on the instant. The conspiracy was ended. We could resume our journey in peace.

On the top of the grassy hill-gap we turned to view the town which lay behind us in the hollow. The tawny trees in the parklands were going down in grandeur. Over our thatched cottages the evening smoke hung : the river was a silver sickle lying at the cliff foot. At the mouth of Cloone, Mary-without-Stain stood up brown and dumpy behind her dark-red railings : she looked down with benevolence on Bovenizer's and Folan's —on Flung Dung and the Maid of Erin. We were able to make out the figure of Little Angel, the old sacristan, as he pottered about the small green lawn in front of the mortuary chapel or deadhouse—a small building clinging to the epistle side of the church. We saw the bald patch that was the market-place just out of Cloone and behind Bank Place. Beyond the market-place was the ball-alley with handballers moving swiftly and silently within its three walls. The town spire was high, slender and graceful.

Beyond the town the river was hiding and re-appearing in the far plain. We saw the rabbit-brown bogland lying between the lowbacked hills. Here and there patches of clean autumn emerald spoke for fields that had yielded vividness as a result of intense industry. After the fields came the broken sandhill wall on the south coast of Fanore. Then there was the sea : over it hung an evening sky that was inching upwards to purple in the full west. We turned our backs on that world and faced for the declivity into Littero.

When again we had joined the road, people appeared at the half-doors of cottages to see us go singing past. Farmers' sons stowing cows watched us inscrutably from the darknesses of stall openings. Old wives doing mysterious chores in haggards straightened their backs and looked wistfully after us. Children ran to cottage doors to tell of our approach ; as we passed by we saw small curtains twitching in the cottage windows. One of the girls had an acquaintance in a roadside cottage. She rushed ahead of us, and leaning on a hedge of privet, called over the half-door : " Hello Han ! "

" Mother of God, where are all the Cloonies off to ? " A

red-faced woman was framed in the doorway. She had been baking bread : she now began brisking her hands on her sides.

" We're off to an American wake ! "

" Where, achree ? "

" In Littero."

" An' who's leavin' fleece-lined Littero ? "

" A Bridie Bowen : her mother is an aunt of Finn Dillon's."

" Well ! Well ! Nora Dillane's daughter ! Where in America is she headin' for ? "

" Bostonmassachusetts ! " Always we took it as an unbroken mouthful of sound : this was because we had heard it pronounced thus from infancy and had never thought it to be other than one word.

" Is she the wan who's friendly with the Meehan boy—he that's the hurler, an' whose father keeps a stake weir ? "

" How do we know ? It gives us more than we can do to keep track of our own coortin' ! "

Han's laughter rang out above ours. She looked at Finn's studded belt. " And so this is the Prince of Cloone ! " She looked at the young women. " And which of ye is the princess ? " she asked.

It was difficult to embarrass Finn : we saw that he was then embarrassed. No one responded although it was a plain opening for gibing. Covertly we looked at Finn and Shoon. She had idled a step or two aside and was plucking at the golden privet leaves. Her brown beret sat on the cascades of her luxuriant fair hair. Her body was slender.

Han invited us inside. We refused, pleading the hurry that was on us. She came out to mid-road. Before she said good-bye, she looked down at our boots : " Ah," she said, " there are the feet that will be jaded before morning ! "

We laughed at the novelty of her saying. We laughed, too, in disbelief. How could all creation jade us ?

II

We were in Littero. There was the river, the three waters plainly legible on its face: the old tide, the ebb and the true ebb. In each of the tiny sweet fields were bunches of red calves. Small black Kerry cows were there too, crammed, so it seemed, with milk, the tips of their black horns bright white. The piers flanking the wooden gates were upright posts of cut stone with hinge-rings bolted through them. What thorn trees there were seemed sucked inland. Clean turkeys were everywhere, piping in their foreign tongues. The Wyandotte hens were plump, clean and busy by the dry stone fences. The hedges of the roadside were solid walls of fuchsia, the leaves black as evergreen, the scarlet flowers decking the darkness of the leaf wall or making a brilliant pathway where they had fallen by the bushes. "Tears of God," the Gaelic-speaking Littero folk called these fallen flowers. At a small bridge over a stream we clapped our hands and watched the trout dart. We passed by bush-covered boreens that would be splendid places for telling a girl how lovely she was.

Whenever an old woman passed us, perched on the high seat of a trim donkey cart, we wondered at the glory inherent in her arrival. The silver wires of her hair, the warm brown of her Paisley shawl, the cart orange-red in colour with the shafts and chamfers tipped with black, the bridge of the straddle painted with farmer's blue or brilliant emerald, with maybe a sprig of red-gold beech leaves in the brass-studded winkers to confound the late flies—all these formed the perfect enhancement for the peace of the old woman's face.

From the mouths of the people we met we experienced the lovely lilt of Littero. Their speech was close to the Gaelic: at this time they were narrowly balanced between losing and holding it. The low snug stone-roofed cottages, lime-white and strong, sat at right angles to the road. Hanks of silver onions gleamed through the slats of the drying-sheds.

Littero was a pocket in the country as Cloone was a pocket in the town. Thus it was that as we walked along the scarlet-edged roadway we began to feel kith and kin of the place. We came upon a rowan tree beside a cottage by the shore. The fading green, the red, the white! We came to a dip where there was a churchyard by a stream: here the gable of a ruined church stood amid the old awry Celtic crosses. Standing on the roadway Finn Dillon selected a spot where the limestone bones of the world were thrusting up through the surface. He stood still and called on us to pay him heed. "A man from Littero," he explained, "comes home late from the fair once a month. As often as not he is a little the worse for drink. He gets out of the cart here, takes his stand on this outcrop of limestone and looks directly towards the gable of the old church beside which his father lies buried. He then raises his voice and shouts: 'Father, will the poor be poor always?'" Finn laughed, and looked at us. "Listen!" he said.

He turned his face towards the ruined church. "Father," he shouted, "will the poor be poor always?" Clearly the echo returned from the spotted stones. "Poor always!" Staunch and steady its answer was, as if, indeed, it told God's Gospel truth. We laughed at the folly of the echo—between us we hadn't a crown in our pockets, yet, where was the loss? Could riches buy a single leap a Cloone lad would give into the sky?

In a roadside field we saw a turkey cock and some turkey hens. The cock was in the full sail of sex: so that he looked as if a single puff of breeze would send him floating in the air. Free and fair, men and women both, we laughed at him. The laughter was neither prurient nor prudish. The honesty of the bird had reduced life to its brave essentials. The young men laughed because of the antics of the barred and bronzed arch-rascal, his dewlaps and wattles fully aflame: what they saw in him was a caricature of the ridiculous heroics of the courting male; the young women laughed because in the counterfeit timidity of the turkey hens they identified the mock-meekness of the courted female. A deeper significance lurked in the laugh, but it, too, after its fashion, was honest. Slight as the incident was, it added a relish to our journey: afterwards the matured laughter on our tongues was peppered with an adventurous memory something like the tang of radish.

In the long house that lay end-on to the road, Mrs. Bowen welcomed us warmly. Approaching the place we had noted that the stone outhouses were strong and well-filled. Entering the kitchen we had found the weak tang of the estuary in every item of gear.

Mrs. Bowen was all bosom and ready tears. She was unlike Finn Dillon's father. When she had finished embracing the girls, she began shaking the young men's hands. "I'm thankful to ye for comin'," she said. "I'd rather a weak white calf from Cloone than a strong bullock from Littero. Where a person is born, he is branded with that place forever. Forever!" she said. Then, brightly, "Forever Cloone!" We laughed, not without a queer pride.

Then: "Gi' me a look at ye an' I'll christen ye. I was schoolmate to yeer fathers an' mothers." She went from one to the other of us. When she saw me, she turned quickly and looked at my sister Mary. "Holy God!" she exclaimed, "will ye look at the chestnut skulls of the two Macnamaras!" To Madcap O'Neill she said softly: "Dark Jack O'Neill is in you, girlie, but which of his three wives I couldn't rightly say." Madcap told her. When Mrs. Bowen came to Shoon Lawlee she ran her fingers through the cascades of the girl's hair. "No denyin' that!" she said, "I've heard of the lovely old name they've put on you. Shoon, isn't it?" Shoon nodded. Nora Bowen then said: "Shoon Lawlee: that's a name royalty 'd be proud to have! The nicest name we have on a girl here is Sive Munnelly." She placed the accent firmly on the ell. Half to herself, she added: "Sive Munnelly an' Shoon Lawlee. They're lovely: they're old: they're Irish."

Turning swiftly, she upbraided her husband for not coming forward to welcome us. He smiled sheepishly. He was a small thickset man with bristles in his ears and nostrils. To each of us in turn he tendered a limp handshake.

We were chastened by the sincerity of the welcome.

" This is Bridie. 'Tis she is goin'," Mrs. Bowen said. The mother was in the girl's face : as we looked again we saw the father. She was what we in Cloone called an honest transaction ! She was a pleasing but plain girl of twenty or so. Her plaited hair was wound like a crown on her head. She seemed reserved. She drew back from us and fell into quiet conversation with her cousin, Finn Dillon.

The broad airy kitchen was coming to life. The children of the house were there : mostly girls they were. There was one boy of about eleven. His name we found was Owen. Owen Bowen ! We said it softly to ourselves and laughed, thinking of how the mother had relished the sound of the girls' names. Great deference was paid to Owen—it was Owen this and Owen that : his name was first on everyone's lips. This was because he was the only boy in a fleet of girls. It was a matter of pride that the holding should " remain in the name." Owen it was who would be king when the father and mother had grown old. He would bring in a strange woman whose fortune would release the last lingerer among the girls. Owen would rule the sweet fields, the flitches of bacon hanging from the rafters and the onions in the shed. It was because of Owen that the girls would, one helping another by paying her passage, cross the ocean with slender hope of ever returning. Out of all the Bowen girls, one, if she were lucky, would remain at home and marry a smallholder content to accept a token dowry.

The Cloone girls hung their coats on a row of pegs beside the door of the upper room. We traipsed into this room and sat around the table on which the marriage delph was laid. We sat there prim enough, boy alternating with girl. The girls kept smoothing their dresses over their thighs. It was a penance on us to hold back our laughter. Mrs. Bowen bustled in and out with Bridie at her heels. The golden tea began to spill into china cups that had blue-gold borders.

The walls were painted a dark scarlet and the cream jug on the table was of such a colour that one would have thought it had been dipped in red wine. Dusk had gathered in the room, so Mrs. Bowen lighted the lamp and set it on mid-table. The lamplight itself, possibly because of the colour of the walls, failed to illuminate our faces fully. But the linen tablecloth proved a wonderful reflector of light as also did the white-painted boarded ceiling. We were thus seated on the periphery of a strange brilliance. As the young women's heads moved with the conversation, the light and the absence of light played quirks with their faces. At times it would bring Shoon's olive face to an attractive pinkish hue, or succeed in whitening the features of my sister Mary. In these unusual surroundings, the food inexplicably became mysterious and enticing. On the tablecloth we could see the faint pattern of the arms of the four provinces of Ireland, also a round tower and harp. The little sugar bowl was delicate olive-coloured Belleek and the sugar seemed cleaner and precious because of the good ware that held it. Beneath the linen was a heavy dark-red chenille cloth—the delph shifted soundlessly on its pile; the tassels of the chenille were heavy on our knees. Bowens had just killed a pig, so we were served with fresh pudding.

When the meal was drawing to an end, Mrs. Bowen said sharply: "Bridie! Cut the currant cake for the Cloone lads!"

Whatever way it was she said it, her voice sounded incredibly funny. A small bout of tittering went through us. A laugh can be the most imperative of all calls of nature. Mrs. Bowen was at the sideboard: Bridie had gone into the kitchen for a breadknife. No one dared placing his or her mouth to the lip of a cup while the memory of this tittering remained. Finn Dillon could hold back the most intense laughter: he looked questioningly all around the table—his thin lips were easy in a half smile. We kept pleading with him, wordlessly : For God's sake, Finn, make a joke of any kind, good, bad, or indifferent, before we shame ourselves ! You have a leg in both worlds ! You alone can save us from humiliation ! But Finn kept us slowly roasting : he even dared to take a sip of his tea and while his mouth was firm on the cup his cool eyes quizzed us. All the while the need for laughter was punching great holes in us. Now, I thought, we of Cloone are humbled for ever.

Mrs. Bowen had found the breadsaw in the sideboard : she sensed the quietness behind her, and bringing the currant loaf and breadboard to the table, began to cut the loaf and at the same time make animated conversation. What she was saying seemed to accentuate our dire need for laughter. The great home-made loaf fell in slices before the knife : as one man we dared to follow Finn's cold speculative gaze and look at the bread slices as they fell, hoping to find sanity in the sight of this ordinary domestic phenomenon. The currants were not plentiful in the loaf. Suddenly, when the smallest titter would have set us aflame, Finn Dillon stopped chewing, struck the table with his fist and pointing at the loaf, said : " Cripes, lads, a currant ! "

In the nick of time the relief came. We bubbled over and fell sideways. We laughed until we cried. Mrs. Bowen dropped the knife on the table and placing her two hands around Finn's neck began to press his head between her bulky breasts. " How could you be good," she said, " an' you to be got off that melted rogue of a brother o' mine ? " Finn's cries to be released were muffled. After she had finished punishing him, she kissed him warmly. I concluded that she was immeasurably proud that Finn had inherited the roguery of the Dillons.

There was a smattering of music from the kitchen. We had heard the neighbours filing in and had noted how, as we ate, the conversation had thickened beyond the room door. Laughter and banter were thrown hither and thither. Then we heard passages of " puss-music ", a kind of lilting-humming that some countrymen are adept at. I listened carefully as a boy emitted shrill weird music on an ivy leaf. Suddenly there was a grand rumpus as a newcomer came in the kitchen door. Silence followed: this in its turn was broken by yelps of encouragement. We then heard one bar from a concertina. One bar only, and we of Cloone were ripe for the Kingdom of Heaven!

Not so the sheepdog of the house who at the sound of the music sat on her haunches and began to howl as if all the desolation of the world had descended upon her.

In the kitchen we watched while the white prized shell sand was being swept off the floor. The green broom drove the powdered shells flying into the ashes of the open fire. From all corners of the thronged kitchen, Littero faces peered at us. Because of us they spoke English, reverting to Gaelic only when the knowledge of English idiom was inadequate for their purpose.

By this time our girls had mingled with the Littero girls. Women have that virtue: they can, always with a sudden warmth and comradeship, enter one another's worlds.

Now and again Bridie or her mother rose to greet new guests. Once, Bridie did not rise to greet a newcomer: he was a tall young man with jet black hair and jet black eyes. His ears were lying close against his head. Attention was focused on him as he entered. Bridie Bowen looked down at her hands in her lap. We had no need to be told that this was Ulick Meehan, whose father owned a stake weir on the estuary.

From a corner by the hob the concertina began to speak from between the musician's fingers. The beat of life was in the tide of the tune. Our bodies were already jigging though we gave no outward indication that they were inwardly straining at their bonds. The music seeped up to the head. We were reared to recognise this type of rhythm and none other. The men looked at the women. It was a new, eager, yet restrained look. There were unspoken pacts and treaties without words. I looked at Madcap: her eyes fell. I was certain that they had been on me before I glanced in her direction. When again her gaze lifted, she answered yes, yes, with her eyes. At the back of my mind a question was being asked: would this, now, here, what-was-present, help to solve I-knew-not-what riddle?

The music fell to the beat of a square set. Mrs. Bowen was smiling and blinking her eyes. Then she said loudly: "Let the music not run to waste, in the name o' God!"

The young men had got themselves into a cluster in mid-floor. Their heads were close together as they began a meaningless conversation. From under the visors of their caps their eyes were roving; their glances were confirming previous agreements made with young women. I watched them narrowly: I was endeavouring to trap a Littero man as he called a girl. The difference between rejection and acceptance in a girl's eyes was so fine that only a Littero man could have told which was which. The music grew surer and the shoe of the musician requiring. After an especially demanding phrase of music the women swept quickly from the walls, and each took her place beside the man who had called her.

Heads high, shoulders square, eyes set, lips tuned to a quiet delight. . . . Grace, pride, precision. . . . Colour, movement and music. The snow-white walls and the shadows on them. Your partner's body understanding yours. Her body moving on a pivot at the wheel of the set so that a finger-tip could control it. The watching farmers' eyes fell first on the shoes, then climbed to scrutinise the faces of the dancers.

In Cloone we took pride in our dancing: for a whole winter we had delayed an itinerant dancing-master who was anxious to make his way into the west. Twice, as he was on the point of pitching us to hell, we made him blithero drunk; twice also we stole his breeches. Every night we kept practising in the Rookery, the beginners having their legs marked so as to facilitate the dancing-master who stood out before them. The right leg was marked with a sugawn or hayrope tied above the calf, the left similarly marked with a gad or withy. It was hard work as we responded to : " Down with sugawn, up with gad," or " Drum on sugawn, Lift with gad."

At last, when we had the master's brains picked we laughed at the fellow and released him for the benefit of the west. Overlate he appreciated the point of our conspiracy ; first he cauterised us with his white-hot tongue, and secondly—unpredictably this—thereafter picked inordinate pride out of our dancing prowess. Among the women, Madcap O'Neill was perhaps the best we had : when I danced with her we both sensed that we had been freed of inner trammels.

Each figure of the set caused us to sidle away into new mood patterns. At the dance's end there was always the sudden jet of delighted breath. Then came the monosyllabic thanking of your partner who had been strange sib to you for the duration of the dance and whose manner of saluting you thereafter would be subtly conditioned by the memory of that sibship.

During the night I danced with a Littero girl. She was a plain-faced, plain-bodied young woman. As we danced someone called her Sive. I knew then that I was dancing with Sive Munnelly. When I said : " You have a lovely name ! " she began to glow. After a while, she asked : " Which of yeer girls is Shoon Lawlee ? " I indicated Shoon. For the rest of the dance, Sive's eyes kept returning to Shoon. I saw then what was in her mind as exactly as if I had been reading it out of a book.

Between the dances there were songs. The shy country fellows could not sing except when hidden behind a rampart of three or four other lads. The girls sang, too : singing, they remained seated. To stand while singing was reckoned a foreign affectation. As they sang they kept looking at their limp hands. The words of the songs told stories that were sad beyond sadness ; the tunes were arabesqued with trills and grace notes. Some of these airs had weathered a score of ballads set to their music. The singers of Cloone had old songs: those of Littero had older. This was because the seaboard was closer to the Gaelic. I kept translating the names of the Littero songs into English, and right royally they sounded: "Jimmy my Thousand Treasures," "I am Asleep and Do not Awaken me," "Take a Blessing From My Heart to the Land of my Birth," "Journey to the Country of the Ever-Young," "My Lovely Brown Boy," "The Blackberries," and "O, Fort of Gold." The exclamations from the onlookers, too, were unusual: "Noted!" "Glory on you, my flamin' boy!" "A devilish fine quatrain, that!", or "Wisha, my shinin' blade!"

A tierce of stout was tapped in the back porch; when the drink began to have its humorous way with the men, they ventured to give recitations. One was "Butte, Montana", a long narrative half-poem of an Irishman's privations in the silver-mines; another—an astonishing medley of irrelevancies—was titled "The Shower of Old Hags", and a third was the sly recitation of "The Skelligs List." This last, an annual doggerel verse, implored, abused and reviled matrimonial laggards: it urged them to take advantage of the aberration in Church Law by which Shrove, or the Season of Marriage, was extended into Lent in the monastery in Skelligs Island, which lay some miles off the coast. Twice during the night we felt the first pangs of weariness, but strong tea in the room revived us. Towards morning we felt fresher than ever before.

As it was brightening for broad day, Bridie Bowen and Ulick Meehan walked out into the yard. For a long while they remained at the gable-end of the house. There seemed to be little lustre in their conversation, only the sober making of plans.

Bridie then returned to the kitchen. I noticed how her face brightened as she saw in the doorway a tall oldish man who had just entered. He was dressed in a navy-blue fisherman's jersey. He spoke deeply and slowly: "At the lobster-pots I was," he said by way of excuse. He extended his great hand. "Goodbye, Bridie!" he said.

"Goodbye, Donal," she answered.

"God go with you, girl!"

"And remain with you, too."

He turned away, then looked back uneasily. Smilingly he said: "The evening you poked your finger between the wicker! And Lord Lobster was at home!"

"I remember!" Bridie said. There was small uneasy laughter. She looked at the index finger of her right hand.

"When are you off, Bridie?"

"A bare hour I have, Donal."

"Time for a row in the old pot," he said. "A last row!"

His mouth was pleading through his whitening lips. The bristles on his chin were lit with morning silver. Here was a man who scorned red loam. It was plain that herring was branded inside in his head.

The bystanders took up the appeal. One last boat ride—then never no more! The memory of it would be a talisman of Littero. We Cloonies who were caught in the knot of pleaders felt the soft force of the Littero mouths all around us. Bridie's mother came up.

"Do you wish to go out in the boat, child?" she asked.

"I do, mother."

"Off with you, then! Everything will be ready when you return."

Ten or twelve of us, mostly Cloonies, set off for the shore which lay beyond the small dunes. The dunes were two fields from the house. Donal, accompanied by another man, went off to procure the oars. Madcap, a Littero fellow, Ulick Meehan and Bridie Bowen came first. Finn Dillon, myself and some others followed. Shoon and Sive Munnelly were together.

Among the stragglers was my sister Mary. She was inclined deliberately to lag. I turned and saw her in company with a tall, awkward fellow: he had a face the colour of leather, his lower jaw was undershot and his cheekbones were high. He seemed foreign and native at the same time. I had seen her with this man many times during the night. It was obvious that she was poking fun at him, for he was so droll and slow that he seemed a perfect foil for her. Yet, when I glanced back at her, her expression changed quickly. She was warning me to keep out. Her emerald beret was sitting on her chestnut hair ; her hair fanned fully outwards as it fell on her shoulders.

We scrambled over the last stonewall and then there were only the sandhills between us and the sea. Bridie Bowen's eyes kept darting from side to side as if seeking for something on the ground. All the while she kept up a semblance of conversation. Suddenly she rushed forward, then crouched and carefully lifted something from the grass. When we had come up we saw that she was holding a perfect cup mushroom.

For a moment or two she was wholly withdrawn. She remained crouched, with the mushroom held between the index and second finger, just as she had held it while plucking it. She looked to left and to right to discover if the mushroom had a comrade. When she realised that it was alone, she put her two hands together and let the mushroom roll over into them. She kept looking at it and smiling as if she were holding a fledgling. She brought the mushroom close to her face. The little vessel of her hands imprisoned its aroma while she smelled it deeply. Next, she tilted the mushroom to the morning light so that she could peer between the stem and the cap and there spy out the delicate hidden rose-gills. When she rose she seemed a different person. Watching her, Finn Dillon's face was filled with a spurious sunlight.

" A mushroom," she said, perfunctorily. Her left hand closed carefully around it.

The tide had turned, and had left about thirty yards of clean fawn sand. There was only one turning wave.

Beyond that wave the estuary to the far shore downstream and upstream was quiet, silent and level. It resembled an old mirror inlaid between the headlands. The morning was wholly trapped in stillness. In the east the sun was climbing upwards behind dim clouds that were edged with the mingled hues of pewter and lilac. The west was bright as if the hidden light from the east had leaped over a barrier near the zenith and had flooded the west with its greenish wonder. On a rampart of rounded stones above the high-water mark a glass net-float, as if responding to this signal of the west, had lighted its green lamp. Beside us lay an old wicker lobster-pot ; its broken rods had peeled to reveal the cream of its wood. On the blue thistles at the edge of the sandhills blue moths fluttered. The moths offered welcome evidence of life—these only, and the one turning wave. The salt of the open sea was in the air, but it was chastened.

About ten yards from the tide-lip the boat lay on its side. It was anchored in the sand. Donal and the other oarsman came up.

An awkward old muller that same boat was ! After a struggle we succeeded in getting her to ride the almost silent tide. Eagerly the Cloonies piled in, all except my sister Mary, who remained on the shore. The tall country fellow stood by her side. Mary pleaded dread of the water.

Finn Dillon, Ulick Meehan and Bridie Bowen sat on the same thwart, Bridie on the outside, with Ulick in the middle. With her left hand she held Ulick Meehan's sleeve. Her right hand was loose, but careful, about the mushroom. Though she could not be called beautiful, the coil of her hair made her a crowned queen.

" A short circle, Donal," she said.

" Right, a-girl," Donal replied, driving the oar with the full force of his back. The clean sand slid under us ; it was faintly crazy-paved by the light from the stirred water about the boat.

When we were a short distance from the shore we began to sing. Our singing drew Mary from the dunes. The rich light on her hair seemed unusually bright. I envied her standing there listening to the singing coming to her from over the water. I thought : she will lose the song for an instant in the breaking of the single wave. Our voices must have carried far down- and up-stream. Looking towards the mouth of the river, I saw a cottage by the shore about a mile and a half from us : as I watched I saw a white cloth move slowly above its half-door. Bridie Bowen raised her arm in answer to this signal of farewell.

So easily and slowly did we ride the dead tide that the glass of the brimmed estuary was scarcely flawed by our passing. Bridie showed little emotion, only an earnest keenness at every triviality. Once she looked over the side of the boat : she then changed the mushroom from her right hand to her left hand, and leaning over, trailed her free hand in the water. She withdrew her hand and looked at it. It glistened.

Between the song snatches, Donal kept saying : the world he'd give to be captain of a red vessel, maybe a Bratt boat from the Baltic riding the true ebb, her decks glowing with Baltic timber. He kept decrying his way of living, saying that if he had his time over again he'd seek his fortune in the world instead of doling out his life on a griping circumscribed plot of ground where he had grass for two cows and water for two hundred. All the while his tune kept returning to the one note : herring, herring, herring.

As we sang " Terence's Farewell to his Love," my sister Mary left her pedestal on a small sandhill and walked forward to the edge of the tide. Close beside her the tall fellow moved. The level sand did not make his gait less ungainly. The song was a lonely one and fitted the case we were in. As we sang, we were half-conscious of offering Bridie Bowen the memory of our singing : the other half of our chanting was born of the sheer love or sheer need of it. When we came to the turn of the song, Mary placed her hand into her beret and raised it aloft. The brilliant green of the beret stood out against the mound of grey sea stones. The colour of the beret was insanely beautiful : its tiny brilliance balanced the low dun shoreline.

Mary was singing, too. She wasn't a good singer: once, owing to the time-lag due to the distance between her and the boat we heard her sing a bar by herself. The water and the morning were charitable to her voice. It reached us rich in honesty. When she found that she could not keep time with us, she waited for a verse to end, then half in mimicry, half in passion, shouted: "Forever Cloone!" Abruptly she doused the light of the beret in her pocket and turned towards the sandhills. Her companion obediently lumbered after. He towered over her, as in protection. Watching her go, our singing became all passion and the boatman pulled more strongly at the oars.

"Turn, Donal," Bridie said.

Returning to the house, we saw that the pony and trap were on the roadway beside the gate. Bridie was to drive eighteen miles to a town in the east to take advantage of a Sunday morning excursion train to the Cove of Cork. The lovely gaiety of the boatride ebbed from us.

The girl's father was standing at the pony's head. He was wearing his best frieze coat and new Sunday cap. The old trunk and the tattered case were in the trap. The mother was standing directly inside the kitchen door. She was dressed in her house best: she seemed unsure of her hands now that they were idle. The sisters stood in a bereft school by the door of the room. At the other side of the fire, Owen was standing.

As Bridie entered the thinly-crowded kitchen, we became conscious of the silence and its implications. Tentatively, we began to talk in little groups; about the boatride and the singing and the flicker of cloth from the cottage downstream and how the green beret had seemed so vivid on the shore. Bridie then went forward to the fire. She took the tongs and drew out a glowing coal of turf from the core of the blaze. This she broke to embers with the tongs' tips. She sprinkled a pinch of salt on the gills of the mushroom, then balanced it on the glowing coals. She went to the dresser and took down a small plate and set it at the head of the table. From a drawer in the table-end she took a fork.

Owen was watching her carefully. She crinkled her face at him as she passed. Then she crouched at the fireside waiting for the mushroom to roast. When it was roasted, she took it up, twisted the stem off it and set the mushroom cup on the plate. Again she grimaced at Owen, then beckoned to him to come forward. Slowly he came to the table head and sat down to eat. She took the fork out of his slow-moving hands and broke the mushroom into four pieces. He looked at her again as she handed him the fork. He took a piece of the mushroom on the tips of the fork-tines, gingerly placed it in his mouth and began to chew upon it, dropping and raising his jaw in a stolid manner. He gave four or five chews, then when his jaw had dropped he let it hang there and his eyes became irrevocably fixed upon her. Then the great tears came, and the small pieces of chewed mushroom flowed out over his lower lip and stuck to the spittle on his chin. We were all watching. Bridie thrust forward to the boy; she grasped his shoulders and ploughing her open mouth down on his, kissed him fiercely. The sheepdog bitch nuzzled up between them and began to lick the salt tears from the boy's face. Watching them, Ulick Meehan seemed suddenly to become strained and drawn.

The woman of the house took down a bottle of holy water. She sprinkled some on her daughter: "In the name of the Father, Son and Holy Ghost," she said. Then, "Let us make a start, in the name of the One God!" She took her shawl from a nailed reel behind the door and threw it loosely across her shoulders. It was good to see the green-and-black shawl of Cloone amid the tan Paisleys of Littero. Bridie looked her fill at the kitchen and walked out the door.

In the yard we formed a haphazard procession to the little bridge which lay in a road-hollow about a quarter of a mile east of the house. This was the traditional place of parting for those who were emigrating from Littero. First came the father, leading the pony by the head. Two neighbouring men walked with him, one on either side. The three were talking of commonplace matters. Immediately behind the trap came the mother and Bridie. With them walked those neighbours who were their closest friends. Behind these came the other daughters —Owen had remained in the house. The rest of us who had been at the wake made a raggle-taggle behind them.

As we passed each roadside cottage, the woman of the house came to the door to wish Bridie goodbye. Behind each woman stood her man, his heavy hands weighed down with shyness. Each of the women gave a soft eager rush at Bridie and enveloped her. We heard blessings, and shreds of blessings: " That you may be lucky, my grand girl . . . every step of the road, my jewel ! " A bedridden crone, who said goodbye to the girl from her bed just inside a hinged window, ignored Bridie after a single casual goodbye and drawing her black headshawl from off her ears, kept saying to the girl's mother: " There's hope from the ocean, Nora, but none from the grave."

At the bridge, we all clustered around Bridie and touched her for the last time. She drew Ulick Meehan apart. They spoke crisply to one another, as if verifying what had been already verified. They shook hands limply and turned away from one another.

The father was ill-at-ease. He was holding the pony's head while mother and daughter embraced. He gave a frightened look at the pair of them, then took his seat in the vehicle beside the second eldest of his daughters. He kept his head low. Heavy and dark his face was. Bridie sat into the trap and closed the door behind her.

" Go on out, pony ! "

At the first clop of the pony's hooves, the mother's spirit broke. She threw her check apron completely over her head, as if she were making a bogeyman to amuse a child. From beneath the apron emerged the sustained open-mouthed notes women make when they are in the extremity of desolation.

The mother turned and walked towards the parapet of the bridge. Her gait was steady : almost it appeared that she was careful to ensure that her grief would not detract from the dignity of her carriage. Her small daughters watched her : each made a minute bereft noise in mimicry of the mother. Each, too, turned and walked a few steps towards the bridge wall. To me, it appeared as if the mother was instructing the single girl who would remain behind how to behave when, in the course of years, her daughters would leave her and go across the sea.

III

It was that morning, returning from the American wake in Littero, that I came close to Madcap O'Neill.

It was a fine morning, though to me it appeared unreal and brittle after the exciting night. My sister Mary had gone off before us—inevitably the tall gawk was with her. Finn Dillon had a gaggle of others with him as he went away.

The night had given each of us something to ponder upon.

It was Sunday morning. " Eight o'clock Mass at Stonewall," Finn had said out of the corner of his mouth before he left us. Our postscript was : " Then we can sleep for the day." We yawned : mention of sleep had made us momentarily weary. By this time it was after six o'clock.

Standing on the roadside at a small distance from Bowen's house, Madcap O'Neill was talking earnestly to a Littero man who had been paying her a good deal of attention during the night. From where I stood loitering with only one of my eyes on her I saw the dark blue headlands crouch about the estuary. Like animals they were, their ears flat on their necks.

Idly I tried to convey the impression that I was waiting for a companion other than Madcap : I could not be sure whether or not she was watching me. Her free laughter forced me to a decision : with a gesture of impatience I turned for the road that led to Stonewall. Although my mouth was filled with a low tuneless whistling my lips remained dry and rebellious. I had scarcely gone a few yards when I heard another whistle behind me : *d' s; d' s* : I could clearly visualise the way the making of the whistle altered Madcap's face. Petulantly, I turned. " In a minute, Ches ! " she called. I saw the man come closer to her : whatever he was saying now appeared to possess the characteristic of urgency. I glanced irritably in her direction, then began to kick some sods on the roadside. The man with Madcap threw me an eye. I then realised that Madcap was signalling to me through renewed laughter. But I did not choose to read her signals. Feigning the breaking of my patience, I walked quickly away.

Madcap's light footsteps sounded behind me. " You could have waited," she said, angrily.

I was afraid my tone of voice would betray me, but—what was there to betray? I asked myself. " Why should I wait ? " I asked her quietly.

"I wanted to be shut of that fellow."

I whistled my unbelief, then said shortly : " I thought you were putting on an act ! "

Her angry breathing was clearly audible.

After a few steps she said : " To hell with you, Ches Macnamara ! " Here was a flash of the old fire that had won her her nickname. Here again beside me was the sprite who had tickled sea-trout and pitched the watching bailiff to the seventy-nine devils. Latterly she had softened. People were forgetting her childish escapades and were calling her Alice or Allie. This was because she was mature.

I could find no anger with which to meet her anger. We walked on in silence for perhaps a hundred yards : she was treading on the edge of the scarlet road carpet of fallen fuchsia flowers.

This I recall quite clearly : Madcap was wearing a new

showerproof coat. The smell of it was exciting me in a curious manner. Then: a gambit I'll try, I said to myself.

With counterfeit anger I said: "If I was married to you. . . ."

The instant she replied, I realised clearly that she knew it was a gambit. There was no reality—as yet.

"You'd what?" she said.

"I'd beat the lard out of you!" I said. "Once on weekdays and twice on Sundays for good measure!"

(Galileo tapping with the heel of his awl on his window pane to attract the attention of a prospective bridegroom. "So you're gettin' married, son? My advice to you is to beat the lard out of her, wance on weekdays and . . . twice on Sundays—for good measure! Ha-ha-ha-ha!")

She said: "That's the handy gab of a cobbler who never had the pluck to own a woman of his own."

"That doesn't make it a whit the less valuable," I said.

"Not to me, Ches! Not to me!" As on a finger-snap we were out of the sham and into the earnest.

"Yes, to you!" I said. "Your body I'd break or your pride."

"Neither my body nor my pride!" The dark wall of fuchsia foliage was towering above us. I looked down at her shoes: one small shoe-ball then spun grinding down the red and puce fuchsia heads.

I looked away at the blue headlands.

"A brave gay night it was, surely!" I said, lightly turning the topic aside to learn if that was the way she wished it. Whilst speaking I looked tauntingly over her shoulder. She did not reply. I knew then she wished me to pursue what I had been pursuing.

"Or else you'd break me!" I broke in. "The wide world I'd gladly give you except the trifle you'd demand. I'd sweat blood because of you. But supposing it was that you made an issue of the getting of a trinket—that it was my will or your will, then, my black girl, I'd not allow you to get the upper hand of me." I paused, then said : " The moment you stopped makin' an issue of it, I'd raise you up on a throne and pelt you with roses of gold ! "

She threw back her head and laughed. I knew then that she had trapped me in immaturity of talk. The laugh showed up my inadequacies. I hated her because she was cool. It was not the first time that my flamboyance had undone me.

She ceased laughing. " At your age, my chestnut foal," she said patronisingly, " every young man talks like Aristotle or King Solomon. It's because you can't become accustomed to the novelty of being free of swaddling clothes. It's because. . . ."

" Two years younger than me you are, Alice O'Neill," I said. " And yet you talk like the Hag of Béara ! "

Again the laugh—this time with an abrupt ending. We faced one another on the road. The smell of her raincoat had renewed my sense of excitement. " Aye ! " she said, " two years younger than you I may be, but here's a fact you should be acquainted with. Between sixteen and twenty, age for age, a woman is three times cleverer than her one-ager of a man. The moment I stop making an issue of it ! " Here her laughter was harshness itself. " The moment I cease being a woman ! You're a simple fellow, Ches Macnamara, and for you life will be a simple affair. A single kick between eighteen and twenty-two. A hound running random into the high meadow, then curling up into a contrite heap on the hearthstone for the remainder of its days ! " It was her turn to look out over the estuary. When again she turned, her tone of voice had altered. " Look, man, do you never wish to crash forward to the footstool of the Lord God Himself, crying out and out and out : ' Hey, Almighty God, here I am, Ches Macnamara, saddler's son, from Cloone, Ireland ! Words I like and music ! Women I have begun to discover ! ' Do you never. . . ." The fury of her voice faltered and broke. Her nostrils flared : her upper lip was beyond discipline. A madcap she was surely.

I tried to laugh yet could not. Her intensity had disconcerted me. For a small space it seemed as if we were moving in a curious dimension of sub-reality. Perhaps it was the queer morning light which already was full silvering the river to the west. I was puzzled and contrite. The pendulum had swung very close and yet I was blundering. Books I could read and understand but not the simple signals of a woman nor the language far underlying language. That which underscores the lifting of a hand or the most casual glance ; that which is most economical since nothing of its fabric is designed to go to waste.

Even now I can hear my own low voice, saying : " You want to know, Allie, if I feel like that ? "

Her voice was strained. She kept looking steadfastly ahead. " What is it to me ? " she asked.

I said : " This mood must not idle away. It is . . ." I hesitated, ". . . of value. You want to know if I feel as you have described ? You *must* know with accuracy what I am speaking about."

" No *must* there is about it ! "

" The kind of talk we are now having, there is a *must* about it ! Look ! what we strive to trap in words, now, between man and man, no ; between woman and woman, no ; but between man and woman, yes ! Allie, is it not so ? "

" I don't know what you're talking about ! "

" You little liar ! " I almost shouted.

She did not grow angry : I knew then that she wished me to continue speaking. I was close to crying out with vexation.

Wheedlingly, I said : " Somtimes I am sure what it is I want ; sometimes I am unsure. Maybe it's power or understanding or charity : maybe it is a need to be wholly individual, or to be wholly merged. Something forceful it is : that I *do* know. It bears some relationship to a small snatch of brightness balancing with its intensity the whole beige world. There are times when I come very close to it. Sometimes I stretch out my hands to grasp it and the instant I say to myself, ' Christ ! but I have captured it at last '—it's gone ! As if it had been frightened away by the very fact of my appreciating that I had imprisoned it! Sometimes it takes the form of a phenomenon that is bright, tiny and fragile: a Red Admiral butterfly with its wings at full span: at other times it is dark, large and powerful like a coal-black sire-horse, the polish on his haunches pulling its own white light from even an indifferent sky. Maybe, Allie, I'm talking mad. But if that is true, then you are also thinking mad. And if two people can hold conversation with mad symbols or mad sounds that each understands, then they have evolved a sanity of their own. I wish I knew what it was I strive after. Whatever it is it pulls the harrow across me. Allie, tell me what you think?"

Her spirit had gone back to its lair. "No concern of mine it is," she said, with sulkiness.

"You trollop!" I said. "You set a match to a barn of straw and then walk off with a shrug of your shoulders saying 'What has this blaze got to do with me?' That's a woman's dearest office! You, the Madcap! A timid, shivering little slut, afraid of an idea that is lying asleep in your head."

She accepted the wounding in silence. Together, I in anger, she in pain, we walked onwards through the morning.

My angry mind would not have it end thus. Of a sudden I caught her roughly by the arm and swung her round in a half wheel. My mouth was close to her mouth. We were almost one when the face of Edith Mallory seemed painted on the intervening air. The picture made Madcap more secure. Then we, who had swung so close, were apart.

"A cowardly slut!" I shouted.

"No!" she said. Her eyes dropped and her tired head dangled. I could scarcely believe that but a few minutes before I had set a torch to her spirit. She said hopelessly: "It's only. . . ."

"What?" I said, eagerly more than angrily.

As she looked up her face was full and open. I had a silly

trick of youth—of trying at moments of intense emotional opposition to project my entire will into the soul of the person who opposed me. As I tried this trick with Madcap O'Neill I fancied that she was conquered, where, later, I knew that she was simply recognising. (Age for age, she had said.) Her eyes fell on my fingers where still they continued to grasp her harshly by the arm. Her eyes ordered me to release her. I obeyed, silently compacting that in return for the release she should explain.

She chose her every word. " There is a ripeness of feeling," she said. " Of ideas, also. Without this ripeness there is nothing. Its coming cannot be hastened. Good fortune it awaits : also its own plan—an explosion of nature, a mating of time and place, a common or opposing mood of the persons concerned. What I speak of is finer than fine. This ripeness may come through affection thinned out to the snapping point. It may come, too, through what on the surface seems brutality but which in truth is the inversion of true affection. These are slender things—I cannot explain them further."

Sure and cool she was.

" A question there is that must be answered," I said ; " then the conversation between us is ended."

" Answer it I shall," Alice O'Neill said, " provided it does not rob me of. . . ."

" Of your pride ? "

" Yes ! " she said, frankly.

I asked my question : " Do you hate me ? "

There was no sudden surprise on the woman's face. Her eyes were steady upon me. Blacker than the raven's wing her hair was, gathered as it was to the waist of an hour-glass on the nape of her neck. The hip-red bow lay horizontal on her upper lip. Her nostrils that I had often seen open in the flare of anger were now closed and resigned. " There are times," she said, gravely, " when I hate you more than anyone in the world. Just as there are times when you hate me with a bitterness that is brother to my bitterness."

I grew limp. The bright brass pendulum had swung away. We walked on side by side. I lacked the grit necessary for the grappling with the ideas that had begun to beset me. The memory of the happenings of the night and morning seemed to make a spun wheel of many colours. The smell of the raincoat came from the right of me: it was insistent above the tang of the morning grass. I knew that the smell of that coat would haunt me: I realised that in drapers' shops in far towns Madcap O'Neill and this green-and-amber morning would come leaping out of a pile of raincoats to the right of me. Aye, and with the vision of the woman would also come the angry agony of these half-understandings, these blunderings, these recriminations.

We had come to a crossroads. For the second time that morning I heard the Cloone whistle coming from the bush-lined boreen that led away to the right. Finn Dillon was standing in the roadway, looking in our direction. He beckoned to us to come forward, signalling to us to exercise caution as we did so. His companions were peering through the roadside hedge. I heard a man's voice raised in anger.

When we had come up, Finn said to me, with undertone laughter: "Your sister Mary is in a right hobble!"

Peering through the bushes, we saw a farmer standing in the one empty block of his galvanised hayshed. He was looking up to where the stored hay almost met the roof. A ladder was close by. At varying heights in the hay, where it had been cut down with the hay knife, there were landings or benches. The farmer was dressed only in his shirt and pants: his feet were thrust out into mud-white unlaced brogues. He was holding a double-barrelled shotgun in tight angry hands.

"I'll give ye while I'm countin' five to come down out of it!" he roared. "I had a haybarn burnt out over that class of coortin'-smokin' before. Come down, I warn ye!"

From our ambush we looked up towards the top of the hay: the dark space above looked innocent and wholly without life.

Under his breath, Finn said : " Sweatin' blood poor Mary must be, herself and the lamp-post of a man ! "

The farmer fired a shot in the air. We all jumped.

" The next time I blaze," he said, " I'll make a strainer of yeer two hides ! "

" The child was tenderly nurtured," Finn Dillon said mockingly of my sister Mary.

The farmer's wife came to the door of the house. She had an old coat thrown over her shift. " Come in, Phil ! " she called to her husband. " The child is bawlin' with the mortal terror o' the shot ! "

" Let him cry away ! " said her husband. Again turning to the barn, he roared : " Are ye goin' to come down, after I seein' yeer heads ? "

" Do you know him ? " I asked Finn Dillon.

" Of course I know him," Finn said. " He's Phil Connor of Kilshone." After a pause, he added : " Mary Macnamara is long enough in the oven." Leaping over the fence into the haggard, " How're you, Phil ? " he said brightly.

The angry light in the farmer's eyes died reluctantly as he recognised the newcomer. " That you, Finn ? " he said, off-handedly. He resumed his upward glaring.

" Early you're shootin' crows ! " Finn said.

" Crows that ate with a knife an' fork ! " the farmer said. " A doxy an' her fella on the top bench of the barn. Two lots of hay burned in this locality, latterly, as a result of that class of carry-on. Besides, the priest is pulverisin' the pulpit, askin' the farmers to set their faces against it."

" The priest ? " asked Finn, mildly incredulous.

" Yes, the priest ! " said Phil Connor. " This game is worse than sheep-worryin' by a good measure."

" Awful pious you've got all of a sudden," Finn said darkly.

" What you mean, Dillane ? " The farmer had turned ugly in the twisting of a hand. His wife was still standing in the doorway, watching the newcomer and her husband.

Finn spoke quietly and with the suggestion of a smile : " A knowledgeable cobbler from Cloone tells me that Phil Connor of Kilshone never failed to break a horse or snare a woman. A proverb he has about you. 'Never a heifer' . . . ."

" Talk aisy, will you ? " said the farmer, glancing sharply in his wife's direction.

Finn grew bolder. He raised his voice. " Some of ye bucks turn into walkin' models once ye find yeerself on the wrong side of fifty. Whisper here, Phil Connor. Wasn't there a foxy woman on the side of Foilnanean you used be payin' attention to for a fine while o' years ? So much so that in the end, the cows of that locality refused to have anything to do with hay, so shot it was with the long strands of her redgold hair."

We were standing at a gap in the bushes. There was no further need for concealment. Finn turned to us. " Payin' coort ! " he said. He jerked his thumb backwards in the direction of the farmer. The gesture imputed to Phil Connor all the blackguardism, raking and philandering that ever was done in the span of Ireland.

" Lower your voice, you blackmailin' get, or it's ten to one I'll give you the entrails of the gun ! "

For a moment Phil Connor was balanced between laughter and anger. Laughter had it at last. We smiled our relief.

" I'll take my oath that it's some of your tribe that is up there," he said.

" Jealous you are," said Finn, " because you're on the threshold of age."

Balanced again. Then, with candour : " Jealous I am, Finn," the farmer said. " Why should I deny it ? "

The way Phil Connor said it, it was the purest of laments for lost youth. Then, lowering the gun : " Where were ye, Finn ? "

" At Bowen's of Littero. An American wake it was."

" H'm ! Always good-lookin' fillies o' women in Littero, in my time. The river is not so harsh on the skin as the open sea. An American wake, is it ? Lucky ye came this way, or an Irish wake we'd have had here ! "

" Go in, Phil ! D'you hear the child complainin' ? Go in, Phil ! Your wife will be famished ! "

With a flash of fire, the farmer said : " I've a good mind to make ye promise toll for releasin' the pair upstairs. A huntin'-dog or a thrush's cage of wicker or maybe a peal salmon when the time for peal salmon comes. But I've thought better of it. Maybe ye'd eel out of a bargain of duress. Bad to be gettin' ould, Finn ! And contrairy ! " At the hayshed, he shouted : " Ye two up there : remember it's by the skin o' yeer teeth ye're gettin' off. An' as long as ye go night-walkin' again, pass by Phil Connor's of Kilshone."

" Old, is it ? " said Finn, luring his anger from the barn. " If you showed your good teeth to advantage, a bevy of women 'd come marchin' after you." Instructing us, Finn said : " Teeth are a great index to vitality."

Lowering his gun, the farmer took this with the quietness of disbelief. Then, when Finn least expected it, Phil Connor pressed the trigger of the lowered gun and fired the other shot in the air. The explosion was close to Finn's ear. Finn leaped with fright.

" The devil's skewer to you ! " he said. " You frightened the daylights out o' me ! "

" Your nerves are at fault, Finn Dillon," the farmer said as he walked away.

When the farmhouse door had closed, Finn called out : " Mary Macnamara ! " My sister immediately thrust her head out from the dark recesses at the top.

" Is he gone, Finn ? " she whispered in terror.

Finn cupped his hand around his mouth : " He's lookin' for more cartridges ! " Mary ejaculated. " Come on, Peter," she said. " For Holy God's sake, come on ! "

I was guffawing as I looked at the benches of hay with my roly-poly sister floundering on the top of them. I was thinking of the seven mattresses and the pea.

Her coat scrawled with hay, her emerald beret thrust baw-ways on her head and her dignity vanished, my sister Mary descended the ladder from the hayshed. The leggy scoorloon of a man scrambled down after her. You should have seen the pair of them footing it for the hedge. Mary, a dumpling : the big fellow, a crouched, angular picker of stars. Uproad they ran. We followed them, hullahooing derisively. When we caught up with them, Mary's companion made to laugh the incident off. His laugh was deep and peculiar. Our laughter stopped the instant his began. In this we but obeyed a signal of Finn Dillon's, who had suddenly chosen to receive the countryman's broken explanation in a chill elderly silence.

The copious comic gestures of the awkward fellow were obviously born of, what was for him, unusual excitement. Finn looked downwards at the countryman's boots. We followed Finn's example : every man and woman of us except Mary was looking downwards. The tall fellow made a half attempt to hide his boots. But they had nowhere to conceal themselves on the open road. Finn walked all around him, still keeping his eyes fixed on the boots. We exchanged significant glances : then we sent our eyes scuttling post haste back to the boots. Peter—for this was the name Mary had addressed him by—was puzzled : he looked down, turned his boots sideways, then looked at each of us perplexedly.

" Don't take any notice of them," said Mary. " They and their looking at your boots ! "

" What's wrong with my boots ? "

We were all down-glancing : our faces were grave.

" Don't mind them, Peter," said Mary. " They'll drive you off your head if you take notice of them ! "

Peter was squarely huffed. " Faith, they won't drive me off my head," he said. Then : " My boots are every bit as good as their boots ! " How deep his voice ! His eyes were widely spaced above his Oriental cheekbones. His lower jaw was like a rock. He had an open-air face weathered to leather. His eye was bright with slow-burning anger.

Finn widened his hands as if he had failed to make sense out of the other's outburst. He walked towards the fence. He looked out over the fields, which at this point were slightly below road level.

Conciliatingly, Mary said: " Don't you see, Peter ? "

" To hell with you, woman ! " Peter said stolidly. " An' to hell with the lot of ye ! " he said to us. " Smart Cloonies ! Mockin'-birds to a man ! " He leaped heavily into the low fields and tore away. " The back o' me hand to ye ! " he shouted before he tore through the bushes of the far fence.

Mary watched him go. She was half-laughing at us, yet half-angry for losing the man.

" He's a decent fellow, anyhow ! " she said, with a sigh. " He didn't lay a wrong finger on me ! "

" Thin blood ! " said Finn Dillon, turning away. " Ireland is no more ! "

We all laughed. Mary continued to look over the fields to where the man's head was bobbing above the bushes. She began to smile, then to laugh. Regretfully, she turned. The women closed in about her, linking her.

As we approached Stonewall, we looked to see if the priest's hawk was on the cross on the point of the church gable. When we saw that the bird was not there, we knew that we had plenty of time for Mass. The people outside were waiting for the bell to ring. We joined the waiting worshippers, who for the most part were leaning against the long stone wall. The young priest cycled up: a falcon was balanced on the swathed handlebars of his bicycle. He dismounted, then cast the hawk into the air. The bird swung on its strong wings, drove forcefully upwards, then planed down and perched on an arm of the cross on the gable. Watching the bird as it circled, the sunlight was lost and found on the people's faces.

The bell rang. The sound peeled the people of Stonewall from the wall and fences. We all trooped in to the chapel. The priest was beside the main door as we passed in. He was slowly taking cycle-clips from his trouser-ends. He eyed us carefully. I saw his tongue make a carbuncle in his cheek. I wondered what it was amusing him: then I noticed the tell-tale scrawl of hay on the back of my sister Mary's coat.

The chapel was poor in its appointments but the altar and the high lancet windows above it were good. The reredos was of light-green marble. The family pews were box-like in shape, with small awkward doors that made it hazardous to enter them. In our endeavour to crowd in somewhere we kicked timber loudly so that the entire congregation turned to eye us. A kneeling woman charitably indicated an empty pew and nodded to us as if urging us to enter. Mary and the other girls did so: they were not subsequently disturbed so that we came to the conclusion that the pew had been owned by a family that had since died out in the parish. We men knelt near the back of the church.

When the boyish priest came on the altar, the windows over his head dwarfed him utterly. The glass was unstained and the novelty of the western sky was visible through diamond panes over the priest's head. The clouds we saw passing by had, for us, the effect of pointing the sacrifice. In our church of Mary-without-Stain in Cloone the windows over the altar were stained with a representation of the coronation of Mary in Heaven.

During the Mass, Madcap's hair caused my eyes to forsake the altar. Now and again the sound of the sacring-bell recalled me to a sense of what was proper. As I stood at the Last Gospel, I could not help appreciating, with a sense of wryness, the wisdom and the knowledge of Saint Paul, for he it was who had first decreed that women should keep their heads covered in the house of God.

# CHAPTER IV

I

*IT is Christmas Eve. Between Little Angel's hands is the bell-rope. In five minutes time he will ring the evening Angelus. When the old sacristan draws on the rope the candle-lights in the windows of Cloone will leap up making a haphazard heaven that is compact of faith and custom.*

*The belfry, a simple structure on four tall timber legs, stands beside the little church of Mary-without-Stain. Its roof is barely adequate to keep the rain off the bell's back but fails to preserve the bronze from the green stain of the weather.*

*Little Angel is dressed in his festival best : he wears a frayed stiff shirt-front that is white beyond whiteness, a black cravat, a priest's coat that does not over-betray the years (the priest died when the suit was comparatively new) and heavy black boots with the metal quarter-tips on the inside of the heels. When serving Mass Little Angel has no need of a sacring-bell—the instant the priest places his hands over the chalice Little Angel snips his tips smartly together to warn the worshippers. For many, many years these tips have rung in the advent of the Lord at every consecration in Mary-without-Stain : they will ring Him in at Midnight Mass tonight. Familiarity has made us devoid of wonder at the phenomenon of the ringing boot-tips.*

*Little Angel is hatless ; his white hair curls away from the collar of his coat. The only operative hinges of his body seem situate in his buttocks. The rustiness of the small of his back has latterly been his most bitter affliction.*

*Over the old man's head the bell is full-mouthed and silent. Little Angel looks at the face of his watch : it is four minutes short of the hour—in our part of the country we disregard the custom of the Catholic world and ring the morning and evening*

*Angelus at seven instead of at six o'clock. Little Angel fears that if he delays the ringing until the precise stroke of seven, the more sonorous bell of the town church will beat him to the first stroke. Thus he is caught between the millstones of anticipatory delight and possible chagrin. He makes a brave resolution : when it is half a minute short of the hour he shall ring the bell of the church of Cloone.*

*While Little Angel is savouring the delight—even the adventure—that lies before him, the Marys of Cloone are waiting tremulously. The traditional law of the people is clear and unequivocal : let a tall candle be set in every window, lest Mary, the Mother of God, should again come straying and she big with child. Let ye make compensation by yeer candlelights for the time long ago when she went straying unwelcomed in the darkness. If there is a young Mary in your house, let her set a light to the candle ; if there is no Mary among ye, let the youngest child do it—he'll live the longest and send the custom the farthest. Do what ye're told, let ye ! Soon enough the world will flow over us !*

*The Marys of Cloone are waiting for the first stroke of the bell. Fully expectant is each Molly, Maura, Maureen, Mane, Maisie and May.*

*The night is frosty and the sky thronged with stars.*

*For Little Angel this day is his birthday in Christ.*

*Each small Mary stands on the hearth holding a sliver of bogpine in her hands. She is ready to thrust the sliver into the turf flames the instant the bell sounds. The Marys are of many types : one owns lovely limbs that some day will prove a constant delight to her husband's fingers ; another has a stammer that ties her face in engaging knots whenever she endeavours to speak ; another is an idiot whose lower jaw cannot be shouted shut, and yet another is a cripple who has to be lifted from the fire to the waiting candle on the window.*

*Mostly, however, the Marys are curly-headed and brown-eyed.*

*When the bell rings out we will all be lifted high on a wave of traditional excitement.*

*Little Angel can wait no longer : he draws on the bell-rope. The bell-sound flows out, firm and true-hearted. The order of strokes for the Angelus is three threes and a nine. Little Angel strikes the first three ; then he waits.*

*The old man stands in the middle of the running rings of sound. He is peering down into Cloone as if enjoying the result of his blessed mischief.*

*For a moment it seems as if the sound of the bell has had no effect on the cottages. Then one window answers with its faltering light. Window after window follows suit. The bell now sounds the second three strokes : it is upbraiding the laggards. Star after star is born in low Cloone. That which was dead has leaped alive ; that which was lowly is exalted !*

*Warm brown or lemon-coloured lights are still up-springing. Over the lights the sound keeps downpouring—if the bell-sound could be said to have any colour it is the colour of gold. The night air seems filled with the legacy of our sublimation. Window after window is twinkling. The countryside beyond Cloone is now responding : the span of land under the domination of the bell is demonstrating its age-old obedience. Lights are showing where unsuspected cottages lurk. In the windows of the long farmhouse of Dark Jack O'Neill—how true and valiant the candles are standing amid the darkness ! Across the river, candle after candle glows, revealing with accuracy the spot where cottages lie concealed in the night.*

*" And the Word was made flesh and dwelt amongst us . . . Hail Mary, full of grace. . . . "*

## II

How the autumn had flown, and the winter come in ! I was now twenty-one.

I could scarcely remember how it was that Christmas had sneaked in the door to us. Things had happened that had amused or angered or tolerably interested us. A lad from

Fannowbane was reported to have set a squirrel afire—we cursed him black! A professor in Dublin had stated that it wasn't true to say that the most nutritious part of the potato was next to the skin—this pronouncement caused high disputation in Cloone where we had always held that the reverse was true. Old Font had thought up three nicknames which were apt and accurate.

A Sheehy woman from one of the glens in the foot-hills to the south gave birth to her seventh son in a row—the neighbouring old women had gathered in, gravely placed two earthworms on the palm of the child's right hand, closed the hand to a fist and, finally, tightly bandaged the clenched hand with strips of old linen. Then they prophesied that when the fist was opened and it was seen that the earthworms had turned to dust, the boy would grow to manhood possessing a cure for many evils.

A young milliner from the town had been persuaded by a Cloonie to wash her hair in stale urine as a remedy for scalp deficiencies: this had sent us off on immoderate bouts of chuckling. Almost, we were successful in driving one of the Hibe lads daft by telling him he'd get bald just because a drop of brine from a fresh flitch of bacon suspended from a hook on a kitchen ceiling had fallen directly on the crown of his head.

Meanwhile, Three Cheers reckoned it his duty to keep reminding us of the speedy passage of time. Almost every night of his life he got drunk and went through the same ritual. Standing in mid-road he would cheer and clap his hands together.

Clap! Clap! Clap! Thus his hands. Then he would shout: "One of these days ye'll all be dead! Look at yeer lives! Flowin' past ye like mad! Ha-ha-ha! St. Patrick's Day it is an' the shamrock lies at the bottom of yeer cups. Ha-ha!" Clap! "The Old Fair of Cloone it is an' our small place is thronged with the colour of Ireland." Clap! "Summer it is an' the rhody-flowers are paintin' the salmon-pools puce. Ha-ha!" Clap! "Race-time it is an' the country girls are singin' for men from beside the hurdy-gurdies. Time goin'! Time blowin'! Like fair mad! Christmas Eve it is an' Molly Font is comin' up Cloone with an elephant of a goose trapped in her oxter." Clap! Clap! "Flowin' away yeer lives are!" Then, throwing up his cap: "Three cheers for life!"

So, here it was, Christmas Eve. Molly, the merry-eyed ringletted wife of Old Font, had gone up Cloone with a young goose under her arm—the bird was to be roasted for Women's Christmas. Seeing her pass their half-doors the old women had emerged to thumb the bird and give their opinions on the purchase. It was true for Three Cheers: our lives were flowing!

Finn Dillon, Young Font and myself came home from Midnight Mass in Mary-without-Stain. We passed between Flung Dung and the Maid of Erin. The Chinaman wore what resembled a soup-tureen on his head and was dressed in a pink-and-black mantle. He carried a gold stick in his hand. Strange that we had taken Flung Dung to ourselves and even cherished him: this was a ready facility with us of Cloone—the making of the abnormal normal. By her side the great-breasted Maid had a Round Tower stunted to a baton while at her feet crouched an eel-headed wolfhound. I laughed, recalling that Old Font had said that in the event of a Famine the Maid 'd suckle the parish.

The click of Little Angel's tips was still true and sharp in our ears. Looking back over our shoulders we could see the sanctuary-lamp of the small church: its light was not so clear as usual for there had been Benediction after Mass and the church was still dimmed with the smoke of incense.

The roads, the flagged pavement and the small band of cobblestones between the flags and the cottages were bone-dry. Cloone was thronged with people returning from the church. For the most part these people were standing in threes, talking.

Old Tim Fennell, the mason, now had a broken hip and was being helped home by his grandson; as he moved, the old man made a semi-circle with the lower part of his body.

Metal Belly, the bellman, walked home in mid-road—he did not stop to gossip, yet those who saluted him received a courteous and dignified reply.

Finn was in high humour: he was humming "*Christ the Saviour is Born!*" We parried the greetings thrown to us. To the greeting of a young person, we replied laughingly: "Aye, a happy Christmas and a goose!" In response to an older person, we said with gravity: "Many happy returns and a good many more of them!"

Jack the Hibe broke away from a knot of young men standing beside the Rookery and came out on the road to join us. Too late he realised that Young Font was in our company. There had always been bad blood between the two families which had reached its climax on the night when Young Font had bitten off the lobe of Jack the Hibe's ear. When Hibe realised that Font was with Finn and myself he made as if to pull away again. But we had a tradition in Cloone that if your bitterest enemy offered you friendship on Christmas Day it was neither right nor lucky to turn your back on the extended hand. Finn Dillon knew this, as did the rest of us, so he called out in a reprimanding exclamation.

"What is it?" Hibe asked, half-turning. His voice was part eagerness, part pride.

"Let ye make friends!" Finn said shortly.

The men standing beside the Rookery turned to watch the small drama.

Hibe walked coldly away. Then, remembering, he stopped dead in his stride. "Manners it is to wait to be asked," he said in extentuation of his fault.

Finn turned to Young Font: "Ask him!" he said, shortly.

After what seemed a long pause, Font said directly: "I'm askin' you, Jack!"

Jack the Hibe came back. The pair shook hands. The men on the pavement turned away and resumed their conversation. Young Font shed his surliness as if it were a cloak he had dropped down. The four of us walked abreast. The stars sang in the high sky. We eared the air as if trying to catch the far faint treble of the firmament.

Living was good ! Three girls came dancing against us. When our docility had lured them quite close, Finn extended his arms and made a mock spring after them. " My Christmas box ! " he shouted. They broke away squealing, semi-hoping we would pursue. We went on through Cloone. The girls called gibes after us but we did not turn to reply. As we went, we heard their voices rising and falling in disappointment.

In every window a tall candle was lighting. The candlestick was a turnip, topped and tailed, then holed to take the end of the candle. The candlewax was of three colours : blue for the blue of Mary's cloak, red for the blood of Jesus, and white for the light of Heaven.

Through the space over the half-doors we could see each kitchen festooned with holly leaves laboriously threaded to make garlands. Branches of laurel were thrust behind the pictures of the patriots. The kitchen walls were newly limed and the dresser freshly golden-grained. On the shelves of the dressers the blue willow-pattern delph stood resplendent. Some of the large ancient dishes had been broken many times and had been stitched with lead to hold them together. On the clevvies, or small wall-racks, china dogs and lustre pigs glittered. On the wall of every kitchen the light of the great turf or bogdeal fire was superimposed on the light of lamp or candle.

On the seats of the settle beds directly opposite the doorways the old men sat looking hopefully out into the blue moonlight.

Dick Gaffney lived with his mother in the cottage next to Finn Dillon's. Dick was a man close on fifty years of age. Twenty-two years before he had been suspected of having committed a small theft in the town : since then he had never stirred outside his own door and had eked out a poor living by tying flies.

Finn went into Gaffney's. Young Font, Jack the Hibe and I followed. Finn raised his face in enquiry to Nan, Dick's mother. As the woman nodded an affirmative, Finn went into the bedroom. I stood at the room door. The others remained in the kitchen speaking to the mother.

Dick was seated at a small table at the bedroom window. The indoor life had made him blanched and soft-fleshed. On his forehead were two white bumps. His hair was black and thinning. He had shaved specially for the feast-day.

As we came upon him he was replacing salmon flies in a tin cigarette-box. His lips were set on the wing of a salmon fly: this was a habit of his—bringing the feathers to a moustache point so that he could properly admire his handiwork. After replying to Finn's Christmas greeting, Dick said gleefully: "They'll shortly be runnin', lads!" He was referring to the first run of the spring salmon which was due in late January.

"Runnin' they'll be, like fair mad!" Finn said.

For a while I watched Dick's hands move lovingly: I saw the tiny vice and the tweezers he used in tying his flies, also the tin box of feathers. A freshly-tied Bulldog was in the grip of the vice: the varnish on it was still drying. From where I stood at the door I guessed that the size of the hook was four 'ought. Like every man in Cloone, I could, at a glance, break down a salmon fly into its constituent parts: Golden Pheasant tip, tinsel, red floss, tinsel again, a scrap of yellow toucan at the front, a scrap of red toucan at the back. Then blue floss with three or four winds of tinsel over it. Silk tying all the way. Shellac varnish on the final tying above the eye.

Finn looked into the box of flies. "Murderers to a man!" he said, admiringly.

"Not bad!" Dick said, gratified.

The box of materials was a magpie rag-bag. Macaw, jungle-cock, blue jaywing, blue seal fur, pig's wool and teal. The skies, caves and sties of the world here in microcosm. The great out-of-doors was trapped by proxy here in Cloone. I named the flies: Black Doctor, Lee Blue, Dunkeld, a bastard Sandy, a half Silver and Red, Thunder and Lightning, and The Bulldog. The Bulldog was the pride of Cloone. On the bench, too, were home-made minnows and half-completed colleys. Each of the colleys had a drunken wriggle on its back.

Hanging on the walls of the room were rods in the process of being mended; also four or five reels taken apart. From a picture, a pair of gaffs hung. One had a lucky hazel handle. The handle of the other was telescopic—I guessed it had been sent up from the hotel in the town for repair. "Gaffney for gaffs!" I thought, and then began to smile.

To Dick Gaffney, Finn said quietly: "A bare week and the New Year will be in the door. Let you be makin' up your mind!"

This was the Finn who had been made Prince of Cloone.

When Dick Gaffney spoke, we saw that the pride in his handiwork was replaced by a rodent terror. He pleaded: "I'm happy as I am, Finn. Honest to God, there's nothin' I require!"

Finn said: "The mother is old and she won't be always here. It would please her greatly if you moved out among the people. Tomorrow is the Wren's Day. Everywhere in Ireland there will be jollity and laughter. If I don't say these things to you, who will?"

Dick was abject: "The noises 'd go in an' out through my mind," he said. "Let me pass, Finn Dillon!" With a wan laugh: "Don't ye all come in to see me? I never lack company! This time twelve months, if God spares us, I'll do as you say. Yerra, what signifies a year in the life of a man? What signifies one penny among seventy pennies?"

Dick's trembling fingers slowly took a rosary from the clutter on the table. This he dropped among the feathers. There was no sound as the rosary fell. His delicate fingers closed the tin box.

Finn paused: he was thinking as I was thinking, that there was some symbolism in the placing of the rosary among the feathers. Perhaps isolation had made Dick extra cunning and he had invested that trivial act with solemnity, knowing that both Finn and I would seek for an unusual significance.

Sighing, Finn said: " This night twelve months, if God spares us all, I'll ask you the same question again."

" I give you my word I'll do as you ask, then ! " Dick was over-eager. Anything to be rid of Finn.

" If I'm here, I'll hold you to it," Finn said.

On our return to the kitchen, Font and Hibe looked questioningly into Finn's face. Nan Gaffney had her back turned and was idly rummaging in a shelf on the dresser. Finn's face was filled with a sense of failure.

" Good luck, Nan ! " he said.

" Good luck, boys ! " Her fingers were finding it difficult to keep up the pretence of searching.

As we were passing the cottage of Brink-o'-the-Grave, the old midwife and layer-out of corpses, Finn Dillon halted, then went forward and quietly pushed open the half-door. We followed, moving close behind him. There was no light in the kitchen, save that of the Christmas candle which was set in the window. Brink-o'-the-Grave was crouched over a small fire. She was recovering from a broken hip. Her wits were said to be failing and her fallen lower eyelids were as red as red ink. Sixty years before she had been a cheery young married woman. Then one, two, three, four, five; directly after birth her children had died one after another. To crown her woe, her husband had then sickened and gone. In the old woman's mind that happy time was as remote as the world of legend.

Brink-o'-the-Grave was mumbling softly to herself. We heard her rosary rattle. Speaking in Gaelic, she began to scold Almighty God, saying that He had forgotten to call her name.

Finn stood behind her chair. " Forever Cloone ! " he said quietly. Brink-o'-the-Grave was not startled—it is impossible to startle the old.

" Who have I, at all ? " she said. " Which of my hundreds

of sons has come to see me this Christmas Eve ? Speak up, an' tell me who I have ! "

We had all stepped into the kitchen. The old woman kept her face turned to the small fire.

" Finn Dillon it is," said Finn.

" God prosper the Prince of Cloone ! " the old woman said. " His place he knows, and his duty to the old. Ay ! Finn Dillon. I borned him as well as the others. He had a caul : I have it here in my coffaleen." She touched her breast, where her string purse was hidden. Over her shoulder, she said : " You'll never be drowned, son ! "

Finn laughed : " The hangman is oilin' his rope for me, Mary Liz," he said.

" God forbid ! " said the old woman, cutting the sign of the cross on herself. She then realised that Finn was not alone. " Who else have you with you ? " she asked.

" Young Font, one of the Hibes, and Ches Macnamara," Finn said.

" I borned them all," Brink-o'-the-Grave said proudly. " Young Font—a breech birth : his body covered with a white down that soon melted like the froth of the river. All the Hibes slipped greedily into life like eels. Ha-ha-ha ! Aisy money for Mary Liz ! Ches Macnamara—it wasn't Ould Font christened him. 'A chestnut foal,' said I, the minute I cleaned the blood off his skull. Ha-ha-ha ! A chestnut foal makes a chestnut colt." Then : " Come forward, son," the old woman said to me, " an' let me see how the candlelight ketches your head o' hair ! "

I did as she requested. The others had begun to laugh softly. I had the wit to stand a little off the direct line between the old woman and the candle-flame. Her open red eyes remained on me for a few moments. She made no comment. She then turned her attention to the fire and resumed her mumbling.

" What way is the body treatin' you ? " Finn Dillon asked.

" 'Tis a thing o' the past, boys," she said. " I'm on the brink o' the grave ! "

Finn was eager. He came a step nearer to the old woman. " Tell me, Mary Liz," he asked, " are you afraid o' dyin' ? "

The old woman looked up. " Indeed then, I am not, my boy bawn," she said. " The way I look at it is this : I had no pain comin' into the world an' I'll have none goin' out. The Almighty God is woeful good : He puts a blanket of forgetfulness across your shoulders on your entry into life and another at your departure. I'm ready to face Him the very minute He knocks at the window."

For a moment or two, no one spoke. The old woman then raised her head. " Leave me be, boys," she said. " Tonight bein' the night it is, my kitchen is thronged with dead."

We left her there, discoursing with her comrades.

Although it was a night for cabin-hunting, Hibe was very diffident about going into Font's. Young Font pressed him to enter before him. I saw the old fellow's hand instinctively tighten about the crook of his stick as he saw Hibe come in the door. He glared at his son, mutely asking out of eyes of fire why he had brought this man to their floor. Old Font's wife looked sharply at her husband. The old man took the rebuke : he lowered his head in humility, then raised it in pride. His beard jutted out in truth and steadiness. " What way are ye, boys ? " he said quietly and with breeding. Then to his erstwhile enemy : " What way are you, John ? "

" I'm good, sir."

" You're welcome, son."

" Thank you, sir."

The feud was ended.

" Something for the boys, Molly ! " Old Font said with sprightliness. " It's Christmas time." To us he said : " Sit down, lads."

We sat down.

Molly Font went into the room ; she returned with four red wineglasses in her hand. Concealed in her apron was a whiskey-tumbler : this she hid behind a jug on the ledge of the dresser. The old man's face fell when he saw only the stemmed wine-glasses in his wife's hand. Molly took a bottle of port from beneath the curtain at the base of the dresser. She poured the wine ; the old man licked his dry lips.

" A drop for yourself, Molly ! " he said huskily and with counterfeit solicitude.

Handing us the wine, Molly laughed. " Ploughin' his own furrow the rascal is," she said. " I married a fox ! " Addressing her husband directly : " What'll you have ? "

" The juice o' the barley," he said, then added, with a sigh : " There aren't many more Christmases left in me."

To us, Molly said : " Ten Christmases ago he began playin' that tune an' he hasn't reached the chorus yet."

She poured him out a good bumper of whiskey : his eyes and mouth relished the passage of the spirits from the bottle to the tumbler.

Old Font raised his glass. " Forever ! " he said.

" Forever ! " we responded.

The old man began to speak of time long gone. During his recital of the glories of bygone Cloone his wife kept sighing dismally in order to provoke him. Afterwards we ate the giblets of the goose. During the meal I couldn't keep my eyes off the semicircle that had been bitten out of Jack the Hibe's ear.

# CHAPTER V

I

A FROSTY light filtered into Cloone on the morning of the Wren's Day.

In ones and twos we came out of the cottages. Each man was crazily dressed: blouses, cardigans, Fair Isle jumpers and old fancy dresses were there aplenty, while the common factor of our attire was a green sash. Our variegated headgear, too, was not untouched by phantasy. I laughed when I saw one man wearing a hand-made cap of rabbit-skin. The step-dancers had light low shoes.

Almost all wore false faces, which we called hifiddles. A lazy minority had masks cut from dark cloth. Our musical instruments included four or five fiddles, three melodeons, one concertina, four kid-skin tambourines and a mandoline. Neither the rib-bones, which Jody Shea used as castanets, nor the mouth-organ which Jack the Hibe played with palm-punching were reckoned as instruments in the true sense of the word.

Then there was the hobby-horse!

Of this possession we were inordinately proud. Very few bands of wren-boys could rise to such glory. The animal's head was carved from a single block of timber: in colour the head was stippled grey while the furious nostrils and savage mouth were painted a brilliant red. To the head was attached an inverted cradle of canvas-covered wicker on which was set a small saddle and toy stirrups. Behind hung a generous grey tail, plundered tuft by tuft from the grey horses of the country-side.

This contraption was designed to be borne by a pair of men: to Badger Breen was usually entrusted the post of being front man under the horse. He it was who manipulated the two strings which controlled the lower jaw of the timber animal.

Children went off into hegs of laughter at the antics of the hobby-horse; they rubbed its nose and pulled its tail and offered it whiskey so that its hind legs would turn stone drunk.

Finn Dillon was Captain of the Wren. When he had marshalled us there were more than twenty men present. Finn was wearing a green fez over a blood-red mask. He had on a brilliant red coat with the inevitable green sash. About his waist was clasped the Belt of Cloone. In his hand he carried a black silver-mounted swagger stick.

He took his stand in front of us with his face turned towards the mouth of Cloone and the town. We lined up behind him in two files. The hobby-horse took up its position directly behind Finn. Young Font led one file, Hibe the other. Each one of these sub-leaders carried a decorated holly-bush from which dangled a dead wren. By this time the light in Cloone had grown stronger.

Finn Dillon shouted an order, waved his swagger-stick and gave the first few steps of the Wren. Away we went down Cloone, the music bringing the sleepy youngsters tumbling to the street and their elders to the doors to wish us success for the day.

The girls came too, each hurriedly binding her hair and pressing hansel money on the leaders. Abernethy Bovenizer came out from under the Chinaman to greet our treasurers with silver: straightaway Murray Folan popped out from under the Maid of Erin and roughly beckoned the man with the string bag to his side of the street.

Our band was dominated by the skin and bell with the gadgets crushing down the slender hairline music of the fiddles. Those of us who could claim that our mouths were free of musical instruments began to raise the Song of the Wren:

*" The wren, the wren, the King of all birds, on Saint Stephen's day he was caught in the furze.*
*Although he is little his family's great, so up my good woman and give us a trate.*
*As I was goin' to Ballinawle, I spied a wren upon a wall,*
*I upped with my stick and brought him down and carried him into my native town.*
*Mrs. ———, she is a good woman, she'll give us a penny to bury the wren,*
*So up with the kettle and down with the pan and give the poor wranboys something ! "*

Outside the great houses of Bank Place we made our first halt. We glanced up at the windows, each of which was six times bigger than the largest window in Cloone. We formed a wide irregular ring on the black asphalt road. One of our fiddlers came forward and began to address his music to Finn Dillon's shoes. I saw Finn brace and relax his body with the true step-dancer's delight of anticipation. He handed me his swagger-stick, then laughed nervously and threw back his head. Beneath the red cloth mask I saw his nostrils widen. The music called insistently, even to our hobnailed boots. Tantalisingly, Finn let bar after bar of the music flow past him. Suddenly his pointed shoes inserted themselves into the flow of the tune.

It was a treasure to see Finn Dillon dancing. He had good carriage, good execution and good poise. His arms were limp. His face was dead. Though his shoes were revelling in their extraordinary emancipation on the black road, yet they were willing prisoners in the bonds of the music. The glory of the moving shoes almost set us crying with delight.

The great windows over our heads screeched upwards. We saw the well-fed women of the banks lean out on the sills, their morning breasts heavy in their blouses. At the mouth of Cloone I saw Madcap O'Neill and Shoon Lawlee stand watching. For once Shoon did not give the impression of being remote : Finn Dillon had also seen her and straightaway his shoes took on an addition of glory. At the end of the dance Finn leaped high in the air and then came to rest for a moment in a semi-bow.

Over our heads hand-clapping began. The white money began to fall in a shower. Finn ignored it. One of our collectors came forward and picked up the silver, doffing his hat to the windows as he did so. We lined up and marched away. The frosty sun lighted on our emerald sashes.

II

It was still morning when we turned our faces to the country. As we climbed the hill outside the town we found the hedges on their northern sides edged with frost. The air lifted us up, so buoyant it was. To the south we saw where the mountains climbed gradually from the green of woolly pines to the whiteness of unmelted snow. The sun-licked countryside to the north lay before us : it seemed to have been placed there solely for our delectation. The whitewashed houses winked us a merry welcome. Between the outracing headlands the far estuary was an inset of planished silver. We smiled out at the countryside. We knew what lay in store for us out there : laughter and jollity, bantering and philandering, eating and drinking, dancing and the singing of songs.

So up with the good music ! The raucous gadgets had green or gold or blue guts as they shrugged open. Knuckles and wedges kept pounding heavily on the tambourines. The fiddlers' elbows were working overtime ! We began to smile proudly but shyly at one another. Ashamed of this small display of feeling we vented our emotions in coarse laughter and small absurdities. The roadway frost was crunching under our heavy boots. Now and again the glitter of Finn Dillon's swagger-stick was high and mighty in the country air. When the breeze came it was like a cold blade placed upon our jaw- or cheek-bones. Badger and his fellow-carrier had emerged from under the hobby-horse to take a breath of fresh air. The din of minor wren-bands floated towards us from across the fields. The gulls were whitening in the morning sky. The world was fresh, fair and lovely.

We were welcomed in the labourers' cottages and in the long low thatched dwellings of the rich farmers. We made our way up mud-pocked boreens and boreens of dry gravel. The morning began to speed by.

The daughters of the strong farmers loved to dance with the masked men. Their fathers were not keen on this practice but here it was that tradition had them gagged. Since the manner of living on the soil was governed by the dowry and its concomitants, farmers thought that their daughters were hardly likely to find suitable mates among wren-boys, straw-boys or mummers. But for the daughters the Wren-day dancing was an adventure: dancing with a masked man, you never knew who it was you had, whether a friend or an enemy, a bold gallery man or a sly sleeveen.

Lanigan's of Teeradounaigh was a fine farmhouse set among trees on a hillock. Old Sean's family consisted of five grown but unmarried daughters. The fact that he had not a son was a sore blow to Sean Lanigan. It was now a certainty that the farm would go out of the name. The flagged kitchen floor gave out a hollow sound when danced upon. In the old days Lanigan's was reckoned a noted dancing-house: it was even said of it that a cow's skull had been buried under the flag of the hearth so as to add resonance to an old dancing-master's steps. Old Sean Lanigan, the present man of the house, was rotten with sense and money both. He had frowned upon the dancing his father had encouraged. Signs by, the people said, his five daughters had been left on his hands without mating. The truth of this comment the old man had latterly realised, hence the relaxation under which we wren-boys were grudgedly welcome.

When we reached the house we found that an army of neighbouring women had gathered in, and were waiting for us.

They were sitting around, their tongues ripe for tip or banter. We chose our partners from among them and danced a set on the floor: old Mrs. Lanigan kept looking at our shoes to see if she could guess our breeding from the way we cast our legs in the set. The old man, dour and non-committal, sat in the corner to the left of the fire.

Young Narrie Lanigan came to me in the dance. She was the youngest. I knew her well by sight.

"Ye'll be havin' a wran-dance one o' these nights?" she asked between our steps.

"Supposin' we are," I said, "would you come?"

She said: "I'd give the world an' all to go, but my father would claw the walls!"

Half-joking, yet all in earnest, I then said: "How are you goin' to get a man for yourself, if you don't display what a fine style of girl you are?"

"I'm easy in my mind about that same," she replied. "It's the highest notion in my head to be a nun."

"You are in your tail-board!" I said. "That gamey eye of yours would upset a nation."

With that she fell against me with the dint of laughing. I laughed too. Her father looked up sharply. He glared at the pair of us, then glanced harshly across at his wife. So it was the woman who had pleaded for the custom of open house to be kept up! I was masked: the old fellow glared at the hair struggling from under my cap. He knew me for the tradesman's son I was. Narrie did not seem in dread of her father. She was the youngest—perhaps he had a kindly corner in his mind for her. Before I could resolve these difficulties, the figure of the dance bore her away from me.

Shemus Goff sang a new ballad and then old Sean Lanigan gave us a crown; he gave it to us readily, hoping to get rid of us. We thanked him and made for the door. All the girls came with us. Thronging around us they were, as if loath to let us go so easily.

Suddenly, Narrie Lanigan said: "Are any of ye fond of fox-terriers?"

"Here's your man!" Finn Dillon said, catching Jody Shea by the wrist. Jody's lip covered his upper teeth as an indication of pleasure. A wheelwright by trade, it was a sight to see him shoe a wheel on the gravel strand below Cloone: as he struck all round the red ring of the wheelband he kept dancing like a dervish on the flames that rose from the burning felloes. Jody could cry over a sick dog with the facility of an Englishman.

Narrie and Jody looked at one another.

"The grandest belly of pups you ever seen," the girl whispered.

Narrie and Jody moved toward the hayshed.

"Will we be in the way?" One of our men had sensed the reluctance of the women to part with us.

"Whether ye will or not, I can't prevent ye comin' with us!" Narrie said skilfully.

She danced ahead. We followed. The women followed after. Suddenly Narrie stopped and put her hands on her hips. Her eyes hardened as she looked first at the men, then at the women and finally back again at the men. For a fleeting moment she resembled her father in the corner.

"Ye needn't be thinkin'," she said to us men, "that I'm cockin' my cap at any of ye. An' 'tisn't away from my father's vigilance I'm gettin' but as little!"

"Show us the pups, strong farmer's daughter," Finn Dillon said.

"That I will, wren-boys," she said.

Our social positions were thus clearly defined.

The terrier-bitch and her five birth-blind pups were lying on loose straw in an idle pillar of the hayshed. In the intervals of sucking life from their mother the pups showed how wrinkled their heads were. Narrie crouched down. Gently she took a pup off a teat and placed it against her own cheek.

Each of us men experienced in imagination the tenderness of her cheek's caress.

" Oh, the dote ! " she said, caressing the puppy. Archly she looked up at us. Of a sudden there moved among us men and women a strange unreality. The women began to laugh softly. Imperceptibly they were mingling with the men : their movements made a slow dance—an old dance which has the virtue of being always novel. Every eye present was fixed irrevocably on the pup which was still against the girl's face. A second time the women laughed : then they fell strangely silent.

We men stood in a broken semicircle ; the women were moving slowly in and out among us.

The bitch had begun to growl.

" Easy, Sheevra, darlin'." A warm strangeness had entered Narrie Lanigan's voice.

Jody Shea was on his grug. Little noises of endearment came from the fixed mouth in his fiddle-face. Before long his hand crept out and stole a pup.

" A dog ! " he said, turning it over.

" Mine's another ! " said Narrie Lanigan.

They both laughed. Her face was as frank, open and engaging as the art of her womanhood would allow her. The mask made Jody Shea grotesque and anonymous.

Among us who were standing the uneasiness broke out afresh. The rustle of sun-brilliant straw was not potent enough to break the spell that had fallen upon us. Behind us an idle pulper stood, the green paint chipped from it. Among the women had begun afresh the subtle movements that concealed the deepest implications.

I glanced at Jody : he was meshed in his love of pups and was innocent of the drama behind him.

" Can I . . . ? " he glanced up at the smiling girl.

" Next time, maybe," Narrie Lanigan whispered. " This time they're all promised."

" How are they split ? " Jody Shea asked.

" These we're holding are two dogs," she said. " The three remaining under Sheevra are bitches." Narrie Lanigan smiled, then added : " Maybe, wren-boy that loves dogs, you'd like to christen the pair that we have in our hands ? "

" You're comin' at me sudden," Jody said, grim and humourless. The pup in his hand had a tan saddle and two tan ears. The pup Narrie was holding had no markings whatsoever.

Narrie looked up laughing : " Have ye a tongue in yeer heads, lads ? " she asked.

One of the men spoke up. " Call them Finn and Ches," he suggested.

" Finn and what ? " Narrie asked. Her face had taken on a quick eager flush.

" Finn and Ches—short for Chestnut ! "

Narrie smiled lazily, then asked : " Which of ye is Finn and which Ches ? "

" Have sense, woman ! " Finn Dillon said. " They're the names of two dogs Oisin had, long before the days of Christianity in Ireland."

" When I was going to school, Wren-boy Captain, it was Oisin's father, Finn, who owned the pair of dogs. And if my memory serves me right, their names were Bran and Sceolan."

" The girl is a scholar ! " said Shemus Goff.

Narrie Lanigan continued : " It was Oisin who rode off on horseback with Niav of the Golden Hair. They rode to the Land of Ever-Young and dwelt there for three hundred years." The sound of banter had momentarily ebbed in her voice.

The way the girl nuzzled the pup's head against her cheek constituted a sore provocation for us men.

" We've a horse, too ! " said Finn Dillon.

" Bigod, we have ! " said a muffled voice from beside our steed. " Too well I know it ! "

" And we've a Land of Ever-Young," said Young Font. " Forever Cloone ! "

Badger worked the jaw of the horse so that it clapped up and down.

Narrie Lanigan stretched out her hand and took the pup from Jody Shea. She now had a pup in each hand. She dandled them singly as if weighing them. Then she put the two old-young heads together and brought them close to her face. She pursed her lips and murmured small endearments. For a moment or two pretence became earnest. When she remembered that she was playing a game her tongue and eyes began to revolve slowly as if under the compulsion of a lovely malice. The women amongst us were intent on the blind faces of the puppies ; although each woman's mouth was doing its best to avoid mimicking Narrie Lanigan's mouth, her cheek could not escape the vicarious touch of fur moving across it.

Narrie was still crouched with a pup at each cheek. " Oh, the Chestnut ! " she whispered. " Oh, the Finn ! " Secretly, under their lashes, her eyes were uptaunting. Into the puckered noses of the little animals she whispered : " I love Chestnut ! I love Finn ! "

I looked down at the blind furred ball that was my namesake. His crinkled snout and sleep-loaded eyes were fast against the girl's cheek. I suddenly realised that my mouth and eyes were longing to supplant his !

The girl was still murmuring, as if she were alone : " I love Chestnut ! I love Finn ! "

Sheevra whined.

From among the women came again the laughter that was rich and deep. They were quietly delighting in the antics of Narrie Lanigan. They continued to look down. In their attitudes there was a tenseness as if they were awaiting a blow. The women knew that Narrie was interpreting them aright—that she spoke for everyone. We were too indolent or spell-bound to crystallise the common thought that the barriers were down. Here was what we all sought. Man and woman of us equally after the limitations of our gender. Here was the pure edge of living. Through the awkward eye-holes in my hi-fiddle I looked steadfastly at the women.

Another truth I realised: women are at their best when looking at an animal suckling her young.

The men seemed asleep and yet fully conscious. All except Jody Shea whose love of dogs had made him less than alert. Over his head the game went on. Played with important trifles it was. It was the first pretence: it will be the last. We of Cloone had no misconceptions. Practising on us they were, these strong farmers' daughters. And with good reason, too! What else were we all seeking but the fugitive and laughing happiness? Whenever the men made a movement, their boots stirred the heavy scent of the straw. It rose as powerful as sin is powerful. These movements of the men begat other movements of the women until all our steps had become part of a drowsy dance. We had sorted ourselves out by instinct, the women taking the initiative yet concealing the fact that they did so with an art that was artless because it was natural. Woman close to man then, ostensibly for the purposes of conversation. We were aware that we were rocked on a tide deep and lovely, yet fraught with danger for the senses.

When the strain was almost insupportable there arrived the laughter and the consequent delighting relaxation.

The old farmer broke the spell that lay upon us. Coming forward from the farmhouse door he clashed the iron wicket-gate with what seemed unnecessary loudness. He walked out towards the roadway. There he hawked harshly in his throat: menace was implied in the manner in which he cast his phlegm on the gravel. He glared at us, once, twice: then turned his face towards the northern sky. Narrie glanced at her father: she seemed amused at his antics.

Jody Shea was still intent on the young terriers. He suddenly realised that the woman was paying him but scant attention. Wanly he said: "Have you christened the other three yet?"

"*Ach!*" she said, "they're christened long ago." She spoke almost with irritation.

" What did you call 'em ? " Jody asked.

Narrie Lanigan smiled. She did not readily reply. She knew well that she would be asked the second time.

Deliberately Finn walked into the trap. " What did you call the other three ? " he asked.

Behind the masks we tightened. We knew that the question would open up a fresh field of dalliance.

The crouched girl looked up. " The one on the left is Madcap," she said. " The one on the right is Shoon."

All the girls laughed. Freer the laughter was by a good measure.

Finn straightened. " You're a lovely fencer with words," he said. " The man who wins you will never be lonely." He turned away.

Foolishly, I thought the trap had fully snapped. " What are you goin' to call the pup in the middle ? " I asked.

So slow she was in answering that I was momentarily deceived. Before she opened her mouth, however, I knew she had me.

" I don't rightly know as yet," she said carelessly, holding me pinned with her eyes. " I'm thinkin' of gettin' an English name for her—one that turns its back on tradition. One out of a book, maybe. A name like Marion or Priscilla." To one of her sisters behind her : " What was that fancy name I was telling you of the other day ? "

" Edith ! " the sister said.

The full laugh was on me. Loving God ! Did the whole countryside know of my affairs ?

" Aye, Edith ! " Narrie Lanigan said tolerantly. " It will serve till I think of a better."

Here was a different sharpness from the sharpness of Cloone. More roundabout, too, the wit was and greater care taken in the spreading of the nets.

Like the turn of a hand, her mood changed. She put the pups down beside Sheevra. Doing so, she said : " Down with Chestnut ! Down with Finn ! The milk is on yeer mouths yet. Yeer eyes aren't even open. 'Twill be many a long day before ye go huntin' in earnest!"

As she rose she smoothed her dress over her good young body. Then she tossed a wing of her hair off her face. She grimaced at us men, and speaking as it were for all the women present, said: "I've a boy of my own! One that could lick any of ye with his right hand tied behind his back. A tall slender hurler he is and he owns acres upon acres o' good red ground. I was only gamin' with ye, wren-boys. There isn't enough of money in the whole of yeer funny Cloone to buy my little finger!"

Finn was back again: slender profile, green fez, red mask, light dancing shoes, sash, and Belt of Cloone. "Money you want?" he asked her directly. "That, or the man?"

"Money and man, both!" she said. "I'll not marry for money, but I'll marry where money is."

Finn had recovered his balance of tone. "Many a fine filly harnessed herself to a poor cart," he said. Turning sharply, he walked away.

She followed him, almost bitterly. He rounded upon her suddenly. They were face to face. Her face was daring his. At the end of the little battle the woman's face it was that fell.

"I'll not dare you with my eyes, wren-boy," she said. "Although I know you haven't the harnessin' o' me, you might leave my mind betwixt an' between for many a year to come."

Finn laughed. Half in earnest, half in fun, he said: "'Tis hard to beat you, Narrie Lanigan, whether you're frank or not frank." Then he said brightly: "Put your mind at ease, big farmer's daughter. We're encouraged to marry our own women. We don't like goin' outside, no more than ye do." He turned to the other girls: "It was pleasant meetin' ye, women," he said. "It was pleasant gettin' a crown from the man of the house. It was lovely clashin' words with ye as if it were slender swords we had. Whatever fun ye had out of us, we had equal fun out of ye. A fair transaction, wasn't it ? "

" Fair enough, Finn Dillon," Narrie Lanigan said, " and no bones broken."

" No bones broken at all, my girl," Finn replied. Then, sharply, to us : " Fall in ! "

The mood was shattered. We fell in and marched away.

III

At about one o'clock we split up into twos and threes and set off in different directions to seek our dinners. Finn gave us strict instructions to re-assemble within the hour.

Finn, Young Font and I went off together. We had not gone far before we were invited into the house of a small farmer. " Have ye e'er a mouth on ye, wran-boys ? " he called to us from his farmyard.

" We have, indeed ! " we replied.

" Sit in ! Sit in ! Ye're among friends. Ah, when I was out in the Wran long ago. . . . "

The children of the house were very silent as they sat down to the table with us. We regretted that we had not brought along the hobby-horse so that they could make delight by offering it sups of milk from a tin panny.

As the meal began, the farmer's mother, a very old but sprightly woman, came up out of the west room. We stood up to greet her. She started involuntarily on seeing Finn Dillon's face and when she was told who he was, smiled ruefully and confessed that his grandfather had courted her when they were both young. Fondling Finn's hands, she shed slow tears and then said, half in and half out of earnest : " Now that there's friendship between us, son, you'll not forget to attend my funeral ? " Finn said, yes, yes, that he would, but added the sensible caution that God spoke first. The old woman seemed satisfied with this reply and then took her place among the children to mouth her small meal in silence.

The dinner over, we thanked the people of the house and hastened back to the agreed-on meeting-place. Most of the others were there before us : they were in good spirits after the meal.

Finn chafed as he waited for the stragglers to arrive : he was worrying lest the Farranmacoo wren-boys should reach the village of Sradeen before us.

On the hurling field the lads from Farranmacoo were traditional enemies of ours. They wore red and white jerseys : these colours, they explained, signified blood and linen. They hurled in their bare feet and were demons to double on a ball. It was a badge of pride with them how close they could go to a man's skull with a swift pull on a seasoned ash hurley. Rarely did they set a hand to a ball : they were merciless with a rival team fond of handling the leathern *sliotar*. When a Farranmacoo man heard an opponent's finger-bones rattle under the blade of his hurley, or saw the blood spurt from a foolish outstretched hand, he was jubilant. He leaped high in the air, and shouted " Fingers ! " From the sideline came an answering echo of " Fingers ! " as the oldsters of Farranmacoo yelled with glee. Such a blow they reckoned a victory for the old style of hurling : to a man they were opposed to the new style of handling and dilly-dallying with the ball.

As I thought of the hurlers of Farranmacoo, I looked at a scar on one of my fingers and felt a reminiscent pain seep into it. I put my finger into my mouth and began to suck it idly.

Soon the laggards came up.

About two miles from the hollow in which Sradeen lay we stopped the music and put our best legs under us. A pony and trap came drumming after us. Hearing a shout we turned : in the trap we saw Dicky Hickey and the farmer who had given him a ride. Dicky was dressed in his wren suit but his mask was high on his hat. He was carrying a tambourine which, in proportion to his size, seemed enormous. We waited for him to catch up with us.

(In the morning I had gone into the Rookery to rouse him for the Wren but seeing him curled up in the feather bed against the mountain that was Streaming Blood, I hadn't the heart to awaken him.)

"The curse o' the crows down on top o' ye, man an' boy o' ye, ye ill-spoken illiterate shams, ye scum o' Cloone! That ye may perish an' melt an' dwindle, every man-jack o' ye, not to wait for me this mornin' above all the mornin's o' the year! That the crows o' God. . . . "

The heavily-built farmer who owned the pony and trap was leaning back on his cushioned seat, breaking his heart with laughter at the astonishing fury of the little fellow.

Finn Dillon succeeded in pacifying Dicky Hickey. At first the little chap was eager to get out of the trap and join us, but finding that the farmer was travelling in the direction of Sradeen he remained in the vehicle. He made sure to slam the door tightly so that those of us who had grown lazy were forced to walk. This he reckoned a suitable punishment for our omission to waken him.

The trap pulled out to the van of our procession and as Dicky Hickey kept urging the pony onwards we were forced to move at a smart pace. Dicky kept screaming at us: "Bad scran to ye for laggards! D'ye want a Farranmacoo boy to be the first to plant his claimin' claw on the cross of Sradeen?" This was an allusion to the cross-country races in which the competitors had to touch the cross of Sradeen before returning to the winning-post.

As we approached the brow of the hill overlooking Sradeen, we were one and all fully short of breath. By this time the trap had reached the hill-crest. Dicky now began to gesticulate and shout: we rushed forward against the acclivity and, reaching the hill-top, looked down into the village of Sradeen. Many of the houses were semi-hidden in the bare trees but through a break in the serried rods we could see the great limestone cross standing below in mid-village. Upriver, behind the white reeds, lay the ruined abbey of Sradeen. The spotted stones of the walls seemed locked in the sleep of the centuries. Downstream lay the mill. The waters of the river were unruffled and the trees were faithfully etched upon it.

Dicky was pointing across the valley at something on the road that descended to the village from the north. At first we could see nothing: then of a sudden we glimpsed the Farranmacoo wren-boys marching forward. The sunlight caught the colours of their costumes. For a moment or two we stood silent. In this span of silence the small fife and drum band of our rivals struck up "Brian Boru's March," a tune in which the music ceases abruptly and, in the resultant pause, the musicians give vent to a fierce battle-yell.

We waited for the yell: full of menace it bridged the valley. Directly after it, as if to crown the defiance of the roar, came the double thunder of the Farranmacoo big drum. The sound seemed to paralyse us: with sinking hearts we realised that we had no means of throwing back the challenge. Each of us in his own mind began to reckon which was the better—a hobby-horse, mute and ornamental, or a drum that could return a challenge with double thunder.

"Run, blast ye, run!" Dicky Hickey's screaming roused us.

Finn Dillon began to race downhill towards the village. Fiddlers, gadget players, singers, mouth-organ players, dancers and tambourine strummers, we all followed. The hobby-horse ran, too. The Farranmacoo music ceased abruptly; clearly we heard their captain urging them forward. Then were borne to us the agitated cries of running men. As I looked across the valley, I saw the big drum, which was being hurried forward by two men, catch the southern light and shine like a moon of cream on the frosty day. I could also see the red and white jerseys which had been borrowed from the Farranmacoo hurling team: this was the blood and the linen that we hated. Downhill we raced, the farmer urging on the pony as fast as he dared on the incline.

When we reached the level ground below we saw the Celtic

cross about two hundred yards uproad from us. A knot of men standing idly about it, suddenly realising that a race was in progress, sang out gaily to the doorways of the village. People began to emerge. Swiftly grasping the situation they began to cheer the contestants. As we raced onwards we noticed that with every step the knot of people about the cross was growing larger. Dicky Hickey was standing upright in the trap : he had snatched the whip from the farmer's hand and was laying it doughtily across the pony's back, the while he chattered like a monkey. Times he screamed at the pony : times he turned back to exhort or abuse us.

" Forever Cloone ! " he screamed. " We'll show them how to play Napper Tandy for the priest ! "

This was an obscure gibe flung at the Farran boys.

Finn Dillon, wee Jody Shea and I were racing in the lead. Our early start had given us an advantage. The Celtic cross seemed deceptively near under the bare looping rods of the chestnuts. Then I saw the first of the Farran men : despite his costume I recognised the fresh stride of Fennell, who was the captain of their hurling team. Finn Dillon saw him at the same time : he moved forward fluently on his lightweight dancer's shoes. Fennell's appearance drove Dicky Hickey berserk. " Forever Cloone ! " was now an undistinguishable mess of sound in his mouth. Finn Dillon pulled to the front until he had drawn level with the pony's head. It now seemed a certainty that we had won the village.

All of a sudden there was an outlandish tattarara in our rear. We heard a scream as of intense pain. Finn and I stopped and turned : we saw that Badger Breen had fallen under the hobby-horse and that those following him had piled up to form a struggling mound on the roadway.

" That's that ! " Finn Dillon said, with a deep sigh.

High-pitched screaming rose from the pile of bodies. We went back and began to unravel the tangled men. The roadway was littered with our wren-boys : one man was mourning for his broken fiddle, another was gaping at a great hole torn in his tambourine, yet another kept gazing aghast at the battered skull of the mandoline his aunt had sent him as a present from Philadelphia.

Finally we released Badger from under the squashed cradle of the hobby-horse : his nose was racing blood and he was screeching meela-murder.

Of a sudden Finn said : " Bigod, lads, look ! "

The farmer in the trap was seized with a sudden frenzy : he had snatched the whip from Dicky Hickey and was flaying the animal forward. As Dicky was a sorry equipoise for the farmer, the vehicle was swaying dangerously on its springs. The mannikin was standing almost upright on the cushions of the seat : he continued to strike the pony's hindquarters with the flat of his tambourine. The cymbals of the tambourine agitated the pony more than did the lash of the whip. Seeing the misfortune that had befallen our hobby-horse, and noticing that our leader had stopped and turned, Fennell had slowed down. Then, with a start, spying the costumed figure in the trap, he began running again. This time he was racing at his full heart. The people of Sradeen had now become partisans : some cheered for Cloone, some for Farranmacoo. The onlookers began to raise the war-cries of the hurling field : " Up Farranmacoo ! " they shouted, then, " Forever Cloone ! "

The pony and trap was first to reach the goal. So abruptly did the farmer draw the animal to a halt under the limestone arm of the cross, that Dicky Hickey was projected on to the animal's back and escaped disaster only by clutching firmly at the breeching. The farmer, with singular presence of mind, grasped the mannikin by the seat of his pants and jerked him back into the vehicle. As Dicky saw Fennell racing up, he threw his tambourine at the cross : it skidded off the limestone arm and went floating away into the crowd of onlookers.

We began to scream : " Dicky's won it ! " " Bigod, but he's won it ! " " Glory on you, you lovely mannikin ! " " Forever, forever Cloone ! "

Fennell raced up and touched the cross with his hand.

"Curse o' the crows on you, rise me up!" Dicky screamed at the farmer.

The farmer caught Dicky by the small of the back and raised him up to the horizontal cross-piece of the monument. Dicky clutched his arms about it, then began to claw upwards like an acrobat. He thrust his boots into the two ornamental circles beneath the point of intersection of the cross. Clasping his arms tightly about the upright, he began to scream incoherently. The people of Sradeen cheered him to the echo. Some one threw him up his tambourine: he banged it in triumph against the cross. His face mated with the grotesque Celtic interlacing on the monument.

Fennell looked up at Dicky Hickey: "Stop your jack-actin'," he said with severity. "The race is mine!"

Dicky put out his tongue at Fennell: the bystanders rewarded him with a cheer. The applause put Dicky in excellent spirits. He took off his coloured cap and set it on the pinnacle of the cross where a leader of the Irish people had once rested his hand while addressing the people of Sradeen.

By this time we had all come up, the Farranmacoo fellows as well as our own band. White spittle appeared at the corner of his mouth as Dicky began to berate Finn and myself.

"Gulong, ye parcel o' moth-eaten highwaymen!" he cried. "Ye were whipped a cripple only for Dicky Hickey's tambourine. Now maybe ye're sorry ye left without me." Then: "Huhoo! Forever Cloone!"

The bystanders raised their caps and cheered.

"The village is ours," Finn Dillon said quietly to Fennell.

"Ours it is!" said Fennell. Then: "Line up!" he snapped to his men. The men bringing the Farranmacoo big drum had just trundled up.

"Fall in!" said Finn Dillon.

We fell in at one side of the cross, the Farranmacoo men at the other.

"By the left . . ." Fennell sang out.

" By the left . . . " shouted Finn Dillon.

Dicky Hickey screamed : " They're goin' to play Napper Tandy for the priest ! "

This was the obscure traditional gibe. The Sradeen people thumped one another in glee and laughter. We of Cloone hooted derisively.

The Farranmacoo big drummer had his drumstick poised. On hearing the taunt, he lowered it. Not without difficulty he bellied over to the front of the cross. " 'fore God," he said, looking upwards, " if I get my fingers to you, I'll grease the gridiron with what there's of you ! "

" Fingers ! " yelled Dicky Hickey.

Badger Breen was still dabbling at his bloodied face. The gore-pied handkerchief loaned him a savage appearance out of all proportion to his valour. He placed his awesome face against that of the big drummer, and said : " D'you think or imagine that we'd hould lookin' at you while you'd be doin' it, you ugly bladder o' lard ? "

The drummer handed his sticks to one of his own men. " Here ! " he said, with resignation, " help me unhook this god-damn drum. God stands witness to what I've endured ! "

While the drummer was being assisted to unhook his drum, Badger was solemnly doffing his wren-blouse and jacket. " Once and for all . . . " he said, " it'll be settled by blood."

I wondered what would happen now : Badger Breen wouldn't fight a fly.

Just as the pair were ready to square out from one another, the Sradeen people started to whisper : " Bullug ! Here's Bullug ! "

Bullug was the local Sergeant. His name was widely feared. Bullug is the Gaelic for belly.

" Put on your coat, bostoon ! " I shouted to Badger Breen. " Here comes Bullug ! "

I saw Dicky Hickey hide beneath the upright of the cross.

All sorts of prehistoric dragons were cut on the shaft : these served Dicky royally for the purpose of concealment.

Now that he knew the fight could never take place, Badger was slow to part company with his truculence. If anything, he grew more belligerent. Matters were somewhat the same way with the Farranmacoo drummer, who was a stout mallet of a fellow.

Still struggling into his sergeant's jacket, Bullug puffed up. He was an enormous man. A slight cast in one eye made him resemble Polyphemus ; it seemed that the deep lines in his neck could have been drawn only with a knife recurrently dipped in black ink. He was bare-headed and the hair was cropped close to his outsize skull. A road melted through the people : he came into the centre of the ring and saw the blood on Badger's face. Lazily he viewed the pair of prospective boxers, then, ever so slowly, he seized them by the collars of their jackets. His left hand made a rat out of Badger : his right made the stout drummer look shrivelled and shrunken.

Bullug puffed himself back to his normal rate of breathing. Then he smiled at the crowd with his entire face. The smiling became concentrated until we had the illusion that it was emerging through his white eye. The smile was the smile of a playboy child who scarcely knew his own strength.

" Ha ! " he said, " just when I have subjugated Sradeen, I get—hah !—imported disturbers from the sublime districts of Farranmacoo and Cloone. Hah ! With the Irish people it doesn't matter whether it's Christmas, Easter or Patrick's Day. Day in, day out, it's nothing but fight, fury and blood, smoke and the worst of language." Viewing the combatants directly for the first time, he said : " Well ? "

There was a deep silence. A fond smile played about Bullug's mouth.

Just then Dicky Hickey thrust his head out from behind the Cross of Sradeen. He rested his chin on the great semicircle that ringed the point of intersection of the arms. " The village is ours, Tub o' Guts ! " he shrieked. " I won it square with my tambourine ! "

Bullug dropped the pair of would-be boxers. Badger fell to the ground with the suddenness and the unexpected nature of the release : the Farranmacoo drummer, though he did not completely fall, was hard set to hold his stance. Bullug looked up at the cross, then rubbed his poll in incredulity. He walked around to the back of the monument, then returning to the front, grimaced gaily and with intense good humour cut the sign of the cross on himself. With mock piety he addressed high Heaven : " Holy You, Utter Divine and Adorable Creator of Heaven, Earth and the Five Elements," he asked, " is it the way 'tis rainin' leprechauns ! "

The crowd guffawed. Towards the end of the guffaw a note of scoffing entered into it. Bullug turned. At his turning, the laughter died. Its dying was without frayed edges : he killed it as a choirmaster kills the chanting of his choir.

Dicky Hickey, who still clung closely to the cross, resembled a pup apprehended in wrong-doing on a carpet.

Bullug renewed his skyward scrutiny. " Hey, small man ! " he roared—Dicky almost lost his grip on the cross with the terror of hearing the sergeant's voice—" what in the name of thunder are you doin' up there clingin' like a leech to the holy cross of Sradeen ? "

" I won it fair ! " Dicky said, in a shrivelled but eager voice. He appealed to the crowd. " People of Sradeen," he pleaded, " talk up an' bear witness that I won yeer village fair ! "

The Sradeen people gave a roar of affirmation. As Bullug turned the roar died. The sergeant crinkled his great face. Ponderously, and in his own good time, he said : " Sub-jug-ated ! " Ruminantly, he eyed the people of his kingdom.

Fennell came forward. " There was no fightin', Sergeant," he said. Indicating Badger, he continued : " This fellow fell under his hobby-horse. We were racin' to see who'd touch the cross first an' so have prior collectin' of the village. I touched the cross before any of the Cloone fellows."

From the sky came the small voice, gathering courage as it went on: "You painted liar an' picked impostor, what about my tambourine?"

Bullug roared: "Hold your tongue, Toby-jug!" Turning to Fennell, he asked: "What about his tambourine?"

Finn Dillon stepped forward. "Dicky Hickey threw his tambourine at the cross and touched it before Fennell did. We're claimin' that the village is ours!"

Bullug turned to Fennell. "Can you answer that?" he queried.

Quietly Fennell said: "We're claimin' that the tambourine doesn't count!"

"Bidamn!" said Bullug. He laughed and swung his tremendously long hands—it was worth a fortune to see Bullug do just that. "Ye have me in a proper pucker," he said, not without gaiety. "I must cogitate this thing over."

Growling the while, he sat on one of the stones that leaned against the pedestal of the cross. He continued to draw ponderous breaths. The crowd tightened its ring so as to hear him debate the matter with himself.

"It's the story of the Red Hand of Ulster born all over again," Bullug said. "How the chieftain cut off his left hand and threw it into the island so as to beat the other chief he was boat-racing. Hah! A diff-ic-ult problem!"

On the outskirts of the crowd a youngster struck the big drum with his knuckles. Bullug sighed deeply at this mark of disrespect for law and order. Conscientious and loud-voiced men chucked the young offender about. I could not help looking down at the broken ribs of our hobby-horse. Arbitrarily I transferred my gaze to the sticky chestnut buds on the boughs over my head.

There was a cough from Dicky Hickey at the top of the cross. Bullug cast his sound eye skywards. "If 'tis a thing," he said, "you let fall the smallest drop of water on the crown of my head, whether it's through pure dread, natural weakness or common bla'guardin', I'll take you down an' stuff my bad tooth with you."

Sradeen was shaken with laughter. Bullug let the tide of noise ride over him.

"Which o' them owns the village? Hah! God direct me! I'm not Aristotle an' I'm not Solomon!" He beat his belly softly with his fist, as if to intimate to the people of Sradeen that he was well aware of his nickname. "Hah! If it's to be solved it's my opinion it must be done so by another competition. What competition? I'm blessed . . . ! A toss of a penny? No! A sickly finish to a noble race. A game of hurling? Not bad! But no hurleys are available. A fight? Blood is ugly—in the abstract!" (Bullug looked as though he lived on goblets of it.) "Three forty-ones in cards? Too anaemic! And yet . . . a competition it must be. Well! Well! Well! Well!"

Thereupon Bullug closed his eyes and lapsed into a kind of trance. In this trance he began to hum a "come-all-ye." I saw Shemus Goff close his eyes and listen with rapt attention: he was striving to pick up the ballad at the first go.

"*An' all the lamps was lightin', except the wans was quenched;*
*An' I did nothin' to no wan, an' no wan did nothin' to me.*"

High over the heads of the crowd a brown handball came soaring. It struck the tranced Bullug full in the chest. One of the crowd captured it as it hopped. The little incident was over in a flash.

Bullug was now wide awake. "Gi' me that!" he shouted to no one in particular. The man who had caught the ball hesitated for a moment, then came forward and handed it to Bullug. It was a good ball of almost translucent rubber. Bullug hopped the ball once. The crowd laughed. Bullug caught the ball and looked harshly at the crowd. He tightened his fist on the brown handball. The crowd watched the ball grow smaller and smaller. So completely did he close his fist that it seemed as if the hand contained nothing. The crowd had never before seen anyone do this to a handball.

Turning to Finn Dillon and Fennell, Bullug asked : " Have ye a handballer apiece ? "

" That we have ! " both replied together.

" Settled, thanks be to the Man Above ! " said Bullug. He clapped his hands down sharply on the taut cloth covering his thighs. " Slat ! Slat ! " said the cloth on his pants. The Sradeen people looked at us in triumph as if mutely inquiring whether we had ever before seen the equal of their sergeant.

Bullug stood up : we began to marvel anew at his size and girth. He opened his mouth to speak. Before he could do so, there was an exclamation from the top of the cross. No one paid Dicky Hickey the slightest attention.

Shemus Goff was speaking sagely to himself : " This is shapin' well ! " ; that was how I read his lips.

Dominick Foy was a tall black lantern-faced young man : if he shaved in the morning his face was blue with stubble by noon. He was addicted to handball as another man is addicted to drink. When Finn Dillon called him, he stepped forward from our ranks. Moddera Magee stepped forward for Farranmacoo : he was a small blacksmith with fair skin and a shock of light ashen hair.

" Stand before me ! " Bullug ordered. The pair took their stand before him. They removed their masks.

" Three games of twenty-one aces each," the Sergeant said. " Whoever wins two out of the three games gains the village of Sradeen for his band of wren-boys. Follow me ! " He turned and walked in the direction of the ball-alley.

When Dicky Hickey saw the crowd ebbing from around the base of the cross he was overcome with dismay. " Hey ! What about me ? " he called out. Bullug returned and gazed up at him. " Jump ! " he ordered. He opened his arms wide and thrust out his chest.

A look of awe appeared on Dicky Hickey's face. Gingerly he placed a boot on the portion of the arm beyond the circle.

He stood almost upright. Removing his hat from the cap of the cross he crushed it on his head. Desperately he grasped his tambourine, then summoned all his courage for the leap. At the last moment his valour fell apart : " I couldn't do it ! " he quavered.

" Jump, you gnat ! " roared Bullug, " or 'tis there you'll hang till the clap o' dark ! "

Again Dicky gathered himself : then he jumped. Bullug caught him lightly. For a moment or two he held Dicky in his arms. He opened his mouth to its full width. Dicky's face twisted fantastically with fear. The great mouth came nearer and nearer to the little man's face. Then, at the last moment, Bullug growled with laughter and gently set the mannikin on the ground. Catching Dicky by the hand, the sergeant led the re-formed procession across the village.

Those of us who were first took up our places on the long seat behind the alley. The crowd piled on the mound behind us. Bullug seated himself on the middle of the seat with Dicky Hickey squirming fast under his left arm. The Parish Priest had come up : Bullug grabbed him and tucked him under his right arm. The priest was very old : he was very careful of his umbrella and kept folding the pleats over on one another unceasingly. Through the subsequent roaring and confusion, he reiterated " My ! My ! " in a mild yet reproving tone of voice. Once he meekly ventured to say, after a terrific bout of cheering : " Tck ! Tck ! Red blood ! "

Finn Dillon had an undertone word with Fennell : both captains then called their treasurers aside. Five pounds eight shillings and sixpence we had in our kitty. The Farranmacoo treasurer withdrew an equal amount from his store. These sidebets were bound together in a large strong handkerchief and given to Bullug to hold. Receiving the moneys he laughed loudly and struck his fist against the handkerchief-ful of coins.

" I'm the marker ! " Bullug shouted. Then he added : " Any objections ? " He twisted his face around to the crowd, which resolved itself into lifeless faces that became volatile the instant he turned away.

Dominick Foy and Moddera Magee were now stripped to the waist. They had procured canvas shoes. Dominick's white skin belied his jet countenance. The teats on his breast were dark-brown against the fair skin of his body. He was wearing a pair of wrist-straps which served to show with accuracy the facile way in which his arms swung. Moddera's skin, also, was fair by nature but had been darkened by his work in the forge.

Dominick and Moddera began to play for the village of Sradeen.

While the games were in progress, Dicky Hickey was jigging as with electricity under Bullug's arms, Shemus Goff's lips were moving in a slow rhythm, and Young Font's eyes were alive with pride. That same pride I had often seen in his father's eyes as he was telling us of our traditions in Cloone. Finn Dillon's face had gone a shade paler. The Sradeen people had divided loyalties : some were cheering for Dominick Foy and others for Moddera Magee. They buttressed their partisanship with further wagers.

Moddera was far better than we thought he was : he used the Scotch toss, which we in Cloone had outlawed as being unfair. Taking his stand at the tossing-line at the left-hand side of the alley, he tossed the ball high up to the right of the front wall, whence it screwed off to strike the right-hand sidewall. Then it swung soaring out high and brisk and as often as not reached the left-hand wall and finally struck the ground. With this toss, the ball had four distinct screws to it : as a result the hop was wholly unpredictable. Sometimes the ball spun crazily backwards towards Moddera who had tossed it : sometimes it seemed to adhere to the face of the sidewall. When Dominick drew on the bewitched ball as often as not his hand sliced empty air.

Moddera kept making ace after ace in this fashion until we saw to our dismay that he had pegged up two gates of aces.

Cloone had got off to a bad start—already we were ten points down!

All this happened to the accompaniment of rounds of applause from the Farranmacoo supporters. At a word from Finn, Dom Foy moved in and began to take the toss on the fly, striking the ball firmly before it could reach the floor of the alley. This was so successful that after a few aces the Scotch toss was abandoned.

Under Bullug's right arm, the priest was restless. Bullug chided him, saying: "Sit down there, Father, an' don't let me hear a gucks out o' you!" As an afterthought, he asked: "Was your turkey tender, Father?" Without waiting for a reply, Bullug said: "So was mine!" The priest continued muttering "My! My!" and caressing his umbrella.

Moddera won the first game, Dominick the second. The third game brought every remaining person in Sradeen out of doors. For the greater part of this, the last game of the three, it was level pegging all the way. Dicky Hickey by this time was a pure lunatic and Bullug's left elbow was providing an ineffective strait-jacket. The Parish Priest was in a realm beyond astonishment. Badger Breen was voiceless—he lacked even the strength to murmur "Forever Cloone!" As we cheered and danced at every feat of Foy's, the ball kept ringing on the butt of the wall. Dominick's face had gone deadly pale: the skin on his body had whitened, while at the same time the teats on his breast seemed to darken. Clearly defined by the straps, the wrists swung backwards and forwards to an effective rhythm. He knew that if he were beaten, he dared not face the old men of Cloone.

Towards the end of the game, when he looked a certain winner, the occasion got the upper hand of Foy: for a while he played wildly, losing ace after valuable ace. Again a sharp word from Finn Dillon steadied him. Once only was an ace in dispute: both contestants turned appealing faces to Bullug for judgment: this he delivered immediately; "Ball in play!" he growled. After a bout of wretched handball, Dom Foy seemed to find surety and poise : he reverted easily to his initial deceptive laziness of style and returned the ball low and hard to the base of the wall. When he had finished a bitterly-contested ace with a butt that sounded like a rifle-shot we of Cloone embraced one another. From that on, the game was Dom Foy's.

The three final aces ! Tally ! Look sharp ! Game-ball !

Dominick killed the game-ball. He rang it hard and low and true. Turning to us in quiet triumph, he first looked meekly at Finn Dillon. Finn nodded and smiled. By this time the whole world seemed to be cheering for Cloone.

Bullug stood up. " Foy, the winner ! " he shouted. " Sradeen belongs to the wren-boys of Cloone ! "

Dicky Hickey had escaped from under Bullug's arm : he ran full pelt at Dominick and embraced him around the thighs. He kept thrusting his face against the pit of Foy's stomach. Shemus Goff walked a few paces aside and began to try out a line of a new ballad.

Finn Dillon returned a pound from our winnings to the Farranmacoo lads. Fennell had the reputation of being a proud man—at first he was reluctant to take the money. Then he smiled and, thinking of Galileo the cobbler, said to Finn : " We shall rise again ! "

" Fall in ! " Finn shouted.

We fell in. Finn stood out before us. The stick had resumed its glittering. Behind Finn came the hobby-horse, its ribs punched back into some semblance of normality. One of the men had lifted Dicky Hickey on his shoulders. Dominick Foy was pulling on his shirt : his face was bloodless. The youngsters of Sradeen were looking up into his face as if eager to learn the secret of his prowess.

" By the left . . ." Finn Dillon said.

Our battered band struck up " The Cock o' the North." The youngsters of Sradeen took up the lilting of the air to their own words : " Yip—i—ay—dee ; Yip—i—ay—dee ; Up the Cock o' the North ! " We paraded down the village, then swung around and strutted back to the Cross of Sradeen. As we went, we were showered with white money. Bullug stood under a great chestnut tree in the midst of the vanquished Farranmacoo men. He had his arm around the shoulders of the disconsolate big-drummer and was thumping the drum in time to our music.

Uphill we struggled by the north road out of Sradeen. It gave our musicians all they could do to keep the music going as they pushed against the incline. On the crest of the hill, at a point where they could not be heard in the village below, they stopped playing. The half-hearted strains of " Brian Boru's March " floated up to us. As one man we drew a deep breath, then looked at one another in triumph and laughter. We turned our faces to the bright dole of countryside that lay before us. The day was waning. Every moment of it was precious. Soon the sun would pine and die behind bars that were edged with gold.

It was past eleven o'clock as we crossed Grey Bridge. Then we were almost at home. By this time, we were straggling in weary twos and threes. A great moon was rising over Cloone: it had whitened the eastern gap of the river valley. The same moon was reduced to an erratic daub in the flurry of water to the left of the gravel-bank in mid-river. As we moved onwards into the sleeping town Finn Dillon formed us up for the last time.

" Hold yeer heads high, for spite ! " he exhorted.

He was speaking to listless men. By this time even the lazy music was overlively for our leaden legs. We had walked close on thirty miles—the stepdancers must have travelled farther if the raising of the foot may be counted as a step. Passing through the town square we tried to march in as soldierly a fashion as we could. There were no onlookers. We swung into the mouth of Cloone. Flung Dung and the Maid of Erin looked down on us with equanimity. Our tired tongues began to rehearse the telling of the day's wonders. We were glad to see the pressed-down cottages of home. Youngsters climbed out of bed and thrust their faces against the small-paned windows as we passed. Forms darkened the mellow squares over the half-doors. When our music stopped, the shouts of welcome beat against us.

"Ye had a gay Wran, boys ?"

"Well, lads, so ye're back ?"

"Ah ! Blessin' o' God ! Blessin' o' God !"

"Life is to the young an' to nobody else !"

The old people had begun their grumbling.

Streaming Blood was leaning against a cottage wall. He was heavy with drink. The music did not succeed in turning him. Spying him out, Dicky Hickey doffed his weariness : he ran over and inserted himself between the bulk of the big man and the wall. Then he began to scold Streaming Blood and to tug fiercely at his jacket.

At the crossroads we saw Caherdown : he was wearing his good black overcoat. His white shirt was like a light in the darkness. We saw his uplifted varnished cane catch the light like an erratic moonbeam. He tried to roar us a welcome but failed. He was well blowsed but by no means footless. When we had come up, he fell to embracing us maudlinly.

We felt deflated. Our boots were our bosses. We broke away from Caherdown's clutches. From the cottages came the smell of frying meat.

## CHAPTER VI

I

IT was the night before the Old Fair. From the twin pubs at the mouth of Cloone came the sound of tremendous tantivy.

Spring had fully won in: in the surrounding countryside the hedges and trees were thick with foliage and the new grass was driving the cattle daft with delight. We had watched spring come, each day lengthening by the scarcely perceptible "cock's step."

There was every indication that it would be a great fair.

With drovers roaring fore and aft, cattle poured down the roadway into Cloone. Capacious high spring-carts drove past, moving at a reckless rate: in these vehicles sat cast-clothes men, cushioned on enormous piles of cast-off garments.

In Cloone proper the road had become almost impassable, what with jarvey-cars and caravans and gigs and other vehicles that still persisted from a bygone age.

A strange clan of tinkers had come in from the West of Ireland. Catfooted fellows they were: it was delightful to see them maintain their gravity against the downward tug of alcohol. They had their encampment on the commonage to the north of the cottages between the haggards and the farm of Dark Jack O'Neill.

As yet, these westerners held their peace with their southern brothers; we reckoned them unusual folk since they could be obsequious and disdainful at the same time. They asked: "E'er a copper? Ah, God love you!" Then, receiving or not receiving, they walked proudly away, moving as if on tip-toe. One fellow had a variant on this theme: with a bright candour, he queried: "Have you e'er a coin for a fellow who's sick from drink?" The beard was bursting out through his face and his eyes were sunken. "Dadda Christmas is dead!" we told him. Then, when we did not expect to find it, we saw the sudden savagery in his eyes.

Cattle continued to blunder in: they were lowing desolately until they had brought our mood to a similar pitch of loneliness. Beside the bridge, on the boreen that led north from it, and on the edge of the common at the back of the haggards, standings were being erected. Rows over pitches suddenly flickered up and at the point when it seemed that nothing could prevent them from bursting into flame they were speedily smothered. Fighting would be premature. As yet the fair was as cold as stone.

To all of us, except to Caherdown, the prospect of the fair was highly exciting. Caherdown was mortally afraid that his precious cottage-front would get soiled with the fair-day dung. Directly in front of his cottage he was at that moment engaged in placing the bulwark of an old trestle. Almost it seemed as if he were preparing his cottage as for a state of siege.

With the first whisper of spring, Caherdown brought his little dwelling to the highest point of cleanliness. In the flower-bed between the cobbles and the wall, the green leaves of Tom Thumb nasturtiums were already over the ground. The front wall had been lime-washed a faint primrose and the door and the half-door stippled red and yellow. The window sashes were of a surprising whiteness and the timber surrounds had been touched with a good emerald. For the sides of the windows Caherdown had chosen a modest sky-blue. The roof of the cottage was thatched to the veins of nicety and the thatch looked as if it had been freshly combed. The single chimney was painted primrose to match the front of the house. On the thatch directly over the door a house leek grew: this was believed to possess the virtue of keeping the house safe from the danger of fire.

"Embattled, by hell!" Caherdown said truculently to Finn Dillon and myself as he readied his trestle. "This night twelve months I was here. A bumpkin drove his beast against my threshold. I accosted the fellow. He had the temerity to say: 'You and the likes of you would be sick, sore an' sorry only for my equals!' O-o-o-h! O-o-o-h! His equals! The low mean skulking Druse!"

"What did you say to him?" we asked. Making conversation we were—nothing more.

"What did I say to him? By God, if it was words he wanted, I had them. And if it was fisticuffs he was seeking, his search was ended." Caherdown knotted a soft white fist. We gazed at it in feigned admiration.

(Finn Dillon had that morning received a letter from Shoon Lawlee who had gone working to the city early in the New Year. The sense of distance in her eyes had gained a passing victory. Finn was happy: a chance remark of his led me to conclude that Shoon's letter had more than hinted at her feelings of isolation and loneliness.)

Together with Finn, I entered the Rookery. The lamplight was warm on the thronged house: looking at the chimney of the lamp made me recall that it was here that our rebel cobbler had recounted how Galileo of Pisa, newly released from prison, had pointed at the sun and exclaimed: "And still it moves!" At this, the climax of his story, the lamp chimney had cracked with a loud report. The women crossed themselves, thinking it a sign from God, but Old Font had laughed and nicknamed the cobbler on the spot.

Tom and Martha Goggin were working like dervishes. On the hearth was a roaring turf fire: from the crane above it hung a kettle which never seemed done spitting water into enormous brown teapots. I noted the lodgers: I saw sly cast-clothes men, check-coated horse blockers reputed secretly rich, a boneless wonder seated meekly by his prosaic wife, a street strong man semi-awake after his meal, a toothless wheel-o'-fortune mother nursing a pair of chalk chanticleers, a maggieman mounted in wall-eyed guard over his spy-holed barrel, a gnarled ballad-singer deep in professional conversation with Shemus Goff and a fat rags-clad umbrella-mender whose naked navel responded gaily to his drunken breathing.

In a corner of the kitchen sat a middle-aged coloured fortune-teller with dark eyes, short crisp curls and transcendently white teeth. His fingernails were inclined to be purple. From time to time he lifted the cloth from a long cage and held secret conversation with his budgerigars.

At the head of the table sat a young man making roses out of coloured crêpe paper. His lips smiled in sympathy with the movements of his deft fingers. I thought that the sudden vision of the roses and the fingers and the smile above the work taken as a unit constituted a treasure. From her corner by the hob, Dolly the Rose quickly looked at the rosemaker: immediately her face was touched with the gold-leaf of joy.

The excitement engendered by such a night invariably caused long Tom Goggin to launch a verbal attack on his short wife. When she had transferred the black of the hob to her nose, he had the excuse he sought. "Look at her!" he stormed: "an' she not up to the border of the kitchen! By the cut of her you'd think her that clever that you could set her mindin' mice under a hat. A peepshow we are! Bigod, if 'twas a thing we bred, our sons could play hurley under the bed!"

Martha did not reply.

Finn drew Tom aside a step or two. He glanced covertly around the thronged kitchen. "A question I have to ask you, Tom," he said.

"What is it?" Tom asked suspiciously.

Finn whispered: "Which of these is the Flea-man?"

Tom's face held its complete rigidity. His blue eyes opened

to their full width. "What do you mean—Flea-man?" he asked, not over-sharply.

Finn took Tom aside another step or two, presumably in order to ensure absolute secrecy. "They tell me there's a man at the fair has trained fleas," he whispered again. "You pay money to view them under a microscope. He has a hair tied around the fleas' necks and a scrap of a monkey nut rigged up as a carriage. Rumour says that he's half a millionaire." Finn then solemnly crowned all his previous insults by saying: "If he hasn't made out this place, he's nowhere!"

"Are you insinuatin' . . . ?" Tom began, with a dangerous calm.

Politely, Finn said: "I'm insinuatin' nothin'! Yes or no, is he here?"

Tom's breathing was asking God to give him patience.

Finn continued, his fingers assisting in the explanation: "The genius who owns the fleas went to immense bother to catch them—mostly on sleepin' lascars in Singapore. These fleas are not like the Irish fleas. For one thing, they're a lot larger. And another thing—they're more intelligent!"

Tom took the air in gulps. He raised his voice. "Finn Dillon," he said, "will you go up the field, ease your buttons, drop your britches on your ankles, an' let a fair gale o' wind to your buttocks?"

Fortunately, Tom Goggin's statement struck a pocket of silence. The laughter shook the house.

"Oh!" said Finn Dillon coldly, pretending to be aggrieved. Turning, he addressed the crowded kitchen: "Ladies and gentlemen, strangers that you are, that's the kind of talk that passes for wit in Cloone." To Tom Goggin he said: "Hell, but you'll want me yet!"

We went out. The last thing I saw was the roses in the semi-light. Dolly the Rose was still transfigured by their beauty.

The fine rain had begun to fall. The flagstones were dropdappled in the dark. One could almost sense the grass thrusting up through the world.

II

It was eleven o'clock. Metal Belly, barefooted and dressed only in his trousers and shirt, was crouched over his fire. The lamp was lighting. The bellman was saying his prayers in a deep voice: when his mouth opened in praying the rosy inside of his lips and his well-preserved teeth contrasted pleasantly with his dark beard.

His prayers finished, he looked at his great silver watch. This he had inherited from his father. The watch had hands that were surprisingly slender.

Gruel was slowly bubbling in a black saucepan which was balanced on embers beside the fire. From behind the hob a cricket chirped peacefully. Outside in Cloone the cattle continued to pour in for the fair of the morrow. "Hurrrr-oo!" they lowed, the slender r's clearly audible through the wide-mouthed bugling sounds.

Rising, Metal Belly went to the dresser. Taking down a jug, he retraced his steps to the fire. Into the gruel he spilled some milk, then added a pinch of sugar and a pinch of salt. On the head of the table the bellman then placed a deep blue willow-patterned plate. He was stooping to take up the saucepan when he heard a sound of low knocking on the front door.

Metal Belly glanced sharply around. A spar of timber was wedged against the door so as to buttress it against the buffetings of the hill-cattle.

For a while the bellman stood motionless. Then he replaced the saucepan on the now dark-and-grey embers. Padding to mid-kitchen, he growled: "Who's out?"

He heard a moan and a gasp. "The blessin' o' God on you, master. Let me in out o' the night!"

A young woman's voice! And Metal Belly a moral man!

"Who's out, I say?"

"A travellin' woman."

"What do you want from me?"

"Nothin' much, master." Again the woman moaned. "A gripin' pain I do get full in the pit of my belly, in pardon to you. Let me in, master, an' may the Lord relieve you in your hardest hoult."

There followed a sound as if her shoulder had been flung heavily against the door. Powerfully, Metal Belly could sense the woman outside. For a span he listened carefully.

"Go 'way from my door, woman!" he growled at last.

Metal Belly walked to his small front window, carefully drew aside the blind, and peeped out into the street of Cloone. Of the woman he could see nothing. His sharp ears caught the insignificant swish of fine rain.

He replaced the corner of the red holland blind and padded back to mid-kitchen. The gruel was still at its dull bubbling.

Again the woman's voice came, this time in full whining: "Weaker I'm gettin', master. Let me in an' may God send you sovereigns to jingle."

Metal Belly paused irresolutely.

As if sensing that she had gained a foothold on his compassion, the woman continued: "Perished an' famished I am, after travellin' through country where you'd be quenched before anyone 'd come to your aid. Let me in, I ask you in the name o' God!"

Metal Belly stood with his back to the little fire. Clearly he could hear the heavy boots of the passers-by noising in Cloone. From the upper murk of the wall, the dead patriots looked down upon him. Charles Stewart Parnell was there: he, too, had been a moral man until he had succumbed to such a voice. Metal Belly thrust his feet into his great boots.

" A heat of the fire, master—in the sight of God that's not much ! A record for hospitality ye have here in Cloone. The stones o' the road can read the good Irish in ye. ' Forever Cloone ! ' as ye say. Quick, master. ' Forever Cloone '. . . ."

The password and the pride. . . .

Metal Belly took the spar from the door and drew the bolt.

He saw a young tinker-woman dressed in the bright western shawl. Under the shawl she carried a basket. Slowly she came into the light. The shawl was as bright as the bog in the height of summer ; under her tartan skirt she had the carriage of a Dresden figurine, had it been brought to life. She stood in mid-kitchen, her body swinging easily in the lamplight. A wing of her hair was athwart her temple. Although her hair was not fully fair by nature, wind and sun had bleached its more generous strands to the colour of full cream.

" The blessin' o' God on you, master," she sighed. The tone of her voice was balanced between victory and mendicancy. Walking to the fire, she extended her hands, palm outwards, to the heat. Turning, she smiled at the bellman. Her every action was invested with a strange confidence. Slowly she placed her basket on the end of the table and returned to the hearth.

Brown eyes, dark skin, good free poise ; the whites of her eyes were alight in her brown face. Her shawl hung loosely from her shoulders. Surprisingly, she was wearing high-heeled shoes of lizard skin, more than likely the relics of cast-off finery. She had bangles and ear-rings of brass. A large open leathern purse depended from her belt : this purse was studded with brass geegaws. Her clothes tinkled whenever she moved.

" Ah ! " she said, smiling. Then she looked around.

Metal Belly had bolted the door. He began to pace up and down from front door to back door at the kitchen's end.

" Ah ! " the woman said again. " Better I feel already with the dint of the heat."

Her roving eyes smiled as they lighted on the bell on the edge of the dresser.

"Can I sit down, master?"

She had already seated herself on the sugawn chair on the hearth. The shawl, as it slipped from her shoulders, had the wonderful colours of western Ireland, where the land is poor and where Nature compensates for poverty with the bright useless gauds of lichen and heather.

She failed to keep her eyes still. "Fine to have a home, master," she said quietly. Then: "You're the bellman?"

Grudgingly: "I'm the bellman."

Turning on the chair, she faced him frankly. Hitherto, Metal Belly had been looking only at her profile. Now he could view her fully under the lamplight. Her blouse was loose and made of shiny stuff. Her tartan skirt was full and flowing. From where her knee was hidden under her dress to the point of her hip, that was what instantly troubled him. He dared not look at it again.

"The heart is the life," she breathed, abandoning her whine. "And the voice comes straight from the heart. You have a fine deep voice, master."

Metal Belly glanced at the basket on the table. His glance showed him tie-pins and camphor balls, brooches that were names written in brass wire, and small badges of the Sacred Heart cut from red baize with serrated edges. As if angry with himself for the betrayal of his eyes he broke in harshly: "Your pain—is it gone?"

Limply: "Relief I get when I turn my body to the fire."

Her eyes lighting at the sight of the saucepan of bubbling gruel, she looked smilingly at Metal Belly. For answer he strode to the dresser, then set the jug of milk, a bowl of sugar and a clean spoon on the table. He made a sound that she interpreted as an invitation to eat. He took his seat on a chair near the room door where one of his ears could carefully sift the noises of the street.

" Blessin' o' God on you, master," she said again.

She poured the gruel on to the plate. Eating, she bore a resemblance to a cat. From where he was seated in the murk, Metal Belly reckoned he had the advantage of her : she was in full light while he was in shadow. The woman knew this and, after her fashion, she, too, reckoned she held the advantage of position. Once, with the spoon half-way to her mouth, she said wheedlingly : " Have you ne'er a one belongin' to you, master ? "

" No ! "

Her tongue came out to tip the gruel. " Lick alike we are so, bellman," she said.

After a while she sighed, then said with small emphasis : " Although the world is all colours, I'd give all I ever owned or saw to have a home ! "

Metal Belly growled : " 'Tis a wonder you wouldn't get a man for yourself ? " The instant he had spoken he realised that he had made the error of enmeshing himself in her affairs.

The tinker-woman took her time about replying : " Once, I had a man," she said between tantalising spoonfuls, " a well-behaved class of a fella that you'd quickly tire of." She laughed freely. " I, that had a tinker for a father and a true-born gipsy for a mother. I that had inherited the wildness of two worlds. . . . " Again she laughed, as freely as before. She then looked steadily at Metal Belly as she said : " A woman doesn't respect a man who's not able to give her a weltin' if she deserves it." Significantly, she added : " A powerful pair of arms you have on you, master ! "

" Your man—is he dead or alive ? "

With her left hand, the woman lifted the falling wing of hair from off her forehead. " Dead he is, an' well dead," she said quietly. " A bare year we were wedded an' then he fell off the board of a spring-cart at the fair of Cahirmee when he was weighty with drink. A simple hurt, as road-hurts go, and yet it swept him. One child I bore him—the spit of its father

—it was too quiet to live. Married I was at nineteen an' widowed at twenty. That's the road, master." She took a generous spoonful of gruel : raising it to her lips she continued to read the bellman's face.

Both waited : they were listening to the sound of hooves passing by outside. The noise passed : Metal Belly's voice was hollow as he said : " They tell me there's little shortage of men on the road."

The woman smiled, then said placidly : " I could have my pick an' choice of many men, but the gipsy in me has made me particular. Blood has been spilled on the head of my half-invitations to the young fellows. Something inside in me cries out for them to fight. Across the Shannon I'm well-known, master. The telly-wires buzz from fair to fair as one Sergeant warns his comrade : 'Here comes Trouble-o'-the-World ! Watch out ! The young tinker-men will spill blood before the night is done, all on account of Trouble-o'-the-World ! ' "

" What way were you christened ? "

" In Kilkerrin in the County Galway the *coonig tawried*—the priest said—that I was Sibby Mawn. In the West I go by no name except the one I told you."

" Trouble-o'-the-World ? "

" Aye, Trouble-o'-the-World ! "

" Were you never in this direction before ? "

" Never, master. A mad fit took us westerns to see the south where the fools of farmers knew nothin' of the gladar-box for by-the-way makin' bright new coins. So we've all come ! The Wards an' the MacDonaghs an' the Mawns. What tinkers have ye here in the south, master ? "

" Cartys an' Coffeys an' Briens, mostly."

" Do they speak the old Irish ? "

" Aye, they have a gibberish o' their own."

" The five hidden languages of Ireland I have, master. Isn't that somethin' to boast about ? The Sheldru, the Romany, the two gammons—the broad an' the narrow—an' also a fair smatterin' of the lost language of the wanderin' masons which they call Bearlager na Saor." She finished her gruel.

Metal Belly turned his face away from her : " If 'tis sufficiently heated to the fire you are . . . " he began. Turning to look at her face, he broke off.

The woman said, evenly : " 'Tis you'd look the grand man on the steps of a caravan. Did the road never tempt you, master ? "

Metal Belly abruptly stood up, then took the hasp off his bedroom door. " The sooner you're away, the better," he said harshly. " I want to get a blink of sleep." He glanced significantly at the face of his father's watch.

The woman stood up.

Quietly but surely, the tinker-woman commented : " Some men die, never knowin' their limits. Some that could not be bound with a hempen rope, could be led with a thread of silk."

In silence the man and the woman listened to the snipping of the cricket.

Metal Belly said slowly, as if grudging every word : " You're an uncommon woman ! " Turning his back on her, he looked at the rafters. His voice hardened when he said, with sternness : " You can be goin' your road ! You won't ketch me with your talk. I'm a moral man ! "

Off at a tangent, she said : " I'm a terrible woman for colours. Look at my petticoat ! " She showed a slash of red petticoat. " Look at my shawl ! " She indicated the grandeur of her shawl. " Look at my brasses ! " Her brasses twinkled and flashed in the lamplight.

Metal Belly said nothing, nor did he turn.

Trouble-o'-the-World came a step closer to the bellman. Her voice was now level and urgent : " In the old days we used to jump the budget, but now it's a travellers' priest in Athenry." Suddenly her voice rang sharp and true as she delivered the core of her message : " Master, did you never think o' marryin' an' of siring a child ? "

Metal Belly made no reply : from the top of the dresser he took down a blue-enamelled candle-sconce. He lighted the small stump of candle in it. " If you've finished your talkin'," he said with reined fierceness, " I'd be thankful to you if you went your road."

As she broke into loud hysterical laughter, Metal Belly's face hardened with indignation and anger. " Easy, woman, with your cacklin'," he said. " Do you want to advertise to all Cloone the fact that you're here ? "

She made her face grave. " Sorry I am, master ! " Only her eyes were contrite : her body indicated little contrition.

Metal Belly had thrown open his bedroom door. He then turned and set the candle-sconce on the ledge of the dresser. He snatched up the woman's basket and thrust it at her. Her eyelids were down as she smiled at him. The smell of camphor came up between them. As he went to open the front door, Trouble-o'-the-World reverted to her whine. " Without hurt or harm to you, master, you could go into your room an' I'd put the hasp on the door so you couldn't come out. I'd spend the night by your fire an' 'tisn't anythin' out of your purse I'd take."

" That'll do, woman ! " the bellman said fiercely. " My name is a by-word for morality in Cloone ! "

Trouble-o'-the-World flared up. " An' so am I a moral woman ! " she said. " I'm full in dread of hell an' the clock that ticks for ever." She laughed freely. Looking around her, she said, sadly : " Sweet God, what I wouldn't give for two at a table an' the door closed ! "

She still made no move to go.

Standing before her, Metal Belly was grim-lipped. The woman opened her shawl unnecessarily wide. She was setting it to climb on her road-bleached hair when she thought better of it and allowed it to slip to her shoulders. The high shoe-heels were kind to her : they now stilted her up and played fair with her body's natural swing and poise. Her tongue roamed provocatively in her mouth. As on an idle notion, she moved away from him towards the dresser.

She rattled the bell with her fingernail so that it noised faintly. She then ran a whimsical finger round the brass rings on the handle of it. Watching her, Metal Belly's eyes became strangely filmed. Suddenly the woman's hand resolved itself into a clutch which closed on the polished bell-handle. The bellman was not warned in time. The woman then fully gripped the bell. As she took it down from the shelf, the clapper idled once. The sound seemed magnified by reason of the tension that lay between them.

The bellman was roused from his drowsiness. " Leave that out of your hand ! " he said sternly.

The bell was touched by the lamplight. Also the blue-enamelled candlestick on the dresser began suddenly to possess a power of colour out of all proportion to its importance.

Slow, cool and arch, half-jokingly yet deadly in earnest, the woman said : " I have you in my power, Mister Bellman ! Suppose I gave your bell three great bangs, wouldn't all your Cloone hear the sound of it ? Aye, an' you a moral man ! " She laughed like a child. Then, as a token of her earnestness, the clapper idled again. As on a hand's turn her face turned wholly vindictive.

" By the Livin' God ! " Metal Belly said, in dismay rather than in anger.

He turned away from her, his limp body indicating failure. Of a sudden he spun and sprang at her. He clutched for the bell : between them it fell to the floor where their struggling feet banged it over and over. The suddenness and ferocity of his attack surprised her. For a while she fought him, then, unaccountably, she seemed willing to accept her punishment. Catching her by the wrist, Metal Belly swung her fully round. His black beard jutted into her hair. Now they were face to face. His face was convulsed with anger and his breathing was laboured. He stripped his teeth at her.

" Treacherous bitch ! " he said.

Trouble-o'-the-World spoke upwards into his convulsive face, the tone of her voice implying hush-hush: "On the street," she said softly, "the gaudy thunderous voice you have! A check shirt an' a red scarf would 'vantage you, Bellman. Rings as big as sovereigns in your ears! I to put a piece on my head an' give out the gibberish of the stars. Lashin's o' money we'd make, us two—more in one week than you'd make in a lifetime clappin' your ould bell the while you're buried alive here in Cloone!"

"Slut!"

The bellman started as a boot clattered on the cobbles outside. There came a loud knocking at the door. The woman smiled and lidded her eyes. Metal Belly was still holding her by the wrist. He glanced at the blind of the front window: it was secure.

Raising her mouth almost to his mouth, Trouble-o'-the-World taunted in a low voice: "I to scream an' where's your reputation?"

The knocking became louder. "Hey, bellman!" a voice outside said.

To the woman, Metal Belly said, with low-pitched but terrifying urgency: "Talk, an' I'll swing for you!"

The man outside said, harshly: "Let me in, bellman. A message I have for you."

"Give your message!"

"To hell with you! Let me in from the dirty dripping sap of your thatch! That an' the penetratin' rain that's fallin'."

Metal Belly looked down at the woman. Her shawl had fallen. It made a coloured heap on the dun floor. Steadfastly he looked at her as he boldly told the first lie. "I'm in my pelt!" he shouted, at the same time thrusting the woman away.

Trouble-o'-the-World backed to the dresser and folded her arms across her breasts. Her face was filled with prodigious good humour. Her mocking provocative eyes were roving up and down the bellman's body.

The man in the street laughed raucously : " God 'lmighty, man, what if you are ? I'm of the male species myself. Let me in, blast you into the pit of hell ! "

Metal Belly raged left and right like a caged beast. " Who're you blastin' ? " he roared. The venom he should have turned on the woman was now being vented on the intruder.

The voice outside diminished to puzzlement. " I'm only a messenger, man ! " it said.

" Give your message ! "

" Well . . . Quinn, the auctioneer, says that at ten o'clock tomorrow mornin' you're to announce the followin' through the fair of Cloone an' the streets adjoinin' ; ' To be auctioned at Folan's yard at the hour of noon, a prime lot of pedigree in-calf heifers, the property of Thomas Arthur Dawson of Bohershee House.' D'ye hear ? ' An' the streets adjoinin' ! ' Those are his very words. Have you the proclamation ? "

" I have ! "

" Are you sure ? "

" Go to hell ! "

" Well. . . . " The puzzled voice grew fainter as the man's boots backed away. When he was some yards from the door, the messenger recovered his courage. " By God ! you lousy chunk of a bearded crier . . . " he began.

Metal Belly clawed wildly for the bolt and threw the door fully open. The noise of the messenger's boots clattered up Cloone.

Breathing heavily, Metal Belly returned. He bolted the front door. Angrily he picked up the bell and replaced it on the dresser. There was an instant of fine drama as he stood still for a moment and looked deeply into the woman's face. Then, taking a mug, he dipped it into a gallon of spring water which stood on the ledge of the dresser. As he drank, his sideface was turned towards Trouble-o'-the-World. She was looking at him, marking how he drank with powerful masculine gulps. Afterwards, he took the candlestick and walked to the room door. Still he said nothing.

As he entered the bedroom the woman marked the riot of colour that was the patchwork quilt, the picture of the madonna over the iron bedstead and the daffodil-distempered walls. The candlestick was like a strange blue flower floating on a place of quiet waters. Metal Belly closed the room door.

The woman seemed in no way inclined to place the hasp on the bedroom door. Alone in the kitchen she examined everything thoroughly: first she went quickly to the dresser and touched each article of delph in turn with her finger-tips. A thin smile played on her lips as she scraped the bell with her nails. Doing this she bore a marked resemblance to a cat.

Metal Belly was still creaking around the room. The tinker-woman heard him stumble to his knees at the bedside. Once he forgot himself and prayed aloud into the patchwork quilt. The woman remained in an attitude of keen listening as she waited for another powerful snatch of prayer to reach her. In this she was disappointed.

Her inventory of the kitchen at an end, she sat beside the fire. After a time she heard the candle gutter as Metal Belly blew it out. Then she heard the bed creak beneath his weight. She remained seated before the fire, with her shawl across her shoulders. After a time she looked up at the lamp. She rose and blicked it out. The smell of smoky wick took the kitchen. Boiled the burner should be, she thought—that much at least she knew of the affairs of houses. Removing her shoes, she padded around in the darkness for a few moments. There was a small suggestion of dancing in the way she moved. Then, with a deep sigh, she again seated herself on the chair before the fire. She heaped turf behind the embers.

Outside the fine rain was still falling.

Metal Belly was not asleep. His hands were clasped tightly behind his head. The hair of his beard had mated with the hair of his chest. The man might have been cut from fumed wood. "Lead us not into temptation," he repeated quietly under his breath. His voice was level and not imploratory. Chinks were open in the lightly-sheeted door; thus he could follow every movement of the woman in the kitchen. Even when the lamp was quenched he could follow her as she padded between the door and the firelight. For hours he remained thus, his lips sometimes moving in prayer. Once he said, half aloud: " Mary of the Immaculate Conception, pray for us ! "

In the morning when he awoke, the bugling of cows was filling Cloone. Instinctively he stretched out his hand to the bedside chair to grasp his watch. His groping fingers grew more agitated. Suddenly he sat up. He looked down at the bedroom floor to see if the watch had fallen during the night. Leaping out of bed he roughly searched the bedclothes and the pockets of his coat. The pockets of his breeches he turned inside out. The dawn of full realisation made him drop the trousers to the floor. He snatched open the room door. The kitchen was empty. Deflated, the bellman sat on his bed, his strong black shanks protruding from under his nightshirt.

Slowly but powerfully his hands resolved themselves into fists.

A small black Kerry cow had thrust her nuzzle against the window of his bedroom. Her eyes were filled with a mild savagery. Her delicate horns were perfectly symmetrical. Dully, Metal Belly marked a single thread of milk falling from her mouth. This web caught the sunlight. All of a sudden the cow lowed fiercely.

## III

Hooves, paws and shoes had brought the wet cow-dung underfoot to what appeared to be an olive pattern in stucco. The wild statement of the fair was so indigenous that scarcely anyone stayed to analyse it. For foundation the tumult had the lowing of cattle and the bony rattle of their hooves as they were urged forward on the limestone road. The sound of ash sticks beating on the bones of the rumps of the animals was garnished with the feverish barking of sheepdogs, the loud " Hey-hey ! " of the shouting drovers, the granular defiance of the buyers and the wheedling and mock-blustering of the ubiquitous tanglers who were forever rushing forward to forestall the thrusts of errant cattle. As bonavs were being transferred from one rail to another, their screeches of protest made a continuous ear-splitting sound ; small wonder this, since the correct manner of lifting a suckling pig was to catch it firmly by the ear and tail.

I stood where a buyer and seller moved slowly towards the clenching of the bargain.

Standing there listening to fair-day ritual, with the cart between me and the sun, I saw the morning sunlight strike directly to a bonav's ear. It made a redness like that of a single seed of fire seen in a dark kitchen on a night when the lamp is not yet lighting. I stood watching the point of scarlet shine before it should vanish utterly. The bonav with the amazing ear had its wet noseholes flat against the break between the laths of the cart-rail. Prudently I held my position so as to keep tally on the wonderful light ; once I made a movement to the left and lost it : once I made a movement to the right and again lost it. I stood directly in the middle and, look you ! there was my ruby flaming in the morning.

" Hello, Ches ! "

Madcap O'Neill was passing by : she had a white enamelled gallon on her arm.

" Where are you off to ? " I asked.

" Strippin' a cow for my father, I am. He's standing her beside the bridge."

" Wait ! " I said. For the last time I looked at the ruby. As if understanding what it was I wanted, the little pig sturdily held its place.

We walked on together.

" What were you watchin' at the rail ? " Madcap enquired.

" Nothin' ! " I said.

" You were watchin' the sun strike through a bonav's ear till it blazed like a red coal."

" That's right," I said.

Prudently we guarded ourselves against the horns of the cattle. At last we came to where her father was standing the cow in mid-Cloone : the cow had not been milked since the previous night : this was to give her bag a good appearance for the fair. Now that the beast was sold, there was no further point in leaving her unmilked. It was with a certain sense of gladness that Madcap set about her task. The father led the cow against the limestone wall of the bridge. At first the milk-jets struck harshly against the bottom of the vessel but as the milk rose gradually the music in the vessel changed in tone. Dark Jack paid little attention to either of us for he was in deep conversation with a farmer. I put my back against the wall and watched Madcap's cheek where it lay firm against the flank of the cow. It was with a certain element of pleasure that I noted, too, the skilful movements of her hands.

Whistling idly, the umbrella-man strode through the fair. His navel was no longer in evidence. Next came the man with the armful of paper roses : his coming made Cloone seem a coloured kingdom. The strong man came to the half-door of the Rookery and growled out into the morning : the time was not yet ripe for him to do his act : before evening his long whip would startle the jaded fair with sounds like pistol shots.

Behind us, in the boreen, out of the direct traffic of the fair, the canvas-covered stalls were set. White sheets were spread beneath the eatables which consisted for the most part of plum-duff, Peggy's leg and heaps of bull's-eyes. There, also, was displayed the local Sugar Rock as well as edible seagrass or dilisk and hillocks of boiled periwinkles. Set apart in wicker baskets were the orange-coloured cockles that would be measured in a fluted glass and sold to farmers avid for the unusual fare of the seashore.

I saw men sneak into the empty cabin which was the shebeen for the day.

When the cast-clothes man held up a man's under-pants, the gathered countrywomen began to laugh. The cast-clothes man was Stentor himself—his voice scooped caverns in the air.

" Here ! Pull it an' draw it an' drag it, ma'am ! It's double-breasted an' it's iron-chested. It'll rest over your man's belly and stick to his back with the worthy courage of a poor man's plaster. Here it is, long in the leg, wide in the waist and capacious in the seat where your poor devil of a husband will need it. Come now, let ye bid me, before the curse o' the crows lights on the top o' ye for the secondhand reception ye're givin' a strollin' but generous draper. Come now while the iron is red an' the smith is sweatin'. Come now, I say, come now. . . . "

I saw the paper roses move away through the fair. For a little span they remained perched in beauty on the backs of the cattle. Again, after a splendid movement, they dallied beside a cart-rail that seemed to have lost all the glory of its new orange-red paint on the arrival of the wonderful blooms.

Returning with the half-full gallon of milk swinging between us, Madcap and I passed a group of tanglers kicking up a great rumpus. In the midst of them I saw Badger Breen : so vehement was he in his talk that the corners of his mouth were carrying white dry spittle. We passed Galileo, as, with his pig tied by the hind leg, he urged it to the fair. We passed Jody Shea who was swopping a dog with a tinker. We passed Malachi Flanagan, a painter from Cloone, who was dressed up in his Sunday grandeur with his signet-ring resplendent on his finger.

Outside Caherdown's trestle a tall country fellow saluted me out of the corner of his mouth. " Hollo, Macnamara ! " he said. There were four slow rural l's in his hollo. So deep was his voice that it seemed to carry with it a suggestion of its own echo.

For a moment or two I failed to recognise the man who had saluted me: then I saw that he was the big country fellow whom we had rescued from the hayshed on the night of the American wake in Littero.

He looked at me, then solemnly spat out. He looked at Madcap. With shattering directness, he asked us: "Are ye two company-keepin'?"

I left the answering to Madcap.

"Maybe we are, and maybe we aren't!" was the best she could do under the circumstances.

For a while he said nothing. He was holding the end of a rope which was tied in the form of a headstall to a braddy—or utterly mischievous—cow. The cow had a dallaphookeen or blindfold fixed across her eyes.

The country fellow spat again. Slowly he said: "Ye'd make a good couple. Oppusits ye are." He did not smile. "Will you strip my cow, young woman?" he asked Madcap. "Her dug is so almighty heavy that it's trappin' her."

"I will, indeed," Madcap said and at once took milking-seat on the end of Caherdown's trestle. Glancing over the half-door I could see inside the cottage the bright fresh-shaved face of Caherdown. He was glaring at me as if he were enraged at finding me aiding and abetting rustics in their infernal trafficking in milch-cows.

The countryman and I spent a while glumly eyeing the jets of milk as they spurted into the vessel. Suddenly he said to me: "That sister o' yours—have she e'er a fellow?"

On the query, Madcap slowed up in the milking.

"I thought you were goin' strong there!" I said.

"Leave off your bla'guardin'," he replied angrily. "I got plenty o' that before!" As a token of his earnestness he struck his ash crop heavily against his boot. Then he said: "Will you carry her a message for me?"

I looked at Madcap. "The milkmaid is a great messenger," I said.

As he turned to Madcap the sound of the milking diminished

in strength until it had become a small purr vouching for the world alive.

Placing word after deliberate word, the country fellow said :

" I was thinkin' it over an' I came to the conclusion that the Macnamara girl would suit me. I asked my mother about it, too, an' she said that the Macnamaras were respectable stock."

" Faith, we won't give her to you without a set of papers ! " I said.

" What papers ? " he asked stolidly, turning his attention full on me.

" Her breedin' right an' left," I said, " for four generations back. The whips of brains her cousins had will be mentioned. We won't leave her go to you bare an' lone, my decent countryman. She'll have her lines like a pedigree dog."

This put him cogitating for a span. He looked at Madcap's face : although she had her face fully averted to the flank of the cow, he could see that she was smiling.

He rounded on me. " 'Tis plain to be seen," he said, " that there's nothin' to be got out of you but roguery an' knavery. Every second word out of your mouth signifies somethin' different to what my intelligence tells me it is. Although we're livin' within eight Irish mile o' ground of one another, we're speakin' two different languages. I've a mind, Ches Macnamara, to up with my stick an' bring it down across the crown of your head an' teach you a lesson in civility."

The game had gone far enough. Madcap said to him : " Give me your message ! "

" I'm in two minds," he told her sturdily, " whether I will or not."

" I'm sorry ! " I said. " Forget what I was sayin'." I turned away. When again he was facing Madcap, I made it my business to look covertly but keenly at his face.

He kept shifting from one boot to another. From time to time he glanced down at the jets of milk which Madcap had now restored to a normality of rhythm. He seemed to be stolidly analysing Madcap's profile. I held my eyes fastened on him. A rawbones, he was, if ever there was one. His right boot was scuffing in the dung. Madcap, also, was watching the boot out of an eye-corner. Not now in the manner we had watched it on the morning of the American wake as we ragged him on the roadway. When again he began to speak, the tempo of Madcap's milking instinctively slowed down. Then it stopped altogether. It was as if the heart of the world had ceased to beat.

Slow, square and sincere—every word was a solid block: "I'll put no two words in it," he said, "my girl of the Neills. Listen well to what I say. A good deal will depend on the manner in which you carry my message, whether you put the colour o' fun on it or the breath of earnest. For me a good deal will depend on what ye two women say to one another when my message is delivered, for you'll then be a lookin'-glass for Mary Macnamara. So I'm requesting you, decent girl, to do nothin' in empty chaffin', which is a born habit of yeers here in Cloone." Here he was moved by emotion. "I ask you to do this because my life is as valuable to me as any of yeer lives is to ye." Again he paused. "It's costin' me a great deal to drop for ye the screen o' my pride. So, please to remember, girl bawn, that while you're talkin' to her that it's a pair of lives you're jugglin' in the palms of your hands an' not the two blind tits of a cow."

Madcap's eyes had burned down to two bright embers. Her head seemed fixed irrevocably against the cow's side. Her hands were idle on the teats. For us three the thunder of the fair had changed to the silence of stone.

"What'll I be tellin' her?" Madcap asked. The unusual level nature of her voice made it the voice of a stranger.

We waited until the countryman had finished beating the grey never-polished toecap of his boot with the knob of his ash-crop. His face was haggard with the effort of honesty. He turned away from us and looked down over cattle-filled Cloone. My eyes followed his. I saw what he saw—the paper roses moving through the dark press of men and beasts.

" Tell her . . . that I was askin' for her. Tell her that she needn't bother overmuch about money. Tell her that although our holdin' is tidy, it's without encumbrance . . . that there's only my mother in the corner an' that she's easy to live with. Tell her that, before the face o' Christ, I'll treat her fair."

The man looked down at his toecap. He then added in such a low voice as we could scarcely hear : " Tell her she do be troublin' me."

How long we three stayed there wordless I do not know. Below us, from beast to beast, the roses were bearing their brilliance, uttering their single shout of triumph over dung and dirt. Madcap was looking up at the man with surpassing wistfulness. Suddenly I knew that this man and none other would sire my sister's children. Nothing could stand against this honesty, least of all a woman's mind to whom finesse was the very breath of life but to whom, also, the novelty of a straightforward attack was beauty—breath-catching and rare.

All the while below us, the glorious roses moved through the fair : red roses and white roses and roses of old gold. Absurd roses of purple and blue ! I turned again and looked at the man. He was still invested with solemnity and dignity. What sort of children would be begotten between the body of this gaunt rawbones and that of my plump sister ? I vetted him. Six feet two inches : a jaw like a ridge of hills. My sister was a dumpling, or the makings of a dumpling. I could see her face gathered for a laugh, grow ugly, then grow engaging and finally explode in crinkling nuttiness. And in the middle of my conjectures, dear God, there were the roses !

I tried to fuse the countryman's face and the face of my sister and bring the resultant face to the composite face of a cherub. A cherub of rose, swinging in a cradle of wicker.

Always the roses ! It was a difficult task I had set myself for I was modelling in wax that was physical and metaphysical.

The milk had resumed its thoughtful purring as it lanced into the gallon. I realised that Caherdown's trestle was now biting deeply into my back. I noted the beast's access of peacefulness. I was also aware that Madcap's spirit had moved a precious inch closer to mine. Because of this small treasure of living we two had found and had shared together ! And all the while, as we three were bound, below us in the fair, weaving in and out through the drabness, through the shouting and the clamour, the roses continued to burn with their extraordinary flames.

There was a period to beauty. Abruptly the bond snapped. Of the countryman, Madcap asked shortly : " What name is on you ? "

" Peter Stack."

Briskly : " I'll deliver your message, Peter Stack."

" I'm thankful to you, my ripe black girl." If there had ever been a hint of beauty in his face, it had now vanished.

Madcap was steadily milking. For a while there was placidity. But even placidity cannot last for ever.

The blindfolded cow gave an unpredictable lurch, then tossed her head up and away, almost upsetting the gallon of milk. It was as if all the pent-up feelings of rage against the irk of her blindfold had suddenly overcome her. She blundered on to the flagged pavement, knocked down the trestle, leaped clumsily over it, then broke through the half-door and went careering headlong into Caherdown's kitchen.

Peter Stack shouted wildly and lumbered after his beast.

I confess that I swore with joy.

What a scene was then enacted in Caherdown's kitchen ! From his Lordship came an outraged roar that defied all mimicry. There followed the challenging clatter of breaking ware ; the side of a cup (with an ear adhering to it) bounced expertly over the threshold and, displaying a resilience that was astonishing in delph, leaped gaily out on to the cobbles. There it stayed swinging like a see-saw, seeming to say as it swung: "Here I am! Here I am!"

Peter Stack had followed his cow into the kitchen. His entrance had the effect of nullifying Caherdown's efforts to eject the beast. Yells emerged to awe us. The plop of falling cowdung was overborne by an anguished roar from Caherdown. A low blast of protest came from the throat of the bewildered animal. Then followed the noise of metalware crashing. This in its turn was followed by curses and profanity. There came an immense jangle and crack—I judged this to be the large earthenware jar which Caherdown's immediate neighbours were accustomed to borrow in order to carry porter to the bog. On the cobbles the semi-cup had ceased its swinging. We heard indignant screams, then came the noise of Peter Stack's stick flailing the cow's rump. Unexpectedly came the rip of cracking timber; peeping over the half-door I saw the white flesh of wood torn from the bedroom partition. There was a rattle of brass and immediately afterwards we heard an astonishing cannonading as the room door was torn off its hinges. When Caherdown's voice reached us, we adjudged it truly berserk. It was now obvious that his boot was trenchantly at work. Through the kicks I heard Peter Stack's menacing voice, saying: "Aisy! Aisy! Blast you for a man, be aisy in yourself!" Further profanity followed. We had one tantalising glimpse of the cow's nose thrust against the kitchen window. To Caherdown, Peter Stack shouted: "I'll give you the stick if you don't be aisy!" His Lordship seemed suddenly to be in a corner and was valiantly trumpeting for assistance.

We saw the cow's head at the doorway. Relieved of her blindfold, she stood there sounding the outside world. She seemed oblivious to Peter's crop belabouring her from behind and the diabolical objurgations of Lord Caherdown. She eyed the overthrown trestle as if mutely marvelling that she had managed to overleap it while she was handicapped by the blindfold. Madcap had retreated to a safe distance.

The cow gave a sudden jerk out into what, for her, constituted the comparative tranquillity of the fair. I was almost trapped against the thrown trestle. Into this trestle the cow now blundered: there she remained balanced for a moment with forelegs fully locked. Again the trestle swayed and, unexpectedly, resolved itself into a large triangular rat-trap. The snapping of this trap brought the cow's front legs to the ground, consequently the cow herself, consequently Peter Stack who had been pushing from behind. The collapse of another of the horizontal spars of the trestle had the further effect of projecting Peter directly on to the cow's hindquarters. Lord Caherdown followed after, his talons deep in the countryman's hair. Trestle, cow, Peter Stack and Lord Caherdown were then heaped in a screaming, struggling, objurgating, bellowing, protesting heap on the street of Cloone.

Crack! The trestle gave up its ghost. The cow was free!

Bravo, mammal! Away through the fair! Cut your swath! Let every man look out for himself! The good God alone knows what you have suffered. Away, cow! Inform all creation of the choking and belabouring you have endured till cow could endure it no longer. Bravo mammal! Away, cow, away, away, away. . . .

Peter Stack and Lord Caherdown were caught in the wholly wrecked trestle. Caherdown was aiming wild blows at the countryman. I then saw Peter place his right paw completely over Caherdown's face (the paw was generously poulticed with the cowdung of the cobbles) whilst his heavy left hand raised itself to initiate a grotesque caress on the neck of Caherdown's vest. His Lordship's head seemed to bubble scarlet under the impact of the powerful hand. Then came Peter Stack's voice saying, as if chiding a cross child, the while his soiled hands continued their infamous business of caressing, "Aisy, you mad ould bastard! Aisy, I say! . . ."

Rawbones looked up at me and asked plaintively, as if fearful for the sanity of his unborn children: "In the name o' God Almighty, are ye all daft in Cloone?"

IV

In a backwater of the fair Madcap and I noticed the brown-skinned man whom I had seen in the Rookery on the previous night. He was standing against a lime-white gable, smoking what, I learned afterwards, was a cheroot. The smoke from the cheroot gave a foreign-country smell to that quiet pocket of Cloone. Business did not seem to be brisk with him: undismayed he kept chanting away in a monotone, the while he quickly shifted his weight from one foot to the other as if finding the weather cold. Far above his head, behind the highest woolpacks, the sky was as blue as blue enamel.

When this man saw us approaching, his eyes began to sparkle mischievously. The cheroot was given free play until at last it dangled from his lower lip in a manner we considered little short of miraculous. Working fluently at the back of his white teeth, his tongue began to offer us welcomes, blandishments and even admonitions. The future ? Rsst !—there it lay, take it or leave it !

Madcap smiled ; seeing the smile I realised for the second time how grave she had become of late and how she had almost completely outgrown her nickname. The man with the birds and the fortunes and the dangling cheroot continued his chanting, to which he now added an alien smiling, and a quaint but confident bobbing in our direction. His demeanour implied that we two, man and woman that we were, would of a certainty be desirous of knowing what the future held. We had no option other than to approach him.

We suddenly spied the budgerigars—a cock and a hen—sidling out along the perch to where the daylight lived at the front of the cage. Such affection as there was between them ! They were like a young man and a young woman courting in a secret arbour. The colours of the birds were delightful—olive daffodil shot with olive green with dark undulations on the wings. Peering more closely, I made out a paler green-and-gold, and more than a hint of red and grey among the feathers. On the floor of the cage a bell tinkled. The cock pecked at the hen's beak while the hen stood utterly still.

Madcap and myself remained there, watching them narrowly. I saw Madcap's bosom lift. With her eyes pinned fast to the birds, she set down the vessel in a safe place. The hen now began to scold her master for his importunate pecking: such provocative scolding it was as inevitably turned to invitation! Madcap was wholly lost in the courting of the birds: her eyes were greyness itself and her laughing tongue-tip came out to dampen her lips. Watching her eager tongue emerge, I was reminded that my own mouth had of a sudden grown unaccountably dry. The love-birds were now neck on neck and between them lay blandishments, caresses and affectionate reproofs.

I have always been taken by small vividnesses set in large beige or dull areas: this weakness is akin to a madness in me. The single fleck of a red sail by the black islands of the Blaskets to the west, a whin-bush lighting its candelabrum beside flood-brown waters, a crab-apple branch raising its pink blossoms against a sky filled with broodings of thunder, a wine-coloured sycamore stem abruptly revealed where quicks have rendered the wood shadowy, a salmon-fly caught in a shaft of sunlight in an otherwise dark room, the litmus flame of a single rhododendron flower set like a shrine lamp above the hillock of its own dark green leaves—all these commonplace phenomena have the power to move me unconscionably.

So, when Madcap had given the foreign man threepence in return for her fortune and when he had inserted his wand into the cage and had brought out one of the budgerigars upon it, the brilliance of the bird's plumage in that nook of Cloone where the sunlight was not at full strength afforded me a sudden thrust of something bordering on ecstasy. The man's dark smiling face was lit by his perfect teeth; the cage was as dun as dun; the bird was set like a green flame before an altar

I could not name—it was little wonder then that I experienced a surge of credence for whatever mumbo-jumbo of fortune the brilliant bird would select.

First it was the sunlight strained through the bright blood of the bonav's ear ; then it was the roses. Now it was the bird ! For me this was good fortune—thrice in one day to have drawn so close to the bare bone of beauty.

I felt myself tear upwards. The spring earth roared in the lust of its own loveliness. For me the world seemed to be rocking in a gigantic hammock. In the highest sky the ponderous clouds kept changing their patterns. The cattle never left off their bugling. The men were still at their fair-day laughing. Madcap stood beside me, eager, vibrant, and wholly alive. In the white vessel the ivory milk lay placid and unruffled. The man's face grew darker. His teeth grew unsupportably whiter. The flame that was the bird was still splendidly brilliant. The flush of spring, of life, crept up along Madcap's neck and conquered her face. Under the black latch of her hair the woman's face was good to see : it was a memory I would hold for ever in my heart's centre.

" Whom shall I marry ? " That was the question the bird would now answer.

The man smiled. Seemingly at his bidding, we both laughed. Our laughter was not untouched with hysteria.

The bird hopped along the wand and then bowed ; it tugged resolutely at one of the envelopes racked in a box at the edge of the cage but failed to withdraw more than a corner of it. Abandoning its tugging, it looked about as if seeking approval before essaying for the second time. The man made sibilant reprimanding noises : he jerked the wand to restore the bird to a suitable sense of responsibility. Again the bird dipped and this time drew out a triangle of the same envelope. Yet the man did not seem to be satisfied. Madcap's teeth were now to be seen for her lips were lax with the eagerness of anticipation.

At the third attempt the love-bird fully withdrew the

envelope. This the fortune-teller smilingly handed to Madcap. Surely and quickly he replaced the bird in the cage, thrusting her into the darkness lest her flame should blind us both. Accepting her fortune, Madcap laughed nervously. I saw her fingers tremble as she tore open the envelope.

She glanced at the letter, then read it. Her slight laughter broke the tension. I put my head close to her shoulder and read with her :

" *My dear Elephant,*

*The sensation of Romance is at the heart of every good man and woman. It is a treasure you must appreciate and guard. Do not don love like a cloak nor cast it from you like a cloak. Somewhere roaming the world is the one who is created for you. Perhaps he knows you : perhaps not. It may be that at this moment he is standing by your side : it may be that he is in a distant land that is to you little more than a name in a book of colours. But believe the green bird ! Wherever your lover lives you may be certain that Providence will guide his burning lips to* your *burning lips. Possess yourself in patience ! Neither vexation nor anxiety can hasten the moment of moments. Be calm ! Your beloved approaches. Farewell.*"

" *PHOTO OF YOUR BELOVED ON THE OPPOSITE SIDE.*"

Madcap turned over the card. We saw an old bewhiskered face—the mouth spread in a hilarious grin and the eyes bulging with infinite good humour. Underneath was written the legend :

" *MY HUSBAND !* "

My dear Elephant !

We both laughed. The fortune-teller was smiling and nodding tolerantly. His cheroot had ascended to the horizontal. As the smoke from its tip came out into the morning air we both braced ourselves against the magic of its alien smell. Instinctively our eyes closed. When again we looked, the flame of the bird was scarcely to be seen in the recesses of the cage.

The stranger had resumed his chanting. It was clear that he had abandoned us. Gradually the noise of the fair reasserted itself. We heard the voice of the cast-clothes man reviling his dull-witted customers.

We passed Shemus Goff: it was too early for him to begin his ballad-singing. To Madcap he said with a shy smile: "A drink o' water, ma'am, an' may God bless the cow!" This was what the clever townie had said when he knocked at the farmhouse door.

Madcap raised the gallon to Shemus's lips. The milk was hot. After taking a tremendous draught, Shemus lowered the vessel, thanking Madcap as he did so. He began smacking his lips. Madcap and I looked into the pail: we saw that the level of the milk had fallen considerably lower than we had anticipated.

"God bless your swallow, Shemus Goff!" Madcap said, with feigned ruefulness.

Before the ballad-singer left us, he remarked: "Fairs are wonderful inventions. They hold the world an' all of attractions if looked at in the proper spirit." We watched him go towards the bawling cattle: he was walking slowly and thoughtfully.

V

Night had fallen over the fair.

Besides Finn and myself, there was Jody Shea, the lover of dogs; Dom Foy, Young Font, Badger Breen, who was a little the worse for drink, two of the Hibes, and nine or ten others. "Spread out through the fields flanking the boreen," Finn Dillon had ordered. "Get between the main encampment on the common and the single fire. And remember! Don't move in on the tinkers unless they come after us."

Each man tightened his grip on his ash-crop.

Finn and I went first. We alone knew the full story: the others thought that the tinker-woman had come to the bell-man's door hawking baubles and had stolen his watch which was lying on the table. Metal Belly walked at a little distance behind us, keeping well to one side of the boreen: he told Finn that he did not wish to face the woman again. "I wouldn't trust my hands on her," he said.

There was a slender moon. From the main encampment of the tinkers came the sound of drunken singing, rising and falling like an eastern chant: we turned our ears to the song but failed to recognise either the tune or the words of it. These western tinkers, we knew, were lithe, yellow-skinned, black-haired folk—of a totally different breed from the tall sandy tinkers of the south who, realising that they were outnumbered, had vanished at the first hint of invasion.

Finn and I, walking ahead, came closer to the lone fire on the edge of the boreen. Trouble-o'-the-World, her back turned towards us, was sitting on a stone beside it. On our approach, a red terrier growled from beneath a cart which was drawn close to the fence beyond the fire. The woman continued combing her hair. She did not turn. In the dim light we saw that the comb was yellow and that its teeth were strong. The woman's hair was a cream-and-dark cascade, curving and flowing and falling over her shoulders. She swayed as she combed. Below the hair was the shining blouse, then came the tartan skirt. The shawl of wonder was thrown in a careless heap on the ground beside her.

As we drew still closer, the rhythm of her movements altered: she began to tug her head violently and almost viciously away from the teeth of the comb. There were times when her struggling revealed the good pillar of her neck.

At last she turned her face fully towards us. Addressing us, her voice, by instinct, assumed the whine of the mendicant, which was completely at variance with the independence of her body.

" What hour of the night is it, boys ? " she asked, as if indeed measured time held any importance for her. Calling us boys indicated that she wished to place us outside the pale of her reckoning although we were almost as old in years as she was.

" Facin' for nine," Finn Dillon said shortly.

" Thanks, an' God bless ye ! " Her head bent low and her body became taut. Her face was curtained with her free hair. She pretended to poke the fire as she waited for us to pass on.

Finn stood his ground ; the woman looked steadfastly at his boots ; her gaze then stole slowly up along his body. Reaching his face her eyes wheedled and her body made ingratiating movements. Suddenly she braced herself and became wholly independent.

Finn drew a step closer : " We came from the bellman," he said. " It's about his watch."

Sharply : " What watch ? "

" When he awoke this morning, it wasn't on the chair beside his bed."

" Are ye shidogues ? " Again the reversion to the whine.

" We're not ! " Finn Dillon said shortly.

Sibby Mawn laughed her relief. As on a thought, she gathered her hair to a rope. " Often an' often, I stole a watch," she said, in a reminiscent tone of voice. " Once I stole a green chenille tablecloth although I had no table to set it on. Once I had a stolen ring on my finger when, through the window of a pub, I spied the Sergeant approachin'. So I asked a countryman to loan me his big box of ' Take-Me ' matches. An' then, boys, I hid the ring in the bottom of the box an' gave it back to the fool. An' when the Sergeant came in. . . ."

" About the bellman's watch ! " Finn broke in.

The woman widened her eyes. With a sharp movement of her head, she brought me into her survey.

" The bellman must be a man o' means," she said tolerantly. " He keeps upstandin' errand-boys."

" There are two ways out of every difficulty," Finn replied evenly ; " the easy way and the cross way."

" Wisha, gasoor," Trouble-o'-the-World said pleasantly, " youth is gay ! This mornin' above all mornin's there must have been whiskey in your mother's milk." She laughed. " Supposin', for the sake of argument, that I admitted havin' the bellman's timepiece, what in the name o' the shinin' God do ye two hope to do about it ? "

" You have the watch ? " Finn asked sharply.

" Tck ! Tck ! Tck ! Childer do be always askin' questions ! Sometimes a woman feels inclined to answer an' sometimes she doesn't." For the first time, she showed venom. " Go away, sweet sonnies, before I let a screech out o' my mouth an' drag a roarin' cataract from Connacht down on the top o' ye ! "

Finn looked into the fields. The Cloonies were there, spread out and alert. They were watching the fire. The woman understood.

" Four to one the Westerners are," she said quietly, " an' they're red drunk."

" Red drunk," Finn said, " is dead drunk ! "

" They have fancy weapons. Pincers to pull the strings out o' yeer hands, kettle-bars to draw the white maggots out o' yeer brains, maggie-sticks to cut the skulls off ye as if they were large foreign nuts. The lucky among ye will have marks to show to yeer grandchildren. I'm askin' ye to go away."

There was her hair downstreaming. There was her face clear-cut against the firelight. There was her throat. There was her bosom rich and poised beyond words. And there, of a sudden, was her laughter troubling the world !

We heard the clatter of a boot on a loose stone behind us in the boreen. As Trouble-o'-the-World turned quickly and glanced in the direction of the sound, Metal Belly stepped back into the darkness. Noting this, the woman threw back her head and again laughed provocatively. Such laughter could have only one outcome: we heard Metal Belly's boots come closer. At first he walked slowly and sorrowfully; then we heard him step briskly as if he were acting from an inner urgency. As the footsteps drew nearer, the woman began to twist her neck about as if she, too, were under compulsion. I saw the firelight dance through the loose strands of her hair.

When Metal Belly was standing beside us, Finn and I instinctively drew back. The man and the woman might as well have been completely alone. The remnants of mockery were still on Trouble-o'-the-World's mouth.

Metal Belly towered over her. "I heard you laughin'," he said harshly.

"I meant you to, Bellman," Trouble-o'-the-World said lightly. "A trick it is as old as Eve."

"I'll bandy no words with you," Metal Belly said. He was breathing heavily. "I want my father's watch that you stole from me, after I givin' you the be-in out o' the weather! The silver watch I took out of my father's dyin' hand. The watch that timed th' announcement o' th' meetin' of Charles Stewart Parnell. It that never went wrong in fifty years! I treasure it second only to my bell. Give it back to me peaceably an' go your road."

Trouble-o'-the-World laughed, but not so surely as before.

Metal Belly took a step closer to her. His dark hands descended. His right hand made a cream-and-black rope of the woman's hair. Trouble-o'-the-World did not move. The bellman twisted the rope on his finger, then shifted his arm suddenly so that the rope coiled around the back of his hand. Almost caressingly his roped hand then crept closer to the nape of her neck. Metal Belly was now in full command. We heard his lips say, in a low even voice, "My fingers to be on your windpipe, woman, suddenly sinkin' in!" We saw the hair on the crown of the woman's head tighten with the strain of the tension begotten of the man's hand. The holes of her nostrils grew larger. Then her eyes widened and her face lost the nuttiness of the sun and the wind. As yet her dilated eyes indicated that she accepted the punishment as a type of inverted caress, the sort of hurt a woman loves.

Then, with one sudden sickening jerk that indicated the full ferocity of the caressing hand, the bellman sped the woman's face upwards to meet his own. His black beard was now close to her draining face. Here, as we had expected, was maturity.

" My watch, woman." How hoarse his voice was ! The hair that had been a rope had now tightened to a cord on the back of the bellman's hand.

There was no loose skin on Sibby Mawn's face which she could gather to make a laugh. Still she did not resist. She remained utterly still : her body in its grotesque attitude hinted at—I dared not name it—transfiguration. Once, indeed, we saw the long fingers of her outstretched hands turn to talons and the pupils of her eyes narrow to embers. We waited for the animal-like tearing, screaming and clawing that we felt of necessity must follow. Then we realised our mistake. We saw the woman's eye call her rebel body to heel. We saw the talons die to ordinary finger-nails. We saw the eyes lose their wicked lights and turn to softness and fondness.

Watching, Finn and I took in the subtleties and elusive puffs of womanhood that, to us, were items of education. Trouble-o'-the-World's head slid up and down, as if she were idling to a coup. Her lips drooped and her breathing became easier. For the pair of them neither Finn Dillon nor I had any existence. Then the small fraction of an inch that she moved her body closer to his made Metal Belly release his grasp on her hair. I saw her draw her body down, moving it slowly to her stool of stone. As she moved away, she laughed again, inciting the bellman to further sweet violence. Metal Belly fell into the trap : we saw his hands form terrible Y's which moved towards the woman's neck.

" May Jesus stop ye," he prayed, " before ye choke her ! " Metal Belly was speaking to his own hands.

We watched the hands take the radiant throat. The throat gladly accepted the hands, as though expecting to find in them a strange delight. The man's fingers began to eat into the throat. The woman's face lost colour, yet it did not lose its gloss of exultation. Her eyes, even in the very extremity of her peril, sought his in fondness. The fingers bit deeper. Making a common exclamation at our discovery of horror, Finn and I moved forward. We dragged fiercely but unavailingly at the bellman's arms. When it seemed that the woman was lost, we heard the noise of an altercation before us on the boreen. Badger Breen's voice sang out loudly: "Across my dead body, you Western bloody coiner!"

What a blessing and an error it was to have stationed Badger Breen on the roadway in front of us!

The noise bade the hands stop: we watched them retreat out of the flesh. Trouble-o'-the-World took a great bite of air, then allowed her eyelids to fall and her face to wince. The gesture was not wholly one of physical pain. Ceremoniously slow, Metal Belly let the woman fall; her head, with good fortune, reached the circle of her shawl. She made the act of falling a step in the stairway of her seduction: we seemed to hear a throaty chuckle as she lay prone on the ground.

In front of us, on the little stony road, harsh argument had now broken out. Badger Breen began suddenly to roar as if he had been blinded. Between us and the encampment fires we saw forms grow inquiringly erect. We heard women's cries, infuriating and soberising the lagging, sagging men. Ten—fifteen of the Westerners then meshed out haphazardly from the fires: at first they ran blunderingly in different directions, but on hearing a renewed outcry they funnelled into the mouth of the little road. Already they had begun to curse themselves forward: from their ranks rose a ragged cry of battle. Once again we heard Badger scream as from the very core of hysteria, then his voice was lopped off in mid-cry as though he had been guzzled.

Still lying on the ground where she had fallen, Trouble-o'-the-World opened her eyes and smiled.

Metal Belly walked towards the fence and savagely tugged a strong paling-post free of its encumbrances of rusty barbed wire. The tinker who had downed Badger was standing cautiously in mid-road, peering at us as he screamed for his fellows. Dom Foy leaped over the fence and joined issue with him. Cloonies began to pour in from the fields. Uproad full battle was then joined. Metal Belly sprinted ahead to meet it: Finn and I followed. Badger tried to raise himself from the roadway as we ran past but, failing to do so, keeled heavily into the ditch. We disregarded Dom Foy as he grappled with the tinker and drove ahead to the main brunt. As we ran, Finn now and again leaped high into the sky: he was crying out to the remnants of our men to converge on the point where the boreen met the open common.

We came upon the main fight in the darkness. Metal Belly had already clubbed down one of a pair of tinkers who beset him. Entering the fight I belatedly recalled that the blood on Badger's face had not appeared red but black in the light moonlight. Metal Belly clubbed down a second tinker—so sickening a noise the post made that I thought the man's skull must have been crushed like a shell. The bellman adroitly swung the falling body sideways with the blade of his boot and pivoted it into the roadside drain. Then the Westerners were all around us. I saw a hook of metal from a fire-tripod upraised against the sky. I heard a cart-trace sing out and knock a full echo from the length of a Cloone man's back. Tinkers continued to pour in upon us until there must have been thirty of them in the neck of the narrow road. Their wives and wenches were screaming. Their small children were lamenting in such a tone of incitement that should egg on their fathers to kill us on the head of it. Three or four Cloone men came over the fences. Dark murderous fighting was now in full swing on the boreen.

It was the first time I had fought with the lust to kill on me.

On my entry into the *mêlée* I feared for my eyes, my nose, my front teeth, my navel and my genitals. But when a blow from an ash-crop slurred across my cheekbone, I readily sloughed my terror. A strange glory took possession of me. I heard my own laugh as if it were the laugh of a stranger. I found my body become wondrously compact. My fists were so tight that it seemed as if they could never again be unclamped. My boots—I knew now that I had donned them for assault and for protection. A new discovery I had made regarding the efficacy of my front teeth as weapons. I realised that the cap of my skull thrust sickeningly into a man's face would prove a serviceable battering-ram. Into the fight I went, side by side with Finn Dillon and the others, clubbing, kicking, biting, swearing, shouting, until at last I felt the salt of my own blood on my tongue and the silk lightness of foam on the corners of my mouth.

Here was a lust such as I had never known before!

The only noise the bellman made as he fought was a sudden hiss whenever one of his powerful blows drove home. He towered over us. Young Font and Jack the Hibe were fighting shoulder to shoulder. From time to time the tinkers raised their war-cry—" Mea-yo ! " As best we could, we answered with our throttled slogan of " Forever Cloone ! "

The half-grown sons of the tinkers were now tugging up loose road-metal from the surface of the boreen and were rushing forward to take a poacher's potshot at us. Whenever one of them threw a stone, he straightaway legged it hotfoot out of the fight. The tinkers' dogs poached on the calves of our legs. A tinker-woman rushed amid the combatants, dug her claws deep into a Cloone man's hair and, as she dragged him down, screamed : " Mea-yo ! Mea-yo ! " Three tinkers threw themselves upon the prone man but before they could beat him unconscious we booted forward until the man's body was well behind our files.

We were now fighting in the almost-forgotten style of faction. The tinkers' war-cries had the effect of bringing up reinforcements of men who had been dead drunk or deep asleep by the fires. Every form rushing forward from the encampment gave the tinkers fresh hope and us fresh despair. Across the gardens from Cloone an odd laggard stumbled to our aid. After a particularly heavy bout of fighting the tinkers withdrew: then they massed for the final onslaught. Already some of us had marks to show our grandchildren.

In the little lull, they began to cry at one another as if lashing themselves onward to fury. Awaiting their attack, we formed a broken line in mid-boreen. Metal Belly and Finn Dillon stood staunchly in the middle of our file. The moment preceding their attack was one of intense silence. Then the tinkers came at us, creeping, cringing, crying, yelling and cursing until it seemed to us that the crawling world was peopled by tinkers only. They rushed towards us with their weapons lying on the length of their backs.

This was the moment Badger Breen had chosen to crawl out of the gully where up to this he had lain semi-conscious. Now, kneeling on the roadside, he cupped his hands about his mouth and called out in a loud voice: "The shidogues! The shidogues!"

It was magnificent timing! The word terrified the tinkers. The law was their hereditary foe. Man, woman and child among them seemed stricken to stone. Badger's voice struck them like a reprimand from God.

"Now!" Finn Dillon shouted.

Our rush had communal force behind it. The tinkers were twigs and dead leaves in our path. True, it had been a trick —but they were three to one against us. Also we had ash-crops while they, for the most part, had iron. To right and to left we smashed and tossed them. Their children screamed like ferret-ridden rabbits and led the retreat to the common. Their women howled as their shawls turned to wings in the darkness. The voices of their menfolk took on the traditional note of piteous appeal. What stragglers among them had any heart left to fight, we clubbed down. Down they went, left, right, sprawled, thrown, wriggling and rolling on the rough boreen. Forty seconds after Badger's shout the battle was lost and won.

Smiling through our blood, we turned. We had thought that Badger was joking. Then we saw the moonlight glint on the polished vizors. Cries of warning came to us from the rear of the cottages in Cloone. The bellman and I lifted Dom Foy to his feet—he had been stunned in the fighting. Shaking his head, he set his boots under him. Hibe and Font raised Jody Shea's limp form between them. As best we could, dragging our wounded with us, we hurried through the fence on our left hand and spread out in the fields. Some of the men were groaning. Finn Dillon stood on the fence until the last of our men had left the boreen. There he waited until the vizors were almost upon him: he could escape easily as he knew the lie of the land as well as he knew his own kitchen.

We had gone some little distance when Finn Dillon caught up with us. Dom Foy, ruefully nursing his injured head, was then walking unaided. We split up into separate groups; the bellman, Dominick Foy, Finn Dillon and I stayed together. For a while we circled in the fields behind the graveyard. Then we went over the bounds' ditch into Dark Jack O'Neill's land. Hearing the hurly-burly of pursuit come close upon us, we entered an arched bramble-and-thorn hedge where in summer O'Neill's cows took refuge from the flies. The bellman sprawled on the ground across the ope of the wicker stall. Now and again a low involuntary moan came from Dom Foy's lips.

The noise ebbed into the fields. Over the bellman's shoulder we could see the slender moon set at a jaunty angle in the higher sky: it seemed as if the touch of a little finger would set it rocking against a blue infinity. Below the moon the late light from the town made the houses of Bank Place stand out as if they had been cut from black cardboard.

With an exclamation, the bellman rose to his feet. We followed him as he walked out into the open field. The noise of the hunt was faint and fine in pastures to the left hand. Metal Belly turned to us and uttered another half-strangled exclamation. Unpredictably he keeled over and fell.

We crouched over his fallen body. Finn Dillon lighted a match; when he had brought the hand-shielded light closer we saw that at the roots of his beard the bellman's face was black with blood. His forehead, too, was pale as paper and stone-cold into the bargain. We turned him over on his face and saw where a dark stream of blood had flowed from his poll downwards into the valley at the sinews of his neck. Thence it had leaked to form a wet pool between his shoulder blades and had soaked out to drench his shirt and vest and jacket.

The match died to an ember. I had a nick on my own cheek: it now seemed a thing of small consequence. By the light of a second match Finn Dillon saw my face. His lips parted in anxiety.

The sweat had dried on our bodies: whenever a slight puff of breeze came we shivered under the stars. All was quiet in the direction of the tinkers' encampment. With considerable difficulty we raised the bellman over the fences and made towards the light burning in the kitchen window of O'Neill's farmhouse. Inside we placed the unconscious man on the settle-bed. We threw water on his face and after a while he came to. Immediately he took a fit of empty retching. Presently he recovered sufficiently to put his legs on the ground and his head between his hands. "There's the head I have!" he said quietly. Dark Jack gave him some poteen that his brother had brought down from the hills.

Madcap washed the bellman's wound. She and her stepmother were both solicitous. It was an open country kitchen with every article of furniture and every utensil scoured clean. It was the first time I had seen the place with conscious eyes. Surreptitiously and cunningly I tried to ascertain by deduction the relations that obtained between the girl and her stepmother. To my surprise, they were wholesome.

Madcap went down and roused out a merry medical student of our acquaintance who proved to be astonishingly sober for the evening of the Old Fair; he put ten stitches in the bellman's scalp and also dressed the wound on my cheekbone. Dominick Foy's skull must have been made of sound bone, for one of the blows he had received would have killed another man. Madcap brought us back the news that none of our lads was seriously injured although at least two had been unconscious for some time. Badger Breen was main proud that his body was a mass of blue bruises: he was at that moment stripped to the waist before the Rookery fire with Martha Goggin dabbing his weals and bruises with tincture of iodine. Madcap also brought the disturbing word that one of the tinker-men was lying unconscious on a wad of straw by the camp-fires with the police standing by, afraid to shift him lest he die. This did not worry us overmuch, since tinkers are demons for exaggeration. Madcap also had it that the police had given the Westerners till morning to be out of the place bag and baggage. From the quizzical look she cast me from time to time I deduced that she had heard a distorted view of our relations with Trouble-o'-the-World.

Later in the night we ventured to creep down Cloone. Now and again Metal Belly had to rest on a window-stool. Cloone was deadly quiet. A child's healthy cry came to our ears. The slender moon had climbed higher into the sky. In Finn Dillon's kitchen a light was burning: his mother was up waiting for him with an old coat thrown across her shoulders. Finn lifted the latch and walked in. I held the door semi-closed behind him so as to reduce to a minimum the amount of light that would fall on the street. Finn Dillon's mother was a woman of great dignity: drawing open the door against my detaining hand, she asked: "Are ye injured, men?" I protested that we were not.

When I went in home, I heard the bed creak as my father raised himself upright in the bed: when he had ensured that I was comparatively uninjured, he launched an attack on me:

"Well, may the good Almighty God Who knows right from wrong. . . ." Sharply my mother bade him hold his tongue. "The world is asleep!" she said. My father said: "I don't give a damn if all creation was dead. . . ." My sister Mary began to knock lightly on the partition. "Tomorrow, father!" she counselled sleepily. My father's voice reluctantly grumbled down to silence.

I climbed the ladder to the loft. My body seemed a ton weight and the wound on my cheekbone had resumed its throbbing. Dressed as I was I flung myself on the bed. Sometimes a bed is a thing of great beauty. I dragged the bedclothes around me and was soon asleep.

Reaching his cabin, Metal Belly lighted his kitchen lamp and lowered it. Carefully he washed his face. For a long while he paced unsteadily up and down. He had removed his shoes and was in his stockinged soles. By degrees the colour flowed back into his features. The ashes of his fire were white cold so that it took him a long time to get the kettle boiling so as to wet a mouthful of tea. On the shelf of the dresser the bell glinted. As he lighted the candle in the blue candlestick the trembling of his fingers startled him. He took a deep draught of water, then blicked out the lamp and went slowly to his room. For the first time in thirty years he found his bed unmade. He set the candlestick on the chair where he had been accustomed to place his watch. Of a sudden he threw himself on his knees beside the bed and with his bearded face deep in his hands began to pray.

Now and again he raised his head and held it to an angle of keen listening. He fancied he had heard the ticking of his beloved watch. When he shook his head to banish the delusion, the movement hurt him unbearably. After a quarter of an hour spent thus, he stood up, doffed his clothes and donned his woollen nightshirt. Painfully he crawled into bed. For a while he remained sitting up with his hands clasped on his neck, a posture which he found relieved his many aches. At last with a heavy sigh he snuffed the candle and lowered himself for sleep.

After a while his head jerked around. Then he sat bolt upright. Crazily he looked in the direction of the chair. As on a crash of thought he inserted his hand beneath the pillow. When his fingers gripped his silver timepiece he was taken with a great joy. Then with a fuller realisation Metal Belly's face grew haggard and drained and old.

# CHAPTER VII

I

THAT morning early! As with Finn Dillon I hurried upriver through the woods.

The soft April rain of the night before had ended. It had left its glistening everywhere. Below us the dun freshwater cooled past; it was stealing through the dangling branches of the trees or breaking into spume as it raced over jutting rocks. The smell of late spring was everywhere. The sky to the south we could plainly see: it held the colour of the body of a quill-fly. In the northeast the sun was lost in the overshadowing trees that ranked on the left hand. Grating over us through a gap in the branches a flock of crows moved westwards towards a rendezvous. When we had come to a place where we could see upriver for a considerable distance white strands of gravel were born and re-born on the banks of the twisting river.

The river still continued its chuckling below us. Low over the water, sprigs of willow held fast to their final issue of catkins. The river had the smell of earth disturbed and borne along in solution. From the ploughed loam on the cliff-tops above the rain had evoked the same smell. Here and there in the woods we came upon rich tufts of primroses. A cock crowed in a farmhouse far away. His hoarse delight made ring upon ring of sound move outwards through the clear air.

"Hurry! Hurry!" Finn was saying, not without irritation.

Though he had not discussed the matter with me, I sensed that he had not heard from Shoon for a long while. For my part of it I was occupied with thoughts of the gay night we had at the wedding of my sister Mary and Peter Stack.

We pushed aside the briars on the pathway with our gaff-handles; the gaff-heads were secure in our leathern belts.

The swishing grass whitened our toecaps and brought the eyelets of our slashed shoes to a fine polish. Neither of us wore stockings.

Hurry! Hurry!

If Finn Dillon wasn't saying it, he was inferring it. It was implicit in the way he beat upon the brambles. A heron came flying in our direction, its speaking wings moving dead-centre in the alley of the river-trees. I turned and watched it perch on the ford below us: its erect slenderness then bore little relation to the cumbersome bird we had seen in flight.

Hurry! Hurry!

Everywhere under the hazels was the royal blue of the bluebells. The Japanese sprigs of the opening ash-leaves had an olive tint to their new leaves. On the woodpath before us the grey down had fallen from the pussy-willows. In the baylets of the river the edges of the water were rusty with the shed sheaths of the beech-buds.

We had been up at cock-crow and were out of Cloone without anybody spying us. Finn's gaff-head was unbarbed, mine was barbed. The hazel handles in our hands were silver and brown: they bore with them the morning's sunlight wherever they travelled. Hazel is reckoned lucky.

Hurry! Hurry!

We hurried on through the many greens of April. Sometimes a beech tree would meet us on the pathway; we thought it as bare as a mountain peak, then astonishingly and arbitrarily it thrust out a single branch in full foliage which was a gay pennant over the ragged army of the woods.

The elm, however, was my favourite among the trees: as I walked along I saw it in its many phases: in bud, in tiny green leaf-coins and in the ultimate goodness of full leaf. The sycamore daubed with wine and cream farrowed happily with little sense of public decency. The blackthorn was curtained with its own blossoms. The green on the whitethorn leaves was tender and brand-new.

Finn growled at me : " Still asleep you are ! Hurry ! "

When we came close to the Mallory demesne we exercised greater caution. Now and again, where the wood was less dense, we stopped to ear the morning air. The nearby barking of a dog made us pause for a long while. Everything was artificial with earliness.

We crossed into the Mallory estate. At a cliff foot directly over the river we hid in a rhododendron bush and there, with strong thongs of greenish horse-hide, bound our gaff-heads to the hazel handles. We then proceeded with renewed wariness until we saw the one-arched bridge which was our destination.

Through the high arch of the bridge we could see the white bulk of Mallory Hall sitting on a cliff perhaps half a mile upstream. There seemed to be no sign of life about the house. We glanced upwards at the parapet of the bridge. The noise of the water breaking from under the arch into the deeper pool below dulled our keenness of hearing. Directly beneath us was a hump of sun-whitened gravel beyond which the brown-yellow river ran over black stones. Between us and the bridge was another strand which projected for a distance into the water. The gravel of this strand was fine and seemed surpassingly clean. Directly downriver from the arch of the bridge was a deep pool.

A band of cut stone projected about five inches near the base of the wall of the bridge : this rough ledge continued right under the arch. The depth of the pool below made it a risky matter to attempt to enter the arch itself : side by side we balanced ourselves on the band of stone and trueing our backs against the wall worked our way outwards over the water. It was difficult to negotiate the corner, but we managed it : gaining inch after precious inch we stole into the cool arch. Here we were struck by the loud sound of breaking water. Reaching a point midway in the arch we stepped down on to the green-coloured stones with which the floor of the archway was paved. The water was three or four inches deep and racing strongly. Downriver the pool at its left and right, out of the brawl of broken waters, carried circles of foam.

From where we now stood we noted how the colours of the world had changed. Framed in the arch we viewed the open east with Mallory's house set high above its own lush inch-lands. Remote it seemed and yet perilously close. On the floor of the archway the water had assumed the light hue of green bottle-glass. Looking upriver I felt on my left cheekbone the dwindled heat of the previous day's sun that had been hoarded in the limestone wall. I laughed as I saw the water take Finn's trousers-ends.

The full crimson of the sun leaked through the cliff-rhododendrons to the left of the Hall.

Keeping close against the left-hand wall we remained in an attitude of listening. Soon we realised how futile it was to attempt to discern sounds of danger above the din of the waters. Finn then waded to the upper end of the arch and splashed across to the other wall. I stayed where I was. One at each wall of the arch we glued ourselves to the grey stones. We turned our faces downriver to the deep pool from whence, if fortune favoured us, the salmon would spring.

Our gaffs were firm in our right hands. Our shoes were set squarely on the rough stones. From time to time we glanced upstream and downstream : when our smart scrutiny was ended our eyes returned to the ragged edge of water over the dark pool below. At any moment an angry salmon would come leaping upwards into the water-race.

Time passed. My ears grew accustomed to the noise of the waters—I even learned to hear other sounds above it. My eyes began to ache from the constant watching of the water : after a while I learned that it had a pattern like green tweed. I grew to learn its every ripple, how it was going to fall, how it was falling, how it had fallen. The east side of me had now wholly cooled of sweat. Once, stealing my eyes up from the water, I saw the gleam of Finn's gaff : in his hand the weapon was a grotesque crozier. Crouched there in the arch my companion seemed surer than a machine. I shook my head to banish an access of false sleep.

Over Finn's head and slightly to the left of him a shrivelled tree had struggled into life from between the limestones. I saw how gallant an effort its buds had made to greet the spring. My watching of the sapling was covert. And then, my eyes meeting Finn's reproachful gaze, I became contrite and resolved to hold a sterner vigil on the racing stream.

I saw a tommy-blue alight on the little sapling. The bird frisked about, making the most of the meagre perches the branches afforded. I noted its blue wing, yellow breast, dark cap and cravat. Of a sudden an excited call from Finn Dillon startled me. A salmon was already on the table of the paving-stones, its water-hidden body humped for the onslaught on the thin but strongly-flowing water. Onward it came, charging directly in midstream, a parabola of water and foam looping over its head and back. Gaff in hand, Finn leaped out on to the table. I came, too, jumping for the joints of the stones where my shoes would find surest purchase : to myself I had to confess that I was compensating with ill-timed vehemence for my previous laxity of vigilance.

(We had been trained to gaff salmon in the haggards of Cloone : the oldsters nodding approval or smiling disapproval as we ran with gaffs uplifted and aimed for a ball of paper on the grass.)

Finn raised his gaff, but seeing that I also had my weapon raised, he held his blow halfway. Thus we foiled one another. The fish swerved towards my wall with such a sudden flurry of passion as took me unawares. It passed so close to my foot that I was afraid to strike lest I should drive the steel into my own instep. The fish careered wildly along the wall and then slipped into the calm waters as expertly as a sword slips into its sheath. Behind the arrowhead of its departure, its indolent fin and tail-tip bade us a fond farewell.

Sorrowfully we returned to our posts. Finn had a habit of

smiling in a certain way when he wished to apportion blame. We set about watching for another fish. This time I nailed my eyes to the water. Recurrently I had to shrug myself awake for I suddenly realised that the moving water had for me the effect of an anaesthetic. On recognising the foe I had to fight I turned wideawake on the instant.

A second fish came. I had anticipated a far larger salmon : thus I lost a moment of readiness in the adjustment of the fish to the fancy. Again the pair of us leaped out. I drew back as I saw Finn raise the gaff over his head, twirl it in the air above him and bring it down firmly on the salmon's back. What a swing of silver malediction the grotesque crozier then made ! The mystery in the water resolved itself into a salmon with a broad tail and fighting fins, the frenzy of whose silver jacket was promptly quenched in Finn's armpit.

Finn carried the fish to my wall : where I killed it, using the gaff-handle as priest. A small fish—perhaps seven or eight pounds in weight. Finn then walked to the downriver edge of the paving-stones and threw the fish on to the grasses on the bank. He washed his hands and again crossed to the other wall. We both looked up towards Mallory Hall. Finn smiled grimly, then crouched with the seat of his pants barely off the surface of the water. I followed his example. The sun had exalted itself above the woods.

We heard the slender sound of a man whistling as he passed by on the bridge over our heads. There was no vehicle-din on the sounding-board of the arch far above, thus we concluded that the man was riding a bicycle. Probably a postman—Finn made a gesture indicative of a man carrying a bag across his shoulder. Upriver a single strand on the northern bank gleamed white in the true sunlight.

Finn readily killed the second fish. It had passed quite close to him as he crouched. This salmon was twice the weight of the first. Two fish in ten minutes ! We decided we had enough. Our decision to quit was that of a gambler who has found luck running with him—and it was just as reliable !

Our gaffs were dangling from the armpits of our jackets as we inched back along the projecting band of stone. Finn had already thrown the second fish on to the bank before him. As we gained the grass we glanced backwards at the arch. We saw a huge salmon leap on to the table. Its leap was one of surpassing idiocy; for it flung itself to the right of the heavier stream and thus landed sideways on a knob of stone about which the water was at its shallowest. The stone had raised the salmon's middle almost completely out of the water, so that fin and tail availed it nothing. Writhing on the stone, its red-gold tail heliographed frantically. The span of the tail more than anything else indicated the great weight of the fish. With a tremendous kick the salmon bounded from the point of stone and then lazily eased itself athwart the current which took it broadside and rolled it over and over till it fell into the deep pool below.

If only we had delayed for another minute! Finn and I glanced at one another. The salmon would of a certainty make a second essay. We were tempted and we fell. In for a penny, in for a pound!

We concealed the two salmon in the long grasses on the bank, then resumed our former positions. This time we were keyed up with excitement. Pressing close to the wall, we strove as it were to melt into the limestone behind us.

Now and again I brought my right hand, firmly clutching the gaff handle, close to my mouth and spat fully into the palm of it. I was terrified lest the salmon should run while my palm was as yet unreadied with spittle. Once or twice the false breaking of the line at the edge of the green stones almost set me leaping out into the stream. Finn's eyes reprimanded me for such false reports. The minutes ticked over. The dark pool below the bridge remained barren and mysterious. It seemed never to have held a fish, much less a salmon so large as is seen scarcely once in a season.

The tommy-blue had returned to the sapling and its movements were now causing me the sufferings of the damned.

Martens took the arch, screaming wildly as they drove between us and the tiny stalactites far above. A cart ground past on the bridge over us : its iron-shod wheels made a metal-edged grumbling on the stone quoins overhead. In a downstream flat a water-hen began bobbing like a toy. In the woods below the bridge all the birds in the world, it seemed, had suddenly begun singing : I could hear them even above the rush of sound in the arch. I continued to hold my eyes fast on the water, marking well how it was going to fall, and how it had fallen. I kept keying myself up for the coming of the great salmon.

Then the great salmon came !

It moved lustily forward, keeping rather to my side than to Finn's. Finn gave an easy leap into the stream, then stopped. Like a mad animal the fish came onwards : it seemed eager to atone for its previous failure. It was nosing fiercely into where the stream was sturdy : wreathed as it was in water, it resembled a powerful fist and forearm thrust savagely against the opposing waters. Watching my eyes, Finn stood completely still.

Then, before the fish was where I wanted it to be I leaped out. I twirled the gaff over my head and took aim at a point in front of the salmon's head. Down the gaff-head curved on to the back of the salmon. How good it was to feel the steel bite home !

Music was to me then was Finn's cry of exultation. That cry, too, was the cause of my undoing. It provoked me to imitate my comrade's previous fancy-work with the gaff : in my folly I tried to whisk the great salmon up to my armpit. But the instant the fish left the water I found its fighting weight in all its fullness. I was spun completely round. Tottering, I lost the sense of where the cracks were under my shoes. Inevitably I fell on the slippery green stones.

The fish, on touching the water, trebled its strength : still held fast by the barb on the weapon, it heaved itself fully out towards the stronger waters in mid-arch. Falling and rising and staggering, I continued to hold my grip on the hazel handle. I knew that if the water came between my hand and the timber the prize was lost. The fish was now almost wholly waterborne : it staggered me from stone to slippery stone until it had won almost to the water-curtain at the edge of the green archway. I saw what I knew was my complete peril : the fish—what its instinct told it was its salvation. It fought its way over the edge, then, experiencing the stronger water about it, put all its strength into one fling. And as I still clutched the gaff-handle like death the fish drew me down, head foremost, into the boil of water in the depths of the dark pool.

I felt the water slide upwards inside my dry clothes. How cold it was ! The pool was deeper than I had thought. I went down, my body lazily spinning, until my shoulders struck the rocky river-bed. I still held on to the gaff-handle. Powerful as the fish had been when held as a dead weight in the air : powerful as it had been when struggling in the shallow water of the archway, the full measure of its strength was reserved for my experiencing as it looped me over and over in the deeps of the pool. The roll of the undertow aided and abetted its efforts. Reaching the strong thrust of stream from mid-arch, it played the very devil with me. Fighting back, I came up for breath and then sharply went under again. I had as clear a vision of my antics as if I were watching myself from the parapet of the bridge above. The fish continued to toss and thresh : I was compelled to roll over and over following every loop and ess of its struggles. All the while, I kept saying in my mind : " By God, salmon, you'll not beat me ! "

Once I found myself completely encased in a bag of bubbles. I grimaced, imagining myself an unusual otter. I fought upwards for another mouthful of air : before I went under again I heard Finn's cry. Analysing the cry to find the laughter and the glory in it, I went down to renew my duel. I then tried to tread the river bottom but failed to touch it.

Finally I abandoned my struggling and in an access of craftiness made a virtue of the necessity of following the runaway salmon. Whether by craft or good fortune, my buttocks instantly struck gravel. Immediately I sprang to a full attack on the fish. I rolled and kicked and griped until I had got between it and the deeper water. I then scrambled and fought until I had penned it between me and the shore. I could see the black whiplash of its powerful back: on this shape I threw myself fiercely. My attack turned the blackness to boiling silver: this fury I scrambled before me, always careful that my face would not become wounded on the gaff-point that protruded from the salmon's middle.

Finn came racing across the stones. With renewed venom I fell upon the salmon. It had now fully realised that it was in shallowing water. As it lashed for freedom, I threw my body heavily on the boil of water. The salmon steadily fought me back, striking my face with a head as hard as bone. Once its broad tail smacked me on the side-face. Of a sudden, seeing my opportunity, I sank my teeth behind its nether fin. I could then feel steel on my cheekbone while my mouth was full of the taste of live fish.

Finn's hand closed over the gaff-handle a little below mine. He hauled the fish towards the dry stones: the last of the struggle resolved itself into a tug-o'-war between Finn's grasp on the handle of the gaff and my teeth, which, by this time, seemed to possess a will of their own, and were reluctant to release their hold. For a moment I was onlooker only: then I opened my aching jaws.

Lying exhausted in the shallow water I watched the fish become a loop in the air: then it thumped heavily to the gravel. Finn set about despatching it with hollow-sounding blows of a long stone. When at last the fish was quiet, Finn threw himself backwards on his hands and began to yowl with laughter.

I lay in the shallow water, spitting salmon-scales and fish's blood from my mouth. The actor in me was uppermost: it would make a tale. The salmon gave a final flop and then lay still. Finn was still kicking with merriment: "Holy You, God!" he kept shouting, then, his face filled with sunlight and laughter, he added: " *Areesh!*"—sham-bidding me perform the deed all over again for his delectation.

Within me exhilaration ebbed: I raised my cold body half out of the water. Was there ever a person as rueful as I was? With movements absurdly delicate I removed the last salmon-scale from my tongue's tip.

As I walked up the dry gravel strand the water poured from every outlet in my clothes. Finn had not ended his mocking; when a small anger touched me I strode forward to come to soft grips with him. Horseplay would be a type of celebration for having killed such a great fish. I had already raised my fist to strike at his laughing face when I glanced over his shoulder and saw two men step down through the bushes that edged the strand. One, a burly fellow, carried a shotgun in such a manner that it could easily be brought to the ready. The second man I recognised: he was the small jockey whom I had seen handling Edith Mallory's hound on the day of the coursing match.

Finn's eyes read my face: he also interpreted the reluctance of my uplifted hand to strike him. His keen ears then caught the sound of a stone being dislodged behind him. He turned calmly. Side by side, we awaited the men's arrival.

## II

The man carrying the shotgun was as black as ink; he was also as thickset as a barrel and had the air of being sour and secretive as the result of some obscure disappointment. To give the jock his due he was making an effort to conceal his glee. We saw at a glance that the fat man was boss and the jockey servitor. With every slow step nearer to us, the pair seemed to savour our discomfiture. Once Finn broke his stance. As he did so, the gun in the dark man's hand lifted perceptibly. I shook my right hand across the gravel, pin-dotting the stones with drops: this I did in a sorry effort to bring affairs down from the plane of menace and tension.

This gesture of mine the black bailiff, or gamekeeper, offset by chewing ominously and by sneering at my sodden clothes.

The black-complexioned man halted a few yards away from us : he looked down at the salmon. Still chewing, he began to attack us with words. He placed word firmly on the top of word as if he were piling blocks of stone.

" Mean, lousy, dirty, impoverished Cloone ! Burrow for wren-boys, spree-boys, rakes, rapsters, whipsters, mummers, flagwallopers and poachers ! "

After almost every epithet, he chewed stolidly. The most prodigious chew of all underscored the word " poachers." This was normal taunting : he was provoking us to indiscretion. It was the overture to violence. After the abuse would come blows as jagged as rocks. The jock was spacing his sharp front teeth along a stem of spring grass.

Remorsely the bailiff went on : " Vagabones of all descriptions, night-and-day hang-gallows robbers ! Cock-crow thieves ! " He spat heavily on the gravel. Then : " Cross-got highwaymen ! " His eye-corner requested the jock to second what he was saying : the jock dutifully removed the sop from his mouth, nodded once and smiled approvingly.

Finn Dillon's voice was steadier than it should have been. " Bravery is contagious to a gun-butt ! " he said.

" As cowardice is to a gun-barrel ! "

I had begun to shiver in the April cold. Noting this the jockey allowed his face to become interestingly volatile.

A new note now entered the bailiff's taunting. " Is it the way the breed of ye is sunk in hunger ? Is it how the agile among ye must be sent out into the fields at dawn to pick and sift and forage and glean ? " His sneer postulated that he was confident of drawing us. " Is it the way yeer women are cold-blooded between the blankets so that it becomes pleasant to ye to abandon the bed before cock-crow ? Why don't you answer me, Dillane of the Clever Tongue ? "

" If your gun was on the gravel, bailiff, maybe God would

allow your teeth to float forward on the blood from your gums ! "

More than ever the bailiff resembled a black bull as he brought his gun to the ready. Even when the weapon was directed on Finn's face it did not succeed in riding him down. When I saw the ominous figure-of-eight of the gun barrels, my sudden wincing was not altogether as a consequence of my sodden clothes and the morning air : to me the bailiff's fingers seemed clumsy on the trigger. They could as lief fire as not fire. I realised that if he fired my evidence in a court would scarcely be worth a straw.

The jock held his teeth clear of the stem of grass. His volatile face had hardened and had become drained of blood.

Then the salmon we had thought dead gave a tremendous thump on the gravel. The noise afforded the bailiff a pretext for lowering his gun. As he did so, I shuddered : it was as if somebody had walked across my grave.

The bailiff laughed bitterly : " A shame it is," he said, " to waste lovely lead on carrion crow."

A wagtail came bounding over the stones.

Finn was uncowed. " A choice man you are for words," he said, evenly. " You'd be revered in a palace of chatterin' women ! "

This remark seemed to cut the bailiff to the quick of his finger-nail.

" Christ ! " he said, " you spawn of Cloone ! " He handed his gun to the jockey, buttoned his coat and rushed clumsily forward.

Fighting, Finn Dillon had a peculiar stance. He kept little or no guard to his face ; his two fists, held loosely below the breast-bone, kept moving towards one another and away from one another as if in time to a peculiar rhythm. It was almost as if he were playing an invisible concertina. A trick stance this, as once I had learned to my cost. It was designed to lure a firmer fighter in, in the specious promise of a facile victory.

To offer a lure of this nature one had to be exceptionally agile on one's feet.

I looked down at Finn's awkward brogues. His footing on the strand was perilous for such tactics. I saw the boots seek balance on two rocking stones ; before they could find it the bailiff had blundered in and had crunched his fist along Finn's jaw and neck. It was not a full blow but it dangerously approximated to one. Finn's mouth began bleeding from one corner.

Somehow or other he managed to eel away. The bailiff came lumbering after. I moved a step closer to the jockey so as to intimidate him clear of the fight. Now that Finn's boots were on firm gravel his innocent hands had begun tapping through the dark fellow's guard. His right hand began to idle in, fist after fist jabbing forward into the bailiff's face. The blows seemed light enough : soon it was evident that they had deceptive force to back them. Thrice the fist won home on the jet face : the third blow was a vicious one—a heavy stone behind the bailiff's heel sent him sprawling on his rump to the gravel. The blood poured from his nose. On his feet again, he came in flailing savagely. The fighting now became in-fighting : I saw Finn take a heavy blow and whiten. The bailiff moved in as for the kill.

Then I heard a voice.

For a moment or two previously I had been conscious of the noise of the rumble-bells of harness. The voice I heard was a cultured one. Also, it was deeply imperative. The fighters stopped fighting and all four of us looked up at the spotted parapet of the bridge.

On the roadway above was a back-to-back car. We saw Major Mallory standing upright in the vehicle. As the chestnut horse harnessed to the vehicle shook himself, the rumble-bells rang out again.

" Stop it at once, I say ! "

The bailiff stopped, reluctantly.

" Come up here, all of you ! Bring up that fish ! "

We formed an unusual procession. The bailiff was torn

between natural anger and the acquired habit of subservience. He was carrying the fish. He pressed a navy-blue handkerchief against his nose in an effort to staunch the blood. The jockey, by his alacrity in moving forward, was already exculpating himself.

Not a word was spoken as we walked across the field beside the bridge. The jockey was carrying our gaffs. We crossed the low roadside wall, then waited until the vehicle ground up to us.

Major Mallory was a tall man whose jacket and cap were disreputable yet distinguished. His small fresh-complexioned face was brightened by a white moustache and lavish white eyebrows. Is there such a thing as breeding ? An advantage of birth as apart from rearing and consciousness of tradition ? I smiled secretly when I recalled that I had caressed his daughter in a cave.

" Poachers, sir ! "

The bailiff, who was finding it difficult to breathe, then raised up the wonderful fish. Also he dabbed his nose. Strange that one so black should bleed so red ! The horse leaped, or pretended to leap, at the flash of silver. Antics of the blood, I thought, which had their parallel in human beings—in loud talk and perhaps also in the wearing of disreputable yet distinguished garments.

For a time Major Mallory said nothing ; his grey eyes looked over us not so much severely as abstractedly. I fell to wondering why he had driven so slowly to meet us. To the bailiff he said, quietly : " Put the fish in the car." The bailiff obeyed. Puzzlement was printed on his face.

Major Mallory looked at us again. To Finn he said, abruptly: " What is your name ? "

" Finnbarr Dillon," Finn said eventually.

Turning to me : " And you ? "

" Ches Macnamara."

" Both from Cloone, sir," amened the bailiff.

Major Mallory made a slight movement with the reins, then

drew a half-breath. It was clear that he was grappling with a problem beyond our understanding. The jock understood it—I read it in the little rascal's face.

To Finn Dillon, Major Mallory said: "Are you hurt?"

Finn shook his head and smiled.

Major Mallory re-set his face in inquiry to me: I shook my head. I wondered why he had asked me: suddenly I remembered that as yet the taste of salmon's blood was on my lips. My rocked teeth ached. I looked down: the front of my shirt was drenched with the fish's blood. My downward glance also reminded me that my sodden clothes were clinging to my limbs. This fact the Major noted.

Major Mallory was softly punishing his lips with his teeth. Suddenly he addressed Finn and myself: "Sit in!" he said, urgently. For a moment we did not move.

"Come! Come!" Major Mallory said, "don't keep me waiting!" He rapped with his whip-handle on the rein-rail of his vehicle. His certainty that we would obey him was disarming. He was accustomed to handling bailiffs and understrappers and gillies.

Finn's mouth curved, as with a smile. I knew that he was thinking of Old Font and the spirit of independence he had tried to beget in us. Where, I asked myself, did independence end and insolence begin?

As on an impish impulse, Finn leaped into the vehicle. He sat down beside the Major, placing his boots one on either side of the great fish. Major Mallory turned to me. Again he rapped the rail of the vehicle. "Jump up behind!" he said and, when I delayed added: "You'll catch pneumonia!"

I leaped up. My perch was precarious, as the seat had been notched well back. On a sign from the Major, the jockey leaped up beside me.

"Very well!" Major Mallory said vaguely to the bailiff, indicating that for the present the matter was at an end. The bailiff's face darkened with concealed anger and perplexity.

In silence we drove on towards the main gate on the avenue

that led to Mallory Hall. A child wearing a blue frock emerged from the gate-lodge and swung wide the great iron gates. We rode freely up the avenue. My skin was beyond coldness. We proceeded through arcades of awakening trees, past enormous rhododendron-thickets and irregularly-spaced monkey-puzzles. Before long the jockey and myself were on tolerable terms. A sly wink from him had evoked a smile from me. The Major's ear was too close for us to engage in any conversation.

As we approached the house, the trees fell sharply away and the sky came through. A white iron railing divided the drive from a paddock closely cropped by sheep. Here and there in the open parkland in front of the house were copper beeches which were already assuming the colour that later would mark them out for splendour. The river had curled to the back of the eminence on which the house stood : looking back I saw that I was on the direct line between the Hall and the eye of the bridge wherein we had poached the fish. Everything below was startlingly clear. The jockey looked at me and smiled.

## III

The house, massive and white-fronted, lay directly before us. We drove up to the front door. The jockey, with a final wink at me, leaped off and held the horse's head while the three of us descended.

I crawled down from my seat. I found that, although I had pins and needles in my cold legs, my body had done its utmost to acclimatise itself to the water in my clothing and had even begun to generate its own warmth.

Within, the hallway was surprisingly bright, even after the brilliance of such a morning. The honeyed sunlight was superimposed on the beeswax on the parquetry. I saw a grandfather clock and armour, brasses and swords, a brass *jardiniére* on a carved table as well as oil paintings of an excellence I had never seen before. I saw furniture of bright red mahogany, walking-sticks with silver mountings and riding whips with bone handles. Through an open door to the right I glimpsed a room panelled in oak with brass ornaments hanging on the walls. Oak and brass—a capital marriage, I thought—the small brightness illuminating a large area of dullness. A massive mahogany staircase lifted before us : on the first landing above there was a transverse corridor.

A butler came sidling out. He was small and had a round dropped belly. His eyes were dilated in what I thought at first was a flattering look of surprise. Later when I had seen him in a limited variety of situations I knew that this apparent reaction of astonishment was due to an exophthalmic condition of his goitrous eyes. He had turned his disease to advantage and was thus equal even to the most disconcerting eventuality.

" Sheppard ! This young man needs a bath—very warm water, and also a change of clothing while his own are drying. Master Maitland's will probably fit him."

" Follow me ! "

As I followed the butler, I was swaggering my independence. This, I realised, was a conscious over-compensation for my tatterdemalion appearance.

In a corridor we met an apple-faced maid : the butler repeated, in precisely the same tone as his master had used : " Sweeney, this young man needs a bath, very warm water, and also a change of clothing while his own are drying. Master Maitland's will probably fit him." He made a single addition : " You will prepare Number Two Bathroom."

" It's ready, Mr. Sheppard."

The girl's neat black shoes preceded my slashed brogues. We went along a corridor, her short steps mincing before me : I saw that she was la-di-dawing me. Sometimes the sunlight slanted unexpectedly across the darkness from the right-hand side. Sometimes I had a glimpse of the beauty of rooms through doors unexpectedly found open.

We went up a short flight of stairs. On the little passage-way above I flirted with the maid : this I did by matching my step over-zealously to hers. She continued to be demureness itself.

Entering the bathroom, she turned the hot-water faucet. After a while the water came hissing hot. " Leave your damp clothes here," she said. When speaking, she did her best to steer her voice clear of irony. " You'll find the dry clothes directly outside the door," she added. With something like a flick of an eyelid she had gone.

I looked around me. Bath salts, towel, talcum-powder, soap, loofah and hissing hot water. I drew the bath, allowing the water to come as close to the top as I dared.

The hot water bit into my blood and repaired the morning's damage. At first, so perished I was, I was scarcely sure whether the water was boiling hot or icy cold. I was prodigal with the new cake of soap. My body I attacked vigorously with the loofah. I scaled the old skin from my kneecaps and dug into the hollows of my ankles where the road-dust had stolen through the gapes of my brogues.

When I was fully bathed, I emptied the bath and rinsed myself in cold water. I fooshed the water around so as not to leave a trace of my endeavours. The towel was soft, ample and milk-white. It was such a towel as I had never known before and I frolicked in its folds like a wet terrier on sunny grass. I waited until my body was bone-dry and my hair was well drubbed: then I wiped the mirror clean of condensed steam and looked at myself. By God! I looked hearty. I reckoned it good fortune that I had shaved the night before.

I have said that I felt well and looked well. When I sprinkled the talcum-powder on my body I smelled well. I rummaged in my wet clothes for an old comb. My chestnut hair curled under its strong teeth. I was a changeling! For a moment I was enticed by the idea of working hard and becoming rich: with a shrug I cast the temptation aside as a sure means of spilling God's life on the open ground.

Cautiously I opened the door—a grey lounge suit, a white silk shirt, elegant black shoes and socks were laid carefully on white paper on the floor of the corridor. Soon I was dressed like a duke. The suit was a little tight in the seat: I was mortally afraid to flex my buttocks less the pants should crack open at the seams. The caress of the shirt on my body, arms and upper thighs was such an entertainment as I had never before experienced. The shoes were a capital fit.

I laughed and pranced, clenched and unclenched my fists, looked into one mirror and saw my poll in another, smelt inside the neck of my shirt, then rubbed my hands delightedly. I composed my face for displaying my metamorphosis to the new world I had entered. I felt so airy that I could kick the stars.

Edith ? In my new-found glee, I had momentarily forgotten her. Then I laughed : no woman could alter my present mood of exaltation.

And then, transcendent discovery, I was hungry !

I went out into the corridor : the maid came to lead me back. It was my turn to la-di-daw her. She moved ahead of me : behind the soldier-sashes of her apron and the sheath of her dark skirt, her body moved delightingly. I knew by the jaunty cock to her head that she was amused at the way I had turned the tables on her. My steps now boldly mimicked hers but this time it was as if I were doling out largesse to an inferior. Where the corridor darkened she turned on me. There she dropped all pretence ; she opened her mouth to speak : then, as on a thought, half-turned away. I mistook her motives for turning and prepared my mouth for laughter. She looked directly at me, and said, abruptly : " Look ! When you're with the mistress do something quiet but odd ! If you do, God will be fond of you ! " She shrugged. She had been speaking under strain. She averted her face and tried again. She said : " Last week . . ." then she broke off. I heard her say something about a tinsmith and his fire. Instantly, I understood. I had a clear remembrance of the Major sitting in his cart : he was looking steadfastly ahead while his teeth were troubling his upper lip.

I glanced down at my contrite shoes. I longed to question

her further, but she seemed in the grip of such peculiar forces that I dared not do so.

As we resumed our walk down the corridor, the relations obtaining between our four shoes were on a square and honest basis.

Passing an open door on my right, I heard the soft sound of piano-playing. The notes were softly tumbling after one another in pleasing sequence. I glanced sharply in the open door of what I saw was a drawing-room. Edith Mallory was playing. Her sideface was turned to the doorway; she was wearing a skirt of white tweed and a lemon-coloured pullover. The manner of her playing did not inform me whether or not she knew I was in the house. The maid glanced sharply at my face.

We had breakfast in a small breakfast-room. It was the first time I had ever seen grapefruit. The silver spoon I used was solid and heavy: the table napery was stiff, white and gleaming. After the fruit we had porridge and then bacon and eggs. Major Mallory seemed anxious for the meal to be over.

When he had led us back to the drawing-room the piano was still open but Edith had gone. Major Mallory stepped through an open French-window and on to a well-dressed lawn. We followed. Beside the French-window we saw the white-enamelled hospital bed set in the sunlight. A woman wearing a blue bedjacket was reclining upon it. The jockey was standing at the bedside: he was showing the woman the great fish we had killed: dangling from his hand the back of the fish made a black wedge against the bedclothes. At our entrance the jockey's arm was reprieved from holding up the fish. Not without difficulty the woman in the bed turned around to view us. Her face was Edith's face, grown older and more drawn. Her head was crowned with masses of grey-brown hair.

(" Do something odd, and God will be fond of you! ")

An arc of golden privet ended the lawn, which was divided into pleasant patterns by gravel paths. On this side of the privet, single-headed daffodils, planted in apparently haphazard clusters, were in bloom. Elsewhere on the lawn vivid tulips stood erect from slabs of purple aubretia.

The woman's expression lighted at the sight of the suit I was wearing. The jockey seemed eager to remain but lacked a valid excuse. As he walked around the corner of the building, I smiled to see that he was inclined to totter beneath the weight of the salmon.

To the woman in the bed, Major Mallory said, in a loud stage whisper: "The poachers, Emily!" His manner had softened. His wife rewarded him with a tired smile. In a smiling silence she examined my features with open minuteness, and then her eyes lingered on my damp hair. My attention was caught by the brilliant slash of the scarlet cover of a magazine lying on the coverlet. When the woman had turned to inspect Finn, I pivoted my head to view this picture: it showed a young woman in a scarlet swimsuit diving from a raft.

"How do you do?" The woman's voice was soft.

("Do something odd. . . .")

"How do you do?" we said.

A game had begun between the woman and myself. It was a game of smoke and finer than smoke.

The mirror—inconsequently, I remembered: I had not realised how burned by the weather my face was until I had viewed it against the milk-white silk shirt.

"Please sit down!"

The garden-seat beside the bed was piled with cushions. As on a common thought, Finn and I reckoned it effeminate to sit squarely on one of these. Each of us sat on the space between a pair of cushions, which were of varying thicknesses. Our lopsided posture did not escape the woman's smiling notice. I looked down at Finn's brogues and contrasted them with the shoes I was wearing.

Effort was stamped on Major Mallory's every word. After a while he went away. The woman saw me pitying her husband,

and understood. Her eyes seemed to be experiencing difficulty in keeping away from my hair. I thought of Edith and her mother. Such confidences would be alien to mother and daughter in Cloone. I grew cold: perhaps Edith had already sacrificed me, so that her mother might, in her mind, grow vicariously young. It was a thought born of my temporary pride and self-assurance.

I probed the thought further in my mind: if the mother knew of the relations obtaining between Edith and myself, she would be certain to betray her knowledge. My mind grew alert for the clue-word the woman would surely drop into our conversation: something connected with the sea . . . strand, cliff, wave, crest, gull, sunlight or rock. The magazine cover . . . was it a trap or a wilful ironic comment on her paralysis? A reminder? A warning? An encouragement? A gesture of sympathy? The flicker of a flag from one hopelessly marooned?

The woman's eyes and my eyes were idling away from one another and re-finding one another on trivialities. In the finding there was no time-lag. A statement of Caherdown's then occurred to me: "Between every woman and every man there are subtleties, despite difference of age. A grown boy can look at an old woman and relish her for what she was, while an old man can look on a tiny girl and find joy in the splendour that will some day be hers. These things I speak of are pure and have nothing to do with ugliness."

The woman looked at Finn's belt: "You're wearing a curious belt," she said quietly.

Finn murmured.

My eyes pleaded with Finn to tell her about the belt. (Do something odd. . . . ) But Finn remained stubbornly silent.

"Did you make it?" she asked.

"No, ma'am."

"Who made it?"

"An old harness-maker—he's dead for more than eighty years."

" He must have devoted a good deal of his time to the making of it ? "

" Aye, ma'am."

" Who gave it to you ? "

" It was given to me after a man's death."

I saw a peacock coming through a gap in the privet : although I had never before seen such a bird, I recognised it instantly from the picture-books. The garish bird strutted forward into the sunlight, its small body expertly balancing the volume of its eyed tail. I was vaguely disappointed in the peacock : it scarcely tallied with the splendid reports I had heard of it.

The woman went on : " Is it an heirloom ? "

" It is the Belt of Cloone ! " I said, shortly.

The woman's lips were apart in eagerness.

" It has some significance you are concealing ? " she said smilingly, to Finn.

" It is a half-joke," Finn said. " The man who wears it is nicknamed ' Prince of Cloone '."

" Are you, then, Prince of Cloone ? "

" I am, ma'am."

" How long will you remain Prince of Cloone ? "

" Till I emigrate or die."

The woman's eyes were fixed upon him : " If you should prove unworthy . . . ? "

" I will still be Prince of Cloone."

" Have there ever been unworthy Princes ? "

" Saving myself, no, ma'am."

We three laughed.

The woman tried again, offering edge for edge with Finn's tone of voice. Finn kept deflecting her questioning with his wan smiles. She was not easily put off.

" This belt . . . this . . . honour . . . is it always given to a young man ? "

" Not always. Old men have been Princes of Cloone. One weighed close on twenty stone ! "

After her almost free laughter: "What are the functions of this royal personage?"

"If there is a doubt, he directs."

"You, then, are the leader?"

Finn had been looking idly at his hands. He looked up sharply. "I am the leader," he said.

"Who nominates your successor?"

"I do."

"Before you . . .?"

"Before I emigrate or die."

The woman was insatiable. "How do you intimate your decision to the new Prince?"

"After I've gone, the belt is delivered." With a small gesture, Finn broke the mood. Over-sharply, he added: "It is a half-joke, ma'am!" He looked away to where the peacock was strutting on the morning lawn.

After a time, the woman said softly: "May I see the Belt?"

Finn handed it to her. It seemed heavy in her bed-worn hands. As she was holding it, Edith entered the lawn by the French-window. The mother looked up. I did not fall into the trap of turning. I was watching eagerly for the mother's eyes to seek my hair. Her habits of introspection had made her more cunning than I had anticipated, for she looked directly into my eyes first. To her daughter, she said lightly: "Two interesting visitors, Edith." We rose.

"Mr. . . ."

"Dillon," Finn said. He half-bowed.

"And Mr. . . ."

"Macnamara," I said.

Graciously, yet with a brush of malice, the woman said: "They killed an enormous fish."

Though I had urgent need to do so, I dared not look directly at Edith Mallory. My finger-tips kept remembering the touch of her forearms. Dutifully I looked at the woman in the bed. Craftily, I awaited my opportunity to look at Edith: I was hoping that her pose of confidence was not over-perfect, not indicative of the perfect actress or the perfect liar.

The mother continued : " We have been entertaining royalty unawares."

Finn and I did not smile over-well : whether it was Finn or Edith or myself that the woman was provoking was not yet quite clear.

Edith came forward and began to tuck in the bed-clothes. Her light fair hair fell clean and heavy to below the nape of her neck : at the end of its fall it curled inwards. Her profile had the force of character. The small of her back was narrow : as it fell gradually away it widened to a good young seat. She took a small size in shoes : the calves of her legs were neither light nor heavy. I began to wish for her afresh. The clothes I wore were influencing me strangely. I strove to keep my eyes lazy for I knew that the mother was sharp. Once when I thought that I could with safety look more keenly at the girl, I discovered the mother's bright eyes framed in the yellow angle formed between Edith's arm and body. I dulled my eyes and glanced away.

" Maitland's suit is a perfect fit," the mother said to her daughter. " You would imagine he had returned ! " The woman was tempting the daughter to look at me.

" Yes," Edith said, primly. She thumped the pillows. Her eyes continued resolutely to remain away from mine.

I felt drowsy : the bath, the food and the air of tranquillity about me had induced sleepiness. Here also was a graciousness such as I had never known. Here there were no black rafters as in Cloone, no salt bacon and no strong tea. Here there was no sense of constriction.

The peacock came closer : I thought of the innumerable hat-bands his feathers could ornament. A superstition of ours had it that peacocks' feathers were as unlucky as an un-churched mother : both were believed to be capable of bringing tears to the threshold.

The memory of the bath lingered with me ; the good food

and the drowsing sun continued to render me less than vigilant. Was it under conditions such as these that empires fell or masterpieces were born ? Was this the environment to which ordinary folk would win up as the result of man's ingenuity ? What then ? Would the faculty of man's effort thrive, or die ? Was life to be measured by the blink of silver on a sideboard, or the sunshine on grass that was trained till it resembled tweed ? Admirable was the fall of Edith's limbs moving fluently in the little mystery of cloth. Acting in tune to a lazy inner rhythm, I rubbed my hands down over my thighs. I had once been drunk on whiskey : now I was again experiencing the wicked laze of that drunkenness. The remembrance of smoothly-served food, the touch of fine cloth on my thighs and the wrap of silk to my chest—these were my delightful seducers.

As through a dream I found Finn's eyes upon me : they were slitted to a sidelong hate. Drowsily, I told myself : " To hell with Finn and all he stands for ! " These lawns, this graciousness, *he* saw through other eyes. I felt that life here was the answer to my body's constant supplication. And then I stiffened on a stab of thought : I could win up to this by hard endeavour—or by a trick !

As I looked at Edith Mallory I reverted to my old habit of leaping outside of myself and examining myself as from a little distance. I must have looked like a marmalade cat in the sunshine. I smiled. I was young. The thought of the trick was natural. In the yielding only would lie the hurt. I was drunk with the well-being of the world. To hell with Cloone !

An hour before I was a poaching rascal crouched low in a windy arch. Now, hey presto ! I was a gentleman.

Sin as sin is bad. But sin as a policy is unforgivable. The temptation to trickery died. I raised my eyelids. The woman lying on the bed had been reading my mind.

She raised her hands abruptly. The rings on her fingers caught the sunlight, flashing, I thought, designedly to shoo away my thoughts. My thoughts ran random. Where had the showpiece tinsmith made his fire ? Had he cut his tin here, disc after disc of it making a succession of small silver moons?

("Do something odd. . . .")

Then I must have laughed aloud, for the two women stilled their fragments of talk and slowly turned their faces on me. Edith had her fingers on her mother's hair. Old face and young face were then exactly similar, except for the intervention of age. Loyalty was compelling Finn to buttress me in my error.

The bedridden woman raised herself on her elbow. She looked squarely at me. "Where is the amusement?" she queried.

The answer to such a question I had rehearsed. What I am going to say, I will say, I thought. Because of it I shall seem an utter fool or shall be crowned a minor king.

Turning sleepily, I said: "It is these clothes. . . . It is also something the maid said. . . ."

Mother and daughter waited. Finn Dillon could not be more alive than he was at that moment.

To Edith, the mother said: "Perhaps Mr. Dillon would care to see the view from the edge of the lawn." Finn and Edith walked away.

"What was it the maid said?" Mrs. Mallory then asked.

I was looking towards the hills. "She stopped me in the corridor," I said slowly. "'When you are with the mistress,' she said, 'do something odd and God will be fond of you.'"

Mrs. Mallory's mouth trembled vividly. I was poised on the razor's edge of brutality. That, or else I was approaching complete congruence with the soul of another.

I raised my head and looked directly at the woman. I had resolved to leap the barriers of seven hundred years.

The woman nodded at me to proceed.

I said: "The maid's words have been troubling me. As I sat here, I have asked myself: 'What shall I do that is odd? Shall I clutch the peacock by the tail? Shall I laugh with unconscionable loudness? Shall I speak of the candelabrum of the chestnut and so use a simile that millions before me have used? Shall I protest: "Why should ye have all treasure while we who are filled with the lust of life go wholly without?" Shall I enquire: "What is there to filch that will not walk forward and surrender to the brave thief striding through the sunlight?" Shall I complain: "How I hate this Maitland who shall inherit?" Shall I cry: "The salmon! Who are ye to nail labels of ownership on the quicksilver bounty of God?" Shall I clench my fists, then strut upon the grass which the gentility of generations has brought to the consistency of tweed? Then perhaps having done my something odd, God will be fond of me!' "

My eyes were brutally frank upon the woman. I had succeeded in fusing her into my unusual mood. She seemed perilously close to crying. And to laughing, too!

Finn and Edith had reached the lawn's edge. I saw a lemon-clad arm extend in brave signal to the world. For the bedridden woman and myself, there was a crying of heart to heart over barriers that were down.

"Why do you tell me this?" she asked quietly.

"Because I think that my world is the one you have often dreamt of. Life for you must be symbolised by such things as the blink of tinsmith's fire or a blackbird's yellow bill balancing a dark field ploughed."

The woman and I were one. "Do not stop now," she said. "What you have said is the echo of truth. It is kin to the murmur of a seashell in the ear."

I laughed. With the mention of the seashell her secret was out! I looked to where Edith was standing on the lawn's edge.

The woman was full smiling. In honest query, she continued: "The memory of you both in the cave—was it wholesome?"

I was winning to full understanding.

"You may be damn full sure it was good in the cave," I said frankly. "Better, perhaps, it was on the sand where the heat of the day still lingered. Best it was on the cliff-top. Standing at her shoulder I liked the fall of her limbs." Sharply, I added: "Why should I deny it? Too soon I shall be horizontal for all eternity."

"What is good, is good," the woman agreed.

On the edge of the lawn, Edith turned: she saw her mother raise her arm. Finn's body did not respond. He resumed his looking towards a horizon that was hidden from my eyes.

Edith was gracefully walking towards us. When she had come closer, she saw that our faces were flushed.

"These things should not be spoken of," the girl said, with downcast eyes, as she upbraided her mother for a pact broken.

"What is good, is good," the mother said, using an unmistakable brilliance of tone.

The mother continued to address her daughter: "After the bitter years, I have found that convention counts for little. Look how it has yielded" (here she smiled) "to a poacher transfigured—to a brave thief striding through the sunlight. This tiny upheaval has drawn us three closely together. Is it not so?"

I realised that the woman was addressing me also.

Unaccountably, I had grown sullen and refractory. Abruptly, I said: "Beauty is always in the future or in the past."

Edith looked sideways at me.

"You, too?" her mother asked her.

Edith nodded.

"Liars both!" the mother said. She eased her neck and head back on the pillow. She had recovered a lost gladness. After a happy sigh, she said: "This is the excitement that I crave." To me, smiling: "You have done your something odd. The pattern of nature is so often distorted before its swings to rightness."

I looked around at the grass and the gravel. "The tinsmith?" I asked: "where did he light his fire?"

The mother answered: "On the base of a milk churn, which,

to me, seemed astonishingly heavy. He set it on the gravel. There!" She pointed to the exact spot.

"What did he look like?" I asked. I was still filled with the realisation that my chestnut hair was shining as only a newly-opened chestnut apple shines when it slips from its gourd.

"His cheeks were venous. He was asthmatic. He had a wispish moustache. When he removed his hat, the sweat made a silver line here." The woman drew a finger-nail horizontally across her brow. "He said he was a gay man when he was young: that he played a piccolo through Ireland." She laughed at the recollection.

"You saw the low, slow glow of his soldering-iron?" Purposely I said, "low, slow, glow."

"Low, slow, glow," she repeated. "Yes, it was attractive while he kept the straight sunlight from it. When the sun's rays lighted on it, it quenched. I liked also the circular moons of tin emerging from beneath his shears."

The mother turned to her daughter. "Treasure it, my darling," she said: "it is the dream. The life is different. If the life and the dream were coalesced, we would be gods. He is closest to God who moves the life nearest to the dream. This adventure will be one candle left alight when everything is lost in darkness."

Edith bent her head: a lock of her hair completely broke her expression. Her fingers plucked at the twig she had brought with her from the edge of the lawn.

I laughed aloud. At the sound of my laughter, Finn Dillon turned. His stance accused me of treachery to Cloone. So as to infuriate him, I laughed again.

In Edith's hands the stubborn twig yielded. She was left without an alibi. Then, as we watched the lawn's edge, a hen blackbird emerged from a small tunnel in the privet. It was spring! Finn had already cast his sidelong eyes upon the brownish bird. Employing a reluctant-to-escape gait, the hen extracted a violent cock blackbird from the same tunnel in the privet. She described a grotesque lame circle as she drew the cock after her: each aberration of her gait was designed to afford the cock time to gain on her. True to eternal design the cock gained ground in the arc of the hen's hobbling. This sideways sham-lame arc was an arc of love, of sullen spring, of world coming alive underfoot and of man and beast feeling the revivifying sap. For us, watching, it constituted an act of faith. It was a single gesture rescued from the million million gestures thrown prodigally from the hand of nature: we had had the wit to recognise it for what it was. We were caught in the universal seep. Each of us existed distinct and separate in a great area of loneliness.

Major Mallory came across the lawn. At first he seemed overjoyed at our apparent intimacy, then, sensing the remoteness of Finn Dillon, he identified himself with him. "Come, Come!" he said shortly, addressing me.

When I had doffed my finery, I was myself once more. On the road home Finn and I were alien and silent with one another.

That night we sent Badger Breen to recover the pair of salmon which we had killed and hidden in the grasses. We offered him a third share if he succeeded in recovering them. We described accurately the place where we had hidden the fish. It was late in the night when Badger returned: he swore he could find neither trace nor tidings of the hidden salmon. We gave it over as a bad job.

A week or so later, for no reason at all, Badger began to be recurrently drunk. Night after night he had plenty of roystering-cash: this, too, at a time when there were no fairs and precious little gleanings for the type of person Badger was. At first Finn and I were inclined to beat the lard out of him, but when we heard the neighbours saying laughingly that Badger Breen had got even with us for the many pranks we had played on him, we realised that public opinion was against us. So we let it go.

The morning of the poaching was also the morning on which Metal Belly disappeared without saying a word to anyone. As time passed, the padlock on his door began to burn red with rust. Peeping through the small back window, Jody Shea was able to descry that the bell was missing from the dresser. This, we thought, was sensible of the bellman and in keeping with his character: wherever he went the man had his way of living close to his hand.

At first the old people missed Metal Belly: they were wont to boast about him when seeking an example of an upstanding man with male resonance in his declamatory voice. But old people are nothing if they aren't disloyal, and when they realised for certain that the bellman was not returning, they began quietly but thoroughly to rend his memory. There had always been a queer streak in his family, they averred, and in proof of this assertion they mentioned a grand-uncle of his who had grown an imperial beard and was alleged to have held numerous conversations with chaffinches.

# CHAPTER VIII

I

"IT was not by the blood of sheep or oxen that we were redeemed, but by the priceless blood of the Lord Jesus Christ! And how are we to behave in the face of this extraordinary outpouring of grace? Dare we to betray the sacred brotherhood into which we were initiated by the sublime sacrifice of Calvary?"

The new Dean paused. "I exhort each parent listening to me here today to inculcate into his or her children lively sentiments of purity, chastity and decency. And it is in no unequivocal terms that I warn in an especial manner the young women of Cloone. . . ."

Tall, powerful and stooped, his presence dwarfing the small altar of Mary-without-Stain, the new Dean went on. The old Dean, whom we had loved, was dead. It was a rare thing for the Dean to show himself in our little chapel. Generally it was the curate, Father Mallon, who came: his ways were our ways. Listening to the new Dean's sermon the congregation was taut. Finn Dillon and I knew well what he was driving at: long since Finn had stiffened in his seat.

"The hounds of concupiscence continue to bay the crucified Son of God. God is not mocked!" The Dean paused, then continued in a level tone: "I have come already to this church to tell the young men and women that unless they shun the occasions of sin they are but twigs of purity in a maelstrom of lust. The rebellious arrogance of the wicked angels, the disobedience of our first parents, the horrid fratricide of Cain —none of these sins, deadly as they were, succeeded in making God say, as He said when confronted with impurity: 'I repent that I made man!' Saint Paul says that this sin should not be mentioned among Christian men. And yet, standing here as I do today in this small sacred edifice dedicated to Mary-without-Stain. . . ."

The Dean drew closer to the hurt we feared. In a community as intimate as ours there was little secrecy.

I glanced upwards at the stained glass window over the altar. Wearing a cloak of blue, Mary was irrevocably fixed in the middle lancet. In the Epistle lancet sat God the Father, old and bearded, benign and smiling. He was wearing a three-tiered crown. His smile rendered all man's malfeasance puny. Over Mary's crowned head a choir of angels poured forth vials of grace. The Saviour was in the Gospel lancet: He was dressed in a robe of scarlet. The poplar cross was set on His shoulder. He also was crowned, but not with gold.

"The knouts and whips of the courtyard! The spines of the mock crown! The nails moving urgently between the sinews! The prone Christ! All the sacred agony of the Divine Redeemer suffered because of sins such as the adultery and fornication of mankind. Original justice lost and the body its own betrayer!"

A pause. Then: "The very neck of hell is choked by the adulterous and unchaste! The Gospel states clearly that fornicators shall not enter the Kingdom of Heaven!"

Far up in a cinquefoil over the middle lancet, God the Holy Ghost was depicted as a descending dove. In the evening time, when the pews were brown and warm and quiet, and the sun deep in the west, these window pictures would reach to full glory in the sunlight streaming down through red and yellow and gold, through tiara and translucent cross, through scrolls and quotations on the scrolls.

The Dean now spoke with cold deliberation: "There is a girl among you who has brought her shame home from the city. She shuns the eyes of her neighbours. Her very presence constitutes a scandal to every person here and especially to the young and the adolescent. I ask the young men to run like a redshanks from virtue spoiled. I ask them to avoid the smear of unchastity as if it were the plague of plagues." The Dean paused to sneer. " Aye ! This girl is here in Cloone ! Cloone of the traditions ! The principality that refused progress, and welcomed fornication ! "

Finn Dillon had turned a deadly white : the agony of Shoon returning spoiled from the city was surely agony enough. He was not accepting the chastisement as the old had been trained to accept it. By the manner of their acceptance, the old were implying : " Shoon Lawlee has sinned and shall be punished ! "; the tenseness of the young could be construed as saying : " Shoon Lawlee has sinned and shall be forgiven."

The morning sunlight crept in through the windows of the organ loft. The altar vases were heavy with the grandeur of young summer.

I recalled Lawlee's door closed behind the half-door. Shoon was hidden in the inner room.

Finn pleading : " This makes no matter, Shoon." Shoon saying, with head averted, " Never will it be forgotten for me nor for my people. In an instant of madness I trusted him. He means less than nothing to me now. I'm cursin' the day I left Cloone."

The Dean poured on : " Though she may skulk in secret, yet she shall be brow-branded now and on the Day of General Judgment. Her shame shall be trumpeted out. . . . "

Father, Son and Holy Ghost—God. Omnipotence, omniscience, omnipresence. (The Father and the Son love each other from all eternity and from this mutual love the Holy Ghost proceeds through the will.) Agility, subtility, brightness : these the attributes of the glorified body. The high dove was wingèd as the mind is wingèd. Dove, dove scything a bright circular mile of sky out of the clear light of evening. Paraclete : response ever to the mind's hunger.

Shoon saying : " I'm branded till I die. Between you and me there can be nothing. Cloone and the countryside around it is filled with girls vyin' with one another to catch the eye of the Prince of Cloone." Shoon then smiling her wan smile. Finn saying : " I'll be as fond of the child as if it were my own. I'll swear it on the crucifix if you doubt my word. It's you I want ! You I danced for ! "

Again, the Dean : " Ireland, they say—the world's last refuge of maidenly modesty ! Ireland, they vaunt—where the women are pure and the men respect that purity ! How little do these vaunters know of the foulness that has its existence within our borders ! How little do they dream that we, too, have been taken with the international craze for lust and now possess the morals of four-footed animals ! "

The cat's-tongue of an elm-leaf began to rub against the diamond-shaped panes of a window. Summer was here and Shoon's body was no longer slender. Her face was drawn and caricatured and the prodigal tumble of her hair had lost its lustre. And, lo ! even as I looked, the window over the altar took on a small dole of light. Then came wonder ! Then came colour ! Then came glory !

Shoon saying : " I didn't know a good man when I saw him." Finn coming a step closer : " I'm goin' to keep askin' you ! " Shoon saying sharply : " Quit cross-hackling me ; you're only making bad worse ! " Finn saying : " A damn fooleen you are ! It'll be a short wonder." Shoon saying : " Go 'way from me, Finn Dillon. I can't bear it when you speak to me like this ! " and then adding, in a broken voice, " Tell me again that you were fond of me and that will be a brooch on my soiled blouse. At the Patteran, we were happy—I kept looking out to sea. At the American Wake I had a smile and a wayward wish for every countryboy but I had nothing at all for the Prince of Cloone. It's all over, I tell you ! I'm a limed bird ! The Cloonies will forgive me only against the outside criticisin' world. Here amongst themselves they'll shred me, fearin' I'll prove a pattern for their daughters to follow. I don't fault them—it's their way of life. I've got my eyesight and I've paid dearly for it. Little Angel is an old friend of my mother's : ' Tell her go 'way before the Dean slashes her from the altar!'—that was a friend's message. Let the Dean roast me! The more roastin' he'll give me, the better I'll like it: it may give another girl like myself pause to consider. What tempted me to come home? Churnin' me, you are, Finn, with your presence alone. I wish I had gone to you with clean hands. My youth is to one side. Whenever a girl falls, the old will nod their heads and say: 'Another slyboots, the likes of Shoon Lawlee!' Go 'way, Finn! You're cuttin' the heart clean out o' me as it is. I've dressed a hard bed for myself. Put me out of your head for ever. Go 'way before all my bravery is spent."

No part of the small chapel was now free from the resonance of the Dean's denunciation.

"Mark well what I have to say! If I find an opportunity, I shall make such an example of this metropolitan trollop as shall resound through Cloone for all the span of its bragged-of forever!"

I marked how Finn had wholly stiffened. Dom Foy was pressing his shoulder close against him, lest our Prince should stand up and, shouting denials, destroy himself utterly. Father, Son and Holy Ghost were taking the additional light. The blue of Mary's cloak was deepening.

On the Gospel side the women made a powerful piece of statuary. On the Epistle side the men were dressed in navy-blue serge suits and at the throat of each white shirt a brass collar-stud glistened. The heavy black boots remained unshuffled. The representation of the Paraclete was still prisoned in the pretty cinquefoil. I watched the mother of Shoon: the still set of her shawl indicated suffering. The desire of her immediate neighbours to do nothing, nothing, was proving a positive action. The women bowed down and down under the lash they half-loved. Outside the greenish glass the single elm-leaf lolled out of the red mouth of summer. Through the windows of the Gospel aisle the sunlight came impish and frolicsome.

The Dean crossed himself, then donned the maniple and

chausible. He spread his talons wide over the red-covered Missal on the altar.

The people sighed. As they rattled their rosary beads the tension broke. The women's heads descended in utter abasement.

II

The step of Cloone had grown heavy. The young men became morose. A townie glancing at one of us too idly by half could cause us to stand and stare in such a manner as not infrequently provoked a quarrel. The old seemed inexplicably to have made a small bound forward into time. Young and old among us seemed to have lost a single inch of stature. Shoon Lawlee was destroyed. Finn Dillon was wounded. When it was all over, the girl would go away : she could never again return. In years to come there would be a furtive enquiry from an odd corner of the world—nothing beside. Brink-o'-the-Grave's fingers had lost their certainty : nothing was surer than that Shoon would be reduced to the ignominy of the County Home. The new Dean was harsh : perhaps it was the harshness of a conscientious man. He would scarcely go to the extremity of calling Shoon by name from the altar. The old Dean understood us better : he would gloss over the weaker points of our nature and comment in a kindly manner on our virtues.

Early one morning John Brophy took her away. Her time was near. On his return that evening John gave out little information. On two subsequent occasions I saw Shoon's mother beckoning to him from the gloom over the half-door. The first time she did so, John did not pretend to see her ; on the second occasion he went quickly to Lawlee's door and, having glanced up and down Cloone, said, half-sternly : "You owe me nothin', ma'am. For God's sake don't be drawin' all Cloone down on top of us." Shoon's mother stammered her thanks and slowly closed the door.

And then the night came when a dark intelligence filtered through Cloone. Its breath was like the unseasonable wind of winter. The news broke the hearers wholly. Everywhere about us there was an enormous listlessness in the presence of tragedy. The blow was strong and utter. " Shoon Lawlee has died in childbirth. The slenderness of her body has proved her undoing. Dead, too, is her newly-born infant."

Hearing the bitter word, an old man crossed himself and said : " May Jesus help every mother tonight ! "

A mother shook her head, and said : " Now it is we're suppin' sorrow with a long spoon ! "

Another woman said : " The limed bird ! The meshed salmon ! The mangled leveret ! " This woman was old, and it was common knowledge that she was in her dotage.

All three repeated softly, as if from reverie : " God rest her, she had a lovely name ! " Then they looked to the east where they expected to find the sky at its brightest.

The stars were in the zenith. The 'crake was in the fields. The houses crouched closer to the ground. For once Death lacked its traditional exaltation.

The old men stayed up late that night. They remained seated on the settles and were looking out over the half-doors. An odd greyfellow stood resting his forearms on the ledge of his half-door. The young men were taken with a singular quietness : the young women seemed afraid to raise their eyes. People moved dismally from one to another, verifying that which needed little verification. The hospitable friendly laughing world had suddenly grown sinister beyond recounting. Below in the darkness the river dragged by over its green stones. Our bowels had turned stone cold.

Later I went up to Finn Dillon's. In an undertone his mother told me that he had gone up the hill road. I followed him. I found him standing at a gateway near the crest of the hill. On the roadside a small stream flowed over water-worn flags. Finn was smoking a cigarette and looking to the north.

" Hallo, Finn ! "

" Hallo, Ches ! "

" The nature of frost there tonight," I said.

" Aye," he agreed, " the nature of frost."

Below us the turf-smoke lingered over Cloone. Here and there the light of the as-yet concealed moon touched the thatch and invested it with mystery. I stood beside Finn. We did not speak to one another. After a while he abruptly threw away his cigarette. We then walked up the hill-road together. This was the road along which, in a glad band, we had danced our way to Littero. As we walked upwards the world became edged with a stronger gold. At last we came upon the moon where she lay in her ambush ; with every subsequent step we assisted her to ride the sky and quench the hard brilliance of the stars. Moonlight of such a quality we had rarely seen before : downstream it filled the river inchlands with the blue powder of its light. It struck the surface of the river at a point three miles upstream and changed a pool to a polished shield. On each side of us in the folds of the hills the cabins hid : the warm glow of their happy lamps riddled us with grief. Winding us, a dog barked sluggishly, as if implying that we were objects unworthy of his anger. Higher and higher we climbed, walking step after sombre step. And all the while sorrow like a dark cat padded behind us, measuring his pace to our pace, stopping when we stopped and resuming his padding when again we climbed into the higher ground.

At dusk the following evening, Shoon's body was brought home. She and her child were together in the one cheap yellow box. Bringing the body through the streets of the town was the part that irked us sorest. Yoked to Brophy's hearse were a pair of borrowed horses that had been out of commission for many a day. With us it was a custom for a relative to ride with the driver on the seat of the hearse ; since there were no near male relatives of Shoon's and the remote connections showed reluctance in fulfilling their obligations, Finn Dillon it was who sat with John Brophy. Brophy's side-car came behind, driven by John's father, with Shoon's father and her mother and sister and Jack the Hibe upon it. Bovenizer's tub-trap and Folan's gig followed. Then came various neighbours in their outlandish vehicles. The bog-carts were there but they had not gone far to meet the funeral. Shoon's mother would not have attended the funeral if this were her first child to die, but since she had already buried two sons custom decreed that she was at liberty to be present.

A bunch of us men waited at the crossroads which was about a mile and a half beyond the town. Some of the men had old bicycles, the gear-wheels of which clicked and missed rustily. I shall not readily forget what a chaos of emotions took me at the first sight of the coffin ; as it drew near the men raised their caps and crossed themselves. Then in a posse they closed in behind the hearse. This was the first gesture of shielding. John Brophy slowed down to accommodate the walking mourners. The father of Shoon showed hurt gratitude in his eyes. Shoon's mother buried her face deeper in her shawl.

All along the road leading into the town we met Cloonie after Cloonie straggling out from gateways and cottage doors to join us. As yet the funeral was composed almost entirely of men. At the town bounds the women joined us, the married and the old enveloped in their close-fitting green-and-black shawls and the girls dressed in dark coats with their heads covered. There were perhaps a hundred of them together: standing where the pavements began, they fashioned a black knot of despair. As the hearse approached them, white hand after white hand emerged from the dark garments and the sign of the cross was made repeatedly.

The funeral stopped for an instant as Shoon's mother descended from the vehicle ; straightaway the women closed in around her and caused her to be lost among them. This they did so that not a tittle of her sorrow would emerge to the inhospitable world. We then entered the town proper.

It was between lights in the main street. We dreaded the

lamplight that sprawled sideways out of the shop windows so we asked God to quench it until we had gone by. The peculiar silence that accompanied us was broken by the rooly-booly of the hobnailed boots, the creak of harness and the clop of hooves. In this fashion we passed through the streets of the town.

It was with something approaching a sigh of relief that we neared our thatched principality and saw the single shutter of mourning on the windows of the smaller shops adjoining Cloone. Eventually we halted outside the gates of Mary-without-Stain.

The men then gathered around the end of the hearse and began to look sharply at one another as if to ascertain what four would shoulder the coffin into the deadhouse. John Brophy opened the glass door of the hearse and pulled strongly on the coffin. It squeaked as it moved forward over the polished runners. We then began to speak to one another in ordinary tones. Roughly we said: "Pull!" "There!" "Rise your end of it!" "You, Mick, you!" "Another bit, John!" "Let it come, man!" This handling of the coffin with rude gentleness was part of our male conspiracy: we hoped that the solemn game of fuss would render events natural, would beat them into a shape that we had knowledge of, and would ease the heartbreak of the parents. In fine, more than anything else in the world, we hoped to make the funeral normal.

By this time it was wholly darksome, and the stars were out.

As the coffin moved under our hands, the women as a unit cringed and were recurrently hurt. Those among them whose childbearing days were over, again experienced the sharp daggers of their lyings-in; the maidens received a foretaste of the terrors and joys their bodies harboured, and the adult barren caught a glimpse of glory through the open gateway of heaven. With every lurch of the coffin I could sense the women's bodies weaken as to water. It was strange that I could not find it in my heart to pity them: to me it seemed good that they should be thus wounded. It was an end of their creation.

We shrugged the coffin on to our shoulders; Finn Dillon and Shoon's father were in front; Jack the Hibe and myself were behind. We turned to face the gateway. The mourners made a lane through which we could pass.

While we were engaged in taking the coffin out of the hearse, I had noticed out of an eye-corner that half the chapel gate was open. Little Angel was standing inside the open half: I had presumed that he was making ready to throw open the other half when the coffin approached, and that, as was his custom, he would then precede us as we made our way by the side of the chapel to the deadhouse. From under the back of his black hat his hair protruded in grey lavish curlings. But even as we headed for the gate, and while the ejaculations and prayers of the womenfolk beat softly upon us like hammers of black velvet, the open half of the gate was slowly closed in our faces. I heard a padlock clack. For a moment or two we failed to understand what was happening: I was of the sudden opinion that Little Angel had gone blind and deaf with age and had failed to notice our approach.

The iron gate of Mary-without-Stain was old and heavy—Finn Dillon's grandfather had fashioned it—and here and there the stout ironwork was beaten into broad pieces of metal representing ornamental foliage. Behind one of these iron leaves we now spied the face of Little Angel. Below the face was the soiled white of his stiff old-fashioned shirt front. At first his lips were not moving—he was peering out merely. When he appreciated that we had spied out his hiding-place he began to mutter; this buttressed my first impression that the old man was ravelling in mind. He then removed his hat and made peculiar gestures; we suddenly realised that he was pleading with us to forgive him. "Let ye not blame me, neighbours," he said. "It's a sore turn in the world that an old commodity like myself should slam the gates of Mary-without-Stain in the face of a little angel. But, neighbours, school-friends and old comrades that I've always respected highly, I'm only doin' what I was ordered to do. May God forgive me if it's wrongful orders I'm obeyin'. But obedience is reckoned a prime virtue. Let ye get the Dean to countermand his orders an' I'll gladly read the Litanies over the bodies ye have on yeer shoulders."

Galileo, who, up to this, had been standing aloof at Bovenizer's corner, now pushed his way forward in front of the coffin. His waxed, soiled hands clutched the chapel gate and began to tighten on the red iron. Slowly he began to rock the gate. "What're you pratin' about, you craw-thumpin' get ?" he exclaimed. "Open the gate an' let the corpses pass in !" Little Angel was taller than Galileo : his white face was withdrawn a little lest the rocking gate should wound him.

The old sacristan ignored Galileo : he continued to address us in his sing-song voice. Each word was cut apart from its fellow and given equal strength. "The beauty of my life it would be to open the gate," he said. "But, as a man sanctioned to handle the chalice, I'll obey the Dean. That's what I'll do till my clay is recognised as clay."

Galileo was mouthing incoherencies. He continued to rock on the gate with a tight-mannered fury. The gate was swaying on its old sockets. Of a thought, Galileo stopped and raised himself on tiptoe. He gathered the full of his mouth of spittle and prepared to cast it into Little Angel's face. The clerk of the chapel saw what was coming, yet he did not flinch. At the last moment, Finn Dillon, who was still under the coffin, caught the old cobbler by the shoulder and thrust him back.

Little Angel seemed to be demanding punishment. "Let you not stop him, Finn Dillon," he said. "If he wants to spit on me, let him spit on me. Spit is a blessed thing and is used in Baptism. If he casts it full in my face I give him my bond that I won't raise my cuff to clean it off."

Turning to the crowd, Little Angel said : "Look, neighbours, my face is here !"

Thus offered love in exchange for rage, Galileo was disconcerted. For us there was little profit standing in front of a locked gate with a resolute old man holding the key, so we fell back on to the roadway. We eased the coffin down to our dropped hands and finally rested it on our toecaps. We were reluctant to lower the coffin to the pavement: we had never before seen a coffin on the ground, except, perhaps, at the graveside. There followed a span of irresolution.

From behind the women Shoon's mother raised her voice in small enquiry: her neighbours made noises of appeasement and told her it was a mistake. Shoon's father, a man of quiet nature, was stunned in the face of this development. After a moment, Finn signalled to some of the others to relieve the toecaps of all three of us, except those of Denis Lawlee. Young Font, Jody Shea and Dom Foy then stepped forward and took our places. Finn held quiet counsel with Jack the Hibe and myself. John Brophy left his hearse-horses under the control of Badger Breen and joined us in our argument. He was a man prone to sudden angers, but the fact that he had gone to the County Home and more or less taken charge of the funeral hitherto made it difficult for us to deny him the right to have a say in our decisions. Meanwhile Galileo had gathered a crowd of hotheads about him. I heard him say: "To hell with tomfoolery; break the gate off the hinges!" The men around him poured forward; Finn had to leave us to control them. "We're goin' to the Dean," he said quietly. "Put the coffin back in the hearse."

Finn, Jack the Hibe and myself went off to see the Dean. John Brophy would insist on coming. We set a fast pace into the town in the dim hope that his fatness would prevent him from keeping up with us. Our ruse was unsuccessful, for anger had infused agility into his feet. We passed through Bank Place, traversed Friary Street and went out into Westgate Street. We reached the stepped and flagged passageway of Church Acre, at the end of which the Deanery stood. This was the part of the town which was oldest: the buildings were made of cut stone. Beyond the Parish Church we could see the white curved doorways of the doctors' houses.

As we passed a small shop at the entrance to Church Acre, we caught a glimpse of Father Mallon leaning on the counter. Under the white moon of an old-fashioned hanging oil-lamp he was playing chess with the old lady who owned the shop. The counter was made of sheets of red-and-white embossed enamelled advertisements. In his day Father Mallon had been a grand hurler and had played with Farranmacoo ; many a time Finn and I had stood shoulder to shoulder with him and slung sturdily on the ball with our ash hurleys.

We hurried past the door for we were anxious not to involve him in the embroilment. But, as if he had been waiting for our footsteps, he hastened to the doorway and called after us. Finn returned and held quiet conversation with the young curate : when again he had rejoined us he gave us no clue as to what had passed between them.

We went up the stone steps of the Deanery. Finn tugged on the bell-handle which was recessed in a niche of limestone at the side of the doorway.

To the old housekeeper, Finn said : " We wish to see the Dean."

" Whom shall I say ? " the housekeeper asked, in a faded voice.

" Men from Cloone," Finn replied.

A spurt of interest appeared on the woman's face. She knocked on the door of a nearby room and, hearing a harsh monosyllable, turned the white knob and entered. We set our heavy boots firmly on the polished parquetry. Over us, the red hall-light was deepset in a holder of wrought iron. A great clock chimed the quarter-hour. The housekeeper held the room door open, so that we could enter.

I confess that I would not have been surprised to see a skull on the black marble mantelpiece. Instead, I saw there the Dean's biretta placed beneath an oil painting of Christ being taken down from the cross. The tassel on the biretta was brilliant. A little to the right of the oil painting was a Latin legend, cut deep from a slab of oak ; I had sufficient of Little Angel's Latin left to know that, translated, it read : " Accursèd be he who fraudulently performs the business of the Lord ! "

The great leathern chair, on which the Dean had been seated prior to our entry, was studded at the seams with closely-set brass-headed nails. Standing erect, the Dean was even taller than I had supposed : ordinarily an impression of hunching about the upper chest robbed him of some of his height. On his cheekbones light red veins were crazy and capricious. His grey hair was unkempt. His fingers were grotesquely long, knobby and powerful. He had already brought his heavy eyebrows closely down over his pooled eyes. He billowed out the sides of his soutane by thrusting his hands fully into his pockets. I noticed that his boot-soles were unusually strong. John Brophy and Hibe, who were given to the wearing of caps, had removed them on our entry and were now slowly twirling them in their hands.

" Well ? " the Dean said. We read on his face that he was already aware of the nature of our errand.

So authoritative was his voice in its own natural surroundings that for a moment or two we were struck dumb. It was scarcely a dumbness of awe, but rather that born of an overwhelming curiosity. The way he stood, the resonance of his voice, the veins on his cheekbones, the power inherent in his hooked nose, together with the flesh of the descending Christus and even the uncompromising slogan cut from oak—all these things necessitated on our part such a measure of mental adjustment as forced us into a stunned silence. The Dean was thus afforded the advantage from the very outset.

" Conspirators usually have a ringleader," he said harshly, the while he beat us down with his angry eyes.

Finn Dillon spoke : " We are not conspirators, Dean," he said quietly. " We wish to take a corpse into the deadhouse of Cloone, and the clerk of the chapel tells us that your instructions are that the gates be locked against us."

" Do you question those instructions ? "

" With every respect due to you, Dean, we do ! "

With dangerous calm : " On what grounds ? "

" On the grounds that the girl died after receiving the Last Sacraments of the Church. We contend that her body cannot be denied admission."

" What is your name ? "

" Finnbarr Dillon, Dean."

" From Cloone ? "

" Yes, Dean."

The Dean made a hoarse noise in his throat that remotely resembled a sarcastic laugh. " Prince ? Chieftain ? Ringleader ? The distinction is a fine one."

Finn remained silent.

The Dean went on : " Have you the temerity to come here from your anachronistic clump of thatched cottages and offer me instruction in what I conceive to be my duty ? Are you attempting to define and clarify my duties as Pastor of this parish ? Perhaps I have, as guest, an authority on theology ? "

" I know little of theology, Dean. What knowledge of Christian Doctrine I possess I received from my mother, from the schoolmaster, from stray sermons, from the parish clerk, as well as from the words of the penny catechism which I learned by rote."

" This penny catechism of yours—does it make any mention of the respect due to one of God's ministers ? "

" In a passing manner, yes, Dean. But to me it seemed of small importance when compared with other great truths it contained."

The Dean was momentarily taken aback : " I do not like being insulted under my own roof," he said. " By your words you stand convicted of crossing me in a matter wholly within my province—a question of procedure touching on public morality."

" You misinterpret me, Dean. I did not come here to allow words to jockey me into provocation. Above all, I did not come here to anger you into saying something that in your exalted position you would have difficulty in subsequently withdrawing. Perhaps it would be closer to the truth to say that I came here to plead with you to revise what possibly was a hasty judgment on your part. This I now do."

"I find you an extremely presumptuous young man. I rarely make a hasty decision. You heard me say from the altar at Cloone that I would make an example of the next moral delinquent, male or female?"

"I heard you, Dean."

"There is nothing more to be said. This . . . deputation of yours is now at an end."

John Brophy thrust forward. His fat face was crowded with blood. "Look here, Dean . . ." he began, roughly. Finn tried to pacify him.

"Let the fellow speak," the Dean said sharply. "Is he a doll you have brought along for your jollification?"

"I'm sorry, Dean," Finn said. He fell back a step.

John Brophy said harshly: "What I'm sayin', Dean, is this. We're Catholics an' our people before us were Catholics away back to the dawn of history. It was never known yet that we opposed ourselves to a priest o' God!"

John's anger mounted at the sound of his own voice echoing in the high room. He went on: "But I'm puttin' no tooth under it when I say that if you don't allow Shoon Lawlee's body into the deadhouse, by the Livin' God above us both. . . ."

Finn Dillon thrust John Brophy aside. The Dean's mouth curled in triumph. "Have we descended to menaces?" he asked Finn Dillon. "Have matters come to such a pass in Ireland that a priest is threatened for doing his duty?"

"He has only said what you wished him to say, Dean," Finn Dillon said. "You deliberately willed him into the making of that statement so that afterwards we could be blackmailed on the head of it. You knew well that this man, by his training, is not skilled in verbal fencing. Your victory is a poor one."

For the first time the Dean seemed to be finding difficulty in controlling himself. " Effrontery can scarcely go further," he said in a raised tone. " I have told you of my decision. The matter is at an end."

Replying, Finn kept his voice low: " The matter is not at an end, Dean," he said.

" Are you offering me a further dole of threatening language?"

" I am not, Dean," Finn replied. He paused to rally and to master his emotion. " I will tell you how it is that the matter is but beginning. You are an old man, Dean. Your scholarship is an ornament to our church and people. Your piety, industry and zeal are beyond question. I grow bolder, Dean. It has been said of you that if you had been more conservative in your outlook you would have long since been elevated to the mitre. But I tell you, Dean, that all your virtues are in danger of being cancelled and in years to come at the mention of your name the more bitter-minded shall spit upon the hearthstones and drawing their shoe-soles across it, shall say: 'He was harsh to a girl who fell!' I go further, Dean, and tell you clearly that you are sinning against the virtue of charity which is at the very core of our belief. For this statement you may punish me. You may curl the long lash of the pulpit across my back. I cannot beat you, but you can beat yourself. It comes hard upon me to say this, who have been reared in the tradition that the priest is always right. Late though it now is, I implore you to alter your decision."

Finn paused for a moment: the Dean continued to glare angrily as if unable to trust himself to speech.

Accurately reading the Dean's face, Finn continued: his voice was now charged only with regret. " Now begins the real tragedy," he said. " If our manner of honouring our dead may appear to you to be over-dramatic or cause you personal pain, I contend that eventually good may come of it, since rumour of the story may dissuade persons in high places from abusing the tremendous powers with which they are vested. The argument of deterrent that you have used to exclude this girl's body from the chapel, we now in our turn shall use against you. We have no alternative. Custom demands that we rest our dead overnight in our own deadhouse. It is already dark, and tradition is opposed to a furtive burial in the darkness. These things you already know. True, we have the bitter alternative of taking the girl's body out of the coffin and waking it tonight under her own roof. I feel, however, that the sight of the dead child beside the dead mother would rouse such feelings amongst us as would prove unbearable. For this, I would not accept responsibility." Finn's voice faltered. "We bid you good night, Dean. If you consider that, in any manner, we have been disrespectful, I offer my you humble apologies. You are hardly the man to favour fawners." Finn turned to John Brophy: "Apologise to the Dean, John!" he said shortly.

After a moment or two, John Brophy said: "I apologise."

The Dean remained silent. His face was adamant.

The old housekeeper let us out. As we went down the stone steps heaviness hung in our stomach pits. Father Mallon was standing in the lighted doorway of the small shop. The very way he stood constituted an anxious enquiry. Finn shook his head dismally as we walked past. Turning at the sound of footsteps, I saw the lone form of the young priest step disconsolately down into Church Acre.

When again we had reached the chapel gate, Finn borrowed a pair of low trestles from Bovenizer's. One of these he set directly in front of the gate: the other he placed at the edge of the pavement. We lifted the coffin out of the hearse and laid it across the trestles—the face of the corpse was turned towards the altar. From Brink-o'-the-Grave we borrowed three blessed candles and three brass candlesticks. The candlesticks had twisted stems and were very old. These we placed on the coffin-lid, one at each shoulder and one at the feet. Stools or forms were brought up, as well as sugawn rope chairs. The stools were placed beside the coffin and parallel to it. Finn then set a lighting match to the wicks of the candles.

Since there was no wind the candle-flames stood up peacefully. Seeing the lighted candles, the people went down on their knees; Little Angel, who had been watching us keenly from behind his iron leaf, took off his hat and led us swiftly into the Creed, hurrying on before us lest anyone should snatch the right from him. The instant the prayers began, Galileo's heavy boots clattered away up the pavement of Cloone.

The reaping hook of Orion was crooked in the sky over us. The handle of the Plough was aimed fairly down into Littero.

While the prayers were being said a cocoanut rosary bead kept clinking against the bars of the chapel gate.

Despite the soothing stream of Avés, our minds were in a ferment. It was the first time in our story that we had turned against a priest. We found ourselves at the mercy of cross-tides of feeling. It was traditional with us that, but for the intervention of a priest, Cloone would have perished on an Easter Sunday morning more than sixty years before. On that occasion the greater portion of the town had been burned down. The priest dressed in his vestments had come off the altar at early Mass in Mary-without-Stain to halt the fire at the mouth of Cloone. Only two thatched cottages had been burned, and these were afterwards replaced by the stone buildings of Murray Folan and Abernethy Bovenizer. Thus it was that we were bewildered utterly. With us, the priest was beyond criticism. Every action of his we placed in its most favourable light. It was as if something beloved and beautiful, that was part of us and we of it, had turned to fury at our touch. It was as if the air or water we trusted had become envenomed. Always our Church, as we knew it, had been fair to our frailties: a man erred, grew contrite and was forgiven. After the forgiveness, no rodent sense of evil remained.

When the prayers were ended most of the people dispersed. Some of the women continued to sit around the coffin. By this time the abnormal was reckoned normal. This was due to the firm leadership of Finn Dillon. We reckoned that the story was not so bad: the coffin was close to the house of God—a few paces one way or the other made small matter. Across the coffin-lid and between the twisted stems of the candlesticks the conversation shuttled on commonplace topics. The women had even begun to take snuff out of old oval-mouthed mustard-tins. With each sneeze they prayed for the dead. As Finn and I walked away, all was tranquil at the chapel gate.

III

Not so in the crowded Rookery, where Galileo voiced his views on behalf of an extreme section. At the other side of the fire, Old Font was not so much arguing with the cobbler as resolving his own difficulties and the difficulties of others.

FONT : A people apart they are ! A Gaelic proverb has it : " Don't be too great nor too distant with the clergy." The chastisement of God's servants should be left to God. I'll not remain silent while they are bein' parsed or spelled. Look ! They have wars in their own hearts. When they are young the wind liftin' a woman's hair can maybe start a rebellion. They alone experience utter loneliness. Sometimes when they are old they receive red buttons—this is a small vanity to keep their hearts true until their Master whistles them home. (*Font whistles*).

GALILEO : (*Laughing*). He'll set the grass at our doors ! He'll put the crows flyin' in an' out through our windows ! Have ye forgotten the old coinage of terror ?

FONT : This agony will pass. When quarrellin' with something beloved the mind of man is water.

GALILEO : Your Dean consorts with the rich ! Does he come colloguin' to the firesides of Cloone ?

A VOICE : Father Mallon does !

FONT : I knew an old soldier whose re-openin' wounds had caused him to vomit three kidney-trays full of blood. The holy oils cooled his soul and soothed his fevered face. (*Pause.*) I think that good.

GALILEO: Leavin' their people to rot! Findin' effort laborious an' condemnation easy!

FONT: Cobblers for argument would involve you in the moon. A cobbler's trade is only half a trade.

GALILEO: If the people are to be lost, it is for the want of shepherds. Look ye! Send them out to where others, the best of them, labour. Place them, say, on the rope bridges of the Cameroons where the very frame o' hell is in the heat. When they have learned their lesson, let them return to Cloone. Then or never ye will have clergy worthy of the people.

FONT: Red hot pokers in brass vases on an August altar. The bright blaze of broom mating with the red vestments. I think that good.

GALILEO: I tell ye that the future is without hope! Where, as here, the bright curate has his legs under the old man's table, it is natural that the years will cast him in the livin' spit of the martinet. Tyranny is contagious. Tyranny political! Tyranny clerical!

FONT: They are always in the focus. Narration has turned small actions of theirs into great events. What would pass as a trifle in you and me would look mountainous in a priest after it had been lighted up by the fire of people's eyes. (*Pause.*) To see a priest with his stole on, in a bedroom on a mornin' at a Station-Mass in a house, the hens in the kitchen coop blinded by a sheet—somehow, I think that good.

GALILEO: "Lay her i' the earth:—and from her fair and unpolluted flesh may violets spring!—I tell thee, churlish priest, a minist'ring angel shall my sister be when thou liest howling!"

FONT: Every triflin' happening we have interpreted in terms of faith. Look ye! We find the faith in the cross on the donkey's back, in the crawl of the chafer and in the morning crow of the cock who cries: "Benedicamus Domino!" The charging of everything with our belief—I think that good!

GALILEO: A black wind blew from Paris. They broke the cross-roads dancin' with their curses an' blackthorns. The boys an' girls scattered to lands where their laughter could peal out unchecked. The clergy applied the test of the monastery to the plain people. Altogether they have made it treasonable to dance.

FONT: Let us seek the foundation. Are they pleadin' with the people to rob an' rut? Are not the Ten Commandments aimed as much at the body as at the soul? Is it not a diamond in the spirit that sends them from this green island to labour in heat and loneliness at the ends of the earth? (*Pause.*) To see a priest walk up the quiet nave of a Convent chapel on Sabbath shoes on an evenin' when the Sanctuary lamp is a coal of fire in the dusk an' the tinkle of nuns' prayers is comin' from behind the grille by the high altar—before God! I think that's good!

GALILEO: My friends, listen! An intelligent man wagered that for three Sundays runnin' he'd go into three different parish churches an' in each case find the priest speakin' about money. You know the Gaelic proverb: "Four priests not avaricious—that's four that cannot be found."

FONT: Friends also, here is the proverb in its entirety: "Four priests not avaricious; four Frenchies not yellow; four cobblers not liars—there's a difficult dozen to find."

GALILEO: This intelligent man won his wager!

FONT: An old priest sittin' in front of a presbytery door on a summer evenin'. Snuff on his lapels. He suitin' the parish, and the parish suitin' him. The lads goin' past with their hurley-sticks on their shoulders. The priest glancin' out over his breviary pettin' an' cluckin', turn an' turn about. That's one thing that's good. A priest hearin' a hell of variegated sins in the box, an' in his age winnin' up to the conscious innocence that lies above all knowledge. That's the second thing that's good. A priest at a weddin'—in the middle of love an' yet appearin' superior to it. I still think that these three things are good.

GALILEO: I will not yield a pawn!

FONT: A new priest, his first Sunday on the altar. He

settin' the key in the Tabernacle lock. The congregation wonderin' whether or not he'll open it at the first go. I confess that I find that trivial happenin' both human an' good.

GALILEO : I still yield no pawn !

FONT : They are an aristocracy thrown up by ourselves for we needed one when our chiefs were banished an' set sail for Spain. They gave us respect for what was fine—for learnin', for Latin an' for culture. Each of them comes to the full blossom of personality in his own parish. Let them say what they like about them, but this at least must be conceded : they took a vow of chastity an' to a man they kept it. This, too, despite the fact that they were kings ! (*Old Font strikes his stick heavily on the hearthstone.*) It is not easy to be royal an' chaste. (*Strikes again.*) They led us against the landlords. They urged on their parish footballers, yellin' at them from horseback. There's a statue erected to one of them in a square of a town in the east, an' neither the green stain on the poor bronze nor the bird-droppin's on the pastor's brow can by a whit reduce the glory of his memory in the mind of man. I find that good !

A VOICE : Our predicament is a sore one !

FONT : An old priest on a sick-call tyin' his horse to the pier of a gate, an' afterwards walkin' home under the stars, clean forgettin' his animal with the glee of beatin' the devil for an immortal soul—I saw that in my time. I think it good.

GALILEO : I reckon it an affliction to be born in the brutal West or in a lost pocket of houses or even in a peninsula. Since time immemorial we have lived in a pocket where magic words have more than quenched us.

FONT : Once when a man was drowned I saw a priest set a blessed candle on a sheaf of straw an' send it floatin'. With my own eyes I saw the sheaf come to rest above the spot where the body of the man was swimmin' between two waters. I tell ye the sheaf was directly over the body ! I think that good.

GALILEO : Always there will be those who stand for the mountainy delusion of pastoral infallibility. The delusion that a congregation is docile because no one heckles from the pews. The delusion that a man is stupid because his hands are lacerated from labour. My friends, I advise ye to address a letter to the Pope of Rome an' explain that one of his servants has erred. It is my belief that *he* won't let it pass! The address should cause ye little inconvenience. The Pope, comma, one line; Rome, full stop, another line.

FONT: It is as if the priest were too large an' awkward for normal life. It is only in crises that he is of supreme value. In an event such as now confronts us we need adjustment only. When the people act together, as often as not they act unjustly. Look ye, neighbours, have patience an' God will send us a shepherd with a vision. One will be sent who will show the world what the world has lost.

GALILEO: The world ye live in is blind! It was a King of France, in time of peace, who said: "After me the deluge!"

FONT: What we strive to say here, the world is also tryin' to say in the larger part. We should proceed sage an' slow. Upcountry where the better land is, the case of priest an' people is better. I now yield a pawn. It may be that a man of known character from among us should stand up an' criticise. First he will be hounded, then he will be honoured. This has ever been the human part. But it is far better that a friend should act in boldness an' in bravery rather than an enemy who would, for his own ends, blow embers to flame. An' still I am netted by the small things that I remember. The tinkle of the water-spoon against the lip of the chalice—in that tinkle is the noise of human nature in the presence of divinity. After my fashion, I find it good.

GALILEO: The Pope, comma; Rome, full stop, written on an envelope. Such a letter would surely reach its destination.

FONT: The Faith is ours! We, the people, held it! The cabins held it, not the mansions. We but reflect an' fashion our priests. When we believe firmly an' staunchly, we throw up a sterlin' clergy. When we falter in our belief, like sinkin' Peter in the lake, our priests also falter an' sink. These men are the sensible manifestations of our faith. They pass : what we, the people, believe, goes on. I tell ye this is true !

GALILEO : Your Bishop an' my Bishop it was who said that hell was not hot enough nor eternity long enough to hold the Fenians. Have ye forgotten that sweet gentle Charles Kickham's corpse was denied entry into a cathedral ? What were we Fenians doin' that we should be damned ? Is it a crime to strike off the fetters of tyranny from the limbs of a people ?

FONT : A notable error it is to confuse the messenger with the message or the container with the contained. (*Loudly.*) I now tell ye what is true, so strain yeer brains to the utmost to grasp it. I tell ye that the body an' blood of Jesus are still the body an' blood of Jesus if circumstances warranted that they should be consecrated by a depraved priest in a rusty vessel. I say this, who am not ignorant of the Borgias ! Whenever our priests were good or bad or middlin' or even utterly weak they were thus an' thus as men. The Creed on their lips did not lose a shred of its validity. Their belief was unaltered because of their short-comin's. If men were more than men, God would strike them down in the full elation of their intellectual arrogance. Neighbours, I know this to be the livin' truth. For me it is the fruit of a lifetime of thought.

GALILEO : Ha ! Ha ! Isn't it our brag that each of our priests walks in the footsteps of Christ ? What did Christ say to the woman taken in adultery ? Answer me, or remain silent for ever.

A VOICE : Lord have mercy on the dead !

ALL : Amen !

FONT : Them that prate haven't darkened the doorway of church, chapel or meetin' for nigh on fifty years. Meat-eaters they are on Friday, like a corn-crake. Selected men they are truly to interpret for us the Gospel of God !

GALILEO : Am I the worse for it ? Did any crusadin' druid tip Galileo with his crozier an' turn him into a puck goat ?

Ha! Ha! I live! Do I not? I walk! Do I not? I laugh! Do I not? Ha-ha-ha!

FONT: He lives! As a crab-apple lives when compared to an apple. He walks! Slowly, as a snail walks, in the darkness of his mind's night. He laughs! The echo of his laughter rouses an echo in no listener.

GALILEO: Ye! Ye! There was a time when ye had wooden chalices an' golden priests: now ye have golden chalices an' wooden priests! A delegate of the Holy Pope it was used those words.

FONT: (*Spits.*) For ever takin' advantage of roused passions for his own base ends. Meanness! Slander! Calumny! (*Stands.*) If I were a younger man an' if he were a younger man, by the God above us both. . . .

Martha Goggin came up out of the room. There was silence then. She took her horn rosary from the dresser where it lay beside the statue of the Infant of Prague. She walked to the hearthstone. She looked at us once with punishment in her eyes. Reaching the hearthstone she raised the small crucifix of the rosary to her lips. She was the only woman there. We realised then who it was had held the faith.

## IV

We kept vigil on the coffin until morning. At about half-past two we persuaded the last pair of women to leave. There then remained only five men: Finn Dillon, Jody Shea, Jack the Hibe, Young Font and myself. The open air had been eating the lighting candles at too rapid a rate: before the women went, one of them quenched two of the candles; she reckoned that by burning the candles by ones the coffin would not be without light until daybreak. At three o'clock or so Jack the Hibe and Young Font went home. Finn Dillon and I also urged Jody Shea to leave, but he refused to do so. His method of refusal was peculiar: he grew suddenly morose and covered his small buck teeth with his upper lip. His lower jaw tended to get out of hand. He covered his eyes by angrily lowering the visor of his blackened cap and abruptly turned away. Afterwards he crouched on a stool beside the coffin and did not speak another word to us.

A late roysterer hushed his singing and crossed himself on seeing what stood on the trestles at the chapel gate. A pair of townies made as if to keep vigil with us : these had the reputation of never going to bed at night. We offered them scant encouragement, so after a while they left us to ourselves.

It was cold at the chapel gate, so that Finn and I took to making short excursions into Cloone. We picked our steps carefully in mid-road : the last thing we wished to do was to rouse those who were sleeping directly inside the open windows. Also we did not wish to have it rumoured about that we had deserted our posts during the night.

Each time we turned at the end of our march we noticed that the moonlight on the mountings and breastplate of the coffin was weakening. Imperceptibly, from some secret source, the morning light filtered into Cloone. We then saw the dawn in all its phases : day-break, day-dapple, the bright ring of dawn, real morning, and finally, broad utter day. When retracing our steps on the incline on the other side of the Rookery, the coffin seemed disproportioned and fore-shortened from the angle from which we viewed it. The single candle-flame had weakened under the winning sunlight until the glitter of the stick had become more of a flame than the light on the candle itself. The disconsolate form of Jody Shea was still crouched on the stool. Once, too, as we halted on the roadway outside the Rookery, a light shower began to fall through the first of the sunlight. Looking up at the sky I judged that the shower would be of short duration : I then saw that Jody had risen, had removed the lighting candle from the coffin lid and placed it on the ground between his boots. Seating himself, he crouched over the flame in protection. We saw his hunched shoulder-blades meekly accepting the shining needles of the morning rain. Finn and myself fell to wondering what slender bond lay between himself and Shoon Lawlee—an errand, a compliment, a glance, a dance or even a single fugitive smile ?

With the coming of day we solved what had been a long-standing mystery in Cloone : about five o'clock a black-and-grey sheepdog skulked down the road. His white breast was a real mat of blood. He seemed curiously sated and guilty. We noted well the animal's markings for this was the robber that for weeks had been worrying Jack O'Neill's sheep. Looking mournfully at us, Jody Shea's eyes seemed as though they were pleading with us not to betray the dog.

By this time the sky had become suffused with red-pink. The noises were the noises of morning. Long since the owls had ceased their not unmusical snoring—before full daybreak one of them had flown low over the coffin. We had looked up at the sound of its wings and were in time to see the blunt beak and the eyes recessed in cartooned astonishment. Now also had commenced the rusty-gate clankings of Folan's guinea-hens. A gull over the river valley filled the upper air with its complaints. In the adjoining streets of the town the rooks were squawking in raucous point and counterpoint : their clamour bore an absurd resemblance to the noise made by bamboo rods being beaten one against another.

A small old angler emerged from the town : he wore a tweed hat and had one shoulder permanently cocked. He moved with a determined strut. When he had drawn level with the coffin he caught his hat by a button on the crown and lowered it to the flags. He then crossed himself and knelt on the pavement's edge. As he was praying, I had difficulty in holding myself from christening the many flies on his hat.

Before six o'clock Little Angel came out of his cottage and opened the chapel gate. He shook his head dolefully but did not address us directly. The gate he left wide open. Soon it would be Angelus time. Then came a Western woman who had married into Cloone. She was wrapped in her fawn shawl. As she passed by she glanced half-fearfully at the coffin ; she paused and then surreptitiously crossed herself within her shawl. She did not speak to us. We knew that she held fast to her own ways. Even to our day the West continued to be a place of epic faith : at consecration time the women standing in the unfurnished chapels broke ranks and pressed forward to the altars, crying out : " Welcome, O Lord God ! " Though we did not mention it to one another, Finn and I were well aware of the Western woman's secret. This was it : her breasts were heavy for she was nursing a child—always while nursing she received Holy Communion every morning : returning home, without breaking her fast she bared her breast and thrust her nipple into the child's mouth. Western mothers reckoned this a holy trick for feeding an infant with the body and blood of God.

Two of the Hibe brothers who had been appointed to open the grave in the early morning, then came out of their cottage. One carried a spade, the other a shovel. They knocked at the window of the room in which Dom Foy slept. Dom was at the door in a few minutes. He also carried a shovel. All three went up the boreen by the Rookery to where the graveyard was. After a time the men who were to relieve us came along and our vigil was ended.

## V

The adult population of Cloone attended the funeral : the people came either because of respect or because of fierceness. As it neared the noon hour the people gathered at the chapel gate. Of the handful of townspeople who were present, the majority had blood-connections in Cloone : the rest we suspected of having attended to carry back to the town news of how Cloone had fared in its grapple with the Dean. From this minority we kept strictly aloof.

Among those who had blood-connections in Cloone, two were the wives of wealthy merchants. The shawled Cloone women unexpectedly began to pick a queer pride out of these two women : out of their coats, their good gloves, their high-heeled shoes, their expensive handbags and their discreet but elegant hats. I had often heard these two women being shredded by tongues at the firesides of Cloone ; now our old women gushed towards them with an all-compensatory love. This was because the merchants' wives had publicly acknowledged the kinship. Also they were reckoned brave, tacitly to have allied themselves with us in an event of such seriousness. Their gesture would not readily be forgotten.

The noon Angelus bell we accepted in lieu of a dead bell. This was a small but forgivable cleverness on our part. The instant the Angelus bell had ceased ringing, Finn Dillon gave the signal for the funeral to proceed. We raised the coffin to our shoulders and turned into Cloone. We sorely missed the priest wearing his white cypress : with us such a lack had never happened in the memory of living man. Passing Lawlee's there was an instant of tautness which readily resolved itself. At the gable of the Rookery we turned into O'Neill's boreen and faced for the spotted crosses of the graveyard. The rusted gate was open. We saw the hump of yellow clay —turning away from it, we made the traditional circuit of the burial-ground and returned to the open grave. We were moving slowly for we were conscious of the gaps of ceremony which we knew not how to fill. We lowered the coffin to the sun-warmed grass, facing it to the east which was the point of resurrection. The bottom of the grave was powder-dry ; spade-marks were visible on the yellow walls of the narrow underground room. At the foot of the cross at the grave's-head were piled the rusted bones of dead Lawlees. The sun shone upon us.

We stood there : a green-and-black circle of women with a wide band of men's hats around it. We stood there, each man's two hands as long as one another what with idleness and not-knowingness. All we could do was to glower fearfully into the open dry grave. Old Font broke the tension. His face was melancholy and his fingers were trembling. When his hat was removed and his chin was tilted, his head and beard together formed a long oval. He took the bottle of holy water from the hands of a boy and then sprinkled the coffin. We saw the flying drops become illuminated in the sunlight. We watched them coalesce on the fresh varnish of the coffin lid. We heard them strike the breastplate and bounce off as if they were flying grains of shot. Then the old man cast the holy water into the open grave.

"May the Almighty God . . . " Old Font began : then he broke off abruptly.

We stooped to set the ropes on the coffin and lower it to the grave. It was a dismal ceremony : still it was better than nothing.

We realised the full measure of what we had been cheated out of. At the instant of realisation, we heard the urgent whisper : " The Dean ! The Dean ! "

The Dean came slowly onwards. He was picking his steps over the tussocks of the dead. Father Mallon was close behind him. Both wore funeral cypresses. The Dean made no hurry. The bright tassel on his biretta did not seem agitated. He reached the grassy pathway that led directly to the open grave. The crowd made a lane to admit him. He came forward and stood by the coffin at the side of Old Font. Sullen and silent the people stood. The Dean's eyes circled the crowd of women : each woman then closed the ope of her shawl to a small spyhole through which a single eye could peep without being recognised.

The Dean removed his biretta and made as if to hand it to Old Font. Holding the priest's biretta at Cloone funerals had always been Old Font's privilege. The old man made no move to take it : his face was lean, wiry and fanatical. Over his beard his deepset eyes were fully alive. He continued to stare steadfastly at the biretta but did not raise his hand to touch it. For Old Font this was the ultimate bravery.

The Dean lowered the biretta : a second time he raised it, this time with something approaching supplication. He spoke in an undertone to Font : in his tone of voice there was little authority, simply a signal as between old and old. Old Font raised his hand and accepted the biretta. A woman choked back a sob. Father Mallon's face seemed to have been touched by torchlight. The Dean opened his breviary.

Wind-taken and wind-restored, the Latin that we loved poured over us. Little Angel had equipped us to translate it as it ran.

" *Out of the depths I have cried to thee, O Lord ; Lord hear my voice.*

*Let thy ears be attentive to the voice of my supplication.*"

The Latin was taken from the priests' mouths and flung here and there amid the living hum of summer. The words were late seed from a sower's hand. We were the fertile land hungry for the seed. The Latin was lost and found among us in a manner we found singularly bracing. Through the losing and the finding, the drowsy world exulted in the full smell of life that came up from the rich grasses.

" *If thou, O Lord, wilt mark iniquities ; Lord who shall stand it ?*

*For with thee there is merciful forgiveness ; and by reason of thy law I have waited for thee, O Lord.*"

The impish breeze played hide-and-seek with the sonorous psalm. Our spirits tugged at their mortal moorings and then sprang up into the upper sunlight. Over us poured the throated Latin that was replete with solace. At first Old Font's mouth was sown up with resistance : then despite himself his lips began to move to the words that he found unbearably pleasurable. Up to the blinding place ! Up to where at last beauty shall be fleshed and palpable !

" *Give her, O Lord, eternal rest,*

*And let thy light shine upon her for ever.*"

Up to where there is no such thing as mediocrity ! To where each man's blood snaps the bonds of his body and mingles with the blood of his neighbours to form one shining universal tide. Up ! Beyond the kingdom of boys' kites, beyond the thrones of skylarks ; up to where larksong lives after the larks have gone. Up, to where duffer and sage, loser and winner, hunchback and beautybody are levelled and rocked and cradled in a manner wholly beyond the utterance of man.

Old Font's lips had momentarily recaptured the good red of youth. The tassel on the biretta showed the brilliance that we dearly loved.

The Dean read the " *Let us pray* ! " When the prayer had ended Father Mallon said " *Amen !* " The Dean closed his breviary. There was a small pause. As the Dean took his biretta and turned to depart, Shoon's mother broke the mourning ring and began to cry out in his direction. The instant her voice was heard the world seemed to balance on a slowing wheel of stillness. Again the woman's voice came—this time in shreds of sound. We could not know with certainty what she was saying : from the rise and fall of her voice it was clear that she was asking the Dean if that were all. The Dean turned—he had not yet donned his biretta. The woman came forward a second step. Her husband irresolutely came too, and stood in loyalty by her side. Through the broken sounds, we heard the woman's voice say : " Dean, darlin', she fell an' she rose ! "

We saw the woman's face red as from weeping in the full ope of her shawl.

(O almond-eyed one ! O small poised head ! O dear dead slender person !)

The tassel went down to be quenched by the Dean's side ; after a few moments he spoke. First he addressed the mother, then all of us.

" By nature I find it difficult to say what I am going to say. The first of the deadly vices is pride." The Dean paused, then continued : " I am an old man. If during my life I have done anything of merit in the service of my God, I now place it on the pan to outweigh this my sin." His voice had climbed to where it was sturdy and steadfast. " It lies between my Master and me. Behind the first sin there is the second—

the scandal I have offered to the faith of the people of Cloone. Arrogance and stubbornness and tyranny I mistook for tenacity of purpose. More than anything I have done in my life I regret these two sins. When the moment comes for me to be judged, I pray that the soul of the girl I have wronged will intercede for me before the throne of God ! "

The voice finished arrogant and strong. That, we thought, was as it should be. The Dean donned his biretta. The tassel was brave and high against the light blue summer sky.

The mother of Shoon fell on her knees at the Dean's feet. She fondled his long red hand that resembled a claw ; eventually she placed the knuckles fully home in her open mouth. When at last the hand had relented, she placed it for a moment against her cheek. Then she looked up. " It's a thing of nothin', Dean ! " she said. Then she rose quietly. The Dean went away. There was no more drama. Abruptly we set about the business of burial.

All in all, it was a happy funeral.

The following Sunday the Dean again read Mass in Mary-without-Stain. In our frailty we kept watching out for the moment when he would turn and ask the congregation to pray for the dead. Before the First Gospel he took up the notice-book and began to read. We hoped to find the flaw of excitement in his voice. In this we were disappointed. It was said of him that, when he was a younger man, he had cloaked the reading of the death notice of his own mother with impersonality. Now, as then, his voice was steady as he read : " Your prayers are requested for the repose of the soul of Shoon Lawlee. May the Almighty God have mercy upon her soul and upon the souls of all the faithful departed."

Through the loud amen came the clatter of hob-nailed boots at the back of the chapel. Onward they came, knocking a prodigious tally-ho from the faded red tiles of the passage. The Dean stopped reading. Fiercely the boots came on until the racket became magnificent. Each person's ears were tuned backwards while his eyes firmly held the Dean's face. The hobnails sounded out the old truculence. The people smiled a peculiar smile—it was a smile of pleasure and pride and wryness. Despite the moment of devotion the men were filled with devilment: they made the cobbler run the full gauntlet of public contrition. Where there was room for him in a pew, the end man made no move to allow Galileo enter. For his part of it, the old rebel was too proud to halt and solicit a seat. Watching him pass, Finn's face was tinged with a quaint sad merriment. Holding his jaw high and taut, Galileo clattered onwards: his eyes were those of an officer who had surrendered and had been allowed to retain his sword. He was compelled to go forward to where the gilt gate divided us from the sanctuary; here, out of pity, the man at the end of the last pew of all offered him room. Galileo jerked a sketchy genuflection at the altar and then proved that he was not afraid to show us his sideface as he sat. When he had been rendered anonymous among the congregation, a breath of finer air entered the chapel: looking up towards the stained-glass window I was taken with the delusion that God the Father was trembling with laughter under His three-tiered crown.

The Dean turned to the altar: we saw his talons ride the Mass-book. He seemed eager to claw down Something into Cloone.

# CHAPTER IX

I

THREE complaining curlews swung away from the little river and flew directly over us as we worked on the edge of the bog. The birds moved over the cocoa-brown turf-banks where the sods were spread glistening in the sun, over the miniature white sea of *ceannabhan*, or bog-cotton, over the first and second footings of turf and over the bog-ricks that had been sundried as dry as snuff. Suddenly, tiring of calling out to us, the curlews started away in a long free flight.

In the cutaway, it was hotter than a pot-oven. Side by side with us the women worked: it was almost an adventure to pass a young woman with the fresh smell of clean sweat on her.

The coloured dresses of the women, the shirts of the men and the splash of a hurling jersey on an oddfellow rivalled the brilliance of the foxgloves, of the poppies and of the bugles that grew in the riverside meadows. Pinpoints of colour were everywhere: in the scarlet aberrations of the dock-leaves and in the vitriolic greens and yellows of the lichen underfoot.

Communal work of this nature—*comhar*-ing we called it—was welcomed as a type of holiday. As well as cutting our own turf we of Cloone also cut turf for those who were too old or too weak or too grandiose to work for themselves. Hands were many and the company was good: the weather was invariably sunny—else we would not be cutting at all! There was a general air of picnic: for the men there were great jars of porter; for the women and children there was tea in the open-air: for men, women and children alike there was home-made bread of all kinds as well as a lavishness of milk and butter. Bottles of cream were kept cool by immersing them in the deep bogholes. Work was desultory : if laughter came it had to be served, in or out of its turn. If a man felt like wandering away to the stream for a swim or to the streamside meadow for a sleep there was no one to reprimand him.

From over the rim of the world came the voice of the cuckoo : as like as two peas it was to the soft noise of the wind blowing across the jowls of a pair of different-sized bottles. Between the light clouds and the blue sky appeared an ope of great height ; now and again a jet crow brought down from the upper air a surpassing glistening on his shoulders ; beside him, his brother the scald-crow attired in a suit of black-and-grey was busy foraging at his utmost endeavour. About ten feet off the ground a fluttering skylark tried to hold to a single point of air.

In the east the first hill and the faint hill behind it and the faint faint hill behind that were all three dwindling gradually into the sunsmoke of distance. By the small river the young meadows were wind-touched ; there, too, a garden of green wheat was picking delight out of the flexibility and resilience of its many blades. In a gap beside the bogland a bush cut when in leaf had reddened. Low under the first grasses the shrine lamps of the clover were lighted. On every side was the prone wonder of June.

The bogland was a whole landscape waiting to be eaten by our fires. God was bountiful. In the memory of living man we of Cloone had taken only a small portion of it. Sometimes we looked on the great ridge of rising ground and wondered how many billions of fires were still concealed in it : their flames would curl on the faces of men and women as yet unborn.

Old Font and Galileo were squatting on sacks of straw on a turf bank. They were smoking clay pipes and talking of obscurities. Galileo appeared to be snarling : a stranger would have sworn that the pair were mortal enemies. From time to time Old Font took a red spotted handkerchief from his coat-tail and mopped his face. His black suit was waterproofed with the grease of many meals. His beard was inclined to whiten under the sunlight. For each of the preceding fifteen summers he had said on the occasion of the turf-cutting: "This is my last year with ye." Long since we had ceased taking notice of his complaints.

I was on the turf-bank piking turf. My mind was busy with thoughts. Soon I would have to decide what to do. My mother's voice was ringing in my ears: "The sight is ebbin' from your father's eyes. For God's sake, take the trade!"

Badger Breen was running here and there, making secret signs to his friends and scowling behind the backs of his enemies. He winked at the children as if to reassure them that he, and he alone, had made the world.

In the bog lay everything that had to do with mystery: lizards, newts, hares, tadpoles, frogs, sorrel, peppercress, moths and butterflies. Clouds of midges hung between us and the dark earth. Life was tufted and dry and sunny and free. When man sweated, the wind and sun dried it. Here it was that man had little need to envy the free beast.

The bridges of the straddles shone: they had been painted a loud farmer's-blue. The carts on the torn road were brilliant in new red oxide. Low in the west the sky was hued with a light cinnamon while clouds the colour of pewter were ranked on the southern horizon.

Soon I would have to decide what to do.

We missed Metal Belly. Missed his active body, his black beard, his solemn and moral injunctions. We missed the powerful press of his boot on the treadle of the slean and his competent outward toss of the oblongs of dung-wet peat. We began to speak of him, wondering where he had vanished to and what madness had got into him. We fell laughingly to cursing the Fair of Cloone that had brought him Trouble-o'-the-World. And us dents in our hard skulls!

The day, how sunny! The young girls were gathering the silky-white heads of the bog-cotton and stuffing them into their pockets. A wild drake flew upwards from the bushes by the river. The brindled bird breasted strongly into the summer sky. Below him lay his mate on her nest. I eased my hold on the satiny cotton-boll I had been punishing in my fingers, fluffed it back to airiness, and set it off floating on the breeze.

The girls' voices twined above us in "*Babaro and Oro, My Thousand Loves.*"

Finn Dillon was quiet. Looking back on it, I see clearly that that was a day of boundary, although I did not know it at the time. New and old, sorrow and joy, were then present, side by side.

In the twelve months since Shoon's death, Finn seemed to have aged. He was quieter by a good deal : he was now barely twenty-six, yet already I could see age on his face. There was little or no gibing when he was present. Always he seemed caught in a remote thoughtfulness. He had fallen away from us in Cloone. Strangers were coming to see him and when he was not off on mysterious errands there hung about him a queer air of conspiracy. The truth of it was that the restlessness of a sundered Ireland had now seeped into Cloone : on all sides the statement was being made that whatever freedom Ireland had gained had been won only by force. Finn was constantly referring small local decisions to me. Whenever he saw Madcap and myself together he was given to strange smiling.

A week previously a quarry hut had been raided some miles north of the town and detonators and gelignite taken. The law had then broken in on Cloone : Finn's house was pulled asunder, yet nothing incriminating was discovered.

When noon came, the sky turned to the colour of pepper. Thunder was away to the south, twenty or thirty miles distant ; we saw the tendrils of a thunder-shower swirl in a far bay. The old people assured us that the weather would not break. In the full southwest where a headland was flung bluntly on the sea a wave recurrently broke to a tolerant bloom and slowly subsided. The fire of dried heather, bogdeal chips and small turf had now been lighted and its smell was added to the heavy smell of the bogland. Soon it would be time for a break in the day's working.

I was relieved of the fork with which I had been slowly spreading turf; long since I had tired of piking but was ashamed to yield. Dominick Foy was on the slean and although he was young he bade fair to become such a sleansman as Metal Belly had been.

## II

As I rested on the cutaway, I saw Madcap take up a new galvanised bucket and set off into the virgin ridge of the bog—what we, with peculiar naïveté, called "the high mountain." "If she looks back," I said to myself, "I shall follow her." As every step took her farther away from me, I despaired of her turning. But I had reckoned without a woman's sense of timing: at the last moment she found the excuse she was waiting for—it was a child's yelp from the *ceannabhan.* Madcap turned suddenly: she was hard set not to glance in the direction from which the cry had come. I saw with a surge of eagerness that she looked first at me, and then at the child. I crinkled my face at her in open freedom and awareness. She laughed—a hearty laugh, then turned sharply away.

I glanced around; watching me, Finn's face had turned studious with interest and affection. On his mouth a wan smile had already appeared. This was the last time I seem to remember his lips breaking into that infrequent smile. His mouth was urging me to go. The happy-sad implication of Shoon hung heavily on the air between us. I rose; Finn glanced around to ensure that I was not observed. I idled up the steps that had been cut in a corner of the turf rampart. When those who were tempted to gibe at me noticed that Finn was on sentry-go, they lidded their smiling eyes and held their silence.

Madcap moved before me on the high ground: it was pleasant for me to see her pretend she was alone, and use small subleties to buttress that pretence. Walking the "high mountain" was like walking on mattresses: it was an exercise that readily told on the buttocks, thighs and calves. Over Madcap's head hung the inevitable lark blinking and singing. I glanced back: the turf-cutters had fallen away into the low ground: I had lost the sound of voices and even of laughter.

I was slow to terminate the girl's gaming: my first whistle mated with a curlew's call; thus it suited Madcap not to hear it. Again I whistled. She turned and waited. The sun set the new bucket mad with silver. I heard a cup rattle in it: I knew it was a white cup with a pink rim. Thenceforward my every step seemed of excitement born. Madcap and I walked past the Blue Hole: we halted for a moment to listen to the waters flowing beneath the blue surface and strained our ears in a vain effort to catch the faint boom of the sea waves beating in Poultorann, a sea cave eight miles away. This boom, through a flaw in the land, could be heard thumping recurrently in the Blue Hole whenever the weather was about to break. The silver bucket swinging between us, we walked up the high brown barren land. Although we were happy, yet we seemed at a pleasant variance.

Farmers drawing gravel had eaten a horseshoe out of the mound of the Knockawn: the opening of this horseshoe faced the north, and, as a consequence, was generally untouched by the sun. Through this gap we went. Out of the dimness a pair of sheep ran bleating. Within, the place was as cool as cool could be. For us the sun was quenched and the entire pit was filled with a welcome brown light. Over us lay the strata of clean brown-black gravel. Our eyelids were grateful for the cold air. The bucket was robbed of its brightness.

On the bushes over the well spider hammocks were spread: scaters walked on the surface of the clean water and cress grew in the stream of the overflow. Crouched by the cool well-side we seemed to be living an old tale.

With the full bucket between us (the cup swam beneath the clear water) we struggled to the top of the hillock. On reaching the sunlight, Madcap halted and drank from the bucket: for me it was a blessing that the vessel hid her face as I then had an opportunity of looking at her body and neck, at her young breasts and good limbs. I read her knowledge of my theft in her eyes when she had finished drinking. I then lifted the bucket to my head. I rested my mouth where hers had been: she accepted the tribute in seeming fairness so that for a moment I thought she was flattered. But there is a woman for you! As I gulped strongly, she tipped the bucket and tilted it fully on me. The water poured down inside my clothes. As my belly slopped as cool as a fish's I was taken by a gust of anger. "You daft strap!" I shouted. The rim of the new bucket had been dented by falling on a grass-concealed outcrop of rock but the cup was unbroken.

I was taken with a desire to maul Madcap and knead her body on the grass. This was a new experience with me. Realisation of its full import sobered me: also I was reluctant to do anything that would mar the goodness of that day, the memory of which, instinct told me, would prove an enduring bond between Madcap and myself, even as a glance or a dance or an errand or a spurt of laughter had forged a bond between Jody Shea and dead Shoon Lawlee. Madcap continued to reel with laughter on the sunny slope. First she grew giddy, then wanton. I realised that only her body was speaking to me: I saw with sudden clarity that this alone would not suffice. My fingers that were itching to break her were ruefully plucking my sodden shirt out from my skin. After a while Madcap ceased laughing: this she did as swiftly as a light is quenched. She grew strangely quiet; I saw the puzzlement of a denied woman being replaced by a tenderness. She grew abruptly chaste. She smiled contritely as if assuring me that she would be forever steadfast. How lovely she was when she smiled.

We sat side by side on the cropped grass watching a pair of cabbage butterflies tangle together as they moved over the hillock. Madcap gathered her skirts against her thighs. We could now remain silent in one another's company and yet feel at ease. Whatever lay between us was ripening. We were closer than ever before. Together we had travelled to the Well of The World's End and had drunk of the Waters of Life from a pitcher of silver. My mouth had rested where hers had been. She had seen and understood the gesture. She regretted that her body had almost flawed the day. The wide acres of sunlit bogland were caught in the grace of her throat.

We avoided looking at the near ground : rather did we look at the far spans of distance. Finn was moving among the moving bushes by the river. He seemed as restless as the willows. I knew that he was stream-fishing with a tiny hook, a red worm and a sally-rod.

In a far field which had once been cutaway-bog we saw two horses with stars on their foreheads. We heard a bull trumpet to his red cows in a paddock across the river. We saw a heron rise from the Blue Hole. Just then we saw the puff of smoke rise from the fowler's gun ; afterwards we heard the sound of the shot. A pair of duck threshed upwards from beside the river : the smaller of the two suddenly fell slantwise into the bushes. The fowler emerged from his place of concealment. Finn stood watching him as he went towards the spot where the wounded duck lay. I descended to the well and refilled the bucket.

As if anxious to husband whatever happiness lay between us, we returned by a slightly longer route. At the base of the hillock a rabbit hopped brokenly into the mud wall of a ruined cabin. The rotten timber in the grass-covered window-ope of the ruin I found strangely evocative : here a man had had the necessities of life : a woman, a cabin, a fire, potatoes, salt and the milk of a goat. Here where triumph was relative to a quiet standard, the acquisition of a blue bowl was a pinnacle of delight and the breaking of a lustre jug grief in all its greatness.

The sprigs of lighting bogdeal were frisking in the fire when we returned to the others. Everybody was impatiently awaiting the water. Finn Dillon had ensured that he would reach the turf banks a few moments before we would : when we came up we found him assiduously distracting the turf-cutters' attention by showing them the three red-tipped trout he had killed. Madcap and I slipped in unobserved. The children were in a ring around Finn Dillon : " Show, Finn ! Show, Finn ! Show ! " they cried. The gillaroo trout had tails and fins that appeared to have been dipped in bright crimson.

Old Font was ill-pleased with Finn Dillon's intrusion : he had been telling the youngsters a story when the distraction robbed him of his audience. Seeing the line the old man's finger was drawing slowly across the sky, Madcap and I knew at once the story he was telling : in his grandfather's time people cutting turf in that spot had seen a ship in full sail move across the heavens. They had watched the vessel until at last it had merged with the air of the far northern sky. Afterwards they had seen in the zenith a town with narrow streets wherein people wearing alien clothes strutted graciously as they took the air.

Trust Finn Dillon to make amends ! He showed Old Font the trout and grudgingly the oldster approved of the gesture. Galileo remained taciturn. Since his reconciliation with the Church the single string of fierceness in his heart seemed broken. Now that he was less eager to bend every event to the vilification of the clergy, we found him a poor source of diversion. Times there were when in our perversity we wished he would revert to the frenzy of his spiritual revolt so that we could continue to drive sparks from his metal.

The frying trout gave out an erratic aroma. The workers passed the porter-jars from mouth to mouth ; the pointers of maize bread and the mugs of milk were issued to the boys and girls while the tea was reserved mainly for the women and older boys. The bog air had made wolves of us. Finn quartered a white pot-oven loaf, sliced the bread and then lavishly buttered the slices. He removed the backbone from a fried trout and placed the fish lengthwise on one of the heavier cuts of bread. This he did also with a second fish. He filled two mugs with tea and put colouring and sugar in them. These, with gestures of ceremony, he brought to Galileo and Old Font.

At first the old pair were inclined to wave him contemptuously aside but when they saw the red tippets on the trout-fins—how brightly they contrasted with the melting butter and the white bread—they smiled the young smile of the old and childishly capitulated. Finn nested the two mugs of tea beside them in the heather; the pair were fully gratified but would not have admitted it for worlds. With their eyes fast on the peeping trout they took off their hats—the men removed their black wideawake hats only when sleeping, eating or praying—and, as on a signal, old fingers fell to picking and toothless jaws to munching.

Now and again they spat the bones from them with loud angry noises. This office they performed with twisted mouths and with unmistakable rancour, thus hoping to curb Finn Dillon lest he should feel an undue elation at their surrender.

We made no hurry over the meal. The day was long: tomorrow was another day.

III

That was a day of adventure. As the meal was ending we saw our first 'plane. When first I heard the sound of its engine I thought that one of boys was playing with a "buzzer," which was a toy saw manipulated with a pair of cords. Then I saw everyone looking at the east. Brave and free the aeroplane came across the heavens; the noise of its engine reached us in an intimidating but thrilling growling which was as yet flawed by breeze and distance. The sun caught the wings of the 'plane and transformed the machine to a high bright silver toy. The approaching din terrified the birds on the mountain: chattering with excitement a flock of crows rose from the ground and were then flattened by fear as if they had been struck by the blade of an enormous fan.

I saw a trout tippet stilled on Old Font's lower lip. Open-mouthed, the old men waited : they felt that something new and terrible had come into their lives. After the initial terror, Old Font stood up erect. He had not yet replaced his hat on his head. To us he was rendered gigantic by the unusual angle from which we saw him. The bright machine was moving to the left of his bearded profile : alternately it trailed through cloud-wisps and soared unfettered in the deeper blue. Standing there, the old fellow made a memorable picture. At first his face showed only astonishment ; as the machine passed directly overhead a waxen terror appeared on his features. As the 'plane roared away, this terror was replaced by a mounting sense of indignation. When the 'plane was out of sight, and the children had ceased their joyous cries of : " I see it yet ! " or " Look ! Look ! There ! " there was a moment of silence. Then we all looked up to Old Font to learn in what terms old age would couch its condemnation of youth, for, since truth is truth, we who were young found the 'plane's passing an event of unbearable delight. We realised that the world had suddenly shrunken. We also thought that joy would instantly be everywhere and that poverty would be no more.

Galileo appeared prodigiously puzzled. For him, this should have been a supreme moment. He had always been the precursor of progress in the abstract : its concrete presence was now proving too much for him. He scarcely knew whether to laugh or cry. After a few moments of quivering indecision his features relapsed into feigned senility. Not so with Old Font ! The instant the 'plane was out of sight, he set to work abusing us.

" Ay ! There's man flyin' ! Flyin' in the face o' God ! What senseless creatures ye are, to have yeer mouths open in astonishment ! I can already see the young an' empty-pated o' ye bubblin' over with full wonder. But—riddle me this—will all this ingenuity make man one ounce the happier ?

How often before have I informed ye of the unalterable fact that happiness exists only in the lovely smoke of the imagination ? Is it blind ye are to glory ? I tell ye that such simple beauty as exists, for example, between man and woman can neither be altered nor improved upon."

He paused. " Ay ! Ye'll maybe see man stakin' out the crags o' the planets for the glorification of his own nation. Ye'll maybe see sovereign wonders come to pass. But can ye not see beyond them, to where I have indicated ? Always the heart o' man will swing to loneliness, because he is fashioned in the image of a God Who of His nature is all loneliness. I now ask the young men of ye again, what I asked them in their childhood ; let them riddle me this : what is God ? "

Although each of us knew the answer the oldster wanted, we remained silent.

Old Font raised his voice : " Is there none o' ye fit to answer me ? I ask ye a second time : what is God ? "

Finn Dillon stepped forward and gave the answer. It was neither the answer from the catechism, nor that from the queer apologetics of Little Angel. It was the answer Old Font himself had given us, and had drummed into our heads when we were children.

Bravely as when a boy, Finn Dillon said : " Sir, God is a lamp of light in a well of divinity."

Open-mouthed the children stood : they were fully attentive to the wisdom of their elders.

Although he had received the answer he sought, Old Font's anger did not abate. He raised his voice. " Aye, that is God ! An' now, can ye answer me this ? What is man ? "

" Hey ! "

We turned. One of the men who had tentatively resumed work had called out to us : we turned and saw him gaping down. Below him, Dominick Foy was holding something he had taken from the boghole. Old Font was minded to continue his preaching, but his congregation had deserted. Dom dragged a fistful of grass from the cutaway and began to clean the object.

We crowded round. Old Font remained aloof but it was clear that his anger had been replaced by curiosity.

Dom Foy was holding a piece of metal shaped like a quarter moon with a boss on each of its points. From boss to boss the object measured about nine inches. From the way his fingers were treating it, we deduced that the object was heavy. We waited in an exciting silence. West in Ahalane, on the banks of the river Breek, turf-cutters had found a silver bell which monks had jettisoned into a boghole centuries before as they were flying from the Danes. Thirty miles to the south in a place called Beenagurteen a silver cross was unearthed. North in Antenon they had found a weighty copper vessel: on it were mysterious markings which no man could decipher. Drinaun in the southeast had had the chagrin of discovering four kegs of butter which was as sound as it had been on the morning of its churning five hundred years before.

The object in Dominick's hand had begun to gleam dully against the fair skin of his torso. Even then we did not rejoice. Badger Breen put out his hand to take the object, but Dom turned and without comment handed it to Finn. Finn began to wash it in the water in the bucket. Old Font was sitting almost directly over him. As Finn splashed vigorously in the darkening water we saw the object suddenly slough the centuries and emerge as clean gold. It was a lune, arabesqued, interlaced and embossed. The colour was returning to Old Font's face. His hands had begun to tremble, though not with cupidity—of that we felt certain. For him it was as if the sky had never held an enemy.

Finn offered the collar of gold to the old man: accepting it, Font's eyes were those of a man who is clean bright out of his mind.

"Aye!" the old fellow said, quaveringly. "Aye . . . !"

The collar was lovely: it was if it had been born of gold the day before. I turned to measure the depth at which it had been found. One, two, three . . . seven, eight sods deep. It had been unearthed at the point where the red bog sally had begun—one sod more and there was the yellow clay. Fifteen hundred, two thousand years old, what did it matter? I felt happy for Cloone.

Old Font's fingers caressed the collar. His face was now glowing. He looked up at the sky, as if implying that the object he was holding could challenge the utmost of the sky's wonder. Implicit in his trembling fingers was the brag—that so long ago we had been glorious. That we had not been a painted people living in burrows! That our scribes had had miraculous inks in the dawn of scribing! That our artificers had the skill to cut such beauty!

Slowly and sadly Old Font's eyes travelled from man to man of us. At those of us who were bareheaded, he looked sharply. He saw our hair that either flaunted in tangled mohuls or was slicked back in the English quiff. His eyes never leaving us, he spat venomously sideways.

"The glib gone!" he said harshly.

We looked at one another's heads. We hadn't noticed it before. The glib *was* gone. True, Jody Shea was the very last of us to have kept cutting his hair close to the bone while yet leaving the Irish fringe. Instinctively we looked at Jody and saw that our gibing had been victorious. His hair was now indistinguishable from ours. What foreign enactment had failed to accomplish, we, of our own free will, had abandoned.

Font looked at our clothes.

"The bawneen gone!" he said.

We could almost hear the whirr of the spinning wheel run down as the old man spoke.

He looked at our shirts and jackets.

"The old linen that had a cure in it is no more! The good *breidin* is vanished!" Again he looked at our boots. "The step-dancin' is dyin' on ye," he said. "Soon ye'll be tied to the clay forever." Up and down his bare skull wagged, his expression wistful, sad, and denunciatory by turns. He looked at the cottages that edged the bogland. "God be good to you for thatch," he said: "your days are numbered!"

Dicky Hickey was coming up the passage-way: he was perched on the back of an ass. Old Font cast his mourning eyes on the two empty wicker panniers which were slung across the ass's back. "The last I'll see of ye!" he said sorrowfully.

He then looked brutally at our mouths. "The Gaelic gone!" he said. "A line of men stretchin' out of sight: son and father and father's father passin' a precious vase from hand to hand. An' one poltroon to let it fall! Adorable God, pity us Irish! What will we be in the heel o' time but a mongrel race draggled at the tail of Christianity!"

Font had begun to struggle with his mouth, his eyes and his refractory fingers. At length he ventured to raise his voice.

"For the last time I'll endeavour to instruct the youth an' then I'll raise my voice no more." Again the pause, until he had won his struggle. "I consider it the duty of at least one old man in every generation to pass on the ferocity he has inherited. Often an' often I have told ye of the kind of place ye were born into. I have striven to raise in ye a pride for the noble people before ye who fell in love with human nature an' through human nature fell in love with God." His still climbing voice rocked dangerously, then steadied. "I have striven to convey to ye before now that the young life as I lived it was so thronged with small beauties that you wouldn't think 'twas sons an' daughters of the flesh we were but children of the rainbow dwellin' always in the mornin' of the world."

The old man's voice was now under control. "An' if only the All-Seein' God had seen fit to send us a man with the gift of ink, then maybe the story of our small wonders would go shoutin' through the borders of the nations!"

At the top of his voice, Old Font went on: "Ye! Ye! I ask ye who are as yet young and agile to hold on to the brightnesses of our tiny world and to defend them against the grey-minded penny-souled upstarts whose sole aim and ambition it is to geld Ireland of her laughter."

Still shouting: "An' why do I ask ye to do these things? Because when the day comes for the wise men to poke for the lost secret of the happiness of individual man, it's among people the likes of ye they'll have to begin their searchin' ! "

By contrast with the small body of Dicky Hickey, the ass seemed enormous : almost the ass was an elephant and Dicky the mahout upon its back. The strange loneliness of Old Font had touched us. For a small span our lives seemed measured by the slow ticking of time. We kept watching the collar of gold in the old man's hand as if it were the sole talisman that had the power to redeem us. Then the sun caught the collar and with the flaming of the gold all our past came up like a vomit.

Lord God, but we were bewitched !

Old Font looked around at the ring of us : if he had had a scald-crow on his shoulder he could have stood for a grotesque Cuchulain in the agony of his dying. In the saddest of voices, he said : " The world is closin' in upon us."

Each man then became aware of the great constriction : it was as if the mountains of the south, the bog bulwarks of the north and the dune-line of the western coast had begun to move towards us so as to crush us beneath ramparts of land.

Finn Dillon stepped forward. The breaking of the spell was in his voice. " Things are not so bad, sir," he said. " Man doffs an' dons. That's livin' ! "

Because Finn was who he was, Old Font's voice was edged with contrition rather than with rancour.

" Man fells a tree," he said composedly, " and fails to plant another."

Under the old fellow's scrutiny, we became tranced and dolt-like. Slowly he said : " Soon ye'll be punched out, man after man of ye, lick alike, like so many black buttons." After a while : " God's likeness ! " Old Font added bitterly.

My eyes fell in sadness : when again I looked up I saw that the old man's eyes were set firmly on the collar of gold. He then lifted himself up to his great height. For the first time we realised how many inches age had filched from him. He was filled with dignity. We saw him raise the collar of gold to his breast. His face was a precise measure of his mind's pride. The collar was now under his beard.

There and then I noted, what I had often noted before, that when occasions are unbearably solemn or tragic God offers relief in the form of a spurt of laughter.

The laughter was led by Jack the Hibe. Instantly the feud that was dead leaped to life. Stiff-legged with rage, Young Font stepped forward: he was mortally ashamed at being found in defence of his father, and on this shame his anger fed. " A finished get it was who laughed ! " he said. He spoke to all of us in general but to Jack the Hibe in particular. Jack clenched his fists and came a step forward. Above him the old man continued to retain his sense of aloofness and grandeur.

Finn intervened between Young Font and Hibe. " Hush, men, hush ! " he said. " It has been a good day."

The little drama had left Galileo morose. Cry shame, I thought, that a soul of flame was quenched forever. Would the man now wilt and die ? Would the ropes on his throat never again stand out in rage ? Would he never again reck whether the sun stood or pranced or galloped ? Would his spirit never again flare up at the tinkle of a hairpin on the chimney of a kitchen lamp. Would the God who made the coyote to howl, the wasp to sting and the fish to swim, rejoice that an old cobbler should stand bereft of his defiance ? Would the God who made man to love and to hate with three-fold force—heart and head and body—be gratified to find to what level of mediocrity Galileo had descended ?

The mahout was clambering down from the elephant's back. The loyal duck was in the sky circling over the river where his wounded mate was lying.

Even without turning, I could see Madcap's face. Old Font was still on his pedestal. Dared any man now laugh ? As the water in the pitcher of silver cleared, the wonder of the world waned.

There was no need of speech. We felt—oh, the magic of it !—that our bloods were pooling. Was it a source of shame that we had allowed the vase to fall from our weary hands? How many skins did man slough? If a leader hammered a million men to one man on the anvil of life would that one man be a god or an idiot? What lay at the bottom of the Blue Hole? Had a pair of panniers on a donkey's back in a bog in Ireland eternal significance? Was this the all-important voice in us—that which cried and barked and whinnied: "God! God! God?" Were these the three hungers of man: God, girl and gear? Should we again revert to the glib and re-learn the Gaelic ranns we had abandoned? Was it possible for a man to retrace his steps to bygone beauties?

What significance had the jumble of incongruities that struggled through my mind? Golden collars and black elvers; insect life on the water and the cool ramparts of gravel; the heron's wings and the unexpected wantonness of Madcap; the rabbit in the ruined cabin and the 'plane in the sky; the red tippets of the trout and the faithful bereft duck; the bone of foam at the point of the headland in the south and the breeze that cooled our sweat; the held anger of Young Font and the scald-crows overhead; these and the children dolcing their cheeks with *ceannabhan*? But, hold, heart, hold! I was close to the secret. . . . If I could but grasp it I was fair in the lair of God. God and girl and gear. . . . Follow fast. . . . The secret of the world was then present in the winking gold. The riddle was a riddle no longer. Man was sublimated. Follow carefully . . . Follow . . . Follow . . . Follow. . . .

If only a scream or a silver sound of song would issue from a man's mouth, and stream out upon the sunny world! How my body would bell in answer! If only the world were always held thus in the peculiar stereoscope of living!

Where was Metal Belly? On what quest bent? Did the mouth of his bell no longer eat air nor its clapper strike metal? What village stirred to the nobility of his resonant voice? Scraps of conversation that I had once heard I now regurgitated: clearly I heard Peter Stack say: "She do be troublin' me!" Was Peter Stack part of the epic? I remembered the rose-maker in the Rookery kitchen spinning roses for my delight and for Dolly the Rose's exaltation.

Loneliness struggled over me. A while ago I was almost upon the inexpressible: my fingers had been extended to claw it to the ground. Now it had gone! Perhaps it would return. Why should it be stumbled upon by such as me? Did those who found the secret wholly lose their reason? Was that the curse that fell upon the finder of the treasure?

As it descended from the old man's throat the collar of gold was again touched by the sunlight. Out of an eye-corner I could see Joanie-the-Neck, as we called the heron, standing motionless on the edge of the bogland.

The sunny day was thronged with ghosts.

Looking around me, I saw in the faces of my tranced brothers the wonder that I wished to trap or be trapped by. The eyes of the children were already awakening to mature beauty: unashamedly they smiled as if they had just been recalled from the earnestness of private prayer. I felt myself stronger than the other men. Stronger even than Finn Dillon. What I would catch I would hold prisoner even if I too were punished with severity. Finn turned to look at me. He saw that I was strong and as a consequence he began to smile with the last happiness.

The old man offered the collar of gold to Finn. Finn accepted it; to us, Old Font was saying: "We'll not give it up! It will suit our Prince better than the Belt of Cloone. Far an' wide they'll know him for a Prince indeed!" To Finn: "Keep it, son, an' pass it on to the Prince who comes after you."

Old Font looked at Dominick Foy. "Is that right by you, Dominick, lad?" he asked.

"That's right by me, sir," Dominick said.

"Is that right by the rest o' ye?" Font asked us.

A half-hearted murmur of assent rose.

On Finn's face I read the temptation. One of his thumbs

was deep inside the polished belt. He shook his head. " We'll give it up, sir," he said to Old Font.

The old man's surrender was surprising. He shook his head as if to help him emerge from a dream. " Son," he said to Finn, " put it to your young throat as I did to my old one."

Finn laughed. He still held the collar in his hand. He ventured to look at us, then changed his weight from leg to leg. Old Font had readied his mouth for pleading, when suddenly Finn did what he had requested him to do. As the lune ascended, our eyes stole to apprehend the glittering in the old man's eyes.

The instant the collar had wholly gained Finn's throat, Old Font began to cry. Abruptly the water poured from his eyes. He had seen too much of life to raise his hand to his eyes and thus betray himself completely. We dared not look to right or left.

Finn lowered the gold : only then did Font dry his eyes with his sleeve.

A sudden whisper was heard. Old Font realised that it was a money-whisper. How to oppose it ? Subtlety and pride and craft appeared by turns in the old fellow's eyes.

As if to himself, he said : " The Bell of Ahalane. The Cross of Beenagurteen. The Bowl of Antenon."

To a man, we were puzzled.

Suddenly Old Font said, with a brightness that was all craft : " We'll give it up, so, but we'll ask no money. Provided they call it the Collar of Cloone ! Eh, men ? "

In our minds two worlds had begun to grapple.

" Aye," we said with listlessness, " provided they do just that."

" An' when the memory of us is gone ; when Cloone itself is no more, people will press their faces against the glass-case in the city an' they'll spell out the name o' Cloone. An' then, in earnest, it will be *Forever Cloone* ! Eh, men ? "

" Aye ! " This time we were answering him full-throatedly. To be eternal . . . the hunger of it !

The old man was laughing : " An' when there isn't trace or tidin's of us in the four winds of Ireland, begod, we'll be leppin' alive in the glitter o' the metal. Eh, lads ? What do ye say ? "

" Alive in the metal ! " we gladly echoed.

The good dream of the yellow future we then held. It was better than selling and the squabbling that accompanied the division of the gain.

In the middle of our wonderful mood, we heard the sounds of an altercation behind us. Turning, we saw Dominick Foy trying to drag Dicky Hickey out of the bog-hole. The mannikin looked as if he had been doused in the dark bog-water. I was certain that he had fallen in until I saw the little fellow attempt to throw himself down once more. Dominick lifted him by the scruff of the neck and dropped him on to the soft sward. We pressed forward. Dicky Hickey's claws were clogged with bogmould. As we halted on the high bank and puzzledly looked down, we saw the mannikin tear at the sods with fingers that had become talons. We heard his frenzied cry :

" Where there's one flea, there's another ! Where there's one collar, there also is its brother ! "

What was left then but laughter, which, if the truth be told, is a common denominator of the numerous moods of man ?

# CHAPTER X

I

AFTER the sun, the rain. After the laughter, the tears. How poignant with distance is the last laughter, lit as it is in memory by a dusty sunlight fading from the face of the bogland.

Words willingly go a certain distance: then they turn obstinate. They fall short of meaning or strike to the right or left of meaning. Here I wish my words to go straight to the core of our greatest sorrow. Sorrow like the sorrow concerning Shoon Lawlee, yet darker and more piercing.

I name the sorrow clean: here it is, a knife with edge and point to it. It is the death of Finn Dillon—the hanging of Finn Dillon, my friend. Hanged he was for the loving of his country to such a pitch as wise men would call madness.

I tell the story as I knew it.

The nation was troubled: between North and South there existed the bitterest rancour. Whether as a people we should be two or one—that was the issue.

Arguments mounted until the arguers grew drunk with their own words. Everywhere the young men were restless. Shots were fired in the cobbled entries of a dark northern city. Every shot echoed and re-echoed in the sounding-house of the South. After the shots were heard the drumbeats. The flame of burning houses tawnied the midnight sky. In the smoky darkness Catholics and Protestants tore at one another's throats. Children standing barefooted in the rain cried through the terror of pogroms and counter-pogroms. How we of the South belled our injustices! How they of the North belled theirs ! *Two or One? Two or One?* Now and again a lull came ; after the lull, as before, word begot act, act foulness and foulness abandon.

In the South where on all sides there were young men like Finn Dillon, idealists to a man, some of them not wholly at peace within themselves, the blood bubbled in anger at the recording of each fresh indignity to our kin- and creed-folk in the North. Ireland had always been one, we shouted bitterly. Wherever there is a national bitterness there too is a secret army. The clack of weapons was heard in dark boreens of the Southern counties. Drill commands came from midnight fields. In Ireland that was traditional—events had always followed this set pattern. The young men of the South told themselves that the history of their country had invariably justified those who were extreme.

With a rigidity both savage and intense Finn Dillon kept the young men of Cloone clear of what he was doing. Had he spoken one inflammatory sentence, fifty young men would have followed him on any crazy pilgrimage he cared to name. His new-found friends of the town wished him to speak that sentence. He refused to do so. We saw him less and less. As he grew valuable to others he grew useless to us of Cloone. His errands became more mysterious, his absences of longer duration. Our requests to him for guidance on local importances went unanswered. When he had been absent for two months we loved him no longer. We even said that he had proved a poor Prince of Cloone.

This was before the refinement of his death.

This is the way it was : there was a skirmish in a Northern alleyway. Afterwards a young constable was found lying on the cobbles with a dark hole in his cheekbone. A young man was captured as, firing from a window commanding the mouth of the entry, he covered his comrades' retreat. Even before the papers had been able to state that the captured man had been identified, we knew who he was. Too accurately every detail of description fitted the Prince of Cloone.

Those whom we had been reared to hate, even as they had been reared to hate us, how correct they were in making a hero of the young constable who had died in his duty. In like case we would have acted thus and thus. Sometimes circumstance is an iron all, and we are powerless in its toils.

The trial . . . the land ringing with the name of Cloone. In the courtroom the lawyers capably reduced the clamour of that night to a clear academic issue. Of humanity there was little. True, when women came forward and said : " Yes, I'm sure, quite sure, almost sure, or, even, not quite certain that *he* was the man," we took a certain bizarre interest in their names, wondering what they looked like, whether they were young or old, whether loved or unloved, or what unusual customs obtained in their Northern homes. The battle of wits, how measured it had become ! Cold evidence there was in plenty by ballistic experts : columns of the paper were filled about the accuracy or inaccuracy of a certain micrometer screw. The medical evidences followed. These evidences conflicted bewilderingly.

As yet we never dreamed that a hempen rope was being plaited for the neck of a loved one. In the Rookery each day's evidence was read aloud for all to ponder on. " He'll get off ! " " He won't ! " The issue had now narrowed down to the one-thousandth part of an inch. What an exciting game this was. The stake could scarcely be higher ! The point of pivot was whether it was another constable's gun or Finn Dillon's had fired the fatal shot. Every sentence we distorted to read as we wished it to read. The affair grew still more academic. It had become a matter touching only seers and sages. In it was the half-understood dialogue that we relished.

Abruptly the trial ended. Just as we had begun to believe that the queer exhilaration would last forever. Aye, and afford us fame forever. In a courtroom where dusty red curtains were behind and above him, an old man adjusted a small square of black cloth on his head. The words he spoke struck deep into every home in the land, but with especial savagery into every cottage in Cloone.

" Read on ! Read on ! " we urged quietly. How had Finn Dillon comported himself ?

" Finnbarr Dillon, stand up. Face the jury ! Have you anything to say why sentence of death should not be passed upon you ? "

" My Lord, and gentlemen of the jury ; according to your laws you have given me a fair trial. I thank my counsel. But so long as one square foot of the territory of Ireland remains under foreign domination. . . . "

Why read ? We knew it all before. We could tell exactly what he was going to say. The old men of Cloone had parsed and spelled it for us. Just as the oldsters of the young constable's town had parsed and spelled *their* gospel for him. There was nothing that could be done about it. Why attempt to apportion blame between the wind that blows against the oak and the oak that stands sturdily before the wind ?

Finn's married brother and his father had been in a train before. His mother never. It was her first time, too, since her marriage doffing her green-and-black shawl and wearing a hat and coat. She was a frail old woman with good grey hair. She had small features. The excitement of her journey to the North somehow dwarfed the importance of her errand. Her mind could not cope with all the new strong sensations : it seized on smaller phenomena that were in nowise important. A number of women from Cloone accompanied them through the town and saw them off at the railway station. These women made spirr-sparr of the condemnation as if it were a game clever lawyers played at so as to terrify untutored people. Not so the men, who had long since realised what issues were involved.

After a few days the three Dillons returned. The father and brother were uncommunicative : they were either bewildered, close-minded or grim. The mother conveyed to us a patchwork of trivial occurrences, of which the seeing of her son seemed by no means the most important. She had insisted on meeting the mother of the dead constable and had kissed the Northern woman in Cloone fashion. The pair of women had had tea in the front parlour of a small suburban villa. The room, Mrs. Dillon recalled, had smelled powerfully of beeswax. The china was thin and handpainted. In a corner stood a whatnot laden with seaside souvenirs. The dead constable's mother had shown Mrs. Dillon a picture of *her* son, taken when he was a boy wearing a sailor's suit. Then they had both cried. They cried for the dead lad and they cried for the lad who was about to die. Then these two women, one a Catholic, the other a Protestant, had kissed and parted. And for the short space of their kissing Ireland was united.

With an incredible faith in the virtue of prayer the old women of Cloone besought the Almighty to save Finn Dillon from the gallows. For a time we were buoyed by the talks of petitions and the rumours of appeal. But these came to nothing.

And then the day came when they hanged Finn Dillon, Prince of Cloone. From early morning there was an unearthly quietness in the thatched houses and even in the town beyond. The year was edged with the first of frost. An odd leaf was swinging yellow in the apple trees. At six o'clock in the morning the men had begun to shuffle into Dillon's. Finn's father and married brother were there to give them a quiet welcome. Conversation began: it had to do with trivial matters—this was the old trick of linking the normal to the abnormal. Father Mallon was sitting quietly on a sugawn chair: he, too, was taking part in the subdued conversation. When, at last, the clock struck nine, everyone seemed to tighten. As yet the signal for lamentation had not been given. The telephone line had been cleared for the length of Ireland: Murray Folan was standing by the receiver in the town. And then, Murray, walking with heavied shoes, came round the corner into the mouth of Cloone. He stood in mid-road and made a small hopeless gesture by opening his hands. Young Font had been standing in mid-road opposite Dillon's to receive the tidings. On seeing Murray Folan's hands indicate the end, he took off his cap, walked into Dillon's house, nodded his head upwards, tightened his mouth and crossed himself. Father Mallon stood up. Mrs. Dillon, too, crossed herself, but she did not break down. She looked at her husband : he looked down at the small ripening fire. She tightened her small shawl about her shoulders and walked across the cobbled yard till she came to the path into the haggard. Two girls followed her. Mrs. Dillon continued walking until she came to the beehive. Standing before the beehive, she said quietly : " Bees, my son, Finn Dillon, is dead." Treating bees as members of the household and informing them of domestic tragedies was an old custom among us.

II

That night there was a wake in Dillon's : the wake was a blind one for there was no getting of Finn's body. By now it had been buried in quicklime. All day long the cottages, for me, had resumed their old trick of crouching. The people of the town kept coming into Cloone to tender their sympathy to the Dillons. Their expressions of grief were stilted but sincere. Before noon the crape and the mourning envelope were affixed to the door : part of the legend on the envelope was written in English—the part that stated that Finnbarr Dillon had died for the unity of his country. It concluded with a legend in Gaelic : " At the right hand of God that his soul may stand ! " We had no difficulty in recognising the spidery handwriting of Little Angel.

A wake without a corpse is strangeness itself. The old women sat on stools or forms beside the bed on which Finn had slept. Their green-and-black shawls were thrown back from their foreheads. The walls of the room were dark red in colour, dark as red raddle. On the wall over the bed hung a picture of the Madonna. The head and foot of the bedstead had been draped with old linen sheets : these were bound at the bed-knobs with thin black ribbons. The brightness of the quilt was hidden beneath an old white bedspread. The pillow-case, too, was snow-white and the pillow was shaken up so that there was no suggestion of indentation upon it. Beside the bedhead was a table on which five candles were lighting. The candlesticks were made of heavy brass : three of them had twisted stems. On the table also was a bowl of holy water. The window behind the table was small and deeply recessed.

Finn's mother sat on the chair nearest the table. Next to her sat Shoon Lawlee's mother. Unlike the rest of the women, Shoon's mother did not remove the shawl from her face.

The men were in the kitchen. They had glossed their grief with a dull futile anger. There was no drink : this was because of the kind of a wake it was. Snuff was passed around in saucers. Sneezing, the people prayed for the souls of the faithful departed.

As daylight waned, the people began to throng in. Soon the house was full. The Bowens came from Littero : for some of us the dark fuchsia bells began ringing the instant they came in the door. My sister Mary came in from the country : at her heels slouched Peter Stack, tall and awkward, towering over her like a cliff. Mary was wearing a fawn Paisley shawl with a border and tassels of red and yellow. She was heavily pregnant. Noticing this, every man's eyes fell from her. She did not enter the wake-room : there was a superstition in that. She stood at the threshold of the room and Finn Dillon's mother, understanding how matters stood, walked out to meet her. They embraced fully. In low tones I heard Mrs. Dillon chide Mary for having travelled. I tried hard not to look at Peter Stack's boots. Someone made way for him on a stool by the dresser. At the wake-room door, Mary prayed, standing, then with another girl went to the small room in front so that she would not be loitering under the eyes of the men.

Caherdown was there : he went to extremities of contrivance so as to avoid sitting on a sugawn chair. Of sugawn chairs he was suspicious : he thought the cat or dog slept on them at night and so was afraid of fleas. At length out of mercy someone offered him a hard chair. Straightaway he became comfortable and dignified. Jody Shea sat on a stool under the hob with Dillon's mongrel beneath his knees. All night long, Jody's finger kept making a curl on the dog's forehead.

It was nine o'clock when we heard the lock-lack of a donkey's cart on the roadway outside. The cart halted at the door. Someone lifted a corner of the kitchen blind : outside we saw an old woman and a boy in the going light. The old woman thrust open the half-door. She had bright eyes. She was wholly caught in age. Slowly she entered. Her shawl was not of our district. I did not know her from a stone. Neither, I thought at first, did anyone else in the wake-house. I saw then that a great light had come on Young Font's face. The woman eased her strange shawl backwards. When she spoke we realised that she had a fine voice. " A bed in Heaven to him that's gone ! " she said. " Amen to that ! " we all answered. Hearing the stranger's voice, Finn Dillon's mother had come to the wake-room door. " Are you the mother of the dead boy ? " the strange old woman asked. " That I am," Finn's mother said sadly. " You don't know me, ma'am ? " the stranger said. " I don't, decent woman," said Mrs. Dillon. " Of a Wran's Day," said the stranger, " your son made a promise to attend my burial. An' it's a black sorrow on me that I should have the buryin' of him first." " Again, you're welcome, decent woman," said Finn Dillon's mother. They then kissed as if they had always been fast friends.

Hour after hour we sat there. Our conversation was low and without lustre. Whenever the hairpin tinkled on the chimney of the oil-lamp, we tried hard not to look in Galileo's direction. Yet on the tinkling we hoped against hope that our eye-corners would spy the twin cords tighten on his throat. We hoped in vain.

It was late enough when Brink-o'-the-Grave came : so late it was that we had already despaired of her coming. A hush struck the house as the tapping of her stick was heard on the flagstones outside. I opened the half-door to her ; wheezing harshly she pivoted past me on her broken gait. She was dressed in the regimentals of a bygone day : crimped white cap, red petticoat and black shoulder shawl. Her age, weight and hip were giving her immense trouble. The instant her boot hit the timber threshold of the wake-room, Finn Dillon's mother stood up expectantly. Brink-o'-the-Grave ignored her. She eased her weight on her elbow which she had now rested on the foot of the bed. Her fingers clutched at her breast where, I guessed, Finn's caul was concealed in her coffaleen. She grasped the iron bed-rail and looked steadfastly into the bed's emptiness. Her breathing came heavily. After a while she got out the words. We heard her say clearly, in a half-chant : " Is it there you are lying, my royal boy, O and O and O and O ! You that were gentle and courteous and loving, O and O and O and O ! You that were the essence of gentility and had the fond attention of women, O and O and O and O ! You that stood straight as a staff in a harvest field, O and O and O and O ! "

Immediately the wake-house was moved by a strong duress. We had suddenly realised what Brink-o'-the-Grave was at ! Each woman sat up straight and erect. Each man's body was trembling with anticipation.

Brink-o'-the-Grave was now chanting in the Gaelic : " *O agus O agus O agus O. . . .* "

And then the blood of the old women took tongue : their throats broke into the Irish cry.

Those of my generation had never heard it. The last time the *caoine* was raised was thirty years before. It had then been raised over the four Cloone men who had been smothered in the caves of Lahardan.

The priests had damned it : " Have done with paganism ! " they thundered. " Have some shred of respect for your dead ! " Dutifully the people had obeyed : they buried the cry deep under the layers of their Christianity.

" *O agus O agus O agus O. . . .* "

This was the cry raised by the women over King Brian, over Brian's son Mahon, and over Mahon's son Turlough when the bodies of all three had been unravelled from the slaughter of Danes at Clontarf. Farther back in time this cry had been raised over King Daithi the Raider, his body blasted by lightning at the foot of the Alps.

Our brothers the Scottish had forgotten it. Our brothers the Welsh had abandoned it. Our cousins the Manx, the Cornish and the Bretons knew it no more. Alone of the Celtic edge, we had held it fast.

If what the braggart schoolmasters had told us was true, that once we were a strong wave breaking over the civilised world, then surely this cry raised under the thatched roof of a cottage in Cloone was the last hissing of that wave spending itself here amid the stones of time.

" *O agus O agus O agus O. . . .* "

The cry held the heartbreak of the pipes and the vibratory drone of the harpstrings. These sounds it interpreted when they were most searing and most exalting. Traditional failure and traditional defeat seemed thus ennobled and distilled in the voice-boxes of our old women.

The crumbled Gaelic was in it. The dark places of our language had become suddenly illuminated by the realisation of our loss.

It seemed the first noise and the last noise. It seemed limitless as to glory and sorrow.

" *O agus O agus O agus O. . . .* "

Brink-o'-the-Grave was carrying the anthem at its purest. Snatches of what she was chanting we understood : snatches evaded us. The chanting tended by instinct to fall to the minor mode. At times, when it took to itself an arabesque of grace-notes, the crying approached singing.

Whenever music and agony rivalled, music invariably gave way.

The candles flames did not waver. The chanting was controlled abandon. Moving only from the waist up, the old women rocked backwards and forwards. The candlelight was warm on their sublime faces. Shoon's mother had cleared the shawl from her face, and her lips were thin around the chanting.

The women's fingers mimed the melody.

Hammocked we were in the upper places of sorrow.

" *O agus O agus O agus O. . . .* "

Diffidently at first, but later with increasing confidence, the young women entered the chanting. As if their tongues could keep out of it! Then truly they were heirs to a thousand semi-understood ferocities. The lamentation became grief incarnate. It was wholly without hope of resurrection. Brink-o'-the-Grave all the while remained firm in the higher places of incantation. Once she was there alone. Then a young woman came in far below her. Another entered in the middle. Another and yet another stole into the embodied sorrow, unerringly filling the interstices of sound, weaving and re-weaving until they had made for us there a basket-work of the purest agony.

" *O agus O agus O agus O. . . .* "

It was an attempt by the living to hold converse with the dead. The wailing fined out until it became the most cunning of sounds. This in its turn became still more rarefied until it was appreciated that sound was now broaching on a new dimension.

" *O agus O. . . .* "

A child cried with the plain terror of hearing it. The natural crying of the child and the stylised crying of the women contrasted strangely. The realisation of the inadequacies of the natural crying heartened the chanters and drove them upwards to higher pinnacles of grief.

We heard the words more accurately. The imagery that our minds lusted after was then present.

" *Mo thri thruaighe naoi n-uaire! A stoir dhil, dhil, dhil! A phrionnsa uasail. Run mo chroidhe agus do chroidhe. O agus O agus O, O, O.*"

" My three sorrows nine times over! O dear, dear, dear treasure! O noble prince! Secret of my heart and of your heart. O and O and O, O, O."

Finn Dillon's mother was standing without *caoin*-ing. The wings of lamentation beat about her. She was listening carefully to the beautiful and broken appellations. It was a great honour that for her son the ultimate *caoine* was being raised. It was a sterling compensation for the baseness of his end.

Clearly I realised: after this it will be heard no more. On the realisation I redeemed myself from the bondage of sorrow.

Consciously I saw the blackened rafters brought by the smoke of years to the darkest of chocolate-brown. I saw the sods above the rafters. I saw the smoke-browned whitewash of the chimney breastwork step gradually up as it climbed to meet the thatch. I saw the mirror on the back window covered before the face of death. I saw the clevy with the trinkets and the small brasses upon it. I saw the dresser and the delph. All these things I saw with an unusual clarity that was an earnest of accurate remembrance.

Subtly, the implication of the chanting changed: it now seemed to promise the old that they would be placed in a land where their broken bodies would be refurbished. It had straggled home to the sanity of a common sorrow. This we presently found was a delusion. As on a hand's turn, the wailing climbed step after terrible step until it had reached a fantastic strength and novelty.

" O hound for swiftness, ended is thy running. O deer of

the great antlers, thy proud head is in the dust. O lion not man, thy head is dark with blood. O stripling of the lovely limbs, without fleetness thou art and without life. O and O and O and O, O, O. . . . "

(His small shoes holding the air before they dropped him into the pit where the priest wearing the dark stole waited looking upwards. Those same small shoes also holding the air as he danced on the Wren's Day when the bank-women leaned out fully on their window-sills.)

" O voice that was a manly shout, thou art a weak syllable on the wind. O face that was created for shining, thou art wholly without illumination. O mouth that was fashioned for the lovely O of entertainment, thou art gnarled and embittered with sorrow. O heart that was destined for accurate and compassionate feeling towards womankind, thou art without pulse and without movement. O and O and O and O and O, O, O. . . . "

(Finn's voice rallying us against the western tinkers. Finn's features transfigured in the light from the estuary as Bridie Bowen pressed the mushroom to her face. Finn's breast afire as the sun struck the collar of gold. Finn's mouth puckish with laughter in the Rookery on the night before the Old Fair. Finn's heart twisting in his breast as he saw Shoon Lawlee's eyes narrow gladly at another man's laughter.)

" O star of our midnight, hidden thou art in the coils of cloud. O body brighter than a hound's tooth, darkened and sullied thou art with the encompassing clay. O lover at the edge of the bridal bed, baulked thou art of beauty. O and O and O and O, O, O. . . . "

Now, surely, I thought, the crying must falter and die.

By a supreme effort Brink-o'-the-Grave straightened herself. Fiercely she rallied her arthritic crones for the last adventure into bereftness. The men remained utterly still : it was as if they feared that one untoward movement would jog the chalice of the women's grief. Rung by rung, Brink-o'-the-Grave descended into the deep places of incantation. She went down and down until her voice became a barely audible rattle in her throat. The veins stood out on the backs of her hands as she tightened her clutch on the bed-rail. Then, as if she had chanced upon the very core of desolation, she brought all the women with her, goading and luring their voices upwards into a transport of anguish that was nameless and placeless and timeless. So rare an exaltation did it become that exaltation lost its meaning and grief perished at the very joy of being sorrow.

Abruptly the wailing ended. One after one, we emerged from the bondage of trance. The men held their eyes from the lamplight lest its gleaming should betray that they had been less than men.

III

During the span of our unreality, I fancied that I had heard the sound of harness-bells.

Looking out over the half-door I saw a back-to-back cart under the blue light of the moon. It had been there during the span of lamentation. Major Mallory descended from the vehicle and with his knuckles knocked softly on the ledge of the half-door. Where never a man had knocked before! I noted the white moustache under the well-cut but ancient tweed cap. When someone drew open the half-door Major Mallory asked with diffidence: "May I come in?"

Over his shoulder I saw Edith sitting in the vehicle. She was holding the reins and speaking quietly to the restive horse.

Major Mallory looked up lest he should strike his head against the low lintel. He then stooped and entered the kitchen. All that was gentle in the English way of life entered with him. For us this was a new sensation. We had been taught to spit out at the mention of redcoats. We had been taught to execrate the seed and breed of foreign tyrants. And yet how suddenly lovable the man was despite the fact that he was English of the English ! Although his people had been in possession of portion of the lands of Ireland for over three hundred years, the gulf between him and us was plain for any man to see. In that three hundred years the number of times any of his forebears had been under a thatched roof could be counted on the fingers of one hand. To them our ground was swordland only. And yet when Major Mallory spoke to Finn Dillon's father he sounded forthright and sincere. True, he expressed himself in a manner remote from our mode of expression, yet for the first time we saw that directness and understatement could also possess merit. Insofar as our natures and our traditions would allow us, we respected this man.

Caherdown was speaking to Major Mallory, who appeared slightly surprised at the fashion in which Caherdown was expressing himself. Then I noted a thing that pleased me immeasurably : now that Caherdown was on his own ground his pedantry had vanished. We were filled with pride and delight that Caherdown was neither more nor less than he should be.

Galileo spat heavily into the ashes and morosely dug his small chin into his breast. With something approaching a plunge of joy I spied the angry cords on his neck. Turning his head away, he concealed his wrath and rancour.

Harness creaked and again the deep-throated harness-bells rang. I heard steel sound out as the horse backed the vehicle against the cobbled channel. The wheel ground harshly as it mounted the flagged pathway. I threw open the door and took the animal's head. Prancing strongly forward, the horse drew the vehicle away from the doorway. It gave me all I could do to hold him. Eventually he calmed down. Edith, who had been unperturbedly holding the reins, descended from the vehicle.

We two then stood beside one another. She spoke of Finn Dillon. After a few trivial observations, the conversation became desultory. I began to wonder what there had ever been between us. Abruptly, she said: " After I have gone away. . . . " I nodded. As yet a part of each of us remained unsatisfied.

" As we were driving here," she said, " we met a girl with a pair of terriers at her heels. As we approached, the dogs ran out on to mid-road. The girl called them by name." She paused, then added: " One terrier was named Finn, the other Ches."

There was a long pause. The woman was struggling to express herself. Our hope that some item of conversation would spring open the locked door between us was proving vain.

" My mother sends her regrets." She turned away. We were both at the horse's head. She looked at the high road that led out of Cloone, then said in a low voice: " She says, ' If life offers, grasp it ! ' "

Idly I bit the back of my hand.

" Why do you do that ? " Edith asked. Her voice was edged.

" In the cave," I said, " the back of my hand broke a sea nipple on the wall behind your head. Afterwards I put the back of my hand into my mouth and tasted the salt-water."

She seemed determined to wound me in a small way. A woman is attractive when she is quarter-mocking a man. " My mother knew . . . " she said. " You were angling for mention of the sea so that you could be certain that she knew. She hadn't the heart to deny you. She told me she had to cudgel her brains to include an evocative word in the conversation. When the word was spoken she saw your face leap as she had known it would leap. I tell you this who shouldn't tell you. That business is the province of women. I have betrayed a secret. I do it only because I wish you to think well of my mother. ' If life offers,' she says, ' grasp it ! ' She has had the leisure in which to grow cunning. The common phenomenon of a butterfly's flight can cause her immense pleasure. Or anguish." Then, with upturned face: "It was good, Ches, was it not?"

"It was good!" I said. She held one ring of the bridle, I the other. The horse's head was docile between us.

"There is a question that must be answered. . . ." She stopped. "It is not pride that prevents my saying it. Pride has lost its importance."

"That is true," I said.

"It is the pair of us against circumstance."

I nodded. This was God's truth.

Stumblingly, she went on: "Whatever happens, neither of us wins. It is not rivalry. It is an attempt to predict the power of forces outside of us. Of tradition. Of viewpoint. Of other things. . . ."

(The memory of the *caoine* was between us. Each note hung separate and blue in the moonlight air.)

"What do you say, Ches?"

"You speak first," I said, looking away.

"It is not for me to speak. I am netted by emotion. I keep saying: 'If life offers, grasp it!'"

I said: "That simple phrase has power. If we are not careful it will rule us."

"Let us not say it again," the woman said.

The horse remained quiet, with head drooped. I looked at the thatch, then at the sky above. Edith Mallory and I were beyond pride and rivalry. I looked at her directly with eyes that had grown accustomed to the moonlight. She was as lovely as a willow rod. I had seen willow rods sway on the river-bank. I seemed to see them then. Swaying. All the lovely young women of the riverside. And the rod that was the noblest took to itself the form of Edith Mallory: her face leaped out of the top tuft and her body swung in the pliant grace of the long rod. Perhaps in another land we would be happy. There I would be man only, and she woman. It was a pleasant dream. Was I rooted in Cloone? Were the manacles of tradition set upon me? Was the thatch so agonisingly powerful? Here lay poverty with sometimes such glory and majesty as lay in a daft lamentation. Old Font was now prompting me: his beard seemed close to my ear. Poverty of chattel, only, he was saying. I loosed the bridle ring. I was waiting for it to jingle. I thought: when the bridle again jingles I will decide. So ring, bridle, ring! My life hangs on your ring. Whether I go or stay. Whether the forces that have fashioned me are strong or weak. Ring, bridle, ring! Now there is no pride. Only the pooling of the lives of two people who are suddenly become wise and humble beyond their years. Ring, bridle, ring! Here is a woman, here a man. Small hoops of seeming silver at the corner of a horse's mouth, why do ye not ring? She is lovely as a willow rod. Ring, bridle, ring! The woman senses what I am waiting for.

Then the bridle rang.

I shook my head. She understood. We came together and kissed. The ending was as clean as the incision of a lancet.

The footsteps of a woman came down Cloone. Without turning, I knew who it was. "This is Madcap?" Edith asked. We stood waiting for Madcap to approach.

"Do you mind . . . ?" Edith asked.

"No," I said.

As Madcap was passing, Edith turned. Softly she said: "You are Alice O'Neill?" Then: "How do you do?" Her gestures were warmhearted.

At first Madcap was resentful. Then the tone of her voice showed that she was puzzled. I knew. While I was there she would not respond. I turned my head. Together they walked away. For a long while they remained talking to one another. Major Mallory then came out of the wake-house. Edith returned. I walked up Cloone to where the ground was higher.

* * *

A month later a soldierly stranger knocked at our door and asked for me. He had a sharp Northern accent. When my father called me, I came out of the room. The stranger was heavily built. He looked at my hair.

" You Ches Macnamara ? " he asked.

I nodded.

" A message I have for you." He held out a small round parcel. The instant my fingers touched it, I knew what it contained. I invited the man in, but he refused.

" Married to a Southern lass, I am," he said with a spurious carelessness. Then : " Wal, I'll be goin'."

He extended his hand. Although his jaw tightened, his face betrayed little emotion.

The question was not easy to shape, yet I had to know. " Did he go game ? " I asked abruptly.

" Lak' a prince ! " he said, offhand. As if the point were of no importance and yet of every importance. He looked up at the sky.

" You're sure ? " I asked again.

" Och, aye, surely," he said. " I was there ! "

No doubting his word then. His handclasp was as firm as firm could be. In it I could sense the spare Northern line.

As he went swinging down the street, he looked with interest to right and left. He looked closely into the face of every man and woman he met as if seeking to recognise each from a description given. I saw him look at the Pump, then glance quickly across the road to Galileo's big window. Passing the Rookery he glanced sharply in the open door. Something in his profile made me think he was half-smiling. When he had passed by, Tom Goggin came to the half-door. " That ill-bred bihoonagh will know Cloone again when he sees it ! " he shouted across to Galileo. Galileo nodded. Both old men screwed up their faces to look after the stranger.

" Who was that ? " my father asked.

" A man with a message," I replied.

I went into the back room and shot the wooden bolt on the door. Sitting on the bed I opened the parcel. My fingers began to treasure the age-darkened and supple leather. Slowly I ran my coat-sleeve over the brass bosses. Answering the caress, the belt came fully alive even in the inadequate light.

# CHAPTER XI

I

IN the autumn of that year, Cloone was a brown and white cat sleeping where the last of the year's heat and light was husbanded. The old people seemed to have withdrawn into themselves. A stranger seeing the low quiet homes would have thought : surely this is not a place where minds feud and ambush, where there is despair and hope, together with mourning and exultation ?

The sounds of Cloone seemed markedly muted : even the ding-dong-didero of Dan Dillon's anvil struck less surely on the autumn air. Intermittently the breeze from the southern pinewoods was not untinged by the first of the frost. In the fields behind O'Neill's and on the hillocks to the north the red of the haws had altogether gladdened the hedges.

Preparations had to be made against the winter : we had to make certain of food, fuel, and a secure roof. A pig was killed in each cottage, the turf was drawn home out of the bog and the thatchers were sent for to give each cottage that needed it its cap of golden or brown straw. Afterwards came the white-washing—not always white indeed for some cottiers mixed green or umber or ochre through the wash.

Metal Belly's cottage was whitewashed by one of his neighbours : the bellman had been gone for over a year now and we had long since despaired of his returning.

This was the way it was with us then at the heel of the year : the bacon flitches were glittering among the chocolate-dark rafters and a snug rick of turf stood in the yard with a small windrow of straw beside it. The straw was used as bedding for the ass or the goat or for that rare beast among us, the bony cow. The bees were secure in the skips. The onions were laid out on the little loft to the right of the hearth—boiled in milk at suppertime and flavoured with salt, pepper and butter they had the virtue of inducing sleep and banishing winter chills. On the loft to the left of the hearth the apples lay. The spuds were pitted in the garden or covered with shore-sand in the out-houses. In the haggard the cabbage-greens were sprouting strong and plentiful : how well they would mate with the home-cured bacon all winter through ! The outside of the house was spick and span and the thatch a real item of loveliness. How good then everything was ! The miniature harvest was home. Let winter come ! Cloone was ready.

How good it was to return home after a day spent in the country working with the threshing mill. Dog-jaded, we would stand at the mouth of Cloone, on the open road between the Maid of Erin and the Chinaman. From there we would see the clean cottages capped with good gold, falling tier after snug tier on either hand till they reached the stone bridge ; thence they would again lift at the Rookery door and stumble away on the rising ground until eventually they petered out at the foot of the hill.

How good then !

A struggle had begun in my heart. The outside world, magnificent and adventurous, was calling to me: many a restless hour I spent trying to determine the origin of my heart's battle. Meanwhile I had begun to dabble at my father's trade.

We continued to say : "Forever Cloone." But now the slogan had begun to hold the beginnings of mockery, for with Finn's passing the saying had lost its pride. Each of us was aware that Cloone could scarcely hold out much longer. Thatch, we realised, was doomed.

As Prince of Cloone I did my utmost to hold fast to the standard of fierce individualism I had inherited. But I was a poor type of prince and scarcely fitted to hold candlelight to those who had gone before. Also, in the secrecy of my heart, I scarcely believed in the doctrine I preached.

Yet in this season of late autumn, Cloone confounded those who reckoned her spent. Now she appeared less a crone than a bride. Even myself she deceived sometimes. When I awoke from my delusions I began to lust with all my strength after the hope that if there was to be an end to Cloone it would come with the mercy of speed; I prayed that she should not perish by the loss of small flickers, as with the advent of age bright tooth after bright tooth ceases to gleam in the mouth of a once beautiful woman. I would not have Cloone lose her beauty by dole. Times there were when I craved God to make my fist gigantic so that in a single instant I could if I chose beat her wholly into the brown ground and thus ensure that her memory would be untarnished, intact and treasured.

Life continued to move over us: the noise it made was the ticking of an old brown clock.

At thatching time the weather came crisp and sunny. Night after night arrived wholly windless with the sky filled with fleets of polished stars.

II

The night the wind came. . . .

I remember clearly the evening before that night—how the mackerel-marked sky had blackened at the base and with the dusk this blackness had brutally thrust its way up to the zenith, consuming all the sky-markings, until at last we were left with souvenirs of splendour only in the extreme north and south of the sky.

Later, when the wind came, it had the demeanour and antics of a true friend. It was bustling and noising as though it conceded Cloone her security. The wind made little impression on the thatch, nor to tell the truth of it did it seek to do so. It rustled the rush-thatch on the turf-ricks in the yards and routed the caps of the heaps of spared straw. It even made air-whirls that aped the workings of a fairy breeze. We laughed at the fidgets of the wind, knowing that it had not the power to harm us. Soon, we knew, the rain would follow on its heels. Then the blusterer would lie low.

We had reckoned without the wind's strongest ally, which is fire.

That morning, about three o'clock, the smell of straw-smoke was suddenly in the air. A person balanced between sleep and wakefulness could scarcely be sure at first; at last the wind beat the smell down into the street of Cloone, where it sneaked in through the small open windows. A man rose coughing; he threw open his window and looked out at a white nuzzling world of smoke that straightaway caught at his throat. This man roared into the night: "Fire! Fire! Cloone's afire!"

My mother's cries roused me; I heard the blind crying-out of adults and the screaming of terrified children. I heard a man hammer frantically with his fists upon a closed door. I was out of bed almost instantly. I groped for my trousers. The smoke poured in through the open bedroom window. My father and mother were up and about. Outside in the street the voice was busy baying: "Fire!"; I knew then that the gigantic fist I had dreamed about had clubbed Cloone. I knew, too, that she would vanish as I had wished her to vanish. The knowledge lent me a fierce elation. Dragging on my brogues and jacket I lifted the latch of the front door. The silent smoke entered: outside a man blundered by, his voice filling the fog with oaths. He it was who was baying: "Fire!" I realised overlate that the man was Badger Breen for the smoke had gnarled the true sound of his voice. My father and mother were now in the kitchen. I went out into the street closing the door behind me.

In the street the open hand of the wind was beating down and down. Crouching where the air was purest I tried to aim the fire. Cries, reprimands and expostulations came to me from the hill-end of Cloone. I heard burning timber crackle. As I crouched I was racked by a fit of coughing. The capricious wind then took the smoke and dragged it up, purifying the air of the small world about me. I saw a wide cap of flame some distance up Cloone. As I watched, the light soared high. Three or four thatched roofs together were ablaze; the united flame was sucked up to a point. The sound of the crackling again reached me: it was a completely fierce noise. Straightaway the whisk of the wind beat the smoke downwards and blotted out the vision.

A man ran by me. "Dolly the Rose," he shouted, "has fired Cloone!" The cry of "Cloone's afire!" came from all sides. I then recalled that latterly Dolly the Rose had been sleeping in an outhouse filled with straw at the upper end of the street.

Screaming people continued to rush past me. The wind repeated its former vagary. A second time it sucked the whole of Cloone clear of smoke; taking advantage of this clearance I sprinted upstreet to where a knot of people stood hopelessly watching the flames. A few men spasmodically rushed towards the fire but as speedily retreated. The heat was sharp and concentrated. Old women dressed only in their shifts and shawls stood in mid-road: they were wirrastru-ing at the top of their voices. The prankish wind took their shifts from their legs; immediately a lifetime of modesty caused the old women to forget their terror in the effort of ensuring that their slender shanks and attenuated thighs would not be seen. As I drew near, one old woman turned. "In the name of God Almighty!" she said. Then, recognising me, she added: "Oh, Ches Macnamara, Cloone is no more!"

The mauling of doors and the shouting grew louder. People continued to approach us. Whenever the wind brought the flame to a point, it towered as tall as the spire of Mary-without-Stain. Through a break in the smoke I looked down to the mouth of Cloone: I saw a small knot of townspeople standing in mid-road between Folan's and Bovenizer's. The chapel bell had begun ringing: hopelessly it strove to convey a sense of urgency and danger but succeeded only in being what it was—a high and gentle Sabbath sound. In my mind I could picture

Little Angel standing barefooted on the stones, shuddering as he drew on the bell-rope.

Our fighting the fire was simply a gesture to the future generations, for we knew from the outset that the task was hopeless. For one thing, Cloone was mad with straw. If we had striven to ensure a welcome for the fire we could scarcely have been more successful. In some cases the turf ricks had been built directly against the back walls of the cottages ; these ricks were sure to spring aflame like gunpowder. And even these inflammable ricks had been thatched with straw ! The good season that had almost kiln-dried the turf was now proving itself a false friend. There was little water. The pump never ceased its clanking. All the while the fire was passing from cap to cap of cottage. Sometimes it lulled us into a false sense of security ; in these lulls it consolidated its hold in secret recesses and then even as we smiled at one another it broke out with renewed zeal. The wind had resumed its trick of holding the flame to a point so that we were lured closer. When again the flame beat down, the broadened heat spat hell into our faces. By the light of the fires we saw the faces of our neighbours. Unsuccessfully we tried to converse with them through the fire's roar.

Someone caught at my arm : I turned and saw Jody Shea. " Look ! " he said. I turned. The dark roofs behind me, on the side of the road opposite to where the fire was, had begun to show here and there living and dying sparks. As I drew closer to these cottages I received an impression of hot vapour rising from all the roofs on that side of the road. The wind continued to beat down between the walls of flaming cottages : now and again as the result of the compression of the heat in such a natural oven the mud walls of some of the weaker cottages, which, to tell the truth of it, had been tilted not a little out of plumb with the passing centuries, now kicked fully out into the street. The sound they made when falling was a loud " Phut ! " We started back from the dribbling hard kernels of hot earth. Some of the clay crumbled out fully into mid-road where in the shape of hard marbles it rolled about our boots. With the fall of a wall, the wave of heat curled over us, and for a moment or two the fire-tongue licked over our heads. Then, even as our attention was distracted, the utter devilishness of the wind was measured, for with an effect that was almost magical one of the roofs behind us majestically donned an immense helmet of gold. Then a second roof, three houses down, independent so it seemed of contact with any flame, lighted with the same terrible crest. Still another hitherto silent cottage flamed up angry and high until all the little area wherein we stood dumbfounded was now deep in the orgy of fire. We were forced to move down into the heart of Cloone.

The pump handle was clanking furiously. On all sides men were calling out and cursing. We fought on. Some of the other young men had come up. From door to door Badger Breen went: he was still beating, calling, swearing, crashing, even smashing down a door where despite his tattarara a house remained as silent as if its occupants were stone dead. Unbelievable it is how deep into the pit of sleep some men and women can descend!

"Out! Out! For God's sake, out! Cloone is ablaze! Out, blast ye, out! Sufferin' God, will ye tumble out or be burned alive where ye lie! Out!"

Through the clanking of buckets we heard wailing as well as ejaculations. People were quietening children and reassuring the old. "Son, you're all right!" "Easy, Father, take it easy!" "No, childeen, no, it's not John's night—it's funnin' just the same!" "No, no, my leanav! No! Husheen ho! Hush!" "Oh, Loving God, Tom, Tom!"

The wind was a fiend, an imp, a blackguard; above the houses it had begun scooping great caverns of air which its confederate, the fire, fully filled with its elastic flame. The nature of the fire was equally compounded of venom, treachery and vandalism. Remorselessly it gnawed beneath the fresh thatch; sometimes it leaped like a billy-goat; sometimes, like a grave-faced child, it played " Tig " with us. We were always conscious that hidden in the leaping and flashing there lay the menace.

We had made a chain of buckets to the river. This chain went through the doorway of a cottage, ran out the back doorway and down the side of the clay cliff. The buckets were few and far between. I was at the fire end of the chain. Once as I lifted a full bucket I noticed the bulge on the side of the vessel : I knew then that this was the pail out of which Madcap and I had drunk on the hillside in the bog. The vessel was tarnished and greened with usage.

There was already a hint of daylight behind the eastern hill. The owners of the cottages in the path of the fire had removed their goods. I heard delph falling in the grey light. This was ware that had been stitched and treasured and handed down from generation to generation, used only on special occasions such as a wedding, a wake or on the morning of the priest's station.

Each pailful of water made but a small hiss as it struck the blaze. The soaker of the pump kept squeaking away as the handle laboured. The water from pump and river came overslow. At last we had to concede to one another that our labours were useless : for all the effect our efforts had we might as well have been piddling into the burning cottages.

Through the intermittent smoke mists we saw the grey morning begin to superimpose the true daylight on the light of the many fires.

Holding an old salmon-rod, Galileo was waiting for the fire to leap-frog on to the roof of his cottage. When first I looked in his direction I noticed that the rod was in two parts : then I saw him crouch as he bound top and butt together with a white shoe-thong. I wondered what manner of plan he had in mind for the saving of his home. And then—the old fox !—I saw that whenever the cat's-eyes of sparks appeared on his roof he speedily rustled the fishing-rod along the thatch. Once I saw the agate top-ring of his rod gleam whilst caught against the background of a rising light. The cobbler was oddly fishing with fire. The points of light on his roof went out—all except one, a stubborn fellow that gathered strength apace. Frantically Galileo began to beat and beat with his rod-tip. By my baptism ! but the man was successful. The thatch was wholly dark. I saw by the set of his body that Galileo was elated by his small triumph. But just then a white sudden flame leaped from the undefended back of his cottage and proved how inadequate all his strivings had been. I saw the tongue of fire appear above the roof ridge : quickly it leaped over the sorry dominion of the rod. The lancewood slenderness was then a disconsolate line drawn against the yellow paper of the roof's flame.

The people's possessions were piled higgledy-piggledy in mid-road. Pigs and donkeys had been let loose through the fields and haggards. In many cases the large kitchen dresser had to be left behind—these dressers had been built in the kitchen by carpenters in the old days and were never meant to be removed. I saw several dressers jammed in doorways ; their owners could possibly have released them if they could have mustered the heart to damage the house by smashing down the lintel. This price they seemed reluctant to pay. The pig stan's had been rolled out into the yard and the flitches of bacon were wrapped in damp sheets. All through the salvage the fire kept leaping ; fire-cap upon fire-cap appearing prankishly, arbitrarily, inexplicably.

The old people gathered into a huddle beside me. They were asking that the priest be sent for. This I was reluctant to do. The fire was in mid-Cloone. The old folk followed me as I continued to fight the fire. I pretended not to notice them. They made an uneasy knot, wheezing and nudging at my very elbow.

" In sixty-two the priest saved us ! "

" Ches, we ask of you, through God's blood, to send for the Dean. He'll read out of a book an' the flames will die down."

" Let you not be stubborn, son ! "

Then : " Oh ! Oh ! " as they watched the fury of the flames, and : " Ah ! Ah ! " as a house puttered down.

Galileo was watching his house burn. He had retreated to his mid-road chattels. The cage which contained his goldfinch he had covered with a damp cloth. His brown cat was secure in a box. With his thumbnail the cobbler was picking chars from the top section of his fishing-rod. Sometimes he threw a weary eye at the old people who were still imploring me to send for the Dean.

" Don't stand between us an' the word of God, son ! "

" Your knowledge is not the be-all and end-all of knowledge."

" We're of a separate generation."

" Reared to trust, we are."

" Goin' away from God ye are, son ! "

The morning was now fully grey. Unhindered the flames were creeping under the thatch. The men were silent and the women were fully awed. The children had even ceased to cry. Still the old people continued to implore.

" Reared to lean on blind things we were ! " " Reared to trust things that were greater than we were ! " " Send for the Dean, son ! Send for the Dean ! "

Once, as a flame lifted, I saw the reflected light burnish the façade of Mary-without-Stain. I walked away from the group of aged whiners.

I called the young men together : we decided to cut down three houses on either side and so make a gap which the wind-crazy flames might fail to leap. We marked the three houses. Then we squabbled. Four of the men in our cutting-gang lived in the marked houses. On the decision, they deserted us. Each man took his stand in his own doorway. He stripped his teeth at us and became not merely an enemy but an animal. Nothing was said. We broke our decision. Human nature is human nature.

We went farther down. We picked out four more houses—

two on either side—and made ready to cut the rafters. One of the houses was mine; the other was Finn Dillon's. Our kitchen had been stripped bare. Standing on a short cow-loft ladder, I dragged down the sacking of our ceiling. The kitchen was barely touched with smoke. My mother and Mrs. Dillon came through the back-door from the haggard. I was standing on the ladder: already I had begun sawing through a rafter. Mrs. Dillon had a lighting kitchen-lamp in her hand although by now the strength of the daylight hardly warranted its usage.

" Son! Son!" my mother said. I stopped sawing. Mrs. Dillon held the lamp high. Standing thus I was between lights. My mother said: " Let our house not go down in disgrace! Fire is cleansing!"

In the distance the fire roared.

The men standing at the front door stood silent. They bent their heads, scarcely daring to look at me. To my mother, I said: " You are shamin' me! How can I order other people's houses to be cut down, if you deny me the right to cut down our own?"

My mother said: " The heart knows no laws an' little pride."

I heard the fire pouring down Cloone. The smoke was already around us in soft coils. My mother had turned to speak fearlessly to the men. " Here I was mated to his father. Out of this reckonin' he is! I am talkin' of the time that was there before he was."

Three women showed themselves from behind my mother. One said: " If 'twas a thing the cuttin' of Macnamaras' house would save my own cabin, I, for one, do not wish my home to stand at the cost of a neighbour's heartbreak."

" Nor I but as little," said the second.

The third woman said: " Why don't we all go down together, an' lick the one skillet of misfortune?"

This suggestion was met with a murmur of approval from other women clustered in the yard. Mrs. Dillon raised the lamp-wick.

The old women renewed their plaint : " Send for the priest ! "

There was a commotion at the door. The Dean walked Cloone.

The world was brightening for day. The fire had settled down to a steady roar. I came off the ladder and went to the front door. The Dean was unshaven. More than ever he resembled a heron. The old people gathered round him. " A hard case, my children," he said. He towered over them. The old people were around him, touching his sleeve and fawning on him. The young held aloof for the young are always proud. The belief was the same, but with the youth it possessed an element of briskness. The old lived in the well-worn ways of faith and forgiveness. The old lived by the heart.

Also, I could not help remembering the bitter things he had said about Cloone. I knew it was wrong to remember.

Hobbling after him, the oldsters continued to urge : " Throw the stole on your shoulder, Dean ! "

" The green stole, or the violet stole, or the golden stole or the red stole."

" Aye, or the dark stole if the feast-day suits it ! "

The Dean walked between the roaring houses. He came to where the fire had done its work. The ramparts of the fallen houses were gapped and silent. Behind him, ever hobbling and imploring, came the old.

" The Latin, Dean ! The lovely Latin ! "

" The flames will answer it ! "

" As they answered Father Hartnett in '62."

" The stole ! Out of your pocket take it ! "

" On your shoulders place it ! "

The light broke in Galileo's eyes. If even now he would rebel ! The light died. The Dean looked at the cobbler. Slowly, yet with full deference, Galileo stood up and tipped his black hat. Turning, he adjusted the wet cloth over his birdcage. As on a turn of idle thought he lifted the cloth and ran his finger along the wire bars of the cage. He was playing with his cock 'finch. He was annoying him so as to soothe him. The bird opened his bill and scolded his master.

The oldsters had gathered into a compelling ring about the Dean. I saw the Dean look out over the heads of the old people. His eyes straightly met mine. He said nothing. He looked at the fire, then turned to look down on the old people. Sadly he shook his head, then drew a deep breath. As he walked away, he said harshly : " Let ye fight the fire ! God helps those who help themselves."

At his words, valour drained from the old people. " Welcome be the holy will of God ! " they said. They brought their hands together, then drew them apart. Again they brought the hands together : this time they entwined the fingers and shook the joined hands up and down. They lifted their faces to the sky. They brought their faces down to the flames. They crumbled the intertwined fingers in the agony of their surrender. They turned and walked through the open gateway of the fire. With gestures of deep acceptance they squatted on the scraps of furniture in mid-road. They fell utterly silent.

The townspeople were now helping us. For the most part of it our own bucketeers had given up the job as a bad one. I had given one fellow a bloodied face for his desertion. Each of the men whose house still stood had tired of communal endeavour and now set about swamping his own thatch. This was before he realised that there was no stopping the jolly jumping of the fire.

Caherdown's roof had fallen in : theatrical to the last he began to cry full on my father's shoulder. In the midst of his lamentations he saw that a spark had settled on the sleeve of his good black suit. Fearing that his garment was injured he threshed wildly around.

Cloone was ravelling for sure.

In vain my fingernails tried to find my eyebrows. One of my cheekbones had begun to smart. My hands were blistered. I put my hand on the crown of my head—my palm smelled of singed hair. I stood in mid-road : my emotions had utterly drained away. Dicky Hickey tugged at my elbow: he was gibbering excitedly. Also he was dancing as if he had a call of nature he could not then answer.

"Ches! Ches! Listen to me! Dick Gaffney is in his room. His mother can't get him out. An' listen, Ches! That's not all!" He drew me aside. "I swore I wouldn't tell, but. . . ."

"But what?" I said, wearily.

"Listen, Ches! There's a wad of detonators and gelignite in Finn Dillon's thatch—in the part nearest to Dick Gaffney's room. Ches, I learned it by accident. Finn Dillon found out that I knew. He warned me not to tell. The fellow that was to take 'em after Finn had gone didn't do so!" Dicky had resumed his dancing.

I measured the fire. Sparks were falling and dying on Dillon's roof. Gaffney's crouched silent and ominous beside it.

"Late you left your tellin'!" I said.

In the haggard at the back of Gaffney's, Mrs. Gaffney said to me: "Let him to himself! He'll come to no harm. God protects his own." Drawing her shawl about her, she went to the window of her son's room. "Come on away, leanav bawn," she said. "White child, come away!"

There was no answer to her entreaty.

Gaffney's kitchen was in darkness. The door of Dick's room was bolted. I called on him to come out but he did not reply. I put my boot through the light sheeting of the door. The bedroom was in darkness. I sensed that Dick was in hiding from me. I put out my hand and touched an old washstand on the bed. "Pass me by, Ches Macnamara!" Dick said in such a tone of voice as I have rarely heard a man use. I cracked a match. In the dying light I saw his agonised face framed in the legs of a washstand. He was crouched in the corner behind the bed.

"You'll burn alive!" I said. The match flame died to an ember. Above the smoke of burning Cloone I received the smell of that individual match.

"I tell my beads every night, Ches Macnamara," he said. "No harm will come to me from fire—only from people."

I dropped the dead match-end and tore the washstand from the bed. I flung myself across the tick at him. As I grasped his clothing, he slid down under the bed. I heard the thump as he rolled on the floor. He was now somewhere in the darkness beside me. Again I called to him, imploring him to come with me.

His breath was that of a tired horse. "The cross of Christ I place between me an' you," he said: "that an' the five wounds of Our Saviour!"

I halted and set at measuring his voice. Of a sudden I rushed for it. But he interposed an article of furniture, probably his little table, between me and him, so that I struck my temple heavily against the corner of it. The dark world lighted with artificial sparks. I went down on one knee and covered my face with my hands; for a time I rocked between the in and the out of consciousness.

When Dick again spoke we both seemed to be in a strange world. His voice had lost its beggarman whine. Firmly and without a falter, he said: "A short salmon-gaff I have now, Ches Macnamara. Come after me an' I'll rip you for sure!"

Above me, behind me and beside me swayed the firmed voice. My mind said: In, out; in, out! Before my eyes frolicked an artificial conflagration.

I swung into consciousness, then rose to a half-crouch. My mouth moaned dully. My tongue was reasoning with him, not precisely saying the things I wished it to say. Even as I reasoned, Dick Gaffney kept saying in his new voice: "For certain I'll rip you!" or, "I'll rip you for sure!"

I heard Madcap's voice calling me from the kitchen.

Harshly I turned to the broken door. Whatever it was she was saying, I could not understand it clearly.

"What is it?" I asked impatiently but did not wait for her to reply. Abruptly, I said: "Tell Dom Foy to get everyone away from Dillon's ! Dicky Hickey will tell him why. D'you hear me ? "

" But, Ches. . . . "

" But what ? "

" The fire has jumped. It's next door but one."

" Do as you're told, you stubborn slut ! "

Madcap had gone. The new sweat on my face and the noising in the straw above my head verified that the fire had indeed leaped. The crack in my temple again irked me. I tasted a sour sup in my throat. As my stomach fully rebelled, I was racked with a hollow retching. This retching suggested a plan.

Dropping on one knee, I exaggerated the hollowness of my vomit. As I did so, my ears took in Dick Gaffney's breathing and gauged it as accurately as I could. I drew my hand around me in an arc in the darkness : I was ensuring that this time there was nothing solid between me and him. My hands memorised the items of furniture in the room. I readied my boots then put my hand to my throat, half-expecting at any moment to find a gaff deep in my windpipe. The crackling of the fire sounded as though a thousand rats had got into the thatch.

After an unnecessarily loud retch I dashed aside the light chair Dick was holding, then closed firmly with him. His down-going hand eluded my grasp. The stroke of the gaff went away over my back in a vicious arc. Catching him around the middle, I butted my poll against his head : then suddenly I drove my knee into the pit of his stomach. As he winced away, I tried to double him over my shoulder. But he was quickly endowed with the frenzy which trebles strength, and even as I slung him over my shoulder he shortened his hold on the gaff-handle and drove the point of the weapon fair and full into the flesh of my thigh. The steel bit the full of its mouth on my buttocks and nicked along the bone. This angered me so that I flung him against the wall and guzzled him until he wilted.

With an angry smile, I realised what it was to be a gaffed salmon. Confusedly I threw my mind back to the Christmas Eve on which Finn Dillon and I had visited Dick Gaffney and had seen the gaffs hanging from the pictures. My memory could not tell me whether or not the gaff was barbed.

I took him on my shoulder. The gaff was dangling behind me. It was my ill-luck that the handle was the wrong height: it was neither trailing nor dangling but hitting the ground infrequently. Once, when I made an awkward movement, it stood on its end on the floor. On my way out to the kitchen it continued to strike against my right boot-heel. The front door was standing wide open. I staggered out into the street. Mrs. Gaffney came from the haggard and followed me.

Dominick Foy had ordered the people back: the majority of the onlookers had taken shelter behind the stout walls of the as-yet unconsumed houses. Dom rushed out of a house and took my load from me. Dicky Hickey, ever watchful, came forward and lifted the gaff-handle, so that my pain was minimised. As we hurried away, the mannikin was carrying my timber tail. In a deserted and stripped kitchen where the lamp was still lighting, Dicky withdrew the gaff-head. It was unbarbed. I saw my blood upon the steel. It could have been the blood of a fish.

Prudently, we went to the doorway. Cloone was deserted. Dillon's cottage went up with a roar. Two sheets of light resembling plate-glass windows met in the air above the house, and after the detonation begotten by their majestic congruence, they tore their terror sideways and upwards. Rafters and thatch and sparks decorated the apple-green morning sky. The force of the explosion made the wind temporarily puny. The acrid smell of burnt explosive reached us where we crouched in the deep doorways. Blazing rafters rolled over on roofs where the heat vapour awaited the boon of just such an ignition. Its seed fructifying in a short span, the harvest of fire was everywhere. My mother saw our house take on a helmet of flame.

Five or six of the houses at the end nearest the mouth of

Cloone we could possibly have saved. But their owners had grown listless : it seemed as if their minds had become attuned to the idea of end. When these houses had been stripped, their owners kept repeating resignedly : " Aye, we'll lick the common skillet of misfortune ! "

Full autumn day was upon us. Cloone was ended. I walked the full length of my principality-in-a-jest. The ruin of the Rookery moved me most. Wrapped in the grey morning light, Tom Goggin and his small wife had watched it burn. She, tidy, frail and loyal, was pressed against her husband as their house of colour and adventure moved to its last. Watching them standing thus, I wondered that there had ever been banter between them. I recalled him saying to his wife : " If we bred, woman, our children could play hurley under the bed ! " This was his assuagement for childlessness. Sometimes to comfort himself, he said : " Kings are without progeny —why not Tom Goggin ? " The remembrance of these words enabled me to dream the old pair young.

But perhaps my grief at the Rookery's downfall was a compounded sorrow : it could be that it was an echo of the barony's sorrow—even of the province's sorrow. The fall of the Rookery was certain to engender a sense of loss, not among the fixed and the stable, but amongst those who were homeless and astray on the Irish roads.

In mid-road, the western woman had withdrawn into herself. She was busying herself amongst her chattels. From time to time she looked at the sky where it hung over her own western world.

I looked along Cloone. Galileo had his birdcage in his hand. I saw the sun strike through the beating wings of the caged bird. The resulting whirr of dusky silver pleased me momentarily.

Although, at the very last, Badger Breen now had a conspiracy worthy of the elasticity of his face, it was clear that the occasion had overawed him.

Through Caherdown's open doorway I could see straight to the yard. Against the scorched greenery of his flower-garden, I spied the old trestle—patched, as it was, with parts of a bacon box; the sight of this made me recall the morning of the Old Fair of Cloone. Of the Tom Thumb nasturtiums outside his door there was not a trace. Between window and doorway on each side the walls were down. What remained of his pink-washed walls were irretrievably stained. Caherdown was moving along from pile to pile of furniture and trumperies that extended right down mid-road for the full length of Cloone. For the first time in his life he was condescending to be warm-hearted with his neighbours. He had drink taken and was crying maudlinly about dead days.

Old Font, his face strangely set, was seated on a chair in mid-road. His beard seemed as proud as ever. I could not bear to talk to him. Latterly I knew that he was failing in health, for more than once I had seen the blue as of thin milk on his lips.

We lighted small cooking-fires near the doorways of the burned houses. These were the fires of irony, for they were made of charred rafters and pieces of chopped-up doors. We boiled and spoiled tea. The eating of our breakfasts took up our attention for a while. Every bite we took we masticated to the full.

Draining a mug of tea, I saw that all eyes were turned upon me. I lowered the mug. The eyes had fallen.

The delusion that I was being watched passed as quickly as it came. Was it a delusion? I was taken with a wave of anger. What did they want? Cloone had ravelled—that much was manifest to an idiot! Prince of Cloone—that was a jest that had shrivelled to nothing in the heart of the fire.

All that remained was the mid-road jumble: the beds and the pictures of the saints, the hen-coops and the quilts, the salmon-spears, the hurleys, the sugawn chairs, the chipped enamel chamber-pots, the mirrors framed in fretwork, the pictures of the patriots, the cones of paper in which human hair was treasured lest the devil have his way with its owners, the piggins and the willow-patterned delph, the lustre jugs, the wicker cliabhs and sciaths for turf, the kitchen tables, the clevies or half-mantels, the tea-caddies and the lamps. I saw an extraordinary article of furniture someone told me was a gossip-chair: I didn't know such a thing existed in Cloone. There were fishing-rods galore; also the settle-beds which were seats by day and beds by night, together with old linen, flitches of bacon and onions in pails.

Among the mixum-gatherum of Martha Goggin's odds-and-ends I spied the Infant of Prague. With the coming of the sun the Slav Jesukin took on brightness in the red of his cloak and the gold of his crown. In his hand he held a miniature gilt globe surmounted with a Maltese Cross. I knew that if I lifted the image I would find a coin beneath. This was a superstition we had: while there was a coin under the Infant of Prague the owner of the statue would never lack money.

I looked around me: were the people waiting for me to speak? The townspeople were gaping into Cloone. Some of them came forward. We broke off their gestures of sympathy.

It was now ten o'clock. Young and old were idly looking up and down. As on a resolution, Galileo, who had been seated on a sugawn chair outside his burnt home, stood up suddenly. He dragged a roll of frayed oilcloth from his gear, unrolled it and flung it fully across his furniture. He then pulled his hat firmly down over his eyes. With one hand he took the cage with the cock goldfinch in it: in his axilla he locked his charred fishing-rod. I saw him lift the little box that contained his cat. Slowly he began to walk down Cloone. He looked neither to left nor to right. His face was grave and grey. He hid his eyes under the old black hat. Clump! Clump! he came down the roadway: of a common thought we recalled that a nephew of his owned a small pokeen of a shop in narrow Oldgate street.

Resolutely the old cobbler came on. The old folk, seated on

the chairs, began to call out: "Goodbye, neighbour!" Galileo did not reply: he moved on through the autumn morning.

As Galileo passed out the place where Old Font was seated his neck threatened to become corded. It was as if his will was imploring his body to relax. But harsher memories appeared to be suborning his mind.

Saddened exceedingly, Old Font stood up and watched the cobbler go. He leaned heavily on his stick.

"Gay days we had here, one-ager!" he called out after him. Galileo did not reply. He kept clumping steadily ahead. Old Font sat down heavily.

I stood straight in the cobbler's road.

"You off, Gal?"

"Out of my road!" he shouted.

"Like sheep they'll follow you out a gap," I said. "Can't you wait . . . ?"

Fully the neck was corded now. "Wait? For what? For poverty an' drop-down? If it's charity that's before me I'll take it square!"

I was caught for words. "Gay days we had here, old-timer!" I said. A proper parrot I was, mimicking what Old Font had said before me.

Galileo stopped. He looked me up and down fiercely. "Maybe, yes! Maybe, no! Out o' my road!"

He was old and he was angry. I came out of his road. He clumped away towards the mouth of Cloone. Hearing his own words of denial had crystallised his opposition. He was a rebel again.

The fire had not moved us as this desertion had. If only I had throttled the old fellow! Yet, what he had said was true. There was nothing in store for the old of Cloone but the alien roof, the lowered voice, the unauthoritative opinion, the sycophancy which they reckoned worse than death. The waiting and watching and craving for such a simple amenity as a place at the fireside. The perfunctory muscular smiling at jokes that they did not relish. The appalling pattern of unobtrusiveness. The furtive panny in the inner room. All the feints foreign to independence that inevitably shrivel the heart of man.

From lips that were lonely the calls followed the departing cobbler.

" Goodbye, neighbour ! "

" Good fortune attend you ! "

" That you may be lucky an' that the road may rise with you!"

They called to him also in the old Gaelic, the nostalgia of which they half-hoped he would find unsupportable. I watched the cage in Galileo's hand. No longer was the sun behind the bird's wings.

And so the sickness of going took us, every one. I saw an oldster rise from his chair, grasp his stick and begin poking grimly at his possessions as if the brass ferrule on the stick-end had the power to shepherd the goods together while the old fellow tramped the town in search of dismal lodgings at a small rental. Implicit in every poke and thrust and jab was terror before the inhospitable world. The movements of the old people had indefinably become those of persons who did not belong to anywhere. And then one spoke ; another spoke ; all spoke :

" Wait, Galileo, ould sport ! "

" Wait an' I'll be with you ! "

" Nothin' here but hunger an' want ! "

" Wait, ould stock o' the west ! "

" Wait ! Wait ! "

A man threw back his head and laughed. Beneath his lowered eyelids, his hysterical eyes were fast on Old Font. Through his laughter he shouted : " Ha, ha, ha ! How can a man fill his belly with the memory of gay days ? Ha, ha ! Will it keep out the rain ? Will it fill the pot with meat ? Ha, ha, ha ! "

Badger Breen had loosened his terrier : he was ready to be

off. Dicky Hickey was pulling at Streaming Blood. Caherdown was looking at the sky ; I knew he was enumerating his distant blood-connections in the lanes of the town, wondering who would be likeliest to give him even a grudged reception. Tim Fennell, the old stonemason with the broken hip—his wife was whispering into his better ear.

Old Font was shouting at the fickle. To hell with the old ranter, I thought. As the people made their preparations for departure, he got more obstreperous. At last he became impossible. His son kept striving to hold him to the chair. His wife, too, was shushing him. Breaking from his son's arms, the old man began to shout in my direction. I laughed and turned away.

I watched them go—the knot of people that I had loved. Times there were when we had one joy, one sorrow, one anger and one exaltation. I watched them move like dry sand falling down. Even as I watched them the insistent world kept calling to me. As I sprawled across a pile of bedding I looked at my boots ; one of them seemed rooted in burned Cloone, the other was eager to noise among the coloured cities of the world. My fingers were trying to recover my vanished eyebrows. I must have appeared haggard. Madcap was watching me from a distance : I had spied her a while since. To hell with her, too ! Creation was crowded with women.

Not in the fire of Cloone had we died but here and now when Cloone was ravelling for sure.

Man after man going. Women now following. The women were looking back at where cottages stood—with woman it's always the nest. The last hullahoos of farewell. Boot after boot clumping steadily in the cobbler's wake. (Finn was dead and so was Shoon.) "Forever Cloone !" I said to myself, then laughed bitterly as I blinded my eyes to the resonant untidy road.

I thought : truly, here is the end.

And then, O neighbours of creation ! it seemed as if the Almighty God had abruptly deserted His business of mating the magnificent animals of Africa, of arranging the wheeling of sky-balls and the superintending of the twisting of the myriad elvers in the slime of Saragossa. And had turned His eye on scabby scalded Cloone!

For, look ye, neighbours of creation, beyond limit or barrier whatsoever, beyond the puzzlement engendered by the moulds in which your prayers are cast, beyond the quaint, whimsical or outlandish styles of your windows or chimneys, this is what happened! Ye who feel proud and whose bodies burgeon under public praise, or who wilt in loneliness when the knife of disappointment is turned in the centre of the heart, neighbours dear, this is what happened!

I raised my eyes: all the people were looking uphill towards the brow of the eastern road. For a moment or two my eyes did not follow the eyes of my neighbours: I knew that by instinct and tradition the hill-road was a point of hope: that we looked upwards and to the east when circumstances had become harsher than we could endure. At last I followed the gaze of my neighbours. And this was what I saw.

Swaying on the hill-road was what seemed to be a bright green flame with a horseshoe of red-yellow beneath it. Focusing my eyes, I made out a cowled chimney-pipe angled against the wondrous green of a wagon roof. I saw the piebald horse galloping down: even at that distance the harness bells were clearly audible. On the front platform of the wagon a man was standing. As he came closer I made out his black pants, scarlet shirt, bright waistcoat and yellow headpiece. This man was shouting at the horse the while he drove like mad in from under the morning sun. The small pair of wheels in front and the great pair behind kept churning up the yellow light. The vehicle lurched dangerously.

Stilled as to stone, in the midst of our bedraggled chattels, we watched this crazy oncoming. Here was the brilliance, the bravado, the risk and the colour that we loved. Where the road straightened out into Cloone proper, the man gave the horse the full pistol shot of the whip. Then the complete jangle and ring of harness came true to our ears.

Into Cloone the caravan came : it resembled the chariot of a king. The man on the platform stood as if riding on tall air : surely and freely he anticipated every lurch and sway of the vehicle. He rode like one accustomed to huzzas : his whip was already raised in salute. Where the crowd was thin the people now began to call out. Man after man became loud hurrahdy-boy : clearly we who were watching saw their gesticulations. The vehicle ground ahead, moving between the barrier of furniture and the broken houses. It skilfully took the half-road that lay open to it. The driver seemed to delight in the danger.

With what cries of joy Metal Belly was greeted : " Welcome home ! Welcome home ! "

With whip aloft and royal gliding, the bellman came onwards. He paid no man individual attention. His eyes kept taking in smoking, broken Cloone.

" Welcome home ! "

The old men had taken off their black caubeens and were holding them aloft. The women had begun to wave their green-and-black shawls. Parallel to the course of the wagon on the other side of the barrier barefooted children ran screaming.

Little Angel drew on the bell of Mary-without-Stain.

The deserters had to stand aside to make way for Metal Belly's caravan. At the crossroads of Cloone Metal Belly checked the horse. The black walls of the Rookery were directly behind him. As one man, we thronged forward. For a moment there was a great silence. The bellman looked around at the prone cottages, then he looked at us. How black the skin of his face had grown ! He was aloof, high and competent. Then suddenly we felt unsure of Metal Belly for he had great ear-rings in his ears.

" Well ! " he said at last.

After he had spoken there was a wave of soft feeling. He was not alien to Cloone : that much was implicit in his tone. " Welcome home ! " Quietly now, the voices mingling happily with one another.

Inside the wagon stood a woman. She moved a smiling step in the direction of the half-open door and stood with her head pressed against a mirror. The women looked hard at her. At first they were repelled, for they half-expected to find the arrogance, the wheedling and the enticement. But Trouble-o'-the-World wore the smile of a women appeased. The watching women continued to be shrewd: as yet they were unsure.

The horse was lathered in foam and sweat. Badger Breen took him by the head. It was an entire sire horse, as was right. His back was a cask of strength. Above his impatient head the sky was filled with vivid patches of blue.

"I seen the glow in the sky," Metal Belly said, "so I came fast." His voice was deep. When he looked across to where his own house had stood we were unable to read his face.

"Well!" he said again.

Inexplicably, the glory of his return was dimmed. The chapel bell had ceased its ringing.

Then, when they were minded to turn away in disappointment the women heard the cry of a child from the wagon. From lip to lip of the women the light ran. They started to laugh. Not to laugh so much as to cry out. It was hunger in the form of a laugh. The western woman came forward out of the ranks of the women: throwing her shawl wildly from off her shoulders she laughed out full and free thus sponsoring all the women's hunger. Bold as brass she was and yet brave in a fashion that we welcomed. We now realised that she had been fully fused into our community. Laughing twisted lips were on her when she spoke:

"The child?" she enquired, masterfully. "Is it black or fawn, Metal Belly?" Trouble-o'-the-World smiled at the question yet she did not move her head from the mirror.

"Black, begod!" Metal Belly said, loudly and good-humouredly.

The women half-cheered. The western woman turned in triumph. The men laughed: rich and full and deep the laughter was, tumbling over and over.

On the crowd's edge, a man cupped his hand around his mouth. "Is it takin' after the sire or the dam?" he shouted.

"The sire, begod!" Metal Belly said proudly. Everybody was cheering and stamping and laughing. Men threw one another aside with the dint of an earthen glee.

A bare step behind her husband's back, Trouble-o'-the-World was a cat licking cream from her paws.

What seemed to us to be polished wit was not yet at an end. After the gust of laughter had died, Old Font pointed with his stick. "Hey there, Bellman," he called out, "is it a boy or a child?"

A pause preceded Metal Belly's triumphant declamation. "A boy, begod!" he answered with a shout.

This statement crowned everybody's hilarity. Metal Belly cracked his whip to add point to his brag of breeding. Turn and turn about, we cheered and laughed. Rearing, the sire horse dragged Badger Breen up into the heavens. This engendered additional cries: cries of fear overlaying the cries tokening the undefinable lust of simply being alive. Fearlessly Badger drew the horse to the ground.

The women pressed forward; again the western woman shouted brazenly: "What are you hidin' it for? Show us your infant, Bellman!"

On all sides the cry was taken up: "Aye! Aye! Show us the child!"

Trouble-o'-the-World went deep into the interior of the wagon and brought the child to the door. It was a black-haired boy, the drawn stamp of his father and as healthy as a hound. The sweet skin on his face was the colour of rope. After a moment's hesitation the child clapped his hands and crowed out into Cloone.

Braving the horse's hind legs, the women came forward in a

gay gang. Their voices were shot with the force of maternal surges. Like branches of winter trees, their hands went up. " Give ! Give ! " the hands implored. The horse warned them with the detonation of steel on stone, yet the women did not reck. " Give ! Give ! " they clamoured.

Trouble-o'-the-World handed down the child. He was immediately enveloped in the women's hands. " God bless him ! " they crowed. The young girls skirmished around the heels of the admiring women.

Brink-o'-the-Grave was heard raising her voice from where she sat on the only sugawn chair in Cloone that boasted arm-rests. Seated thus she had spent the morning : the greater part of the span of her enthronement she had devoted to the taking of snuff and groaning.

" Me to be without respect in Cloone ! " she complained. " Me that borned the throng o' ye ! " The old crone again raised her voice. " Did I not born you, Metal Belly ? " she asked.

With suitable gravity, Metal Belly replied : " I was among the first you brought into the world."

They brought the lusty boy to Brink-o'-the-Grave and laid him on her lap. The women kept singing his praises. " Jewel " they called him and " bright young hound," and even " hazel nut," than which no other appellation could be more fitting. Brink-o'-the-Grave took the child in her worn deft hands. She looked up at the ring of praising women. Then she scowled and spat fully on the crown of the boy's head.

" Do ye want to overlook the child ? " scolded Brink-o'-the-Grave.

The women stood rebuked. The spit, we knew, was to take the harm out of the abundance of praising. The women hung their heads in shame.

Brink-o'-the-Grave's old eyelids were fallen open red. The skin of her leathern face was crazied with age. Her nostrils were powdered from interminable snuffing. Her hands were barely able to dolce the child : what they lacked in strength they more than compensated for in craft and experience.

The child gave a single look upwards. For a moment his face was a pure puzzle-the-world. At length he seemed satisfied with his scrutiny, for he began to crow delightedly and then to thump the old woman's knees with the balls of his heels. Black his hair was as midnight. Real sloes his eyes were. The drawn stamp of Metal Belly, you'd say, yet if you closed an eye and looked at him with the sun yellowing portion of his face and the shadows lingering in the hollows of his eye-sockets, he was certainly Trouble-o'-the-World—herself and none other.

The old woman turned the child so that he stood facing her. It gave her all she could do to manage him. Her old fingers ran over his gipsy legs : the legs immediately clambered over the old woman's breasts with scant mercy for her infirmities. "Noble limbs," voted Brink-o'-the-Grave, "an' a grand substantial child."

"God bless him!" the women said in atonement. Seeing their opportunity they crowded in to add further sentences of praise.

"Free in manner, too!"

"In nowise dark with strangers!"

"Strangers!" exclaimed Brink-o'-the-Grave. "Where, under God, are the strangers?"

The child made a glaum for the red eyes, but Brink-o'-the-Grave forestalled his clutchings. Then the young girls of from seven to eleven years of age went down on their knees and crept right under the legs of the thronged women until they reached Brink-o'-the-Grave's skirt. There their lips began to form the silent endearments that young girls form in such a situation. "Cuckoo!" their lips said, wholly without sound. In spite of their utmost endeavours, they failed to hold the child's attention : now and again he offered them a cursory puzzled glance and then turned to gape afresh at the bloody crescents of the old woman's eyelids. The girls were undismayed : silently, their lips working all the while, they sought to find which of them the child would first favour with his solemn or laughing attention. All their blandishments were in vain. Refusing to abandon hope, they went as close as they dared without rousing Brink-o'-the-Grave's anger.

It was the first time I had seen the girls with my conscious eyes. I kept gazing at them for a long time; tragedies and comedies they certainly would have. To me it was sobering to consider that these girls were already fashioning a fresh and powerful pattern of life.

I continued to watch them. The world had not begun with my beginning: nor would it end with my ending.

The girls were now working up to a certain fever. Again and again their hands came up to touch the child. They mortally feared a rebuke from Brink-o'-the-Grave; thus, every time the old red eyes fell on them they swiftly flashed their hands away. But the hands continued to be rebellious and were already trembling with the anticipatory delight of touching the child's limbs. In the end it got so that the girls could scarcely trust their hands. Once Brink-o'-the-Grave glanced harshly down; then each kneeling girl locked her two hands steadfastly between her thighs, so that thus imprisoned they could not betray her.

The child was clapping his hands. The girls laughed. It was a lovely peepshow! High above them as the sire horse shook his head the harness bells began ringing. Brink-o'-the-Grave glanced over the child's shoulder. Suddenly she looked at the laughing girls.

"Jesus an' Mary, girleens," she asked, "is it happy ye are?"

"Happy we are, ma'am!" they pealed together.

"Ye're not frettin' for yeer cauboosheens bein' burned?"

"We're not frettin' at all, ma'am!" the girls answered.

"Glory be to the Mind of God!" said Brink-o'-the-Grave.

The girls did not take their eyes off the boy's face.

Hanging in the blaze of the sire horse's forehead was a brass trinket composed of a horse's head inset in a horseshoe. Everywhere the brass bosses and ovals glittered where they sat squarely on the natural-coloured harness. The chamfered

red-yellow wonder of the upper portion of the wagon door was tricked out with pretty green-and-white muslin. On either side of the door were brass harness-lamps that gave the wagon its eyes. On the low half-door of the wagon, too, was a brass knocker, well polished. Over all like a banner was the devilish emerald of the wagon-roof. For us children of the rainbow it was good to have such colour : it was a symbol that our affairs would end in prosperity.

Badger Breen was still holding the stallion's head : from time to time he glanced about him to see if everybody understood the importance and difficulty of his task. I thought that he half-hoped that the stallion would again rear. Metal Belly still stood on the platform of the caravan : he was greeting a dozen men at once. Old comrades of his looked up at him in a new awe : the bellman had travelled much and his great voice had dominated the bright events of Ireland. He had smelt the naphtha flares under upcountry stars.

And even as Metal Belly laughed and greeted his neighbours a housewall collapsed into a crumble of yellow clay. "Phut !" the wall said, and straightaway the centuries vanished. The children's laughter rang out even through the noise of the falling wall. Once I saw Metal Belly's face darken as his eyes fell on his own tumbled cottage. " How small she is ! " he said to one of the men.

In the interval of time suspended the climbing sun continued to seek out the brass on the mitred-edged collarplates and reins-savers, on the hames-straps, on the rope-edged ovals and on the dip of the horse's collar.

Walking carefully, a woman approached the caravan. Her packing apron was heavily laden. At the steps of the wagon she halted and looked up at Trouble-o'-the-World. From the apron came the careful chuckle of delph. " Your man's valuables, ma'am," the woman said. " Jamesy, my husband, it was who broke down the door."

The woman opened the apron. There again was the riot of colour.

" Well ! " said Metal Belly. He had fully turned. For an instant his features softened. Slowly he stooped. Trouble-o'-the-World kept watching him concernedly. Out of the opened apron he took a lustre jug and a blue imitation Japanese vase. As he chose, we saw the bellman's two lives written on his face. He laughed. It was the laugh of one capable of standing aloof. We knew then that he had decided, for, like his wife, we were fitted to interpret the laugh. Trouble-o'-the-World's face became tranquil once more.

" Thank you, Peggy," the bellman said. " Thank Jamesy for me, too." As he looked up fair into the face of his wife, they laughed at one another as if we of Cloone had no existence.

Peggy asked : " Are the rest mine, Metal Belly ? "

" Yours they are ! " the bellman said, turning.

Slowly the woman closed the apron over the glory her apron contained. She said : " There's your bed an' your beddin', your small stool an' your chairs that creak. Your sheets of old linen an' your alarm clock. Also, your grand Madonna of the Chair."

" Is there e'er a patchwork quilt ? " Metal Belly asked. He laughed provocatively. " An' a blue sconce with a socket for a small candle ? "

" Aye, there's them too," Peggy said understandingly.

" A bargain I'll make, woman. The patchwork quilt an' the blue sconce for me—the rest is yours ! "

Trouble-o'-the-World was remembering : her smile was a sure indication that this was so.

" That's a bargain that's too fair," Peggy said. " Good luck to you an' yours." Again she opened the coarse packing apron that was edged with red bias binding. Upraised by her knee, the blue sconce came up from the deeps of the delph ; she handed it to Trouble-o'-the-World.

" The quilt I'll bring you later, ma'am," said Peggy.

Then she bowed and withdrew.

Dick Gaffney was seated on a bundle of bedding ; the men kept asking him how he liked the experience of the sunlight and the open day. During his time in the darkness he had developed a queer way of moving his hands. His features were paler than a potato-stalk that sprouts in a cellar on hearing the first rumour of spring. He seemed perfectly at ease. Looking at him, the wound in my thigh began to chafe and the iodine with which it had been daubed began to bite me sorely.

Behind the dead houses the apple trees showed the final remnants of life. A single apple-leaf moved uproad where there was no clutter of black thatch. The leaf, urged by a low wind, proceeded slowly on its points like a sea-crab crossing smooth stone.

The girls had thought of a new shift to attract the child's attention. They began to hum-sing the Gaelic lullaby, "Cow with the One Horn."

"*Bo, bo, bo na leath h-adhairce, bo, bo, bo. . . .*"

The child seemed interested. Wide-eyed he watched their mouths. Through their humming-singing the girls semi-smiled at the success of their plan. Brink-o'-the-Grave was now content to let them have this small turn of success for the child's heels were proving over-strong for her knees. When the child's full attention was taken by the humming, the girls as on a signal began to sway in time to the beat of the song. The pattern of this swaying I had seen before—on the night the women had *caoin*-ed Finn Dillon. And then I thought: delight, anguish, love or even anger—women will always reduce these extremities of emotion to the simplicity of a sway.

Madcap was there: the tiredness of the night was washed from her face. Her hair was caught behind her in a braid or plait or coil, that despite my utter weariness, moved me to look at it a second time. Her dress was navy in colour with pin-points of white. She wore a white collar. Her lips were rich red. Seeing how clean and graceful she was made me suddenly realise that I was begrimed.

Little Angel came up the sodden street of Cloone. His

hands were commiserating with us. For once the quarter-tips did not clip as he moved.

We continued to hold time back in an inexplicable reprieve.

Old Font had gathered round him the young boys of from nine to twelve years of age. They resembled birds in an aviary that had been hushed. The boys sprawled here and there on articles of furniture. Old Font was preaching his gospel of Cloone being eternal—he was doing this with a zeal that continued to be close to daftness.

He asked one of the boys : " How did she go, sonny ? "

As if reciting a lesson in school, the boy said in a monotonous high-pitched voice : " From the mouth of Cloone the cottages were capped with good gold an' snug brown straw. . . ."

Galileo's goldfinch was on the move again. Wherever in Cloone conversation turned on goldfinches, this noble bird of Galileo's was sure to be mentioned. Whenever I set him before the mirror in the cobbler's kitchen, he would go off into lovely rolls of high sound. Now with the gold bar brave and clean in his red-gold wing he was going away.

Shemus Goff stood in the centre of Cloone : his gaze was following the departing cobbler. As songmakers go, Shemus knew that he would never be truly great for he lacked that harshness which is always an attribute of greatness.

Do not turn, I told myself. Walk away. Away and away and away. The dream is ended. They are all going now. Slow rolling coin is following slow rolling coin. Their departure is as noiseless as a dream. Do not turn, I counselled myself again. Walk away and away and away. How wide the world is and how filled with wonders and colours !

Metal Belly let a holy oath out of him. We lingered to listen. This was not the voice of the moral man we had known ! The bellman continued to rant and to roar. Blast and blast and blast !

After the initial natural start, nobody paid him the slightest attention. Each man was intent upon his chattels, taking what he could not, for the moment, bear to leave. One man took a terrier. A second took some calf-bound books. A third took a great blue dish. I saw a carpenter quench the glitter of his tools in a straw bass. My father and mother looked with mendicant faces to where the sky was clearing over Mary's townland. Mrs. Dillon looked in the direction of Littero; it was the fall of the year and the waysides by the estuary would be coloured with the blood of the fallen fuchsia blooms.

Metal Belly was now standing on the wagon platform: he had froth on his mouth from calling and from receiving mocking replies. Badger Breen had abandoned his task of holding the stallion's head and the animal was showing signs of restlessness. Metal Belly grasped the reins and drew heavily upon them. The wagon swayed dangerously, then stilled. Behind Metal Belly stood his wife: the boy in her arms was looking at his father with keenest interest. Through a truce in his shouting, Trouble-o'-the-World said something to her husband. The bellman's face showed an angry appreciation of the wisdom of what she had said: he turned and from a shelf inside the doorway drew forth his bell.

When the bell's tongue hit the metal everyone halted. In Trouble-o'-the-World's arms the child clapped his hands and laughed freely. The bell kept ringing and would not be denied. The people of Cloone respected the sound of the bell: it had called their fathers together to hear the uncrowned King of Ireland state that no man had a right to set a boundary to the onward march of a nation. Almost it could be said that this bell had given Ireland what measure of freedom was hers.

Also, the sound of the bell puzzled them. It had a strangeness of note in it. It suggested the wildness of West Country fairs. The fumes of poteen and the hissing spurt of naphtha flares—these were the phenomena its sound implied. It kept ringing until, with slow discipline, all the people had gathered in a ring around the wagon. Then and then only the bell seemed satisfied. With reluctance the sound ran down as the last straggler drew near. Dick Gaffney had been led forward by the hand, as if he was a child afraid of walking in bright light; the chair on which Brink-o'-the-Grave sat was lifted holus-bolus and brought closer to the wagon.

His voice was pitched low and filled with pathos, as Metal Belly said: "In the name of the Adorable God, is there ne'er a Prince in Cloone?"

The assembled people looked at me and accused me with their stares: You! You! You!

Galileo stood at the edge of the crowd. "A lovely chestnut foal!" he mimicked in the voice of Brink-o'-the-Grave. Through the resultant bitter laughter I kept remembering that Madcap would witness my humiliation. And then the old thought occurred to me: I seemed to see the world in terms of its cities and women. In my mind I began to experience the free gait of a young man on an open road. For the moment I was without master and the mouth that could injure me had no existence.

The people continued their unspoken accusations. I turned angry. The excitement of the night had shredded me sorely.

I spat out heavily.

"There's your Cloone!" I said, nodding at the houses. I walked aside a step or two—to where I could see the full measure of the sky.

"To hell an' to hell with you!" roared Metal Belly. The froth on his mouth-corners again took life.

Galileo shouted at the bellman: "A fine one you are to talk—you that deserted us for a woman of the roads!"

Metal Belly's face darkened. "Before God . . ." he began.

Old Font was looking at me piercingly. "Till you emigrate or die!" he said clearly. I gestured my anger at archaic idiocies.

Over the brown hills the world was a fine place. I was young and untrammelled. I could strike the calf of my leg with my palm and hear the voice of lust in the resultant sound. The weariness that was on me would vanish in a night. Beyond the hills were cities with the fullness of adventure in them. Everywhere in the lands women were calling out to be loved. To hell with this craziness of Cloone ! To hell with the tyranny of oldsters !

Tomfoolery had reached its extremity. I turned my back on the people, then walked away.

Metal Belly had leaped from his perch. He stood in front of me with his left hand extended and clenched : his right hand gripped the bell by the brassbound handle. Like it or not, I had to listen to the bellman.

" I'll brain you with my bell," he said, " unless you come back an' direct us, whether the direction be right or wrong."

People, people, people. My people standing quietly by. The world tugging at my waist, saying : Come ! Come ! Here is what your body craves !

I came back. I was still smiling bitterly. I leaped on to the platform of the wagon. I looked about at torn Cloone. What was the story ? Mud in a rampart : mud levelled ! What in God's name was all the fuss about ? To hell with Cloone—let it ravel !

I looked down. It was the first time I had seen all my people together.

If you get a pencil and idly make scrawls on paper, doing it quickly and haphazardly, adding a nose, an eye and an ear to each circular or oval or semicircular representation of a head, you will then have the queer faces that confronted me. The faces were old and young ; battered and serene. I turned my attention to the children in arms and to the girls who were already weaving threads of colour in their lives.

Murray Folan and Abernethy Bovenizer were standing neutrally on the edge of the crowd : Folan was of ourselves while the Palatine's people had brought us understanding out of the heart of Europe. Neither of them wished Cloone to die. Remarks came pelting up from the crowd. Again the bell rang and stilled the angry voices. I was resolved to tell the people the truth. I would set an end to madness. I put my thumbs firmly into the Belt of Cloone. And then, even when my decision seemed steel-strong, I faltered. Had these people stepped down through time with their curious impudences and independences so that I should stand up and betray them? I had stood by and heard Finn Dillon say that man doffs and dons.

Standing there with the people waiting for me to speak and to direct, I stumbled upon the secret I had forgotten.

My tongue would have run away with me then, but my reason kept it in firm check. This was the secret! The houses didn't matter: what mattered was that these people of mine owned an individual lazar-squint on the lighted altar of life. What mattered was that these people had their own and their own and their own. In the sight of God they had something to show. My mind blundered forward to the full realisation that the quirk of individualism in man is more precious than the most precious stone on a golden ring on a king's finger.

So I said: "I echo what better men before me have said. The issue is whether we shall scatter and leave the sites of our dwellings go to grass, or stay here and build again. We had our feuds here: we had our happinesses. When we weren't kissin' we were bleedin'!"

On the outskirts of the crowd somebody laughed. Hold back the tide with a hayfork—that was the implication of the laugh. I grew angry.

"Go, let ye," I continued, "an' be lost in the laneways of the towns or among the boreens of the countryside. Have souvenirs of freedom doled out to ye as a caged lark is occasionally given a green sod. As likely as not the old among ye will taste the charity of institutions—places where the poor meat is cooked in a haunch and the bread kept under lock and key. Cloone had hard times before now. In the days of the Famine our fathers didn't whinge or die. My advice to ye is to spit on public organised charity, than which nothing is more destroyin'."

Galileo laughed bitterly. He then raised his voice and asked:

" Are we to live on perches like hens ? " His query earned him a murmur of approval.

" I didn't born him," Brink-o'-the-Grave said. " My mother told me he was a serpent, even in his crib."

There followed the clamour of warring voices. The bell demanded silence. Galileo was astute enough to ignore the old woman and fasten his grip firmly on me.

" Riddles are the curse of the Irish ! " he roared. " Down the centuries, through all our rebellions, when we sought a clear statement of fact from a leader, all we got was a ball-o'-wax of words ! "

I had to balance each word as a card is balanced against a card. I continued to speak quietly. " We are here four hundred and twenty three people all told." (Secretly, out of pride, I had counted my subjects.) " Ninety four of us are men of workable age, not counting the boys who will work as half-men. Today each householder will mark his site so that in the future there will be no danger of dispute. Then we will take a vote as to whether we will go or stay. If the decision is to go—we go ! If the decision is to stay, tomorrow morning we will start levelling Cloone. In the town beyond us there are three or four young men who are reputed to have the gift of beauty in their eyes. One of these surely has a hankering for a monument and for appreciation. Whoever we select will be well thought of in the Cloone of tomorrow. We have little else to offer him. This man will advise us on the shape and type of house we will build. This time we will build of stone. O'Neill's quarry is ours for the asking. We shall roof with the half-slate, half-stone of Gurranagore : mortal cheap we'll get it or pledge our reputations until we have the money. Here among us we have the masons, the slaters, the plasterers and the joiners. While the weather holds we will work like demons in an effort to get a roof over ourselves and the children. If any man is to get the first of building it must be a man with a family. Till the roofs are over us, we'll manage to live under the carts. We'll not leave here ! It is not a difficult case I have stated. Once ye have yeer minds readied to it, it will turn easy. The walls will walk up, for we shall prove tyrants to ourselves. Then, come Christmas Night. . . ."

There and then I walked into Three Cheers' trap. "Come Christmas Night," he laughed, as he gave his three handclaps to attract attention, "Molly Font will come up Cloone with an elephant of a goose trapped in her oxter. Flowin' like mad yeer lives are! Ha! Ha!" Again he began to clap his hands.

"Come Patrick's Night . . ." I said, though I was smiling.

"Come Patrick's Night an' the shamrock will be at the bottom of yeer cups an' the cold porter will be floatin' around the heel of yeer stomachs. Time flowin'! Ha! Ha! Ha!" Clap! Clap! Clap!

"Come the night of John's Bonfire. . . ."

"Come the night of John's Bonfire an' the children will be leppin' mad through the blessed flames. Yeer lives are flowin' away! Flowin' mad! Ha! Ha! Ha!" Clap! Clap! Clap!

Ignoring Three Cheers' glee, I went on: ". . . the roofs will look as if Cloone had never died. An' this time she'll live forever, because she'll be built of stone."

"Forever Cloone!" Three Cheers shouted.

Lord Caherdown was truly tipsy. His back was turned to me and he was paying no attention to what I had to say. He stood directly in front of Old Font. "My old Patriarch of Constantinople," he began: then tugged tentatively at Old Font's beard; the old fellow's eyes were terribly alive, yet he did not take offence. Rather did his eyes wander and come to rest on Galileo.

Galileo was growling. "You'll put it to a vote!" he said.

Put it to a vote we did. Everyone had a vote, even the children in arms or those in the cradle, for whom their fathers spoke up and recorded what they had to say. Abernethy Bovenizer and Murray Folan were appointed the tellers: they stood in the middle of the road in front of the Rookery and let all Cloone pass between them. One of the publicans recorded the ayes and the other the noes. " Aye " was for building : " no " for not building.

Streaming Blood refused to vote, because, he said he wasn't a native of the place like Dicky Hickey. Before Dicky voted he called Streaming Blood aside and took counsel with him. Metal Belly was given votes for himself and for his son, but not for Trouble-o'-the-World. Caherdown voted a resounding aye, as did Old Font, his wife and son. The father and mother of Shoon Lawlee voted no, no, in low scarcely audible voices. Galileo growled a stern no. Strangely enough Dom Foy did likewise, as did Badger Breen. Martha and Tom Goggin kept arguing bitterly : she was for building, he was against it. Finally the woman had her way and both of them voted for re-building. Jody Shea voted a sad yes for Cloone to be rebuilt. Inexplicably, the western woman also voted for re-building. Metal Belly aye for himself, aye for his child, though he put in the proviso that he, himself, would take to the road. In at least three cases husband and wife voted different ways. Dick Gaffney voted a mild but indelible no. His mother voted as Dick had voted. After a while, thinking that the sun had been too much for his whiteness, we clearly asked Dick whether or not he wished Cloone rebuilt. He repeated that he did not want Cloone rebuilt and added that he had suddenly taken a fancy to travel into the wonder of the town beyond. Brink-o'-the-Grave's chair was brought to the voting-gap : she walked the last four steps and voted aye, aye, for Cloone to be rebuilt. Old Font stood at one side of the gate and watched how each one voted : when a stream of ayes came from a long-tailed family it was good to see the old fellow's face brighten.

When the boys of from eight to eleven years of age passed through, Old Font looked at each narrowly. Under his scrutiny they voted aye to a man. Muttering fiercely at this intimidation, Galileo took his stand on the other side of the gate, but by this time the greater part of the votes had been recorded.

It was evident that the ayes had it two to one. Metal Belly rang the bell and read the result. The men growled soberly. The women narrowed their shawls over their faces. Dicky Hickey turned a glad handspring on the sunlit road.

From man to man, Caherdown went, saying maudlinly: "Ye're plebeian to the last curl of the tail! Ye're coarser than canvas! Incredibly and indelibly vulgar, ye are! *Odi profanum vulgus!* But, by the living God, ye're my own, and I'm fond of ye!" Hereupon he shed a few tears and buried his first chin in his second chin. Those of an even-tempered disposition he embraced. When he came to Galileo he halted, then drew himself up to his nasal aristocratic height. He put out his hands and caressed Galileo's face. "My adorable rebel," he said, in an altered voice. He embraced the cobbler fully, saying: "I love you for the intransigeance that's in you: it's the line of demarcation between man and dog." Galileo remained unalterably morose; catching him by the nape of the neck, Caherdown forced him to look upwards at the sun. Galileo's twisted upturned face was black with venom. Both faces were close together: "And still it moves!" Caherdown prompted.

"Aye!" Galileo said bitterly: "still it moves!"

Caherdown's mood changed: he tightened his grip on the back of the cobbler's neck. His face grew mottled with anger. "Cobbler! Sole-stitcher! Last-lover!" he said: "let me hear you say it!" Into the old fellow's ear, Caherdown again breathed: "We shall rise again!"

Galileo lowered his head. He was pursing his worn lips in his unshaved face. He kept looking steadfastly at the ground. When he looked up, his eyes met mine. I smiled at the arch-rebel, but he did not respond.

Caherdown was still throttling him.

"Say it!" He set a whiskey-kiss squarely on the hole of the cobbler's ear.

Simply to placate Caherdown, Galileo said in a low voice: "We shall rise again!"

Caherdown continued to maul him. He treated the cobbler's face as if it were putty. He tightened his grip on the scrawny neck. Galileo was smiling sadly : he did not take umbrage as Caherdown shouted : " Louder ! You patcher of brogues and pampooties and poor yellow gaiters ! Louder, before I throttle you fully ! "

Galileo still held his face in the same sad smile.

When Caherdown's fingers got too strong for him, he was in a predicament : whether to grow angry or to yield ? He gathered his wind and said in a voice we could all hear : " We shall rise again ! " A second time he roared with the full vigour of his voice : " We shall rise again ! "

This time most of us heard it. It put us almost in the fettle of tears. When Caherdown had choked the slogan out of the cobbler for the third time, everybody was laughing. Then, for good measure of happiness, Caherdown uttered the Raheela Roar.

III

I walked away from my shabby principality.

Instinctively, I turned uphill. I had not gone far when I heard light footsteps hurrying behind me. When she had drawn level with me, Madcap suited her step to mine. We did not speak. I was jaded, embittered and almost physically sick as the result of the conflict of sadness and happiness within me. For me, emotion had come to a dead end. My burns began to blaze when touched by the moving airs of morning. On my thigh the gaff-nick again spoke up. Madcap's eyes, I knew, were recurrently turning sidelong to glance at me. After walking for a while the smell of burning straw fell away from us : then we were where the air was fresh and frosty and the sunlight unmoted. The trees of the countryside were turning tawny. On the roadside an elm tree still held its foliage but its leaves lacked the deep richness they had known in the height of summer.

On the crest of the hill, we stood by a gateway : this was

where Finn Dillon and I had loitered on the night of Shoon Lawlee's death.

Far away I could see the flawed mirror of the estuary beyond Littero. I rested my hands on the gateway—the harsh iron chafed them, so I let them fall to my sides. The palms of my hands were black. I turned to the little roadside stream and began to wash them. With the first touch of the water my burns and bruises lived again. Madcap had not spoken since she joined me. It seemed as if there was an immense barrier between us. Whenever I looked at her, my face tended to turn to truculence. She noted this : her mouth was angry but her eyes kept understanding my predicament. When I had dabbed my face dry with my handkerchief I sat down on a broad brown stone beside the tiny stream. Madcap was still standing at the gate : she was steadfastly looking at the faraway. Suddenly she called to me ; I looked up—her face was averted. So strange was the tone of her voice that I was forced to rise and look at her fully, to find if she were in pain. Her body was as taut as taut. Again she called to me, this time in a lower voice. As she turned to face me, I came closer, and then stood directly in front of her. She hung her head and would not let me see her face.

" Strike me, Ches ! " she said, in a low voice.

At first I failed to understand her. She lifted her face slightly. Her lips—how red ! Her breasts—how braced by nature and the moment's compulsion ! Her face—how drained of colour except where the points of anger or pride or what-I-could-not-name glowed on each of her cheekbones ! Her lashes—how long, hiding her eyes !

Suddenly I understood.

My right hand came up : open it was and eager with anger. I struck her fully on the side of the face. The head went sickeningly sideways. I felt a strange exhilaration take me. Slowly she shook her head free of megrim. Slowly, driftingly, a wing of her dark hair came down over her face. For a moment she allowed me to see her eyes where they were hiding in the thicket of her hair.

" Again ! " she said, quietly.

Again I struck. The head jerked. The mouth that had already been twisted now turned to a full wryness. After the second blow her dry lips again framed the word that I eagerly awaited. The third time I struck with all my force. For a time the head hung limply : when it had lifted I saw the pencilled line of blood come vertically down from the mouth corner. I saw that her eyes were alight with triumph and that her soul was out of its hiding-place. I was unutterably churned.

My fingers became officers of iron, eager to take command. I saw the woman's hair beside the autumn land. It was as if all the walls of the world were breaking.

As we came together, we were breathing strangely. For a moment our bodies trembled : then they were bound.

First I tasted the saliva, then the blood. The blood was better. In the years before us, the salt of it would always lie between us. All the while my mind ranted at the people of Cloone, shouting : Who can break the spirit of man ? What iron circumstance can hoof him down ? I was conjuring them with staircase wit, crying out : The image of The-King-that-was-killed-on-Friday is in you and in you and in you ! How can you submit to regimentation knowing that even the glad cry of a child can drown the world's thunder? How can you be defeated when there is in you and in you and in you that which of necessity must break to a daft shout in the darkness, glory to a leap over a high lath, or, if denied, be trodden underfoot to a nameless perversion ?

Our heads rolled together. Here was goodness ! Here was the spirit, laughing, free and drunken, in a city of mirrors and bells. Here, in truth, was the spirit scorning rope since there are no narrows by which the soul may be bound.

Between us, then, were the crumbs of endearing appellations. All the while we were caught in the slow swirling of our bodies' tide.

A strand of her hair irked my tongue-tip : I spat at it quickly like a cat. For me there was minor joy when the irritation was ended. Over the woman's shoulder and through the woman's hair I saw the green wagon-roof illuminate the dullness below. I saw Peggy walk slowly uproad, bringing the patchwork quilt to Trouble-o'-the-World. I felt unutterably exalted; in the midst of my exaltation I smiled for I had heard something that pleased me mightily: it was the sound of singing rising from the ruins of Cloone.

THE END